BY THE AUTHOR

THE COUNTDOWN CHRONICLES
Kiss of the Mandarins
The Warehouse
Never Go Back
The Deception Covenant
Endgame

ORIGIN TALES
The Brotherhood
Rise of the ACF

VLADIMIR SERIES
Vladimir's Diary
Red Empire
Fifty Years to Paradise

THE VAV CHRONICLES
Vampires And Victims

OTHER WORKS
The Prophecy Illusion
Trinity

Vampires And Victims

Martin M. McShane

The Book Guild Ltd

First published in Great Britain in 2022 by
The Book Guild Ltd
Unit E2 Airfielod Business Park
Harrison Road, Market Harborough
Leicestershire, LE16 7UL
Freephone: 0800 999 2982
www.bookguild.co.uk
Email: info@bookguild.co.uk
Twitter: @bookguild

Copyright © 2022 Martin M. McShane

The right of Martin M. McShane to be identified as the author of this
work has been asserted by him in accordance with the
Copyright, Design and Patents Act 1988.

All rights reserved. No part of this publication may be
reproduced, transmitted, or stored in a retrieval system, in any form or by any means,
without permission in writing from the publisher, nor be otherwise circulated in
any form of binding or cover other than that in which it is published and without
a similar condition being imposed on the subsequent purchaser.

This is a work of fiction and is entirely a product of the author's imagination.
Any resemblance or similarity to names, places, characters, incidents or events
or to any actual person, living, dead or undead, is entirely coincidental.

Typeset in Adobe Garamond Pro

Printed and bound in Great Britain by
CPI Group (UK) Ltd, Croydon, CR0 4YY

ISBN 978 1 91512 299 5

British Library Cataloguing in Publication Data.
A catalogue record for this book is available from the British Library.

Is it better to be loved or feared?
If you cannot be both
Then be feared.

FOREWORD

Of all the many trials and tribulations the poor must endure throughout their lives, none is so great or so unjust as being bled dry. Nobody hears the cries of the poor when they are hungry or out of work or in need of shelter or clothing. Those who help the poor are seldom what they seem. Do do-gooders do good, or do they do what they do to do themselves good? At least when Vampires bleed the poor dry they do so out of their nature.

PROLOGUE

Vampire Houses have, at one time or another, infested every city on the planet. Their Nests go largely undetected because Vampires conduct themselves almost identically to mortals, paralleling them in their vices, virtues, fascinations and failings. As with the living, Vampires can be ambitious, industrious, mischievous, ruthless, ingenious, greedy, philosophical, altruistic, religious, and so on. Some, however, only exist to see an end to their kind. To maintain a façade of normalcy is extremely expensive, so Vampires, instead of feeding on all their Victims, they sometimes work them to death in their factories, mills and mines.

Being immortal, and with so much time to kill, Vampires often immerse themselves in careers, Prosthetist being very popular. The reason behind this is the demand for replacement limbs due to Vampires losing various body parts throughout their so-called lives. If a Vampire loses an arm or a leg or a hand or a foot, despite popular myth, it does not grow back and, being so extremely vain, Vampires would rather end their own existence than be imperfect. Their vanity extends especially to the face, and losing an ear or a nose, or even mild facial scarring, will drive Vampires to Vampicide.

Nobody, neither Vampires nor those who study them, truly knows where the first Vampire came from. There are writings going back to Old Testament times which allude to Lucifer leading a rebellion in Heaven, and during an epic battle between the so-called forces of good and the so-called forces of evil, a drop of the Dark Angel's blood fell to Earth, coming to land on the head of a blind beggar. Becoming instantly immortal the beggar regained his sight, but in doing so his soul was denied access to the Great Universe. Due to the links that exist between immortality, everlasting life and the divine resonating within the Holy Scriptures, many Clergy venerate Vampires; some even devote themselves to individual Vampires, thereby becoming their Familiars. Consequently, many Religniks down the ages have taken the Vampire Oath of Obedience, paralleling that which they have with the Aristocracy to do their bidding by helping them suppress the common people. Despite Familiars longing to be made into Vampires, it is exceptionally unusual for them to be so, mainly because they are valuable as Familiars. There is a Vampire and Ecclesiastical saying which goes: "Whether you be the Lord of Light or a Denizen of Darkness, good help is hard to find and is never to be wasted."

It cannot be emphasised enough just how difficult it is to create a Vampire, otherwise there would be a great many more of them than there are. Even when feeding is carried out to perfection, an Initiate can simply fade away at the very last instant of their mortal life, their soul passing into the Great Universe instead of joining the Legion of the Undead. This is extremely frustrating for the Vampire involved, as the process can take decades, meaning all that time, effort, energy and blood going to waste.

For reasons lost to the mists of time, every Vampire on Earth came to settle in the Carpathian Mountains, but, after gorging on peasant children, local warlords rose up and slaughtered very nearly all of them. Millennia of Vampire evolution snuffed out in a single afternoon. So much suffering had been endured so that Vampires could walk unblistered in twilight or in smog or under overcast skies, but all that progress was lost. Many believed that Vampire Science would eventually allow them to bask in the full and glorious light of the sun without bursting into flames, but all those hopes and dreams were shattered and gone. And for what? A meal. Fortunately, every Prima Vampir, together with 400 Inferiara and most of their devoted Familiars, plus various nether-creatures, were safely tucked away in the deepest granite vaults safe from the stakes of marauding villagers. It fell to individual Prima Vampiri to rebuild their Houses far away from their mountain refuge.

There really was no need for the Vampires to have fed on the local children, as any blood will do for them. But it is the quality and convenience of feeding on Humans that drives them to it, especially children for obvious reasons. The blood of Humans is nectar to Vampires, plus they are so very easy to catch compared with quadrupeds. There are drawbacks to feeding on non-Humans, as the feeder temporarily takes on the characteristics of the source food. With innumerable goats and sheep wandering the lower reaches of the Carpathian Mountains, feeding on these animals led Vampires to become Ovine in their behaviour for some minutes, or even hours, after feeding. The effect can be reversed, or altered, by a change in the food source. Blood 'cocktails' were experimented with, often producing bizarre, and oftentimes enjoyable, results.

Feeding on large carnivores or aggressive beasts can be extremely risky on two counts. Firstly, animals only remain under the enchantment of a Vampire Stare so long as eye contact is maintained; bears, wolves, wild boar, and the like, that slip from a Vampire Stare can attack the feeder, leading to many lower-order Vampires in particular being ripped apart. Their hearts then having to be located and staked in order that their souls may pass the threshold into the Great Universe. Secondly, the feeder, taking on Lupine or Ursine characteristics, becomes a danger to all those around them, including other Vampires. So, why do it? Why did Vampires feed on wild animals in the knowledge they could, in so doing, be destroyed or destroy others? "What is the point in being immortal if you can't have the occasional thrill to pass the time?" being the reason they most commonly gave.

For long enough after they left the Carpathians, Vampires tried, unsuccessfully, to bend Lycanthropes to their will. Accordingly, Vampire scientists undertook experiments to create a Lycanthrope that was not only obedient but would maintain its form without relying on a full moon to transmogrify. And so began the process of creating a Wolf Child or Lupulo, as they became known. The scientists adopted the same process as that used for creating Vampires but using cooperative Lycanthropes as surrogates. Progress was slow, but after a century of trying, the first Lupulo was created from a Lycanthrope feeding on a Siberian wolf cub.

In spite of their post-Carpathian geographic dispersal, Vampire Houses around the globe evolved along virtually identical lines due to them having a kind of 'hive' consciousness. Many Houses integrated with local communities to the extent that the children of Familiars attended the same schools as the food, which caused problems when they saw their classmates being served up as an appetiser or dessert.

★

It was around the Renaissance that Prima Vampiri first fashioned a Treaty with Humans as a way of keeping their race from being wiped out. However, due to Vampires constantly breaking the terms of the Treaty it seldom lasted very long, but it formed the basis for all future attempts at peace between Humans and Vampires. Treaties set out the 'Rules of Engagement' which, *inter alia*, banned Vampires from feeding on children while listing 'permitted food', which has always been highly controversial. Each successive generation of Humans was required to renew the Treaty with the local Prima Vampir. Together they are known as the Treaty Scribes.

As with all cults the Vampire cult has many and various Adherents, Advocates, Disciples, Followers, Devotees and Worshippers. The collective term is 'Familiars'. What is perhaps surprising is the number of Familiars who are also Men of God. Perhaps it is not so surprising when consideration is given to the fact that Vampires are possessed of Eternal Life, something which most religions hold sacred.

The following is from the New Testament:

> *Truly, truly, I say unto you, unless you eat the flesh of the Son of Man and drink his blood, you have no life in you. Whoever feeds on my flesh and drinks of my blood has eternal life, and I will raise him up on the last day. For my flesh is true food, and my blood is true drink. Whoever feeds on my flesh and drinks my blood abides in me forever, and I in him.*
>
> *Amen.*

CHAPTER 1

In a little less than an hour the school day would be over for the older children while it was barely thirty minutes before the younger ones were to be let loose. All eyes were on the ticking classroom clocks as they counted down the seconds. Sitting in the warmth of their classrooms, staff and children alike dreaded the thought of returning to their freezing cold homes. Winter, especially the dead of winter, was when Jack Frost visited and took the elderly, the infirm, the sick and the weak into his deadly embrace. His icicle fingers clawed the life out of all but the strongest. It was a struggle to survive when temperatures remained below zero for weeks on end. In recent years, the Arctic conditions lasted for months without respite. Then there was the smog – the smothering, asphyxiating, choking, all-pervading smog. It seemed to be getting worse. However, for the Vampires of the neighbouring settlement of Storm Hill, the smog provided them cover from the sun's rays, enabling them to go about their business without fear of spontaneously combusting.

★

The poorest of Ravenport's poor inhabited an area in the south of the city situated next to the docks. It was known by all as the Cauldron. Cauldronians were so poor they could not even afford to light a fire in the grate for more than half an hour of a morning and an hour before going to bed at night. During winter months they went to bed early rather than sit and shiver in the cold and dark of their damp homes. Families would huddle four or more to a bed for warmth. Some beds were hardly beds at all; they were old couches or boards placed across the backs of chairs, or tables topped with straw palliasses – anything to keep sleepers off freezing cold floors.

The Cauldron used to be known as 'the Old Town', but its quaint name was changed some hundred years before. Nobody alive could recall the reason for the change, but the area soon grew into its new name. The children of the Cauldron were known simply as street kids, which suited them, for the street was where they played and grew up.

Most families had a half-dozen or so living children, but with child mortality being what it was, gaps would appear between slumbering bodies. Gaps that Jack Frost could crawl into and roam around. Parents kept their youngest children with them in bed for warmth. Their little lithe bodies being ideal for plugging gaps. They would be moved into their siblings' beds when space was needed for new arrivals. It was risky moving a child from a parents' bed, but they were needed to fill those gaps in their brothers' and sisters' beds because where there were gaps Jack called in the night.

On winter's mornings, children, their eyes stuck fast with crusty yellow sleep, would slip from beneath eiderdowns to dress while kneeling on their beds to keep their feet from freezing cold floors. While waiting to be called down to breakfast, they would scrape ice from the inside of their bedroom windows. There was no purpose to it; it was just something they did while waiting for their porridge and cup of weak tea to be served. The scraped ice would sometimes melt into puddles on windowsills. With sufficient melt, water ran from windowsill to floor where it pooled and froze into ice-pennies, which children took and put into dispensing machines to get chocolate.

For Cauldron kids there was never any thought of washing on a winter's morning, or at any other time of the day or night for that matter. Apart from bath day at school, the children simply did not wash. Every Wednesday morning, however, the children of Penny Street School were marched single file to the local bath house to be sheep-dipped in hot soapy water. Charlie Carter, like all the other bathers, had his mother's words ringing in his ears: "Don't forget to stick your head under the water to wash your hair and remember to wash behind your ears." Scuffles invariably broke out between children to be first in line to bathe. This was not keenness on the part of the children for a bath; it was purely self-interest, as in no time the water would turn grey and become topped with a thick layer of cream-like scum. Teachers did their best to maintain order, but the larger kids took no notice of them, and once stripped naked and running full pelt toward the bath there was no realistic way of stopping them. Being last in the bath queue was a life-lesson for the smaller children, who quickly learned their place in the grand order of things. After schools had bathed, locals would demand a complete change of bathwater before handing over their three-farthing admission fee.

★

In thirty minutes, school would be over for the day for the older children, while the younger ones were already making their way out the door, screaming and yelling with excitement as they played a game of snow football or went sliding along pavements. The slipperiest slides were created by children pouring water over flagstones. Some slides were more than twenty feet long. Adults hated them because at their age they were more adept at falling than sliding. The sides of slides were decorated along their lengths with the blood spatters of fallers. The blood remained visible through the ice all winter long unless Vampires licked it for a popsicle. Few parents collected their children from school in those times. This was normal, as kids were expected to make their own way home, playing and yelling and sliding in doing so. With most of the children living within a few streets of each other, and often just a few doors from one another, they were safe so long as they did not stray into the road where they might get run down by a speeding horse and cart.

The fog rolled in at three thirty-five as usual and, as usual, it quickly turned to smog. Being the dead of winter, it was pitch black by four o'clock, with the only light being that coming from the shop windows lining Dock Road. At last the bell rang for the end of the school day. Charlie Carter put his books away and wrapped himself up in his scarf and overcoat. His youngest brother, Patrick Junior, had left at three thirty with his friends and relatives, but Charlie, as usual, had to wait for Jed to turn up. Jed, though not actually a middle child, behaved just like a middle child, being the middle boy of three. He often arrived late to meet up with Charlie for their walk home together, the main reasons being that he was in detention for his characteristic bad behaviour, or he was having one last game of football before heading off home. He eventually showed up at four fifty-five in company with two of his classmates, Maurice 'Moey' Groom and Billy 'Patto' Patterson. Jed's nose had obviously been bleeding.

"Mum'll kill us if you go home looking like that," said Charlie, wiping away the blood from Jed's nose.
"Oh, don't worry about it, it's nothing," replied Jed casually. "I just fell over on the ice and Patto ran into me. He couldn't help it, could ye, Patto? He said he was sorry anyway."
"It's late, so we'd better get home or we'll be in trouble."
"You worry too much, you do, Charlie boy."
"Shut up, Patto, when I want your advice I'll ask for it. C'mon, Jed, let's get going before the smog gets any worse."
"I don't think it can get any worse if you ask me."
"Nobody's asking you, Patto, now let's go or Mum'll kill us."

On smoggy days, which was virtually every winter's day it seemed, the light from the shop windows along Dock Road guided the way home. No matter what, Jed just could not walk past Marsden's toy shop without stopping to look at the things he, nor anybody he knew, could afford or ever hope to play with. Left to their own devices Jed and his mates would have stood for hours pointing at trains and toy soldiers and things made using Build It sets – cranes and bridges and the like. Charlie gave the boys five minutes to ogle at the toys before dragging them away on the promise that they could look at them again on Saturday. Why he chose Saturday he was not sure, as it was only Monday and they would likely stop to look at the toys every day on their walk home.

The boys lost all track of time on their way home as they chatted, joked and kicked stones in a game of pavement football, only realising the lateness of the hour when, at half past five, the lights in the shop windows were turned off. Just as they were about to cross Dock Road the sound of a horse neighing caused them to stop and look around. They knew all too well the number of children run down by horses and carts in the smog and had been warned by their parents to always be careful. "Better five minutes late than not come home at all," they were told. In the smog it was impossible to tell which direction the neighing had come from. The boys stood statue still and listened and waited. They were well used to the sounds made by horses and carts in the smog; it seemed to come in waves, loud then quiet then loud again, but not this time. If a cart came to a sudden stop then wheels skidding over cobbles caused sparks to fly, but not this time. If a horse came to an abrupt halt it created all kinds of noises, from rapid clip-clopping to the animal snorting and whinnying, but not this time. This time there were no further sounds. All was silence. Where was the horse and cart? The only sound was from the boys' breathing, which seemed oddly loud as though it was being amplified somehow.

"Where is it?" whispered Patto in a hiss.
"Dunno. Have you got a light on ye, Patto?" asked Moey.
"Nah. Have you got a light on ye, Charlie?"
"Shhhhhhhh, you lot, I'm trying to listen!"
"I think it's gone."
"How can it be gone? We'd've heard it go, wouldn't we?"
"Ye can never tell in the smog. It does funny things, so maybe it has gone. What d'ye think, Moey? D'ye think it's gone or what?"
"I don't know, but it didn't sound right, did it?"
"Shhhhhhhh, I heard something," hissed Charlie.
"Sorry, lads, that was me," sniggered Patto, pinching his nose and wafting away an imaginary fart.
"Very funny, Patto, now will ye please be quiet, all of ye."
"Yeah! Shurrup, youz!" added Jed, backing his brother's demand for silence.

Charlie, Jed, Moey and Patto listened as hard as they could without bursting their eardrums, but all they heard was the sound of their own breathing. They eventually figured it was the smog keeping the sound locked in that made their breathing appear so loud. A long two minutes passed without any further sounds, so the boys resumed their walk home. As they could not see more than a few feet in front of them they navigated their way by the cracks in the paving stones they had passed every day for years. Arriving outside old Mrs Wainwright's greengrocer's shop opposite Sanderson Street, Charlie and Jed said their goodbyes to Moey and Patto by giving friendly punches on upper arms, which were returned with interest. Barely had the brothers reached their side of the road when a coach pulled by two massive black horses materialised as if out of nowhere right alongside them. It was surreal; not even smog could deaden the sound of such a large rig, could it? Charlie instinctively called out, "Patto! Moey! Run! Run! Whatever you do don't stop until you get home!" In a flash, the coach made off after Moey and Patto. Through the smog Charlie heard the muffled sounds of hobnail boots on cobblestones but nothing of iron rims or shod hooves. There came a single cry of pain through the haze followed by dead silence. Charlie made to go toward the cry, but Jed held onto him.

"Charlie! Don't leave me! Please don't leave me!" pleaded Jed, almost in tears. Charlie had never seen his brother look so frightened. "Let's get home before something bad happens to us!" begged Jed. Charlie cocked an ear to the smog, trying to catch any sound, but all was silent.

"Sorry, Jed, I've got to go and see if they're okay," said Charlie.

"I'm begging ye, for Christ's sake, don't leave me!" cried Jed, pulling his big brother close to him.

"Alright, our kid, I won't leave you," Charlie promised. "Look, we're nearly home, so don't go mentioning any of this to Mum or she'll kill us."

★

When the boys entered the house, the first they noticed was how warm it was, then they noticed the smell of stew – stew made with meat. They could tell the difference between the smell of stew made with meat from that made from just potatoes, greens and carrots – an essential talent for children of the Cauldron. They used this superpower to good effect during charity meals when stews sat side by side on the serving counter. They would unfalteringly point to the stew containing the most meat.

"Where have you two been?" shouted Mary Carter in a right strop.

"Just coming home from school, Mum, that's all, nothing unusual in that."

"And what's up with our Jed? He looks like he's been crying. And there's blood all around his nose. Have you two been fighting again? Have you? What have I told you two about fighting?"

"We weren't fighting, Mum, honest. Jed got hurt when he —"

"I don't want to hear any of your lies, Charles Carter," said Charlie's mum, taking a handkerchief from her cardigan sleeve, spitting on it and wiping the blood from Jed's nose. Mary always called Charlie Charles whenever he was in trouble or she was angry with him. She inspected Jed all over. "Now then, son, tell your mum the truth, you know I won't batter you if you tell me the truth. What happened, son? Did Charlie punch you on the nose?"

"No, Mum, honest a God it was an accident. I was playing footy with Patto and Moey and I fell over and Moey ran into me."

"I thought you said it was Patto that ran into you?" interrupted Charlie.

"Oh yeah, that's right, it was Patto not Moey that ran into me, but it was an accident and he said he was sorry."

"I don't know what to believe with you two. Anyway, your tea's waiting for you. It's stew. With meat. Lamb, a good cut too."

"Where did the meat come from, Mum, I thought we were out?"

"It's from the Storm Hill League of Welldoers. I'd've thought you'd've guessed that!" How Mary thought the boys would guess this was beyond them. "They're always doing nice things for the families of the Cauldron. And they've sent everybody a sack of coal and they're going to do the same every week, so they say." Mary stood smiling, waiting for some reaction, but none came. "That was nice of them, wasn't it?" she asked. The boys just grunted and nodded. "And they're offering to sell us cheap food. Your dad thinks there must be a catch, but I don't. Anyway, we've lit the coal and we're eating the meat, so what the catch is I don't know!"

Mary served the boys a bowl of steaming hot stew with a chunk of bread on the side. A rare treat. They ate their meal sitting in front of the fire, the light from which danced on the parlour walls alongside the shadows of Charlie's sisters who danced too. With the house being so warm the family did not retire to bed until nearly eight thirty.

The sleeping arrangements in the Carter household were: Mary Carter, Patrick Senior and their youngest daughter, Tatty, in an iron-frame bed in one bedroom and the three boys in the other bedroom in a four-foot bed, with Effy and Agnes in a three-foot single in the same room as their brothers. The third bedroom was unusable due to the roof leaking. The kids slept head to toe as best they could, though with a week between baths the smell from the boys' feet was rank. Mary tried to stop them wearing their socks in bed, but after months of complaining she let them leave them on, as the moaning was getting just too much for her to bear.

"Jed?" hiss-whispered Charlie.
"What?"
"What really happened?"
"What do you mean?"
"You said Patto made your nose bleed, but then you told Mum it was Moey. I can tell when you're lying, Jed. What really happened to make your nose bleed?"
"Shut up, will you, I can't get to sleep with you two yakkin' away," snapped Effy.
"Oh, be quiet, I'm just talking to Jed."
"Well, go downstairs and do it."

As the boys made their way downstairs their mum called out wanting to know what was going on. Charlie hiss-whispered to her that they needed the toilet and did not like going in the pot while the girls were in the room, so they were going to the outside lav. Mary shouted back, "Since when have you two been bothered about the girls being in the room? And you should've gone before you came up to bed!" The boys ignored their mum's comments and continued downstairs. The fire was still giving off a little heat, so Charlie and Jed crouched close to it and huddled for extra warmth.

"So, Jerad Carter, are you going to tell me the truth or what?"

"Okay, but don't get mad at me." Jed paused to consider how much he was going to tell his big brother. "Well, over the weekend, me and the mates went up to Storm Hill to have a look around the place. You know, to see if the stories were true or not."

"You're an idiot, of course they're not true. How can they be? Who was you with anyway?"

"There was me, Moey and Patto." Charlie sighed and shook his head when he heard the names of the usual suspects being trotted out. "We just wanted to have a look over the wall to see what was going on."

"What wall?" asked Charlie.

"You know, the one around the what d'ye call it? You know, the hospital thing."

"Not the Sanatorium? You went to the Sanatorium?"

"Yeah. So anyway, it was dead easy getting over the wall. We hid in some bushes and then crept toward the windows when nobody was around." Jed adjusted events in his head before continuing. "There were loads of people walking around inside wearing white coats. Then, guess what?" Charlie shrugged his shoulders instead of guessing. "We saw Stevie Lewis' dad strapped on a trolley; they were wheeling him into a room. He lifted his head and saw us. He called out something. Then the men in white coats looked toward the window so we legged it."

"Stevie Lewis' dad? Are you sure it was him? Mum said he went to London and doesn't want to come back. That's what everybody said."

"I know, but he's in Storm Hill. Honest a God, I saw him and so did Patto and Moey."

"Are you telling me everything, Jed?"

"Yeah, of course I am." Charlie did not believe his little brother for an instant, but as it was suddenly bitterly cold he was not keen to push the point.

"So what happened next?"

"Later on, we told Stevie Lewis what we saw and he went to Storm Hill to see for himself. He got grabbed by the Sheriffs and his mum had to pay a fine for him trespassing on Lord Harbinger's private property. Stevie said we have to pay his mum the money back, but we can't afford to."

"So Stevie Lewis gave you the bloody nose?"

"That weed? Don't be daft, I'd burst him easy. Nah, it wasn't Stevie, it was his big brother Joey that did it. He kicked Patto in the knee too. He ran after Moey, but he was too fast for him." Jed did not like the look in his brother's eyes. "Now, Charlie, don't you go doing anything stupid, it'll all calm down soon and I just want to forget what happened."

"Sorry, Jed, I can't have Joey Lewis hitting you. I'm going to have to give him a good hiding."

"You? Give Joey Lewis a good hiding? He'd burst you easy. If anything we'd have to get Cousin Billy to have a word with him."

"Which one?"

"The one next door of course! Who did you think I was talkin' about?"

"I don't know, there's so many of us it's hard to keep track. But anyway, you don't need Billy Lynch to have a word with him, I'll be the one having a word with Joey Lewis!"

"No, Charlie. No fighting Joey Lewis, let's just see how it goes."

Charlie could tell by Jed's voice that there was more to the story, but as they were now both shivering it was time to return to bed. As they ascended the stairs, Jed asked Charlie if he thought Moey and Patto were okay.

"Yeah, they'll be fine. You know what those two are like, they get away with everything!"

Mrs Carter called out, "What's going on? Did your friends get grabbed by the men in white coats?"

"Nothing's going on, Mum, go to sleep."

When Charlie and Jed slid back beneath the eiderdown poor little Patrick Jnr was freezing cold, so they squished up close to keep him warm.

★

In school the next morning, Charlie and Jed looked for Moey and Patto to find out what had happened the previous night but they were nowhere to be found. The brothers asked around, but nobody had seen them. Moey turned up at lunchtime. He told Jed that he had been to visit Patto in the hospital to make sure he was okay.

"So what happened to Patto?" asked Jed, concerned. Moey told him that he had been run down by a rig the previous evening.
"But he's not all that badly hurt, just a few cuts and bruises and a broken arm, that's all." Jed was about to ask Moey about the rig that had run Patto down when he was hit from behind with an almighty blow that gave him a dead arm. He turned to see Stevie Lewis' big brother Joey lining up to hit him again. "I'm warning you, Joey Lewis, if you hit me again, I'm gonna…" Jed stopped speaking, as over Joey Lewis' shoulder he saw his cousin Billy Lynch marching toward them. The children in the playground quickly formed a fight circle around the prospective combatants. Everybody was surprised to see Billy Lynch at Penny Street School, as he was Catholic and attended Holy Cross School two streets down Dock Road from Penny Street.
"Billy!" shouted Jed. "Don't you go hittin' Joey!" he yelled. "I'm askin' ye as a favour to me, please don't hit 'im." Joey Lewis, who was related to both the Lynches and the Carters, was the same age as Billy Lynch, but was nowhere near as good a street fighter as was the illustrious Billy Lynch.
"Who do you think you are, hittin' our Jed like that?" Billy asked while rolling up his shirt sleeves.

"Now, Billy, I've got no argument with you," stammered Joey Lewis. "Jed and his mates owe me mum half a crown and I've been told to get it off them."

"I'm askin' ye, Billy. I'm beggin' ye! Don't hit Joey. Please!" cried Jed in anguish. Charlie Carter suddenly appeared on the scene and after elbowing his way through the fight circle he removed his coat and jumper and pushed Billy Lynch to one side.

"If anybody's going to fight Joey Lewis it's going to be me," declared Charlie. Everybody fell about laughing and pointed at Charlie.

"I can always rely on you to make me laugh, our Charlie, but go ahead, he's all yours," said Billy Lynch, putting his coat back on.

"Look, nobody's going to fight nobody, okay?" shouted Jed over the laughter. "I need to tell you something, Charlie, but you've got to keep it to yourself," muttered Jed from the side of his mouth. "By the way, our Billy, what are you doing here? Shouldn't you be at the Cat Lick School?"

"I heard there was going to be trouble, ye ungrateful Proddy Dog ye, so I gave up me stew to come and help ye," snapped Billy, though he was smiling.

"Okay, so what is it you've got to tell me? I think I know what it is, but I want to hear it anyway," said Charlie, crossing his arms.

"Hey, Joey!" shouted Jed. "You and our Billy will want to hear this too."

"Right, youz lot, get lost, all of yez," yelled Billy at the fight circle, which quickly dispersed to resume schoolyard games.

Jed began his tale by telling Charlie that he had not told him the whole truth about his visit to the Storm Hill Sanatorium. This was no surprise to Charlie.

"There wasn't just the three of us that went up to Storm Hill that night, there was nine of us, including Patto and Moey," said Jed. Charlie returned his brother a knowing look. "When we got over the wall we saw light coming from one of the windows, so we went over to have a look inside. We couldn't believe it. The place was full of men and women wearing white coats, and there were loads of people lyin' on beds and one of them was Stevie Lewis' dad." Joey Lewis did not seem surprised by this revelation. "Stevie started shouting and banging on the window to attract his dad's attention. Mr Lewis tried to sit up, but he was strapped to the bed-thing. He shouted something, but we couldn't hear what it was. Then some of the people in white coats looked to see what Mr Lewis was shouting at and they saw us lot looking through the window." Jed found the next bit of his story hard to tell. "Anyway," he continued, "we legged it so the men in white coats wouldn't grab us. Then we heard shouting coming from behind us. It was Stevie. He'd stayed looking through the window at his dad. He shouted for us to come back, but we were too scared because we heard people yelling things like, 'There they are' and 'Grab them' and 'Take them inside' and stuff like that. We didn't want to get grabbed, so we kept running. When we got back over the wall we heard Stevie shouting and screaming at the top of his voice. Moey and Amy said we should go back. They said mates don't leave their mates behind. But I said I wasn't going back for anything, and the others agreed with me. Moey and Amy went to climb back over the wall, but we stopped them. Then we heard people shouting and they were getting close, so we ran like the clappers into the woods and made our way home. We felt so ashamed that we didn't go back for Stevie. The next day we heard he'd been fined half a crown by the Sheriffs. We thought that was that, but then Stevie, Amy and Patto said people were asking questions about them and trying to find out who their mates were. Me and the others didn't believe them, but then Stevie said he nearly got grabbed by the men in white coats but they slipped on the ice, so he got away from them. And that's the whole story of what happened," said Jed, hanging his head low in shame.

"That must be why our Stevie won't come to school," said Joey Lewis. "We heard that Patto ended up in hospital after being run down by a rig just like the ones the men in white coats drive. He's terrified. No matter what me mum said she'd do to him, he won't leave the house. He's just sat there, shivering in the freezing cold."

"What are youz lot talking about?" interjected Billy, incredulity ringing in his voice. "The men in white coats only cart people off to Storm Hill if they go mad or something. It's their job! They're supposed to do that to keep them off the streets."

The inhabitants of the Cauldron were long used to having the men in white coats cart friends, neighbours and relatives off to the Storm Hill Sanatorium, supposedly to cure them of their insanities. How people suddenly, and for no good reason, became insane was the subject of much conjecture. Most of those carted off did not end up in the Sanatorium but were put to work as slaves in the factories, mills and mines owned by the Vampires of Storm Hill.

"Is your dad mad, then, Joey?" asked Charlie indelicately. "Is that why he's in the Sanatorium up there in Storm Hill?"

"I don't know. He might be, but I don't know. Mum is so ashamed. Nobody can tell no one about this because if it gets back to me mum she'll go mad at us. She doesn't know about you lot seeing Dad, so don't any of you go mentioning it. Just let her carry on thinking that everybody believes he's living in London and doesn't want to come back home." Joey thought for a moment before adding, "So, Charlie, will you help me get the money off your Jed and the others? We're in a bad way with Dad gone. We're desperate so if ye can help get the money for me mum then please do it."

Charlie and Billy promised they would do all they could to help get Mrs Lewis her half-crown back.

★

The Carter boys felt so ashamed. They had not considered for a moment that, with their father gone, the Lewis household was practically destitute. Even though the older Lewis children were willing to work there was hardly any work to be had anywhere in the whole of Ravenport. The docks was a closed shop, as jobs passed through the hands of generations of the same families, but unfortunately none of the Lewis family or the Carters or the Lynches or any of their relatives had a single Dockers Ticket between them. Another limiting factor for jobs in Ravenport was that employers hired people based on their religion. For example, there were parts of the docks that were open only to Catholics and others open only to Protestants. To help overcome religious prejudice, families would give their children a mix of typically Catholic and Protestant names to increase the chances of them bringing money into the household. At job interviews, applicants would be asked questions about their schooling, their place of worship and which football team they supported to ascertain whether they were telling the truth about their professed religion, though the majority of people doing the hiring and firing knew who was Catholic and who was Protestant. This made things doubly difficult for Patrick Carter Snr, because he had renounced the Catholic faith to become a Methodist and consequently was despised by all those handing out jobs. Worse, Patrick had changed the family name from Lynch to Carter, which angered the Lynch clan. They saw it as him renouncing his Irish heritage. Patrick had been asked time and again why he had done it, but he resolutely refused to say. The only people who knew the reason were his wife, Mary, and his mother-in-law, the fearsome Elizabeth Rose Lyons.

Occasionally there was some temporary work to be had on the docks, but to get it men had to gather outside the dock gates and wait to see if they opened. If they did open then a shop steward, or some similar lackey, would come out and stand on a box to peer down on the sea of men desperate for work.

"Okay, listen, youz lot, we're looking for twenty men today," the shop steward would announce to his eager, hopeful audience, their hollow cheeks and watery eyes staring up at him from sooty faces. Such announcements were always greeted with a mix of cheers and groans from the 400 or so waiting men. "Have any of you lot got a Dockers Ticket?" That 'joke' stuck in the craw of the men stood perishing in the cold and the rain desperate for work. "No? Okay then, have any of you got a Union Ticket?" The shop steward already knew the ones that did. The opportunity for work was the union's way of recruiting new members. "Okay then, that's fourteen of yez, so we just need another six. Any of you okay with heights?" All hands would go up. And so this game would go on until the six were chosen from the shop steward's favourites. He would already know the ones he wanted to hire, but he liked to dangle the carrot of hope in front of those without hope. He and his kind seemed to get some kind of a kick out of it. Familiars are like that.

Walking away, the despairing jobless men would mumble, "I see the usual lot got the work, then!" Remarks such as these would be met with comments like, "They're only payin' half a crown anyway," which would elicit, "That's typical of the bosses, that is, bleedin' us poor sods dry, they are, bleedin' us dry." This would provoke responses such as, "The union should do something about it!" Which would be answered with, "They are! They're in cahoots with the bosses! So long as the union get their subs they don't care." Men would nod in agreement. "If it's not the bleedin' bosses bleedin' us dry it's the bleedin' union bleedin' us dry." Such words would be repeated time and again before the men went their separate ways, ending up in pubs all along Dock Road. While men can afford the price of a pint of beer there will be no revolution in England.

CHAPTER 2

Charlie woke in the bitter cold of the pre-dawn. It was not the shimmer coming through the curtainless ice-covered windows that woke him; it was always the cold that did it, though not so the others. His siblings would lie asleep until Mary Carter's poor-house-morning-chorus-consumptive-croak tore them from their slumber. She sounded like a smoker but had never taken a drag of tobacco in her entire life. In her case, as well as that of most women of the Cauldron, this was due to the price of tobacco, as there were no health concerns connected with smoking in those days. In fact, as tobacco suppressed hunger, it was seen as a boon product despite it costing more than the food it deprived families of. As usual, Charlie remained in bed to keep his brothers warm after his mother's alarm call and to partake in whispered conversations with his sisters, as they usually woke before Jed and Patrick Jnr.

"Charlie?" hissed Effy. "Is it true that Mr Lewis is in the loony bin and not in London after all?"
"Where'd you hear that?"
"Everybody's talking about it. They're saying that Jed and his mates saw him in the Storm Hill Sanatorium when they went up there the other day."
"We're not supposed to say anything in case Mrs Lewis hears about it; she's so ashamed and Stevie won't leave the house."

"I heard he won't leave the house because the men in white coats are after him and they nearly grabbed him the other day."

"Where do you hear all this stuff?"

"Everybody's talking about it."

"Do me a favour, will ye? Stop talking about it. If you keep talking about it then we're bound to get into trouble, so stop talking about it."

"Mum and Dad said that the men in white coats are taking more and more kids to Storm Hill and they're worried that you and Jed'll be next."

This news shocked and angered Charlie. He was the eldest child and it should be him that Mum and Dad told stuff to, not the girls.

"That's rubbish. Anyway, when did they tell you that?"

"Oh, they didn't tell us, we heard them talking to Uncle Billy and Aunty May about it. They're dead worried, Charlie, they're thinking of moving away."

"Where would we go?"

"They're thinking of Nana Lyons' house."

"But that's only a few streets away."

"I know, but they said the men in white coats don't go there for some reason. Anyway, it's time to get up."

"How can you tell it's time to get up? It's still dark."

Just then Mary Carter yelled up the stairs that it was time for the kids to get out of bed. She shouted that she had already lit the fire and they were to come straightaway so that the warmth would not go to waste. As usual it was porridge and weak tea for breakfast. Charlie had heard that some kids did not get any breakfast at all, while kids from the posh parts of Ravenport had chocolate for breakfast. He wasn't sure about that because chocolate was a luxury even for posh kids, or so he believed at least. Though Charlie had no evidence to back his thought up; it just made sense to him that not even posh kids could afford to eat chocolate for breakfast.

Before he left the house that morning to venture out once again into the cold and the smog, Charlie turned to his mum and asked her about the men in white coats taking children away. She looked at her husband before saying that he was not to worry, and then patting him on the head she shoved him and the other children out the door with the instep of her foot.

The Carter children joined in with all the others skidding and sliding their way along Dock Road to their various schools. Most attended Holy Cross School, including nearly all of Charlie's relatives, as the area was predominantly Catholic. Holy Cross was in New Street, two streets down from Penny Street. There was a huge amount of rivalry between the two schools, which often erupted into fights, particularly between certain pupils, one of the main culprits being Charlie's cousin, and next-door neighbour, the fearsome Billy Lynch.

★

When Patrick Carter renounced the Catholic faith to become a Methodist it caused a huge scandal across the whole of the extended Lynch family, but he was adamant that he was not ever going back to Catholicism. "And neither is me wife or any of me children," he had announced at the time. Since then, most of the family, and it was a truly massive clan, shunned Patrick, though they remained friendly towards Mary and the children. They felt sorry for her having to live with 'that heathen Patrick', ever fostering the hope that they could eventually wear Mary and the children down and bring them back to the faith. Charlie and Jed were quite happy being Methodists because the services were short and they were not noticed when they skipped Sunday school to go playing on the swings in the park. His sisters, however, desperately wanted to be Catholic again because they liked the dressing-up and all the ceremony and rituals connected with the religion. They thought

Catholic Priests were better than Methodist Ministers or the Priests of the Protestant Church, who they had in last place in their order of preference.

Patrick was the youngest of fifteen surviving children and Mary the youngest of ten. As they were the 'babies' of their respective families, and with poor people knowing how to suffer through giving, both he and Mary were spoilt rotten, or as rotten as it is possible to be spoilt in poverty. Some of their nieces and nephews were older than they were. A couple of them, being Merchant Seamen, brought back gifts for them, from faraway places, that were the envy of all the children in the Cauldron. Being from such poor families, Patrick and Mary looked after their toys and clothes to the extent that they were in good enough condition to pass on to their own children. Their family of six children was small compared with those of their siblings as well as the families in the area, but they had felt six was enough, so they stopped there. With the recent advances in medicine, hygiene and health, even six children was far too many. The number of children surviving into their teens and beyond was the reason why so many families struggled to survive. The next generation could do something about it by having fewer children, but the families of that generation cursed their ill fortune – silently, and in private of course, especially when Priests were around, but nevertheless they cursed their 'blessings'.

★

The children filed into the school hall in age order from eldest to youngest for morning assembly to partake in hymns and prayers and listen to announcements. The eldest children were now sat on the floor at the front of the hall. They used to sit at the back of the hall but were so badly behaved that the Headmaster thought it best to have them close at hand where he could watch them and punish mischief-makers. The Head's favourite form of punishment was a good old-fashioned caning. Six stripes across the bottoms of bad boys, but not so the girls; they would get a one-foot boxwood ruler across the palms of their hands. There was virtually no pain involved, but the girls would put on an act to satisfy the Headmaster that the punishment had been properly administered. The middling children remained in the middle of the hall, while the youngest were seated on the floor at the rear of the hall. Why the Head thought the youngest children would be better behaved than the older children baffled school staff, as they were the siblings of the older children and had learnt their behaviours from them in the first place. In short, they were no better behaved, and for that matter they were often worse behaved, than their older brothers and sisters.

The Headmaster stood behind the lectern, which was located in the middle of the stage for assemblies, and said, "Good morning, children." After which the entire school assembly chorused, "Good morning, Mr Bawles," in response. No matter how many times the children said this it was all they could do to choke back their laughter. After gagging much of their laughter, the children were about to burst into song with hymn number twenty-three, 'The Lord Is My Shepherd', when Mr Bawles held up his hand to silence them.

"Children! Staff! Before we begin our assembly this morning I have some announcements to make. My first announcement concerns young William Patterson, who I believe many of you know as 'Patto'. You'll be pleased to hear he has been discharged from hospital." This announcement was met with cheers from Patto's friends, and jeers and boos from his enemies. "Settle down now, children, settle down," said the Head, giving the main perpetrators of the disruption the stink-eye. "As it will take some time for him to recover from his injuries he has been sent to convalesce in the Sanatorium at Storm Hill." This part of the Head's announcement was met with gasps of astonishment and head-swivelling from children looking from side to side in disbelief. "I won't tell you lot again!" snarled Mr Bawles. "Settle down or I'll bring out Mr Cane!" he growled, glaring at the main troublemakers. He wrote down something in his notebook; the offenders thought it was probably their names for punishment later. "Now, children, it sometimes falls to me to make the saddest of announcements. Some of you will have noticed that the Lewis children aren't at school today. In fact it is likely we won't be seeing some of them for a while." Behind the Head some teachers were crying into handkerchiefs. "Late last night a fire took hold at the Lewis home. They all escaped with their lives, but several of the children sustained burns. Little Steven Lewis had to be rescued from the house, as he refused to leave it in spite of the flames. He has been taken to the Sanatorium at Storm Hill for treatment, but he is not expected to survive." The entire assembly dissolved into tears and wailing, which Mr Bawles did not attempt to stem. "I know young Steven was very popular, so I've asked Father Grogan to lead the assembly in a prayer for him." Mr Bawles looked toward the back of the assembly hall and beckoned Father Grogan to join him on the stage.

After Father Grogan finished leading the prayer for Stevie Lewis he spoke some words of hope for his recovery. He said that Stevie was in the best place to get the best treatment and asked everybody to pray for him every night before they went to sleep. As the children and staff thought Father Grogan had finished speaking they began filing out the assembly hall, but he called out to them, saying that he wanted to tell them about a trip the church was arranging for the children during the coming Easter holiday. He said there were to be games and prizes and he would let them know more soon.

Charlie noticed Mr Bawles looked furious with Father Grogan after his announcement. The Head and the Priest then grabbed one another by the lapels, turning and spiralling to the back of the stage in some kind of mad fight-dance, hiss-whispering into each other's faces and spraying enough spittle to drown a cat. They then began pushing and shoving one another. Mr Bawles tripped over the curtain at the side of the stage, which almost sent him toppling over. Their arguing continued behind the curtain and some swearing was heard above the hubbub of the children filing out of the assembly hall.

"Did you see that?" said Izzy Sanchez. "I bet Father Grogan could batter Mr Bawles if he wanted to," she speculated.

"You what? No chance! Bawlesey'd burst Father Grogan dead easy. Have ye seen the size of him? He's got arms on him like a Docker!" responded 'Thrupence', the nickname of Arthur Sixpence. Arthur's siblings were nicknamed 'Tanner', which was apt but confusing as there were a dozen of them.

"I wonder where the trip will be to and what games'll be played and —"

"Stop going on about it! If ye want to know then go along to the church after school and ask Father Grogan!"

"I bet ye there's no trip or prizes or any of that. I bet it's just a trick to get us to go to church because they need a few extra bob."

"Well, Jonesy, if you'd stop sticking your hand in the collection plate they'd be alright for money." Everybody laughed because they knew Jonesy stole from the church collection plate while it was being passed around. He would hide behind one of the columns, dip his hand into the plate and wiggle it around to make it sound like he was putting money in, before grabbing a handful of change and stuffing it into his pocket.

"Do you think you'll be going on this trip over Easter, Charlie?"

"Definitely. It'll be great to get away from this place for a while. I hope we're going far away. I'm fed up with the smog. It's been smoggy for almost four and a half weeks solid now."

"Me ma says it's the coal that makes the smog, and with Lord Whatshisname's League of Thingies handing the stuff out to everybody for free it's only going to get worse. That's what me ma says anyway."

"Don't be stupid. How can coal make smog?"

"I don't know, Harry, have you seen the amount of smoke that cheap coal makes, especially when it's damp? And the stuff we get from Thingy's League of Welldoers is always soaking wet, you can hardly light it at times," answered the knowledgeable Izzy Sanchez.

The children arrived at their classrooms, giving one another friendly punches on arms before their lessons began.

★

"What the hell are you playing at, Grogan? You know very well that we depend on the children doing the spring planting over Easter, so what's all this about you taking them away?"

"You don't even pay them the money you get for the work they do! They're just free labour to you, Mr Bawles, just free labour. You ought to be ashamed of yourself. Instead of dragging them off to work from dawn to dusk you should be concerned with the health and welfare of the children in your charge."

"It does them good working on the farm! All that fresh air!"

"Mr Bawles, they're only children and they can't be studying during term time and then be forced to work on the school farm during the holidays. They need to let off some steam."

"Let off steam? Let off steam! They're always bloody well letting off bloody steam! Look at how many of them end up in hospital with broken this or fractured that! If they let off any more steam they'll explode! And where is it that you're taking them by the way?"

"Lord Harbinger has kindly agreed to let us camp on the grounds of his estate for the entire Easter week." Mr Bawles' face went as white as a sheet and his legs turned to jelly at this news.

"Father Grogan, you can't be serious! Take the children to Harbinger's estate? You know what'll happen to them. He'll cart them off never to be seen again!"

"I don't believe the old wives' tales, Mr Bawles, all I see is a philanthropist keen to do good for the benefit of the poor. Why, he's even started giving each household free sacks of coal! And he's giving them meat too," said the Priest, prodding Mr Bawles' chest with every word. "Good cuts, mind you, good cuts, not scrag ends or the gristly innards of glue animals." Father Grogan eyed the Headmaster up and down in disgust before continuing. "Tell me, Headmaster, I understand Penny Street School benefits from Lord Harbinger's generosity, does it not?" Mr Bawles remained silent. "Well? Is the coal you burn from the Storm Hill League of Welldoers or not? No? Yes? I notice you burn it instead of returning it."

"The School Board would replace me if I did that."

"You know, Mr Bawles, I hear say that it is the damp coal that is responsible for all this smog we're getting."

"That's nonsense, Father Grogan, complete nonsense. We've always had smog in Ravenport, always!"

"But not like this. Not for weeks and months on end without let-up. And it's getting thicker and more noxious. Some of the children can hardly breathe it's so thick and noxious."

"Then what should I do, Father Grogan, stop burning free coal? If I did that then the School Board would definitely replace me!"

"So you keep saying, you old hypocrite."

"Now, Father, that's no way for a Priest to be speaking!"

"But it's true, Mr Bawles, and I'm sure you wouldn't want a man of God to lie. You're a hypocrite and you've been bleeding the whole community dry for years, yet it appears somewhat differently in the school accounts. Would you care to explain, Mr Bawles?"

"I'm warning you, Grogan, be careful where you stick your nose. Now get out of my school and don't come back."

"I'll leave for now, Mr Bawles, but as Penny Street falls under our diocese I'll be back to give my regular sermons."

"You can send one of the others to do the sermons. If you ever show your face here again I'll kick you out on your arse," warned

Mr Bawles. Father Grogan walked away lest things got out of hand, leaving the Headmaster to stew in his own juices.

*

Father Grogan was one of three Priests ministering at Christ Church with Father Francis, a scallywag who all the females in the district thought very handsome and many had a 'thing' for, and Father Horan, a fierce, pious, heavy-drinking man of whom everyone was terrified, including every Priest in Ravenport and miles beyond. There were six Priests at Christ Church, but after half of it mysteriously burned down one smoggy night only three could be accommodated; also the population of the area was reducing so there was no need for any more than three Priests.

*

Word got around during the lunch break that seven or eight children had been taken in the night by the men in white coats. Some pupils told how their parents had seen them being trussed up in straitjackets with their feet tied before being bundled into a rig resembling a cage on wheels pulled by two massive black horses. They all swore that their parents had sworn oaths that the rig made no sound whatsoever as it made off over the cobblestones. "It was like a ghost wagon," said some of the older children to frighten the younger ones. The stories got exaggerated as they were passed around, heightening the terror in the minds of those easily frightened, but there was something in the consistency of the tales that made the stories believable as fact. Panic and fear took hold of the children. Charlie Carter attempted to quell the anxiety in the smaller children as some of them were starting to cry.

"Listen, there's nothing to be afraid of. Me and Jed and Moey and Patto saw the same sort of rig on Dock Road the other night. It was there one minute and disappeared into the smog the next. We didn't hear a thing; it was dead quiet. We reckoned it must've been the smog deadening the noise; it was a bad one that night. Honest, it's nothing to be worried about."

"Wasn't Patto run down by a rig that night?"

"Yeah, he was, but the smog was really bad, so it's not surprising that he got run down; none of us could see very far or hear anything very much."

"What did the rig look like, Charlie?" asked one child.

"Was it like the one that took the kids away last night?" asked another child.

"Was it a cage on wheels then, Charlie?" asked a third child.

"I can't really remember, it all happened so fast. I do remember that it was pulled by two massive black horses, though." Charlie's intention had been to calm the situation, but he had made it far worse.

"Nice one, Carter, you've done a great job of scaring them all out of their wits," sneered Lorcan Thorne, as if he cared whether the children were frightened or not. Thorne was one of the Storm Hill kids that had recently enrolled in Penny Street School: a notorious bully and sworn enemy of Charlie Carter. Nobody knew why this was as Charlie was one of the most popular and likeable kids in school.

When the children returned to their classrooms after lunch break it was all their teachers could do to get them to pay attention. They kept looking out of the window, wondering when the fog would roll in off the river and turn to smog. Mr Bawles stomped along the corridors from class to class, brandishing his cane like a Sabre, making swishing sounds as it slashed through the air. He warned the children that unless they settled down to their lessons he would hold them in detention and thoroughly cane them until they behaved themselves. The threat was enough for the majority of the children to sit upright and face forward, as they did not want to walk along Dock Road in the smog, especially after what had happened to Patto.

The school day finished, as normal, at three thirty for the younger children and four o'clock for the older ones. The smog arrived at three forty-five. It was as though it was on a timer. Jed and his mates did not hang around to carry out their usual shenanigans; instead they met up with their siblings so they could all walk home together. They did not even stop to stare at the toys in Marsden's shop window; they just trudged along Dock Road from one cone of yellow light to another cone of yellow light illuminating their way home. They walked with their heads bowed in silence, which was hardly surprising considering the circumstances, but the shop owners thought it rather disturbing.

*

When Charlie and Jed arrived home, Mary asked them where Patrick Jnr was. They told her that he had left school at half three along with all the other younger children.

"He wasn't in detention, I looked in as I passed the detention room," said the well-informed Jed Carter.

Mary went frantic. "Where the hell has he got to, then? You two are going to have to go out and look for him! I'll ask around to see if he's in anybody's house."

Charlie and Jed retraced the well-worn pavements back along Dock Road toward Penny Street, asking people along the way if they had seen their little brother. Meanwhile, Mary went door knocking and eventually found her youngest son eating stew at his Aunty Agnes' house. Mary, though relieved at finding her son, was angry that her sister-in-law had not let her know that Patrick Jnr was at her house. Agnes, known to all as Aggie or Aggie Moan, told Mary that she had told Aunty Vicky to knock on Mary's door to let her know Patrick Jnr was having stew at her house. Mary grabbed Patrick Jnr by the arm to march him home, but Aggie asked her to stay for a cup of tea and a chat, as she wanted to clear the air over the family feud, but instead she broke down in tears.

"Mary love, the men in white coats came and took little Kevin away last night. Our Stella's going out of her mind with worry."

"Why did they take Kevin? Was he ill or something?"

"He took a funny turn about eight and before they knew it the men in white coats were at the door asking for him. They had a doctor with them, and he said that the lad needed urgent treatment, and as the hospital was full he said to take him to Storm Hill and off they went. They stuck him in a straitjacket and everything. Why would they stick a little kid in a straitjacket, eh, Mary? Why?"

"I don't know, love, but I heard that they took seven or eight last night."

"Jesus tonight and tomorrow!" exclaimed Aggie and, crossing herself multiple times to invoke the protection of her God, "It's starting all over again! They're carting off our kids!"

"Oh Christ, don't go saying that, Aggie, you'll put the…" Mary stopped speaking mid-sentence as a sudden realisation hit her. "Oh Jesus, our Charlie and our Jed are out looking for Patrick Jnr. I'll have to run home to see if they've come back. If I'm not there they might go out looking again."

"I'll come with you. I want a talk with you about a few things anyway."

"Tell you what, love, I'll come back later and we'll talk then, okay?" And with that Mary bolted out the door dragging Patrick Jnr behind her.

What none in the Cauldron realised was that each of the children taken the previous night had visited Old Mother McGee's shop, where she had sneaked them a sweetie to eat in secret after their supper. This was how the men in white coats knew where to visit and make their calls. Old Mother McGee was, of course, a Familiar, as were most of those running businesses in Ravenport. There was nobody to protect the ordinary people of the Cauldron, nor was there anywhere for them to hide from the evil that dogged their lives.

*

When Mary Carter did not show by half past eight, Aggie Moan decided to pay her a visit. She had a lot on her mind and Mary was the only person she felt she could talk to. Not wanting to venture out onto Dock Road, Aggie took a shortcut across the grounds of Christ Church. A door opened to her right. From it a wide yellow slice cut through the smog.

"Who's there?" shouted Father Francis. Aggie Moan recognised the voice.

"It's me, Father Francis," she replied. Aggie, like most of the women of the parish, thought Father Francis very handsome. *Too handsome to be a Priest*, she and others thought.

"Is that you, Agnes Lynch?" Aggie moved toward the light.

"It is, Father Francis. I'm making me way to our Mary's. Her lads are out looking for Patrick Jnr, but he was with me and when Mary found out she had to get home in case they came back and then went out again looking for Patrick Jnr, if ye know what I mean Father?" Father Francis knew exactly what she meant.

"Would you like me to accompany you? It's not easy getting about in this smog with the flagstones having raised edges." Aggie jumped at the chance of having Father Francis show her the way.

"Oh, yes please, Father, that's very kind of you, Father. Can I link your arm so I don't fall, Father?" Father Francis looped his right arm for Aggie to pass her arm through. She smiled and pulled the handsome Priest close and off the pair went.

As Aggie and Father Francis approached the house they heard a loud pandemonium being raised in the streets. Aggie ran toward the noise. By the light of the parlour window, she saw Mary Carter standing in the street. She had her head in her hands and was crying streams of tears.

"What's up?" asked Agnes. Mary could hardly speak to reply.

"It's our Jed, Aunty Aggie," said Charlie, "he's missing. I think the men in white coats have taken him away," answered the lad, speaking for his mother.

"Who took Jed away?" asked Father Francis, having joined the group.

"I think the men in white coats snatched him while we were out looking for Patrick Jnr. He was right next to me then a rig came up behind us, so we ran. I thought we were together, but when I turned around I couldn't see him. I called out, but he wasn't there. I looked for him for ages, then I came back home to tell Mum and Dad what had happened. Dad's out looking for Jed now. He's got some of his brothers and their mates with him, so hopefully they'll find him." Charlie turned to look at his mother. "Don't worry, Mum, they'll find our Jed even if they have to tear down the walls of Storm Hill. They'll find him and they'll bring him back home."

"Oh, Mary, it's all my fault," cried Agnes. "I shouldn't've brought Patrick Jnr to my house, but I needed to speak with you. I knew you'd come looking for him and, well, with things being the way they are I couldn't very well drop round, now, could I?" Mary reached out and hugged Agnes.

"Don't blame yourself, love, you weren't the one driving the rig. It comes to something when we can't walk our own streets in safety. Something's got to be done. We can't go on like this!"

"Shhhhhh. Listen. Listen. Is that Dad's voice?" cried Charlie.

"It is. What's he shouting?"

"Dad! Dad! Where are ye? Where are ye?" Charlie yelled. Out

of the smog came Patrick Snr and his brother Stan, followed by a line of ghostly silhouettes.

"We found him. We found your Jed! He's had a bit of a fall, but he's okay. They're bringing him now."

Patrick Snr carried Jed into the house. Mary kissed her son all over his face and then scolded him for causing her so much worry. Father Francis cradled Jed in his arms, making the sign of the cross over him. The men stood around not knowing what to do or say, as they were not on speaking terms with Patrick Snr for renouncing the faith and becoming a Methodist. Agnes ordered them all to go to the pub and sort their differences out. They did not need telling twice and disappeared to the local, which was only forty feet away, as there was a pub on every street corner in those days.

Jed was more seriously hurt than first thought. His arm was so badly injured that Mary wondered whether she should take the lad to the hospital, but as many children ended up in Storm Hill after visiting there she was reluctant to do so. Charlie and his siblings sat vigil next to Jed while Mary went into the kitchen with Agnes to prepare a poultice. Moments later, Stella Malart appeared in the kitchen asking what had happened to Jed and if he was alright. Aggie quickly brought her up to date, and at the end she asked Stella to give Mary and her some privacy, as they needed to have a talk about a few things.

"No, not after what's happened to our Kevin. I want to get to the bottom of this as much as youz two do." Not wanting to cause another family argument the women agreed that Stella could remain.

"I don't understand it, Stella, your Draven's one of them and yet they took your Kevin. Why? What the hell's going on, girl?"

"I don't know, Aggie, honest a God, I'm telling ye, I honestly don't know. I'm going out of me mind and Draven won't tell me anything. He just says that Kevin'll be alright and that I'm not to worry and I'm not to talk to anybody about it."

"I like your Draven and all that, but there's something not right there, Stella, don't you think?" queried Agnes.

"I love him, Aggie, honest a God I love him, but he needs to decide whose side he's on because at the moment it doesn't seem like he's on mine."

"Well, I can't take it anymore, we're moving out," announced Aggie.

"Where will you go, Aggie love?" asked Mary, wiping away her tears.

"Far away from here, that's for sure."

"How will ye manage the rent and that? I know it's not a very nice area, but you're amongst friends here and the rent's cheap."

"Your rent might be cheap, Mary love, but our Landlord is bleeding us dry. When we can't afford the rent he makes us work in his slaughterhouse or cleaning his cellars out to make up the difference."

"There's a few places going in our street, Aggie love, and the Landlord isn't a robber. I don't want you to go, Aggie. We don't want the family split up any more than it already is. And besides, now we're all getting free coal and meat that's another reason for you to stay," said Stella cheerfully.

"That's nothing. I heard the other day that the Storm Hill League of Welldoers have been giving free coal and free meat to the schools around here for ages."

"Those crafty old sods Bawles and McGuiness kept that one quiet, didn't they?"

"Nobody gives you something for nothing. It's dead suspicious if you ask me. There's definitely something going on."

"Have you heard what they're saying? It's the wet coal what they're giving us that's causing the smog!"

"I have, love, I have, but that doesn't sound right to me. Does it sound right to you, Stella?"

"I don't care, I'm thinking of taking a leaf out of your book and getting out of here."

"Where will you go?"

"If we go anywhere we're going to have to move in with Draven's family."

"Do you think that's a good idea, Stella? They're a weird lot up there at Storm Hill and some of their names are very unusual. Where is it they're from anyway?"

"All over the place, all over the place, but I'm not hanging round here waiting for them to take more of me kids away."

"I thought they'd stopped all that years ago. Why have they started again?"

"I didn't mind so much when it was just the tramps that they were taking away, but this isn't on. We need to get the church involved."

"What? That lot are already involved. I wouldn't go near them if me life depended on it," exclaimed Mary.

"Is that why Patrick renounced the faith, is it, Mary? Is it because the church is letting them take the tramps away?"

"Never mind all that, where's Father Francis? Did you see where he went?"

Before either Aggie or Stella could answer Mary's question, Charlie burst into the kitchen to tell his mum that she needed to come straightaway and listen to what Jed had to say. In the back parlour, the patient was propped up next to the fire grate for warmth with his siblings huddled around him.

"Hey, Mum, you should hear what our Jed just said," said Effy hesitatingly. Charlie told everybody to be quiet and just listen to Jed's story. He began with him and Charlie becoming separated and the appearance of the rig. He said he heard voices talking about Moey so decided to follow the rig. He said he could not understand how it could drive so fast in the smog and he soon lost it, but having heard the men mention Moey he made for his friend's house. Jed claimed the rig made no sound whatsoever and neither did the horses pulling it. He arrived at Moey's just in time to see him being taken away by the men in white coats. He ducked inside a neighbour's doorway to hide. Then he heard a deep growling drawing near. He said he did not dare to breathe for fear of giving his presence away. A man shouted, "Shut up, we can't hear anything with your bloody growling, you godless abomination!" Next thing came a doglike yelp. As the man moved off Jed followed to see if he went to the rig. He dropped to his hands and knees and, crawling toward the rig, came face to face with, "a creature. I can't say what it was because I've never seen anything like it before. It was a kind of a dog but not a dog. It looked me straight in the eyes. It had yellowy gold-coloured eyes that could see through the smog. I don't know how I knew they could see through the smog, I just knew they could." Jed said he thought the game was up, but the creature just sniffed him and turned away. Then a man kicked the creature; it yelped and jumped up onto the rig followed by several men. According to Jed, two of the men were wearing white coats, while the third was dressed all in black, "like a Priest, he was dressed just like a Priest." Jed climbed onto the back of the rig and, lifting a cloth, discovered a cage beneath. He heard one of the men say, "Let's get going, they'll be waiting for us to return with our catch."

The rig set off at lightning speed. Jed opened the cage and once inside he saw four bodies lying on the floor. He recognised one of them as Moey Groom. The others were children he knew from school. They were wearing straitjackets and gagged with rags stuffed into their mouths. The door to the cage snapped shut from the rig jolting, locking them all inside. Jed shook Moey. He seemed drowsy as though he had been given a powder from the chemist shop. There was no time to lose. Jed, with much difficulty, freed Moey and the others before reaching through the bars to release the latch. The cage door sprung open, catapulting Jed through the air. He hit his head on the wall of a building before crashing to the pavement. The next thing he knew he was face to face with the creature again. Jed stopped speaking, reluctant to continue.

"What happened next, son?" asked Mary. Jed looked away.

"I don't want to say, Mum, in case you think I'm mad and have me carted off to the loony bin." The children urged Jed to tell their mum what he had told them. "Alright, but promise you won't laugh at me or hit me or anything."

"There'll be no laughter or hitting you for telling the truth, son."

"Alright then. Honest a God, Mum, this thing spoke to me. Not like a person, it was all croaky, but it spoke to me. It told me to run. It croaked, 'Run… run,' so I did." Mary and the other women were stunned into silence. Before they were able to say anything Charlie spoke.

"Mum, I believe our Jed. I believe him, Mum." Concerned with the turn the story had taken, Mary told the smaller children to go to bed.

"Jed love, dogs don't talk. You've had a bad bang on your head and you're probably not feeling right."

"There's more, Mum. It asked me to help him. It did, Mum, honest a God, it did. It said, 'Help… help us,' then it growled and ran away."

"That's it, I'm getting the doctor out to you," said Mary, concerned that her son had sustained a serious injury to his head.

"No, Mum, don't do that!" cried Charlie. "Look, there's not much wrong with Jed, so there's no need for a doctor. The doctor'll just send for the men in white coats and they'll cart him off to Storm Hill and that's the last place we want him to go. Think about it, Mum. Think about all the kids being carted off by the men in white coats never to be seen again!" Just then Patrick Snr arrived home. He was clearly drunk.

"Where the hell did you get the money to get drunk, Patrick Carter?" yelled Mary.

"Now then, Mary girl, don't be like that. All our drinks were bought for us. I didn't even have to pay for a round," replied Patrick Snr, tapping the coins in his trouser pocket.

"Oh yeah! Who was it then that bought you these drinks, Paddy?"

"This fella, never seen him before, but he's welcome back anytime."

"See, Mum! People giving us free coal, free meat and now free beer."

"And ciggies!" added Patrick Snr, pulling a pack of ten 'tailor-made' cigarettes from the pocket where he kept his dusty bag of rolling tobacco.

"See, Mum, see! Free ciggies too! What next?"

"Well, Paddy Carter, while you've been gallivanting in the pub your son's hit his head so hard he thinks dogs can talk. I want to get the doctor out to him, but Charlie thinks it's a bad idea. What do you think, Paddy love? Shall we get the doctor out to look at our Jed or not?" Patrick Snr lit a cigarette and thought for a while.

"Nah, the lad'll be alright after a good night's sleep. If he's not then we'll take him to the hospital tomorrow. Now then, I'm off to bed," said Patrick Snr, scooping Jed up in his arms. "By the way, Mary love, I'm working tomorrow. How about that? I got meself a job."

"Where the hell did you get yourself a job at this time of night?"

"From the fella in the pub. He gave all of us jobs that don't have jobs. That doesn't sound right, but you know what I mean?" With that, Patrick Snr staggered off to bed cradling Jed in his arms. "By the way, love, the bloke said if it gets permanent we might have to move to Storm Hill," shouted Patrick Snr down the stairs. "I'll see how hard it is getting there tomorrow morning, and if it's too hard then we'll have to move."

Charlie glared at his mum and aunties in disbelief; he didn't need to say anything, they were convinced after what Patrick Snr had said, and with all that was going on, it was entirely possible that Jed had indeed heard a dog speak. Later, after Agnes and Stella had left to return to their own homes, Charlie sidled up next to his mum and, putting his arm around her shoulders, whispered, "I don't want to make things worse, Mum, but that thing our Jed saw sounds like the same sort of thing I saw at Nana's house when I was small." Mary told her son she had heard enough for one night and to stop going on about things he had seen in his nana's house. She added that she hoped he was joking, as they might have to move in with his nana soon.

"C'mon, son, it's late. Time for bed," whispered Mary. Charlie kissed his mum on the cheek and wished her a good night. She returned Charlie's and said, "You go on, son, I'll follow you up after I've raked out the fire." As Mary was raking out the fire a loud banging came on the front door. When she opened it there stood Father Francis flanked by two men in white coats. The Priest said that as Jed was so badly injured the men had come to take him to Storm Hill. Mary replied in an off-handed way that Father Francis was mistaken, as Jed was nowhere near as badly injured as first thought and he was now sleeping soundly in his bed with his brothers. Charlie Carter sat on the top stair silently listening to the proceedings in the hallway below. Hearing what the Priest had said, Charlie retrieved the length of lead pipe his father kept for unwelcome visitors from its hiding place. He raised it above his head ready to bash in the skull of anybody who tried to take Jed away. When he heard the front door close and it became evident that Father Francis and the men in white coats were on the other side of it, Charlie replaced the lead pipe back into its hiding place, and as he did so his father whispered from the shadows, "Well done, son. You're a good lad, I'm dead proud of ye."

CHAPTER 3

Storm Hill, its estates, forests, lands and tenanted farms, were bestowed upon Mordred Harbinger by Queen Elizabeth I. Before that time few had heard of him and wondered about his credentials and lineage and what acts he had performed for the young Queen to warrant giving such a large and generous reward. Not even those at the centre of Elizabeth's Court knew what he had done to be honoured so generously. Historians write about the parts played by Cecil, Dudley and Walsingham during Queen Elizabeth's reign, but none wrote about Mordred Harbinger, in spite of him being as important to her as any of her closest and most trusted advisers.

Mordred Harbinger stayed away from Court as much as he possibly could while he played the role of Elizabeth's eyes and ears in the north and even abroad. Those few who knew of him were astonished at the speed with which he gathered intelligence at a time when it took four days to ride from his estate on the outskirts of Ravenport to London. Sometimes, he would appear at Court twice in the same week and on each occasion would bring fresh intelligence and sometimes even news from the French and Spanish Courts. He would turn up unannounced at wherever Elizabeth was holding court and somehow eluded the guards to suddenly appear without anybody noticing his presence until he spoke. Elizabeth thought this a wonderful trick, but not so her advisers. They were concerned that if Harbinger could do this then an assassin could do the same. Elizabeth eventually relented when Walsingham insisted he interrogate Harbinger as to how he gained access to her court without anybody noticing him. Whenever Elizabeth quizzed Walsingham about progress with his enquiries into Mordred Harbinger he could not remember embarking on such a quest. Shortly thereafter their conversation slipped from their minds, as did everything concerning the new Lord Harbinger, and with everybody else it seemed. Sometimes, when Lord Harbinger came up in conversation, people would have to be reminded who he was, and even then the memory of him would not persist for more than a few hours or a day at the most. Yet whenever he appeared everybody knew instantly who he was and carried on as though he had never been away.

It is one thing to be handed a vast estate, but entirely another to turn it into something which can reach down the centuries to become worthy of inheritance. But that is exactly what Lord Harbinger did. As soon as he began building his Manor House there appeared all manner of exotic strangers, few of whom seemed concerned with construction. They settled in the local area as tenant farmers and the like, though their farms were only productive after they hired people to do the farming for them. Others were artisans producing earthenware, metal, woven and cane goods. They were of unusual design and decoration, but being of good quality they were in demand throughout the North West region of England.

As Manor Houses go, Lord Harbinger's Mormant Hall was gigantic, such that it was reported to Walsingham as being a substantial Fortress. The word 'Fortress' implied something military, which in turn implied insurrection. Walsingham took this as his opportunity to do away with Harbinger once and for all, but when he spoke to Queen Elizabeth about Lord Harbinger's Fortress she forbade him from saying anything at all about Lord Harbinger unless it was complimentary. This infuriated Walsingham, but he soon forgot about it and whenever the subject of Harbinger's Fortress came up he would simply enquire, "Oh, how is it coming along? I must go and see it one day." But he never did. After Elizabeth's death the subject of Lord Harbinger and his Fortress was raised with James I, Charles I, Oliver Cromwell, Charles II and so on to Victoria. It was during Victoria's reign that reports of Lord Harbinger and his Storm Hill Estate and Manor House completely evaporated from Royal interest.

By the mid-1800s, Mormant Hall was enclosed behind a high wall, with further protection from view provided by dense woodlands a mile deep. At that time, the estate consisted of fourteen tenanted farms, each with its own workers' cottages; four villages; several hamlets; and a cluster of eight large buildings hidden behind a brick-built wall topped with cemented-in glass shards and hand-cut iron nails to deter inquisitive wall-climbers, escapers and the alike. The largest of these buildings became the Storm Hill Sanatorium, while the others served as gaols and then workhouses. Imagine being incarcerated in a gaol or a workhouse run by Vampires? Little wonder many of the unfortunates who ended up there were never seen or heard of again and had paper records of their existence obliterated from history.

When his gaols eventually emptied, Lord Harbinger exploited the opportunities that destitution brought and converted the old gaols into workhouses. Even though the destitute were not a Vampire's food of choice they were far more nutritious than the lice-ridden criminals Mordred and His Disciples had endured feeding on for over a century.

Social reformers railed against workhouses, and so Lord Harbinger, ever alive to changing situations, closed his workhouses and formed the Storm Hill League of Welldoers dedicated to looking after the poor and needy of Ravenport and its environs. He even built a couple factories and mills to give paid employment to the poor. During this time a second influx of exotic strangers came to live in Storm Hill.

Long before the closure of the workhouses, Lord Harbinger bought up all local mines, with their former owners seeming to move from the area to London never to be seen or heard of again. From his mining enterprises Lord Harbinger had the necessary workforce to dig a deep shaft below the grounds of Mormant Hall in search of water. After finding water at just over 2,000 feet, the miners then dug a labyrinth of underground galleries and chambers which were later lined with stone. Some were fitted out for use as a Vampire Church, shrines, chambers, stores, cells and the like. In all, the miners dug over ten miles of galleries across four levels and hollowed out 480 chambers, with more added over the decades by slave labour.

The residents of Lord Harbinger's villages worked in the various buildings around Storm Hill, but nobody knew what it was that any of them did. Some were clearly artisans, but the occupations of the others remained a mystery. Over the years a few of the names of these strangers became known to the locals, but they were never certain if they were their real names, as they often didn't respond until they realised it was their name being shouted. Males of the villages occasionally married 'outsiders', such as Stella Lynch becoming Stella Malart after marrying Draven Malart, but it is totally unknown for females to marry outsiders. After marrying an outsider, the family would live away from Storm Hill, but, following the wife's death, they would always return there. This pattern did not go unnoticed by the locals and served to heighten suspicion about those living on Lord Harbinger's estate.

Toward the middle of the 1800s things took an unexpected turn after Humans and Vampires fought a bloody war in London. The Humans were led by somebody known as Nana Alice who gave Vampires an ultimatum to change their ways or be wiped out. And not just those in London; oh no, she meant every Vampire on the planet, and she possessed a weapon so deadly to Vampires that they had no choice but to capitulate and sign a Treaty which permitted them to feed only on the destitute and never on children. Successive generations of Humans are required to ratify the Treaty locally; signatories are known as Treaty Scribes. However, it being in the nature of certain Vampires or certain Humans to be ambitious, the Treaty gets broken from time to time, which leads to hostilities, ending only after appropriate tribute is paid to the innocent party and the perpetrator(s) being punished in some terrible way.

*

Storm Hill is situated above the smog line to the north-east of Ravenport. It is an ideal location from which to look down over the city, and especially so the docks. Though Mormant Hall is surrounded by high walls and protected from view by dense woodland, access to it is relatively straightforward. Anybody wishing to call there simply presents themselves at the Gatehouse built into the west wall. Appointments are necessary to gain admission beyond the eighteen-foot wrought-iron gates, but once inside the grounds the only road leads directly to Mormant Hall. The Gatehouse Wardens can sometimes be seen through the bars of the gate, but never outside the grounds. As for food and other essentials, everything that is required for the estate is produced within the grounds of Mormant Hall. It is known to have its own water supply, though how this can be baffles everybody, including experts, due to the depth of the water table. Engineers have speculated that to reach fresh water would require a borehole some 1,500 to 2,000 feet deep, and how 'aqua' sufficient to satisfy the estate's needs could be brought to the surface from this depth baffled everybody. It was rumoured that the estate somehow managed to grow grapes and produces its own wine. Those same rumourmongers put it about that Lord Harbinger distils his own whisky and gin for sale in London. Going by the stench drifting down from Storm Hill into Ravenport's northern suburbs, Mormant Hall must house a large population of pigs.

It is common for the 'Noble Ranks' to use their titles in conjunction with ordinal numbers to differentiate between the holders of the Station. And so, as a title passes from father to son, the son takes the next ordinal number as the 'n'th whatever of wherever. This applied to Lord Harbinger's line, despite there being no evidence of any 'issue'. And so, as with many things concerning Mormant Hall, lack of lineage served to heighten speculation as to what really went on there. Was there an actual Lord Harbinger? Or was some commoner using the title for their own benefit? But with the estate providing the poor of Ravenport with work, free coal, meat and, so it seemed, other 'essentials' such as beer and cigarettes, the population were not as concerned as they should have been.

★

"What! They got away? All of them?" screamed Tyran Skel.

"Yes, my Lord. They must've wriggled free from their straitjackets, opened the back of the cage and leapt out."

"What about the Lupule? Did they not track them down?"

"They seemed unwilling to —"

"Unwilling? What do you mean, 'unwilling'? I've never known them to fail before."

"The Repeste say they took them in the wrong direction on purpose. It was as though they wanted them to escape."

"Perhaps it was Xenka's Repeste that failed and not my Lupule. Bring them all here. Bring Seren too, I'll need her to help me get to the truth."

"What shall we do with the new children? If word gets out, there could be trouble. Shall we release them to show there's nothing for the people to be afraid of?"

"Afraid? Why should the people be afraid? We give them free coal and free food, and at Easter we're allowing their children to camp in the grounds for a week. No, there's no need to release any of them!"

"My Lord, some in the Cauldron are getting suspicious that it's the coal we are giving them that's causing the smog."

"Really? In that case, increase the amount of Somnifir in their food to keep them amenable. But don't use too much, we don't know what they are doing with it."

"What do you mean?"

"Poor people do strange and inexplicably stupid things. Even though they are starving, some of them might sell the meat, while others might eat it all themselves. Some might even hoard it. Who knows? If they ingest too much Somnifir we could have problems, real problems, so just a light sprinkling; just enough to keep them docile and a little forgetful. Now go, and don't forget to summon Seren."

★

Eighteen months previous, Tyran Skel and Xenka Drach led a rebellion against Lord Harbinger and wrested Storm Hill from him. Between them they controlled the Lupule, the nightmarish half-wolf half-Human nether-creatures, and the Repeste, the creatures who drove the wagons at such frightening speed in the smog. Storm Hill's Familiars were made to choose between joining the rebellion or being 'staked'. This was not the staking that 'dusts' Vampires, even though a stake through the heart of a Familiar does for them; this staking was of the type originally practised by Vlad Dracul when he impaled prisoners following battles. Dracul's version of staking was forcing a ten-foot-long sapling through the length of the torso, starting at the anus and exiting through the neck or mouth depending on the skill of the Staker. The end of the stake was planted in the ground, thereby creating forests of corpses, their cadavers swaying under the weight of scavengers fighting one another to pick their bones clean. Staking prisoners in this way had the dual effect of striking terror into the hearts of those who might rise up against Vlad Dracul's rule and, second, his Army were not weighed down by caring for thousands of prisoners.

Tyran and Xenka rebelled because they craved a life befitting a predator and not one where they were only allowed to feed on the drunken, lice-ridden dregs of Human society. They believed that they and their kind deserved good wholesome nutritious blood, not fetid disease-ridden fluid which caused stomach ache or occasionally eternal catatonic stupor. They believed that they saw things for what they were, not some idealised world built upon a Treaty for mollifying Proles.

★

Patrick Carter rose at five for the first day at his new job. He left the house by ten past with his knapsack containing his sandwiches slung over his shoulder. After reaching the top of Sanderson Street, Patrick headed along Heatherfield Road toward St George's Hill. It was a bitterly cold morning, and the smog, thicker than ever, it seemed, acted to keep the cold in. As he stumbled along, Patrick caught sight of several ghostly figures walking ahead of him.

"Are you lot off to Storm Hill by any chance?" shouted Patrick nervously.

"We are. Is that you, Paddy Carter?" returned one of the shapes.

"It is," answered Paddy, very much relieved.

The ghostly shapes belonged to the men Patrick had been drinking with the previous evening. He opened the pack of cigarettes he had been given in the pub and passed them around. The men drew heavily on the tailor-made ciggies, causing them to cough a choking morning chorus. As they reached the corner at St George's Hill, they came upon two men in white coats standing alongside a huge wagon drawn by massive black horses. One of the white-coated men asked if they were going to Storm Hill. Patrick answered saying that they were as they had been hired the night before but none of them could remember the name of the man in the bar who had hired them. One of the white-coated men took a headcount.

"You're two short!"

"That'll be the McCann brothers," said Patrick. "They're lie-abeds, you won't see them before eight."

"We'll send a wagon for them. Get aboard or you'll be late," said a white-coated man.

The wagon took off into the swirling smog at lightning speed, terrifying the passengers into thinking they were going to crash or drive into a ditch and die. However, they arrived at the next pickup point unscathed. There were three further pickups before the rig turned toward Storm Hill. The road was extremely steep, but the massive black horses took it like it was on the flat. Arriving at their destination, Patrick and his companions leapt from the wagon and hugged one another, glad to be alive.

An eerie sight greeted the men. They were above the smog line looking down toward the Cauldron. None of them had ever seen anything like it. Foggy wisps rose up and fell like waves crashing on an ocean in slow motion. Church spires and factory chimneys poked out through the smog as though they were floating in mid-air. The whole scene was surreal. While Patrick's group were standing around like lost children, the other passengers made their way toward a large iron gate. One of the white-coated men shouted, "Come on, you lot, get a move on. You've got work to do!" Their instinct was to turn and run, but where would they run to? Tommy Lyons was the first to move. "I haven't had a job for ages so I'm going in. Who's coming with me?" he cried. Not wanting to be left standing alone in their ghostly surroundings the men formed up behind Tommy and followed him into what they knew not.

★

A mile along the twilit fourth-level gallery stood the cell of Lord Harbinger. He was being kept in a docile state through regular, microscopically small, doses of Somnifir. More would likely destroy him; less and it could be dangerous for his gaolers. The door to Lord Harbinger's cell was guarded by four Vampires. At their sides were four Lupule in full battle armour, their eyes glowing yellow in the darkness.

Tyran Skel entered Lord Harbinger's cell, followed by Seren, in whose icy wake came the Repeste who lost the cargo of children and the Lupulo they claimed had refused to track them. Not wanting any witnesses around, Skel dismissed the Vampire guards. As the Lupule crossed paths they snarled their strange, unintelligible, language to one another. The insults hurled caused a fight, resulting in serious injury to two of the armoured Lupule. Nobody was interested in the fight, but had they been they would have been alarmed because trouble was brewing between the Lupule clans.

"My Lord," began Tyran Skel, "I have come to discuss matters regarding recent events with you."

"If I am still your Lord then why am I shackled to this bed? If it can be called that!"

"Last night, Xenka's Repeste apprehended some children who had climbed the wall of the Sanatorium and saw inside. According to Seren, they witnessed what they shouldn't have. We must take precautions. Even you must agree with that?"

"Your actions will only make things worse. We were forced to leave our home in the Carpathians because we did what you are now doing. It will only take a small spark to ignite the fire that will consume us all."

"If they had used Somnifir they wouldn't have had to flee!"

"You don't know what Somnifir can do."

"Then tell us, oh great one, exactly what it is Somnifir can do," mocked Tyran Skel. Lord Harbinger simply looked into Skel's eyes and smiled. "Smile all you want but your silence risks the survival of the House of Mormant. If there is danger in the way we are using Somnifir then it falls to you as Prima Vampir to tell us what you know."

"Never!"

"It's a pity that you have so little regard for the…" Tyran Skel could not be bothered finishing his sentence. "Well, my Lord, let us return to the matter in hand. You know more about Lupule than any other Vampire. They were bred to be obedient, so, tell me, is it possible for a Lupulo to disobey an order?" Lord Harbinger laughed out loud. "You know, my Lord, if I wanted to, I could shove enough Somnifir into you to turn your innards to dust, so, please, tell me: can a Lupulo disobey an order?"

"It depends on who gave the order, but that's not the whole story. You see, boy, Lupule have evolved over the centuries, just like we Vampires have. The Vampires of today would hardly recognise the Vampires of old and the same goes for Lupule. And they are still evolving, as are we. What they are evolving into I'm afraid I do not know."

"You're lying!" screamed Seren, baring her claws and snarling at the former Prima Vampir.

"Hold your tongue!" blasted Lord Harbinger in a Vampire Howl, the power of which should have propelled Seren across the room but in his weakened state she hardly felt a thing. Tyran Skel stepped in to calm matters.

"Please, my Lord, the situation is critical. You must tell me what you know. We stand on the edge of greatness, but one wrong step and we will fall into the abyss. I need to know if I can trust the Lupule." The Lupulo moved toward Lord Harbinger, her yellowy golden eyes glowing bright in the twilight of the cell, and whispered something to him.

"Get her out of here!" demanded Lord Harbinger. "Seren and the Repeste too!"

"Take them away," commanded Skel, speaking to Seren. "Find out all you can from them about how the children escaped." Seren was extremely unhappy at being ordered from the cell.

"But, Master, I need to question him!" she screeched, pointing a claw at Lord Harbinger.

"I will continue here alone. You have your orders, now go!" Seren did not like being spoken to in this way and howled a Mutanti howl of rage, but, accepting she had no choice in the matter, she ordered the Lupulo and the Repeste from Lord Harbinger's cell. She turned and snarled at Lord Harbinger before following them out.

"I think she was looking forward to questioning you," said Skel, stating the obvious.

"I think you mean she was looking forward to interrogating me. There's a difference. What was she planning to do to me? Dose me with Somnifir to get near enough to practise her dark arts?"

"No, I would. I can't afford for you to kill her, she's far too valuable. Now, my Lord, about the Lupule?"

"Firstly, tell me about the children. How many have you taken? Where are they being held and what are you going to do with them?" Skel thought for a moment before answering.

"The children are flourishing under my guardianship. Instead of growing up in filth and poverty they are being put to good use in our factories and mills. Some on the Ruling Council wanted to reopen the mines and put them to work there, but I would never allow children to work down the mines," he lied. "So, for the time being at least, they are healthy and happy. We've even begun lessons for them."

"You are not feeding on them?"

"Feeding on them? Of course not. Though we sometimes take a Cyathus measure or two, and then only very rarely, for research. And whenever we do we are very careful never to take them anywhere near the threshold."

"What about their parents? Their relatives, their friends? They'll be concerned about them being here. All hell will break loose if they find out what's going on. Please, Tyran, stop before it is too late, you're risking the destruction of the House of Mormant."

"Don't worry about parents or relatives or friends, we're keeping a close watch on them." Skel paused for a moment. "I had Talon give some of their parents jobs. We're going to include them in our experiments. They'll imagine that they're working in a factory. Can you believe it? Humans are so easy to control," said Skel, laughing. Lord Harbinger turned away. "So, my Lord, the Lupule? You said it depends on who gives them their orders. What did you mean by that?"

"I will tell you only because the Lupule could plant the seeds of our destruction. So many have deserted to the other side," bemoaned Lord Harbinger. Tyran Skel stared coldly at the former Prima Vampir while he waited for him to continue. "When the Lupule began breeding we should've looked into their ancestry. Because they are mortal they're as different to one another as are Humans, and being so they are possessed of mortal thoughts and fears and desires and ambitions."

"But they inhabit the nether-world."

"Tyran, Lupule barely cling to the margins of the nether-world. They are as mortal as their Lycanthrope Progenitors. Before Mother Nature bestowed on them the gift of reproduction they had no lineage, but now they do. I suspect they have inherited something passed down through their generations that has altered them and now they want something different, something new: they want freedom; they want independence. Independence from us."

"Freedom! Independence! Have you lost your mind? You are mistaken, my Lord, my Lupule are as dutiful, dedicated and devoted to me as they have always been!"

"But you are Lord of the Lupule, so naturally they are obedient to you. But beware, your influence over them will wane, and when it does they will rip out your throat while you sleep." Tyran Skel was visibly shaken by Lord Harbinger's words.

"Why haven't you said anything before now?" asked Skel sceptically.

"I planned to wipe them out, but… well, we both know what happened. You and Drach led an uprising against me because I was opposed to your plans to increase experimentation on Humans, and I remain against them!"

"But you didn't give my plans a chance!"

"No, and I never will. I will not risk losing my House for a sup of blood."

"Your House? Your House, my Lord? Look around you, you have already lost your House!" spat Lord Harbinger's former Disciple. Skel turned to leave.

"Tyran, mark my words. Watch out for Seren. She calls you Master, but she and her kind have no master." Skel recognised the truth in his former Master's words.

Lord Harbinger lay back on his stone slab bed, closed his eyes, folded his arms across his chest and descended into a deep VSleep.

★

Creating a Vampire is not straightforward. It is not simply a matter of biting a Victim and they magically transform into a Vampire, though on very rare occasions this does happen. The process usually takes years and can even take decades. Despite many Initiates passing into the Great Universe along the way, Vampires believe the effort is worthwhile because they themselves can and do 'die': some from being hunted down and staked; others by Vampicide, either at their own hand, or the hand of a Familiar, or even a wild beast after being released from the mesmerising control of a Vampire Stare, and so Vampire Houses need constant replenishment. Vampicide rates have remained alarmingly high ever since the Carpathian Mountains debacle. The principle reason behind Vampicide is that immortality is not all it is cracked up to be, as after a couple of centuries of doing nothing in particular the boredom becomes crushing, making Vampicide more and more attractive with each passing decade. During the process of making a new Vampire, the Initiate is maintained in a state hovering between life and death until their soul can no longer continue, and it is at that moment they either cross into the nether-life of the Vampire or they pass beyond the threshold to become one with the Great Universe.

After giving up on the idea of bending Lycanthropes to their will, Vampires began experimenting on creating a nether-creature to replace them. They started with the same process used to make a Vampire. They fed on dogs to see if any of them might transmogrify into a Lycanthrope-type creature but imbued with the dog's capacity for total obedience, which, after all, is a dog's greatest quality. It all made sense at the time, despite the fact that up to that point Human Beings were the only creatures Vampires had successfully transformed.

Long before the days of Vampires attempting to create what would eventually become the Lupule, the first of the monstrous creatures known as 'Mutanti' were produced. Many Prima Generatie Vampiri wanted to destroy these 'mistakes', but, with them being immortal, others wanted to understand their potential as Soldiers to protect them from Humans. A moratorium was called to halt all experimentation, but later a vote was taken to continue. This was in the days when Vampires were trying their hand at democracy. Thousands of Mutanti were created, by both accident and design, each one different to the other. Then, after Prima Vampir Osanda Aratare's favourite Lycanthrope was torn apart by a Mutanto called Seren, such experiments were ceased permanently. Seren quickly disappeared to avoid being beheaded.

Because of what had happened to their leader, Lycanthropes demanded all Mutanti be destroyed, but as they, like their Progenitors, were immortal it somehow seemed un-vampire-like, immoral even, to kill them. Besides, killing a Mutanti was not very easy, as they were capable of ripping almost any Vampire to pieces. However, when the idea of Mutanti genocide came about, almost half of them ran away, while the remainder seemed prepared to fight Vampires to the death. A truce was eventually agreed. Those Mutanti that ran away became the stuff of nightmares in isolated communities all around the globe. Witnesses claimed to see Mutanti dragging some poor soul off into the wild, but their accounts were seldom believed. Some witnesses went mad, while most kept their mouths shut for fear of being ridiculed.

The Lycanthropes Council came into being when a section of Vampires wanted to revive the Mutanti programme, at least to replace the numbers that had run away. The whole situation descended into chaos until one of the Lycanthropes came up with the idea of creating a Hybrid from a Lycanthrope and a dog. All sides thought this was at least worth a try. The method used by Vampires to create a new Vampire was used by Lycanthropes to create what they did not know. They took dogs to the threshold of death, as with Vampire creation, then the dog either died and passed into the Great Universe or became a Lycanthrope Hybrid. The process worked so well that Vampires became concerned that Lycanthropes might create these Hybrids for their own use, but they had far too much self-respect to do that.

A major advantage of the Lycanthrope Hybrid was that it did not need to transmogrify, it remained permanently in its Hybrid form. How Lycanthrope Hybrids came to be called Lupule is uncertain, but it started around the time the Vampire nation congregated in the Carpathian Mountains. As with Lycanthropes, Lupule are mortal and so eventually die, usually at around seventy or so years.

After the Vampire nation scattered following the attack on their Carpathian Mountain stronghold, the survivors took with them their Familiars, their Mutanti, their Lupule and hundreds of Lycanthropes so they could produce replacement Lupule. After three generations, Lycanthropes refused to create any more of their own kind through Vampires forcing them to attack Humans. The Lupule quickly came to the edge of extinction until evolution, in the form of Mother Nature, kicked in and they began to breed. The Vampires were astonished at this and wondered what else Old Mother Nature might have in store for the Lupule, but, being Vampires, they soon became disinterested in what was going on with them. What did they care so long as the Lupule ran around doing their bidding?

★

The Vampire House that established itself in the north-west of England was led by Prima Vampir Morfeo Thana who later reinvented himself as Mordred Harbinger, confidant to Queen Elizabeth I. After she made him Lord Harbinger, he started building Vampire numbers after many of his House deserted him to join other Houses; Houses that let them feed as they wished; Houses that were destroyed for their gluttony by Humans such as Nana Alice.

Morfeo started his Nest with a mere fourteen Prima Generatie Vampiri with which to populate the House of Mormant. Vampires require huge numbers of Initiates because during the making they can be lost to the Great Universe in the blink of an eye. Tyran Skel was a difficult Initiate. He went one way then the other and then back again for over a year. His Progenitor tried everything she could but finally had to concede defeat. Even as she walked away, Tyran Skel's spirit defied her by neither passing into the Great Universe nor transforming into a Vampire. She asked Morfeo to try. It was below him to create a Vampire that another Prima Generatie Vampir had failed with so he bit so deeply into Tyran Skel that he passed immediately into the Great Universe. But then Skel's eyes flickered and opened, and the first thing he saw was the face of Morfeo Thana. In that moment a bond was created as exists between a father and a son, which was to become the root of centuries of conflict, as they were as unalike as it was possible for two Vampires to be. Their bond, however, remained strong. Many believed it was unbreakable.

CHAPTER 4

At the end of his first day's work at Storm Hill, Patrick Snr was dropped off by the wagon right by where he had been picked up in the early hours of that morning. He wanted to ask the driver if he could be dropped off further along Heatherfield Road toward Sanderson Street, but he missed his chance; the wagon was gone. The smog was not as heavy as it had been lately, so Patrick's walk along Heatherfield Road was pleasant. As usual, whenever he had work, the children would sit on the sandstone step outside the house in anticipation of his homecoming and would run and greet him like a returning hero as soon as they spied him. All the children of the Cauldron observed this 'ritual'. While the families of working men were waiting for husbands and fathers to come home, the women of the jobless were standing on their steps watching what was going on. "Hiya, I see your fella's got himself some work then." "Where is it?" "Is there anything going there for my fella?" "Ask for us, will ye?" shouted the hopeful housewives.

The neighbour women of the working would answer, "Yeah, he's got a few days, maybe a week, but that's all." "We'll have to see." "He's working down by Speller Lane." "I'll ask him if there's anything going for your fella." But of course there would not be any other work going because if there was then it would already have been snapped up. The men were too ashamed or too proud to do the asking, so they left it to their wives.

Patrick knew his family would be waiting for him, so he whistled to them through the haze as soon as he turned into Sanderson Street. It was said that Patrick Carter's whistle was loud enough to rattle the bones of the dead lying in their graves. The Carter children ran to meet their dad, which was no small feat, especially so for the smaller children, as Sanderson Street was extremely steep. Patrick Jnr, Agnes, Charlotte and Tatty stopped halfway up the hill to await the others making their way back down to them. At least they tried to make it all the way to the top, but they were just too little. The children that lived in the steep streets between Dock Road and Heatherfield Road lacked stamina, largely due to poor quality food, too little of it and bad housing conditions, all of which sapped the energy from their growing bodies. Nevertheless, they were happy kids that knew no different life, though they had heard about kids from the posh parts of the city having chocolate for breakfast. They did not know whether this was true or not, but they were prepared to give it a try should the opportunity present itself; the children of the Cauldron would do anything for chocolate, a fact the Vampires of Storm Hill were well aware of.

The Carter children wrapped themselves around their father's legs, arriving back home clinging to him like a multi-limbed creature from a penny dreadful. Once through the door, Patrick removed his knapsack from his back and went to hang it on a chair in the kitchen. He missed and it hit the floor with a heavy thud. Mary was surprised at this as, empty, Patrick's knapsack should have landed with a 'plip-plop' sound. She picked the knapsack up and opened it.

"Hey, Paddy love, what's this?" said Mary, holding aloft a neatly folded greaseproof paper package containing four raspberry jam sandwiches.

"What are they doing there?" asked Patrick Snr.

"I don't know what you're asking me for, love, they're your sandwiches. Why didn't you eat your sarnies, Paddy? Didn't you like them? Don't you like the way I make your sandwiches anymore?" asked Mary with a sob.

"Ar' hey, love, don't cry. I love your sandwiches, I do. I've got no idea what they're doing in my knapsack. I wonder whose sarnies I ate, then?" said Patrick, attempting a joke to lighten the situation. There had been words between them recently about Mary's culinary skills, and the uneaten sandwiches were a painful reminder of the argument when things were said that were better not said.

"Don't you lie to me, Patrick Carter, you prefer another woman's sandwiches, don't ye?" The children were getting upset with their parents arguing again, so Charlie stepped in.

"Hey, Dad, tell us about your work. What did you do?" Patrick went to speak but nothing came out of his mouth. He stood silent, trying to recall his day.

"To be honest with you, son, I can't remember what I did at work today. Or anything really until I turned the corner at the top of our street." Patrick looked so dumbfounded that Mary and Charlie believed him.

"Did you give your head a bang at work today then, love? Is that why you can't remember what you did? Bend down and let me have a look at your head." When Mary examined Patrick Snr's head coal dust fell onto the floor. "Take your shirt off, I want to see your back," she growled. Mary took a finger, spat on it, ran it across Patrick's shoulders and licked it. "Coal, bloody coal! They've had you down the mine, Patrick Carter, I'm not having you going down any bloody mine." Mary was terrified of Patrick being killed in a mine collapse and her becoming a widow and the children fatherless. Things were tough enough as they were without the breadwinner being killed. "Can't remember what you did today? You're a bloody liar, Patrick Carter, a bloody liar! You're not going back there tomorrow, I can tell you that for nothing!"

"But, Mary love, I honestly can't remember what I did at work, honest. If I did go down a mine I can't remember, but let's see if me spit is clear." Patrick spat onto his hand. "See?" he said after examining the spit. "No sign of any coal dust."

"Well, I don't know what's going on, but what I do know, Patrick Carter, is that you're not going back there tomorrow."

Both Mary and Patrick knew that no matter what was said Patrick would be going to work in Storm Hill, as being so poor they could not afford to be choosy when it came to work.

★

Unskilled men such as Patrick were paid at the end of each working day. They would stand in line, tokens in hand, to swap for a pittance in coins. It was then they would ask, "Is there anything going for me tomorrow, boss?", hoping the answer was a definite yes and not "Turn up and we'll see if we need you," or an outright no. It was important to get in the payment line at just the right time in order to be near enough to the front of the queue in case they were giving out jobs on a first-come-first-served basis, but not too early that it looked like you were skiving. The boss or manager or foreman or supervisor or charge-hand or shop steward or whatever generally did not really care who they hired; they just wanted to get the list filled so they could get about their business.

Patrick was about fifteenth in the pay queue. It seemed to him that the men in front of him were getting the nod that they were required the following day. He was nervous. The family badly needed him to get some regular work, as Mary was at the church and charities almost every day getting what she could. The free meat from the Storm Hill League of Welldoers was very much welcome and it went great with vegetables to make Irish stew, but the charity bins were almost depleted.

"Hand over your token," said the ganger without raising his head. Patrick handed over his token. "Name?"

"Patrick Carter, Senior."

"Does your son work here?"

"No, Sir, he doesn't, he's only a wee nipper still."

"Okay. Pay him," said the ganger to the Counter, and Patrick was paid out his wages.

"Am I on for tomorrow, boss?" Patrick asked pleadingly. The ganger referred to his list.

"Let me see. Patrick Carter, Patrick Carter, Patrick Carter," he repeated while scanning the list of names. "Patrick Carter, yeah, you're on for the next few weeks, might even be a couple of months. Next!"

★

Patrick thought after supper was the best time to tell Mary about him being offered a couple of weeks', even a couple of months', work. She looked him straight in the eye and said, "I'm pregnant and I don't want to hear any of your usual stupid questions about 'How did that happen?' You know very bloody well how it happens, or at least you should do by now!" Mary sounded angry, though she was as happy as she could be. She wanted another girl, but was convinced it was another boy. "That's great news, love, great news," replied Patrick, almost choking. The children hugged their mum, showering her with kisses. "I hope it's a boy," yelled Jed, but the Carter girls chorused, "There's no chance, Jerad Carter, it's definitely going to be a girl this time." All the family were happy and wanted to tell everybody the news, but Mary swore them to secrecy, "Until after it shows, okay? And then it'll be me what does the telling." Everybody nodded their agreement.

Later that night, in bed, Mary whispered to Patrick that she and her mother had been talking. She asked him how he felt about moving out of Sanderson Street and into Evelyn Terrace.

"It's nice up there, Paddy. It sits just above the smog and it's nearer for you to get to Storm Hill." Patrick was not against the idea, as he got on well with Mary's mum, but for some reason he had it in his head that the family should move to Storm Hill.

"What's brought this on? And don't say it's me job, we both know that's not going to last," argued Patrick.

"It was talking with Stella and Aggie the other night, you know, when Jed went missing, that did it. They're thinking of moving and I don't want to be here if they're not around," said Mary unconvincingly.

"I didn't realise you were all that close," remarked Patrick, unconvinced. "Now, Mary love, stop messing around and tell me the truth."

"Paddy love, I'm scared that something is going to happen to our Jed if we stay here. The other night really frightened me. What are the men in white coats doing taking kids off the street? They're not supposed to be doing that sort of thing, they're supposed to be carting people like Mr Lewis off to the loony bin, not taking kids off the streets."

"Maybe they were just putting the wind up them, you know, to frighten them a bit so they don't go wandering too far from home in the smog and that," said Patrick implausibly.

"Do you really think so? I don't know, Paddy," said Mary, unconvinced. "I remember when I was a girl and Mum telling me about that lot up at Storm Hill taking children away to work in their bloody factories and mills and whatever. I remember how frightened I was at the thought of being carted off by the men in white coats. It still gives me the shivers."

"Okay, love, if it'll give you peace of mind then we'll move in with your mum for a bit. By the way, is there anybody else living there at the moment?"

"Oh, just our Alice and our Lilley and their kids, but there's loads of room and the roof doesn't leak. Not like this place. And it's always warm there. I think it's because it's on top of a hill and far away from the docks and the river."

So it was settled, the Carters were moving to Evelyn Terrace to live with Nana Lyons. Patrick and Mary knew Charlie would have mixed feelings about moving, but Nana's house was much closer to Penny Street School than Sanderson Street, so they concluded he would be okay with it. Besides, there was far less smog up there, which was best for all the family.

*

The houses on Evelyn Terrace were originally built for rich merchants who would sit watching for their ships entering the estuary from the windows in the upper rooms. Upon spotting their ships they would rush down to the docks to check on their cargoes and get the goods sold as quickly as possible. The merchants' homes were vast and beautiful, and no expense had been spared in decoration and fitting them out with the most modern conveniences, including sit-down toilets, cellar kitchens and electricity. A light bulb was fitted in the middle of every room and one along each of the four landings. There was even a light fitted in the outside toilet and one in the coal cellar, though these often did not have bulbs in them, as they were expensive for ordinary people to buy.

When Irish immigrants arrived in Ravenport the merchants moved to the countryside and rented them their vast villas. The houses on Evelyn Terrace were easily big enough for the largest Irish families. The accommodation was spread over four floors, excluding the coal cellar. The bottom floor consisted of a cellar parlour to the front, with a cellar kitchen to the rear. All washing of clothes, people and otherwise took place in a single sink in the cellar kitchen. At the end of the cellar corridor stood two doors. The one straight ahead led to the backyard, where the outside toilet was located, and the other to the coal cellar – a dark, dank, smelly dungeon of a place. It was while Charlie lay on the comfy old couch in the cellar kitchen, recovering from one of his many childhood illnesses, that he first saw 'It'. Little Charlie had no words to describe the creature he found staring back at him. He had caught it out of the corner of his eye just as it descended the last few stairs to the basement corridor. Where it had been he knew not. Where it was going he was too frightened to imagine. It stopped in its tracks after it realised Charlie had seen It. Turning its head toward him, it opened its maw to show sharp, pointy fangs sitting either side of a slavering, lolling tongue. It emitted a low purring-type growl. Far from being menacing, the growl was more one of regret; at least that's what Charlie thought it sounded like. He closed his eyes. When he opened them again the creature was disappearing along the corridor toward the coal cellar. Then Charlie heard the door of the coal cellar open with a squeak and close with a snap. He made a solemn, silent vow right then and there that he would never go down into the coal cellar ever again.

The ground floor of the house in Evelyn Terrace consisted of two rooms: a front parlour and a rear parlour. The front parlour was only used for 'best' and contained all the 'best' of everything Nana Lyons had: best china, best cutlery, best doylies, best table cloth, best chairs, best embroidered antimacassar headrests on seats, best curtains. Everything was looked after so carefully and was never mistreated or mishandled so they would last a lifetime, as nobody in the Cauldron could afford to replace much of anything. There was no great value to anything Nana Lyons, or any of her neighbours, had, but if the occasion arose to invite somebody into the house, then the poorest could show they were civilised. The first and second floors of Nana Lyons' house each contained four bedrooms, which was why her daughters and their families used Evelyn Terrace whenever they found themselves homeless, which was quite often, as employment was irregular and unpredictable.

★

As the children filled the school hall for morning assembly they did so with a sense that something was wrong or, if not wrong, something was definitely going on. The teachers looked sad, and a quick look around told Charlie a lot of children were absent from school. After the kids finished wriggling to find a comfortable space on the hall floor, Mr Bawles approached the lectern at the front of the stage. The children looked beyond the Headmaster to the faces of the teachers sitting behind him; they were pale and some had obvious signs that they had been crying. Mr Bawles placed a pile of papers on the lectern, adjusted his glasses and cleared his throat.

"Good morning, children," said the Head.

"Good morning, Mr Bawles," they chorused with the odd titter at the Head's name.

"Children, you will have noticed that some of your friends are not in school today. It is my sad duty to tell you they are ill with the fever. It is not known what fever it is but Sweating Sickness is suspected, as it struck so quickly and so devastatingly. The families living in and around Lemon Street are affected and the entire area has been cordoned off. It upsets me greatly to tell you that some people, some older people, have died, including several former pupils of Penny Street as well as Holy Cross schools." Charlie could not believe what he was hearing; six families in Lemon Street were relatives.

"Sir," called Charlie, "do all the families have the fever or are some of them okay?" Ordinarily, Mr Bawles would not have tolerated such an interruption, but today was no ordinary day.

"That is yet to be determined, but you will not be allowed to pass through the cordon to find out."

"But, Sir, how can we find out if our cousins or our aunties or our uncles are okay?" called another child.

"I have the names of those who are infected and as you can see it's a long list."

The Headmaster turned to the first page and began reading aloud the names on it. Some of the children started crying, which caused others to miss the names they were listening out for. Realising this, Mr Bawles stopped reading and said he would pin the list on the noticeboard outside his office and if any child wanted to speak with him or any of the teachers they could do so because lessons were cancelled for the day. Nobody at the school could recall Mr Bawles being so caring.

As the children filed past the lists of names pinned to the noticeboard, they went over them twice to make sure they had not missed a relative or friend. Why Lorcan Thorne elbowed his way to the front of the queue nobody could understand because he was from Storm Hill and would not have relatives in Lemon Street. When a small child objected to Thorne's line-cutting, he punched the lad in the stomach, causing him to wretch and then vomit. Charlie Carter, already upset at the prospect of finding names of his relatives on the list, cried out, "Hey, Thorne!" When Lorcan Thorne turned around to see who it was calling out his name Charlie rained punches down on him and had to be dragged off the howling boy by two teachers. They demanded to know what the fight was about, but the boys refused to say. The small boy who had been punched in the stomach, however, was only too eager to tell the teachers what had gone on. Both boys were sent off to stand outside the staff room and await their punishment. Charlie felt bad for what he had done and apologised to Lorcan Thorne, saying he was upset, as some of his relatives lived in Lemon Street. Lorcan Thorne said he was sorry too and held out his hand for Charlie to shake and make friends. As Charlie reached forward, Lorcan Thorne landed him a cheap shot on his jaw and setting him on the seat of his pants. Thorne's cronies laughed and pointed at Charlie, calling him names and kicking his belongings along the corridor. Charlie got to his feet and brushed himself off. "I won't forget that, Thorne," he said, trying to sound menacing, but his remark only brought further laughter from

Thorne's cronies who got their pleasure out of making the lives of Cauldron children completely miserable.

There were several boys, however, they would not dream of bullying, one of whom was approaching them from behind. It was Billy Lynch. Just like Penny Street School, Holy Cross had cancelled its lessons that day and so he had come to check on his cousins. When Billy pushed his way through the knot of children the corridor fell silent. Most onlookers were hoping that Lorcan Thorne and his cronies were about to get a thorough pasting.

"Think you're tough, do ye? Well, come and try it with me!" snarled Billy, inviting all-comers to chance their arm.

"We were only messing around, that's all, just messing around. You know us, we're always messing around," cringed one of the cronies.

"Yeah, we're always messing around, Billy, you know us," snivelled another crony.

"Well, you've messed around once too often. Nobody messes with my cousins because if they do I mess with them. Now, who's first?" Billy took up a boxing stance, did his characteristic little hop and marched forward. The gang scattered in all directions to 'bock, bock, bock' chicken noises from the children in the corridor.

"You don't scare me, Lynch," grunted Lorcan Thorne, removing his jumper.

As Billy Lynch was taking his jumper off over his head, Lorcan Thorne attacked him. Billy was taken by surprise and went straight down onto the floor, covering up as best he could. No matter how good anybody is at fighting, if an opponent gets the drop on you it is hard to recover. Hearing a commotion, Miss Williams came to investigate. When she saw what was going on she dragged both boys to their feet and asked Billy where he had come from, as she did not recognise him. He told her what school he went to and that he had come to Penny Street School to spar with Lorcan Thorne in preparation for the upcoming Inter-Schools Boxing Tournament. Miss Williams was not taken in by Billy's story and ordered him to leave the school and not to return. He said that was fine by him, but he wanted to know if his cousins were going home, as they could walk together. She asked Billy who his cousins were and was surprised when he said, "Charlie, Jed, Effy, Agnes, Tatty and Patrick Carter, Patrick Carter Jnr, that is, not to be confused with Patrick Carter Snr," Billy added to the amusement of onlookers.

Miss Williams was good-natured enough not to get angry and told Billy to get on his way when his cousins were ready. After she departed the scene, Billy Lynch turned to Lorcan Thorne and said, "How about just you and me behind the tins by Christ Church after school tomorrow?" Thorne replied saying that he looked forward to it, though everybody doubted he would turn up. With this 'offering out' of Lorcan Thorne, Billy Lynch regained his status as somebody to be wary of, which was vitally important in the fighting streets of the Cauldron.

It was extremely unusual for schoolchildren to be out and about in the middle of the day, which, as it was winter, meant they were walking home in daylight. It was almost the end of the smog season and the walk home reminded them all of the good things they had to look forward to. But this was not a day to celebrate the coming of the sun; this was a day for sadness and mourning. The children spoke very little on their walk home. They did not even kick stones along the pavement as they went, something that did not go unnoticed by shopkeepers. They just walked along in silence with their heads bent to the ground.

When the Carter kids reached Sanderson Street they were surprised to see their mum, helped by neighbours, loading up a horse and cart with all their household possessions. Spotting her children, Mary ran and flung her arms around them. She had been crying.

"Oh God, kids, have you heard the news about the fever in Lemon Street? I hope your Nana Lynch is okay but I can't find out anything about what's going on down there. Have any of you heard anything about what's going on?"

"Mr Bawles put a list of names up on the noticeboard outside his office but we couldn't get anywhere near them."

"Then Charlie and Billy had a fight with Lorcan Thorne and a teacher came and told us to get out," blabbed Effy. Mrs Carter was so upset she did not even pick up that Charlie had been fighting again.

"What's going on, Mum? Why are you packing up all our stuff onto a cart?" asked little Agnes Carter.

"Me and your dad have been talking about it for a while and we're going to move into Evelyn Terrace with your Nana Lyons," said Mary sadly. Charlie looked terrified. "We were going to move at the end of the month but with this fever going round we can't afford to catch it and take it to Evelyn Terrace in case your poor old Nana Lyons catches it from us."

"But, Mum, what about Dad? He won't know we've gone," said Jed in a panic.

"Don't worry, son, I'm going to the place where the wagon drops your dad off and tell him. Anyway, Evelyn Terrace'll be much better for him with his new job. The wagon can pick him up on the corner of St George's Hill and you kids will have an easier walk to school because it's all downhill." Mary was not making much sense. "It'll be great living with your nana. You always have a great time there. The smog very rarely gets up to Evelyn Terrace and you like the kids around there, don't you?" she wittered.

"But, Mum…" whined Charlie.

"But Mum nothing, Charles Carter, we're moving to Evelyn Terrace and that's all there is to it. With Aunty Lilley and Aunty Alice and their kids living there it'll be like going to camp," said Mary cheerfully.

"But, Mum…" whined the girls.

"Not you lot as well? Anyway, it's better than the alternative."

"What's the alternative?" asked Charlie in the hope of persuading his mum that the alternative was better than them going to live with Nana Lyons.

"With your dad's work we were thinking about moving to Storm Hill." Which was a fib if not a downright lie. "He said he thinks his job might be permanent." Which was another fib if not an outright lie. Mary knew the children would not want to move to Storm Hill, despite more and more children from there attending Penny Street and other schools in Ravenport.

"But, Mum, I don't want to live in Evelyn Terrace, and you know why," whispered Charlie so as not to alarm his siblings. Mary dragged him away to a safe distance before replying.

"Now look, I've told you before, there's nothing living in your Nana's coal cellar. If you're frightened to go down there to get the coal just say so and you won't have to go."

"So who'll get the coal then? Jed? Patrick Jnr? Effy? Because if you make them then I'll tell them what I saw and they'll never go down there again!" Mary did not appreciate being blackmailed but the children had a lot on their plates and with the fever going round and kids going missing she played it down.

"Listen, son, we'll make sure the light down there works properly so nobody'll have to go down the coal cellar in the dark," Mary answered sweetly.

"That won't help. It'll just make it easier for it to find us!"

"Look, son, if there was anything in your nana's cellar, don't you think somebody would've found it by now?" Charlie could not argue with his mum's logic.

"But I saw It, Mum, honest a God, I saw It. I even told Nana, but she just said it wouldn't do me any harm. If I imagined it then why would she say that?"

"She was just messing around with you, son, that's all, just messing round with you. She's always messing around. You know what your nana's like with the games she plays; it's just to frighten you kids, that's all. It's all just a silly game."

"Why does Nana do that, Mum?"

"To keep you lot in your beds at night so you don't go wandering around the house when she looks after you," laughed Mary. "Look, son, if you really don't want to live at your nana's house you can go and live with one of your aunties." Charlie did not like the thought of leaving his brothers and sisters at the mercy of the Creature.

"Alright, Mum, I'll go with you to Nana's house, but the kids can't go down the cellar to get coal. Promise?" Mary nodded.

"Lilley and Alice's kids don't mind going down the cellar to get coal. I hope they don't think you're a chicken, Charlie," said Mary with a sly smile. Charlie ignored his mother's taunt and went to help finish loading the cart.

★

The following morning, the house on Evelyn Terrace looked like a battlefield as the Carter children and their cousins got ready for school. Nana Lyons was a stickler for children washing their hands, faces, armpits, crotches and necks at the beginning of each day. She would stand next to the sink to make sure they made a proper job of it. A light dabbing of water was insufficient cleanliness in her book. It had to be a good self-scrubbing, or she would take over and do it her way, and none of the children wanted that. As soon as a child finished washing, they would take their turn at table for a quick bowl of porridge and mug of weak tea and then vacate their seat so the next in line could have their turn. After breakfast the children congregated at the front door so they could walk to school together.

The walk to Penny Street School from Evelyn Terrace was so much easier than it was from Sanderson Street, being downhill all the way. Naturally, the same applied to their Catholic cousins who attended Holy Cross School. The view over the city and docks from Evelyn Terrace was spectacular on clear days, but the cityscape looked as remarkable with church steeples and factory chimneys poking out from the smog. Due to the excitement of moving to Nana Lyons' house, it was only during their walk to school that the children recalled the events of the previous day and wondered what further news they might receive about their relatives and friends behind the cordon in the fever zone.

As the children turned the corner into St George's Hill, a wagon came thundering up behind them driving at breakneck speed. As it passed a voice called out, "Get a move on, Carter, or you'll be late for school, you laggard!" It was Lorcan Thorne shouting while his cronies laughed and pointed at Charlie. The wagon dropped them all off at the bottom of St George's Hill before continuing on to deliver the remaining passengers to Holy Cross and other schools in the area. There were now four such wagons taking Storm Hill children to schools throughout Ravenport.

Thorne and his cronies leant against the wall of a local sweet shop as they waited for Charlie to appear. When he emerged onto Dock Road, the gang ran at him, but were stopped in their tracks by the sight of all the children that had joined the procession down St George's Hill, more than forty in all. One of them called out, "Hey, Thorne, are you looking forward to your fight with Billy Lynch tonight?" The bully winced and answered, "He won't turn up. He's a bigger coward than Carter!" Thorne's cronies cheered his remark but the children of Holy Cross School were not going to take them lying down. "Then you won't mind if we tell him what you said then, Thorne!" Lorcan Thorne's cronies jeered at this. Suddenly, from out of the sweet shop, came Miss Williams. She was sharing a bag of lemon sherbets with Bruce Prince, one of Penny Street's English teachers. They had guilty expressions on their faces, which the girls picked up on. "Miss Williams has got a boyfriend, Miss Williams has got a boyfriend, Miss Williams has got a boyfriend…" sang the girls, only stopping when Mr Prince warned them that if they continued they would be kept back after school.

The Catholic kids carried on along Dock Road to New Street while the Protestant kids crossed into Penny Street. Lorcan Thorne and his cronies walked behind Charlie and his siblings, ankle-tapping them to trip them up. Effy fell over, cutting her knee and making her cry. Charlie turned around to face Thorne, but he and his cronies had already run through the gate and into the playground before he could confront him. Miss Williams witnessed what had happened.

"You mustn't get into fights, Master Carter, because if you do it'll be you that ends up getting into trouble. I'll deal with Master Thorne later, but in the meantime you're not to take the law into your own hands. Do you understand, Master Carter?"

"Yes, Miss," Charlie replied timidly.

"You're a good student, Charlie, and you don't want any blemishes on your record because they might affect your chances of getting into Grammar School." Charlie was absolutely astonished by Miss Williams' words. Nobody had ever mentioned anything about him going to Grammar School before.

"Do you think I can pass the exams and get into Grammar School, Miss?"

"Yes I do, but there are no guarantees. You must continue to study and work hard, and if you do I believe you'll pass the exams and get into Grammar School."

"None of my family has ever been to Grammar School, Miss Williams."

"That's all the more reason for you to buckle down and work hard. If you do well at Grammar School there's no reason why you shouldn't go on to university; but let's not get ahead of ourselves."

"Can I tell my mum what you said, Miss Williams?"

"Of course you can, Charlie, of course you can. Now, get off to the assembly hall, you don't want to be late." Looking at Charlie running into school gave Miss Williams a warm feeling that brought a smile to her face.

★

When Charlie arrived at the assembly hall there was a queue waiting to get inside. The line was moving very slowly. When he got to the front of the queue he saw that the holdup was due to the number of new children being shown where to sit. When he got to his spot on the floor in front of the stage he found a couple of the new children either side of him. "Hello," said the girl to Charlie's right, "I'm Margot Thorne, what's your name?" Charlie thought with that surname she had to be related to Lorcan Thorne; he also thought her voice the loveliest he had ever heard. "I'm Charlie, Charlie Carter… are you related to Lorcan Thorne by any chance?" Margot smiled. "Yes, he's my brother. Lorcan's mentioned your name quite a few times." Charlie thought Margot's smile wonderful. She sounded nice enough, but how could she be nice if she was Lorcan Thorne's sister? "And I'm Maggart Thorne," said the boy on Charlie's left, introducing himself. "Your name's Maggot?" queried Charlie. "Not Maggot; Maggart. I'm Margot's twin brother. You can tell that by how alike we are." Nothing could have been further from the truth; Maggart was as gruesome as Margot was beautiful. Charlie looked shocked. "Don't worry, I'm only kidding about us looking alike. People are always shocked when I tell them we're twins. They say things like, 'When you were born did they mix you up with another baby?' or 'Were you dropped on your face when you were born?' and stuff like that." Charlie didn't know what to say at first. "That's not very nice of them," he eventually said. "What are you doing here?" whispered Charlie as Mr Bawles ascended the stage. "Shhhhhh," shushed Margot, pressing a long, slender, beautiful finger to Charlie's lips.

"Good morning, school."
"Good morning, Mr Bawles," chorused the children, with most sniggering at the Head's name.
"You'll notice we have a number of new children with us today," said the Head, gazing around the hall. "I'm sure you'll make them

feel very welcome. They will be with us while their schools, St James The Less and Kirkdale Middle and Primary, are used as makeshift hospitals to treat those suffering from the fever. There's nothing to be alarmed about, they are from Storm Hill, miles away from Lemon Street." Mr Bawles then produced several sheets of paper from his jacket pocket, flattened them on the lectern and cleared his throat before continuing. "Now then, children, I'm sure you'd all like to know what the situation is in Lemon Street. The fever seems to have abated slightly, but the whole area remains under quarantine. Over seventy people are being treated in makeshift hospitals, as they can't be treated in normal hospitals for obvious reasons. I'll post their names on the noticeboard as before. The children most affected by the fever have been removed to a special isolation ward in one of the wings of the Storm Hill Sanatorium." On hearing this most children, including Charlie Carter, gasped audibly. "We must all thank Lord Harbinger for his kindness and generosity and hope that the children concerned won't be detained too long under his care and are soon well enough to return to be with their friends and families."

"Sir, do you have the names of the children that have been taken to the Sanatorium?" shouted Charlie.

"I do and they will be posted on the noticeboard outside my office along with all the others. And on that subject: it has been brought to my attention that some boys were involved in a fist fight outside my office yesterday morning. To avoid any similar incident, you will file out of the hall in an orderly fashion and wait in line to pass by the lists in single file before going to your classes." The back of the assembly groaned as the younger children knew that the older boys would elbow them out the way to get to the lists without waiting in line. "Lorcan Thorne and Charles Carter, wait behind after assembly, and now, Miss Cartwright, will you kindly take the lists and pin them to the noticeboard," said Mr Bawles.

The children were told to stand and turn their hymn books to hymn number forty-two, 'Guide Me O Thou Great Redeemer'. After a further hymn and a rendition of The Lord's Prayer the children filed out of the hall and, as directed by Mr Bawles, formed a queue outside his office to view the lists pinned to the noticeboard by Miss Cartwright. As predicted by the younger children, the older boys elbowed their way to the front of the queue to give them time for a quick drag on a cigarette in the toilets before going to their first lessons of the day. Meanwhile, back in the assembly hall, Mr Bawles retrieved his favourite cane from the back of the stage, removed it from its velvet sock and got in a few practice swings in preparation for delivering his punishment on Lorcan Thorne and Charlie. He asked them, "Hand or bottom?" They both chose hand. After receiving six strokes each they were dismissed. Walking side by side from the assembly hall, Lorcan Thorne told Charlie he would pay him back for his caning. Charlie whispered, from the side of his mouth, that Thorne could not punch the skin off a rice pudding. The taunt stung Lorcan Thorne into punching Charlie on the arm in full sight of Mr Bawles, who called them both back to stand in front of him.

"What is going on?" screamed Mr Bawles, spraying them both with spittle.

"Nothing, Sir," replied Charlie, wiping his face.

"Nothing? Nothing? It didn't seem like nothing to me, Carter. I'm aghast at the behaviour of you and your tribe. You Carters are always causing trouble. How do you think it reflects on the school when children from nice neighbourhoods, such as Storm Hill, are subjected to people like you and your family?"

"Sir, it was Thorne that hit me, Sir, not the other way round," answered an exasperated Charlie Carter.

"Be that as it may, it must've been sparked by something you said. Lorcan Thorne isn't the type of boy to just go hitting people, now, is he?" Charlie did not know how to answer Mr Bawles' question and so remained silent. "It's obvious the cane isn't sufficient punishment for you, Carter, so I'm going to expel you from Penny Street School forthwith. Now go!" yelled Mr Bawles, grabbing Charlie by his coat, turning him around and shoving him from the assembly hall.

"But, Mr Bawles!" protested Charlie. "That's not fair! It was Thorne that punched me, not the other way round. Thorne punched me!" he exclaimed.

Mr Bawles frogmarched Charlie past the queue standing outside his office and ejected him through the main door. "Get out of my school and do not ever come back!" yelled the Headmaster. Charlie was distraught at being expelled. All he had spoken about with Miss Williams was going up in smoke. His main thought was, however, *How am I going to tell Mum I've been expelled?* Making his way up St George's Hill, Charlie stopped when he heard Jed's voice calling him from behind. He waited for his little brother to catch up, hoping he was going to tell him that Mr Bawles had changed his mind and he was not expelled after all. After Jed caught his breath he told Charlie that the whole school was talking about him getting expelled and they were blaming it on Lorcan Thorne. Charlie replied that he thought Mr Bawles was at fault because he actually saw what had happened and instead of punishing Lorcan Thorne he punished him instead.

"I don't know what I'm going to say to Mum."

"Never mind that, I just saw the list of names and guess what?" Charlie was not in the mood for guessing games so just stared blankly back at Jed. "The kids they took to the Storm Hill Sanatorium, guess who they were?" Even though Jed sounded concerned Charlie was still not in the mood for guessing games and gave his brother a dead-arm punch. "Alright, don't get narky with me just because you got expelled," said Jed, rubbing his arm.

"Sorry, Jed," said Charlie apologetically. "So who was it got sent to the Sanatorium?"

"It was the rest of the kids that climbed over the wall with me Patto and Stevie. That means there's only me left out of the nine of us that saw Mr Lewis." This disturbed Charlie.

"Are you sure?"

"I can read and I can count, so I'm dead sure," replied Jed sarcastically. "What should I do, Charlie? I don't want to be dragged off to Storm Hill like the others, that place gives me the willies."

"It's a pity it didn't give you the willies when you and your mates climbed the wall to see what went on there," answered Charlie angrily. "Come with me to see Nana, she'll know what to do."

"No chance, I'm not getting into trouble with Mum for sagging off school. I'll see you tonight." With that Jed ran full pelt down St George's Hill back to school.

When Charlie rounded the corner of Evelyn Terrace he saw his mum and aunties with shopping bags nestling in the crooks of their elbows. Believing that imparting the news of him being expelled while his mum was in company was his best chance of avoiding punishment he made his way toward her. But it was not to be. Nana Lyons, who was on her hands and knees scrubbing the sandstone step, called for him to come inside; she wanted a word with him.

"What are you doing home at this time of day?" she asked. Charlie thought of lying but did not have it in him to lie to his nana.

"Don't go mad, Nana, but I've been expelled." Charlie recounted the morning's events as his nana sat listening.

"Don't worry, son, you'll be back at school Monday. I just need to have a little word with old Bawlesey to set things straight." Charlie said he did not want to make things worse and begged her not to get involved. "How can things get any worse, son? You've been expelled from school. It doesn't get worse than that. No, son, you just leave things to your old nana." Charlie asked what he should say to his mum when she came back home. "Oh, don't worry about that, she and the other two won't be back until tonight," replied Nana Lyons without any further explanation. "You just have a nice relaxing day. Read a book." Charlie told his nana that he did not like being in the house alone. She asked why that was.

"Do you remember when I was little and I was lying on the couch in the cellar kitchen recovering from being ill?" The old woman nodded that she did. "I don't know if I can say the rest, Nana," said Charlie, sounding apprehensive.

"You were going to say that you saw something, weren't you?" Nana Lyons' words stunned Charlie into silence. "There's nothing to be afraid of, son, he won't hurt you. In fact he'll look after you. He would never let anything happen to you or your brothers or your sisters. He'll be your Guardian Angel." Charlie went to speak but no words came out. "I'll tell you all about him one day, but for now you have to trust me and don't go poking your nose down the coal cellar looking for him. He'll let you know if it's okay for you two to meet. Now, Charlie, I need to go and have a word with old Bawlesey. I shouldn't be too long. If you don't fancy reading a book there's a pile of taters that need peeling and putting into cold water."

"That's alright, Nana, I'll read a book," replied Charlie, smiling.

Nana Lyons went and had her word with Mr Bawles, after which he agreed, in writing, to, "Rescind the expulsion from Penny Street School of one Charles Carter." She went around the classes of Charlie's siblings to tell them that he would be back at school on the Monday and that his expulsion was all just a little misunderstanding that did not need mentioning to their mum. She then went to Holy Cross School and did the same as she knew word would spread there. The children and teachers at both schools were impressed with, and frightened by, Nana Lyons. Billy Lynch was so proud of her. He told everybody that she was his nana too, even though she was not, but in the ways of people like those from the Cauldron she was.

Lorcan Thorne was absolutely furious when he found out that Charlie Carter would be back to school after the weekend, but Margot Thorne told him not to be so horrible to Charlie in future as she liked him and he was a nice boy.

CHAPTER 5

As soon as she returned to Evelyn Terrace, Nana Lyons gave Charlie the note from Mr Bawles rescinding his expulsion and stating he was to return to school on Monday morning. He was still worried that his mum would find out that he had been expelled and that she would want to know all about it but his Nana reassured him, saying that she had told everybody not to mention anything about the so-called expulsion to his mum. Charlie knew if Nana Lyons had said not to mention anything then it would not be mentioned.

When Patrick Snr arrived home that night, Mary quizzed him about what he had done at work in Storm Hill. And again he told her he could not recall what he had done but thought it might have been something agricultural as his boots were covered in mud, as were his trouser cuffs. Once again Patrick's packed lunch was uneaten. "Now this I do know, this I do know," repeated Patrick. "They feed us," he supposed. Nana Lyons was deeply suspicious about Patrick's poor recall of events while at work in Storm Hill and told her daughter that if his memory loss continued she was to forbid him from working there. "Anyway, love, now you have the weekend off you can help with the family chores. Mum's written a list. You're on breaking coal in the cellar." Patrick could not look Mary in the eye. "Erm, I'm working this weekend, love, so I can't help with any of the chores, sorry." Normally, this news would be greeted by loud cheering, as it meant more money coming in and so paid work always took precedence over household chores. "What do you mean you're working the weekend? Sunday too?" asked Mary. Patrick nodded. "What about church? What kind of an example are you setting your children, Patrick Carter?" Patrick knew that the children skipped Sunday school and went to the park instead. He did not tell Mary about it because he saw how happy and carefree they were while playing. Even though Patrick had a grudge against the Church, whether Catholic, Protestant, Methodist or any other, he was determined to allow his children to make their own choices regarding worship.

"Now, I know you're disappointed, love," said Patrick, though Mary was not half as disappointed as the children were if it meant they would have to attend Sunday school instead of bunking off to the park, "but I've got to take the overtime when I can get it. You know that, love. And they're paying me double time, so I'll get thirty bob for working the weekend." No one in the family had ever heard of anybody earning so much money for just two days' work.

"And what about your weekend chores, eh, Paddy? Who'll break the coal in the cellar?" Hearing those words, Charlie went cold. He guessed what was coming next.

"Charlie can do it. He's a strong lad and a bit of hard work won't hurt him. It'll build him up and get him fit and ready for the Inter-Schools Boxing thingy," replied Patrick, putting a positive spin on things.

"I've got to be honest, love, that does sound like a good idea now you mention it. Do me a favour, though, when you go to work tomorrow, write down what work you do so I don't get worried."

"Okay, love," replied Patrick, thinking he had gotten off lightly. "Now, how about me supper, I'm starving hungry," he lied.

Nana Lyons looked across at Charlie. After learning he was going to be breaking coal in the morning he went ghostly white and looked like he was going to pass out. She grabbed him and said, "Come with me." They left the room together. Mary wondered where her mum was taking Charlie but seeing how close they were becoming she decided not to pry. *Let them have their little secrets*, she thought.

When they got to Nana Lyons' bedroom she locked the door and opened the cupboard next to the chimney breast. Once inside, she pushed in one of the panels. It fell away, revealing a set of shelves on which were various things covered in cloth.

"You must never ever come here by yourself," warned Nana Lyons, "Unless I'm no longer around and even so you must never ever speak about what you find here." Nana Lyons took a metal tube from the top shelf. It was about four inches long and pinched flat at one end. It had four holes in a line along the top edge and one hole beneath. "Now, Charlie, I hope you're musical because you're going to have to learn to play this. It's a whistle."

"Okay, but why do I need to learn to play the whistle, Nana?"

"With this whistle you can call the thing, in the cellar. Actually it's called a Lupulo. Don't ask me what a Lupulo is, just accept that's what it's called, okay?" Charlie nodded. "It won't hurt you, but it's not a pet, so don't think you can go treating it like one."

"There's no chance of that, I've seen the size of its teeth. They look like they could chew through a door!" Nana Lyons chuckled at Charlie's expression.

"They can do more than that, son, so don't go getting too confident around Michael…" Nana Lyons didn't mean to use its name.

"Michael? That's a strange name for something like that, isn't it?" Nana Lyons nodded her agreement.

"I had to call him something, so I named him Michael." Which was not the truth but near enough for the time being.

"Does anybody else know about Michael, Nana?" The old woman considered for a moment how to answer the boy's question.

"They do, son, they do, but I won't be telling you who knows about him, and I don't want you to ask about, or even speak about, Michael to anybody but me. I mean it now, son, it's important, Michael's life could depend on you keeping his secret." Nana Lyons handed Charlie the whistle. He blew hard on the flattened end, but no sound came out of it.

"I think it's broken," he said, believing he must have done something to break it. Nana Lyons laughed.

"Only Lupulos can hear it, so be careful where you use it, you don't want to attract the wrong one." This was something else Nana Lyons did not mean to say; she was having a good day.

"Are there more Lupulos than Michael then, Nana?"

"There are, Charlie, there are, but enough of that for the moment, you need to concentrate on learning to play your whistle."

"How am I meant to play it if I can't hear it?"

"I'll show you where to put your fingers for the different calls." After a few minutes Charlie had the basic fingering of the whistle worked out. "That's enough for today, let's go back downstairs before the others come nosing around for us. This is your whistle, Charlie. You must take good care of it and never lose it or lend it to anybody. Promise?" Charlie nodded.

"One thing before we go downstairs, Nana. The creature Jed saw the other night, I think it could be the same sort of thing as Michael, a Lupulo, and Jed said his creature could talk, sort of. Can Michael speak, Nana?" Nana Lyons was surprised by Charlie's question.

"Nothing you'd understand, son, nothing most of us can really understand. Only his own kind truly understand their language." Charlie went to ask another question but Nana Lyons said that was enough for one night and promised she would talk to him before he ventured down into the coal cellar.

★

By the time everybody woke on Saturday morning, Patrick Snr had already gone to his work. He was taken to a different building this time: a factory that made furniture. His supervisor, Dracaena Zayne, showed him and his mates how to operate the machinery. She warned them not to get close to the moving parts, "or your arms will get ripped off," she said, laughing like it was a joke. The factory was light and airy, though a bit noisy, but everybody there seemed happy. Many of the workers whistled while they worked, which Patrick and his friends considered to be a sure sign of the Devil.

At lunchtime all the men went and to a room where there were tables and chairs and a huge teapot sat on a stand next to dozens of white enamelled mugs. And they were clean! It was all very civilised compared to what they were used to working on the docks or in a local factory. Dracaena Zayne sat with the men to eat her lunch. They were unused to having female company. Patrick opened his knapsack, reached inside and pulled out a greaseproof paper package containing two sandwiches made from four slices of bread. One sandwich had jam inside and the other cheese. He had worked up quite an appetite and was rather disappointed by the amount of food Mary had given him. Dracaena Zayne noticed the look of disappointment on Patrick's face and said, "If you want, you could purchase some food from a local shop if you're hungry?" Seeing as he was earning so much money for just a couple of days' work Patrick asked Madame Zayne for directions to the shop. "I'll get one of the Repeste to run the errand for you," she said. Patrick's workmates were likewise incredibly hungry and asked if the Repeste could get them something to eat too as they were all absolutely famished for some strange reason.

After lunch, Patrick opened his piece of notepaper to read what he had written down about the work he had done that morning. Despite reading his own words it was all very vague in his memory.

The memory of the work he had done soon evaporated. When Patrick picked up his money at the end of the day there was nothing deducted for the food he had purchased. Patrick, a proud and honest man, mentioned this oversight to Dracaena Zayne, who replied that Lord Harbinger had paid for the food to show his gratitude for everybody working so hard.

★

By the middle of the morning, everyone at Evelyn Terrace, except Charlie, was busy doing their household chores. Instead, he was sitting bolt upright on the old couch in the cellar kitchen drumming up the courage to go into the cellar to break coal. He felt for his whistle inside his pocket and recalled the tune his nana had taught him to summon Michael. *'What am I doing calling that thing to come to me?'* Charlie asked himself. *'I'd have to be mad to do something like that. I don't want the men in white coats taking me away!'* he joked nervously. A minute later Jed walked into the cellar kitchen at the head of a line of cousins. He asked Charlie if was on the couch because he had finished breaking coal. Charlie did not answer; he just stared blankly at the wall, the other side of which was the door leading to the coal cellar. Jed called upstairs to his mum, saying that there was something wrong with Charlie. She shouted down asking what was wrong.

"Nothing!" Charlie shouted back. "I just, I just..."

"I think he's scared of going down the coal cellar, Aunty Mary," shouted Billy Lynch.

"It is a bit of a dark old hole," Mary shouted back. "So why don't you go down there with him, Billy?" Billy did not fancy that one little bit.

"I would do, Aunty Mary, but I've got me own stuff to do," Billy shouted.

"I've heard there might be rats down there, so that's me out too!" cried Billy's little sister Kathy. Charlie hated rats and wondered if he could use them as an excuse not to go down into the coal cellar.

"You don't want to be scared about the rats, our Kathy, it's the spiders you want to worry about," joked cousin Carol.

"Now that's enough of that, you lot," shouted Mary from the hall above. "Now get back to your chores or I'll find you something to do!" The children marched back upstairs. After they left, Charlie turned to find Nana Lyons standing staring at him.

"Look, Charlie, I wouldn't let you go into the coal cellar if there was any chance of you getting hurt. Now, go on and don't be in a rush. He'll know you're there, he's expecting you."

Charlie did not want to know how it was that Michael was expecting him. As Charlie rose from the couch he felt the blood in his head pumping and surging and pulsating around his brain, pounding and thumping as it went. The din of it all drowned out his inner voice.

Just as if he was in a trance, Charlie walked toward the coal cellar door. Without looking back to see if his nana was watching him, he lifted the latch. The door creaked on opening. He wondered why he had not heard the creak previously. Peering down into the pitch black of the coal cellar, Charlie reached across to the light switch hanging loose on the end of a cable. He grabbed it with both hands. "Do you want a hand breaking the coal?" asked Jed from behind. Charlie almost jumped out of his skin. "What are you doing here?" he yelled. "I just thought I'd give you a hand, that's all." Charlie did not want Jed going anywhere near Michael. "Go away! I'm fine, I'll do it myself. Don't you ever go down into the coal cellar," Charlie sputtered in a panic. Jed was confused. "I always break coal for Nana whenever I visit, so why can't I go into the coal cellar anymore?" Instead of answering Jed's awkward question, Charlie simply repeated that he did not need any help and told Jed to get on with his own chores. Jed walked away shrugging his shoulders and muttering to himself.

After flicking on the light switch, the bulb hanging from the ceiling in the coal cellar dimly glowed a dull yellow. *Why doesn't Nana get a brighter bulb?* thought Charlie. Taking out his whistle, Charlie covered four holes and blew gently into the pinched end of the pipe. He tune was answered by a low purring growl. *It's a greeting!* thought Charlie hopefully. Slowly, tread by tread, he descended into the depths of the coal cellar. He blew on his whistle again and was answered by a low growl coming from a dark corner lit by two flickering candles. But when they blinked off and on Charlie realised they were not candles, or any light; they were eyes. The eyes came toward Charlie. He stood frozen to the spot by fear. Michael stopped just outside the cone of electric light thrown by the measly bulb hanging from the ceiling in the middle of the coal cellar. Charlie was face to face with the creature that had haunted his nightmares since he was a small child. Now that he saw it up close it was truly terrifying to behold but for some reason Charlie was not scared. "Michael?" said Charlie softly. The creature returned a catlike purr. Charlie felt compelled to reach out to touch it but then he remembered what his nana had said about Michael not being a pet and so withdrew his hand. Michael made a sad noise, so Charlie reached out again. This time the creature did likewise and the pair touched fingertips for the briefest of moments before Michael returned to the shadows. Charlie felt elated, ecstatic; he wanted more but somehow knew there would be no more that day.

Charlie whistled a tune as he smashed big lumps of coal into small lumps of coal. Stamping her foot on the floorboards above the coal cellar, Nana Lyons yelled for Charlie to stop whistling. Before he could shout, "Why?" the answer came from above. "Whistling summons the Devil," swore Nana Lyons so Charlie hummed instead. How happy he felt standing there in the dank semi-darkness of the coal cellar, smashing lumps of coal to smithereens, while just a few yards away a creature that could easily tear him to pieces lurked in the shadows, watching him, protecting him. In that moment,

Charlie Carter changed. He would never be the same boy again. "How many buckets of coal do you want me to bring up, Nana?" shouted Charlie. "Just the two will do for now, son," answered Nana Lyons. Charlie filled one of the coal buckets to the brim. It was so heavy it caused him to stagger up the stairs. Reaching the back parlour, Charlie dumped the coal in the coal scuttle by the fireplace. He looked plaintively at Nana Lyons as if to say, "That was very heavy, is it alright if I just do the one?" Nana Lyons, as if reading Charlie's mind, smiled and said, "The second one'll be easier now you've got the hang of it."

Returning downstairs, Charlie found a full bucket of coal sitting just outside the cellar door. He looked around but nobody was there. *Michael must've done it*, he thought. Charlie stuck his head into the coal cellar and whispered, "Thank you, Michael." He thought he heard a purring noise in reply. Charlie secured the coal cellar door and took the second bucket of coal upstairs to the back parlour. Nana Lyons was still there. Charlie told her that a bucket of coal had been left by the cellar door. She told him he had done well for a first encounter but he was not to get cocky or complacent or assume that future meetings with Michael would go so well. "Michael can be a right moody bugger at times, so don't you go pushing your luck with him, my lad," she warned.

★

It was just turned seven in the evening when Patrick Snr arrived home from working in Storm Hill. As soon as he was through the door Mary asked him what he had done at work that day. He showed her the notes he had made and as they went over them his memory of what he had done was as clear as a bell. Mary asked so many questions that Patrick became angry and told her, "Enough is enough, pack it in, I'm not a child so stop it! I'm starving hungry and I'd like me supper!" he lied. Mary told her husband to go and wash his hands or there would be no supper for him. As Patrick turned to go to the cellar kitchen to wash his hands Mary sidled up behind him and said, "Have you forgotten something, love?" Assuming she was still going on about his work, Patrick snapped at his wife, "I've told ye everything! There's nothing more to tell ye! I wrote everything down just like ye said! For God's sake, can't a man have a rest after a hard day's work?" Unmoved by Patrick's tantrum, Mary held out her hand. "Where's the wages? You did get paid today, didn't you? Don't tell me you didn't get paid!" Without speaking another a word, Patrick handed Mary his wages for the day. She counted it out aloud. "Half a crown, five bob, seven and six, ten bob, twelve and six, fifteen bob… seventeen shillings and six pence!" she whooped, beaming a smile. "Now that's what I call a day's wages! Will it be the same tomorrow?" asked Mary. Patrick thought for a moment. "That depends, we did a bit of overtime today, so if we do the same tomorrow then I should get the same money." A thought entered Patrick's head. "Oh yeah, there was something now I think on. After I'd eaten me sarnies I was still starving hungry, so Dracaena said we could buy some food from the shop but she didn't take the money out of our wages. She said Lord Harbinger was so pleased with the way we worked that he paid for us," said Patrick Snr proudly. Mary was furious; how could her husband even think of buying food when they were so short of money? She was about to let rip when Nana Lyons interrupted. "What food did you get, Patrick?" Nana Lyons only called him Patrick when she was angry with him or he had done something stupid or something he should not have, which seemed to be most of the time going by the number of times she called him Patrick. "You know, Liz love, I can't remember. Isn't that funny? I just can't remember. I'll write it down if it happens again." Mary gave him a look that said it would not happen again.

Nana Lyons shooed the children from the room and ordered Patrick to remove his shirt. He looked blankly at her and then at his wife and she at her mother. "Have you gone mad, Mum?" asked Mary. "I want to give him a thorough looking-over. He's eating loads lately and not putting on any weight. I want to check to see if he's got something." As Nana Lyons was a renowned local 'Medicine Woman', that some called a Witch behind her back, who could cure anything with olive oil or inhaling over a bowl of hot tar, Patrick removed his shirt. His body was totally clean. It looked like he had just stepped out of the Heatherfield Road Bathhouse. Mary licked a finger and rubbed it across Patrick's back. It came back clean. Nana Lyons got right up close to Patrick and examined every inch of his upper body, especially so his neck. He thought that if she asked him to remove his lower half he would simply refuse. "You look the picture of health to me. Maybe you're having a growth spurt and just need to eat more," she joked. Despite her close examination of Patrick, Nana Lyons failed to find what she was searching for: the tell-tale marks Vampires leave after feeding; puncture wounds and bruising and so on. She considered examining Patrick's lower half but concluded that would arouse too much suspicion. Instead, she would wait and see if her daughter noticed anything in that region of Patrick's body.

After an incredibly sound night's sleep, Patrick Snr bounded out of bed like a spring lamb, gulped down a breakfast of porridge and weak tea and sprinted to the pickup point on St George's Hill where the wagon was waiting to take him to Storm Hill. While he was living in Sanderson Street, Patrick was in the first group to be picked up but now he was living in Evelyn Terrace he was the very last person to board the wagon, which brought friendly jibes from his mates who joked that he kept making them late. As he sat down, one of Patrick's cousins pointed and said, "What's that in your knapsack, Paddy?" Patrick patted his knapsack. It was bulkier than usual. Looking inside he found his greaseproof paper package contained double his usual number of sandwiches. "That'll be the missus," he said. "She wasn't very pleased when I told her I got extra food yesterday and would've been madder than hell if I'd've paid for it." His cousin Danny said, "I made that mistake too. That won't happen again." The men laughed but they admitted that they all had extra food in their knapsacks and that each had been lectured the previous evening about buying extra food at work, despite the fact they had not actually paid for it. As a result, all the men had 'a little extra' in their knapsacks. Their wives were poor but proud and did not want it passed around that they were not giving their husbands enough to eat.

The Repeste drivers overheard the men's conversation and reported it to their Supervisor upon their arrival at Storm Hill. She went directly to Viserce, Xenka Drach's Conducere.

"My Lady," said Viserce, bowing submissively to her Mistress, "the Repeste say that the men brought extra food with them this morning. Apparently their wives are unhappy that they are being given free food."

"I will never understand these people," exclaimed Xenka Drach. "We give them free food and their wives complain. Go, ensure that a close eye is kept on them. Report anything out of the ordinary; we are at a critical stage."

Viserce knew the job of spying was best done by herself and so joined the men working in the so-called factory. She recorded everything they said and did and helped Patrick write the account of his activities. For their morning break, Viserce brought the men tea and biscuits and persuaded them to leave their sandwiches until the afternoon by tempting them with hot stew for lunch on that bitterly cold day. "On a day like today you need something warm inside you, not cold sandwiches. But remember, not a word to your wives," whispered Viserce coquettishly. The men were enchanted by Viserce's voice as well as her great beauty. Being the class of men they were, they had never worked alongside a female before and consequently felt it would be rude to refuse her anything.

★

On Sundays, everybody in the Cauldron went to church, it being somewhere they could socialise without spending money they did not have. Whenever Cauldronians had people round to their houses they felt compelled to go overboard on food and drink and so forth to demonstrate that they were not as poor as people thought they were. It was all a game but nobody would admit it. In church, to avoid arguments over pew places or standing spots in aisles, worshippers were allocated services to attend but this did not prevent them being full to overflowing. Oftentimes, children had to give up their places to elderly worshippers for which they received a farthing that invariably ended up on the collection plate despite them not wanting to make the offering but felt pressured into doing so by keen-eyed Vergers. Most parents saw this as yet another example of an institution bleeding the poor dry. This tithing-type behaviour was driven into worshippers and is yet another example of how the poor suffer through giving what they have not got.

For Charlie and his siblings Sunday meant sneaking off to the park instead of attending Sunday school at the rear of the Methodist Chapel. Patrick Snr, being against all forms of organised religion and having renounced the Catholic faith, turned a blind eye to the bunking-off. He likewise turned a blind eye to his wife occasionally attending Catholic Mass, something they did not talk about even when it was brought up by 'company'. But with their father working that day, Charlie promised his mum that he would look after his brothers and sisters and give a penny to the plate as the family offering. Mary went to the ten o'clock Mass but Nana Lyons remained at home, saying she would do her praying there as she did not see the need to go to a special place to do it.

During services before Sunday school, Charlie noticed there were a lot of children he did not recognise in the congregation and assumed, quite correctly, that they were from Storm Hill. With so many Storm Hillers now attending local schools, and churches too it seemed, Charlie's interest was piqued and, with his new-found bravery, he resolved to investigate the situation.

After Sunday school was over, children poured into the park, screaming and shouting as they ran around the place like mad things. Charlie introduced himself to some of the Storm Hill children to engage them in conversation to find out about what went on up there. As he did so he was punched from behind. Even before he turned around Charlie guessed it was Lorcan Thorne that had attacked him and his suspicion proved to be correct. The punch winded Charlie so badly he had to take a breather on one knee. "That's right, Carter, you peasant, kneel and pray to me," smirked Thorne, who went to shove Charlie over with the sole of his boot but Margot stopped him. "Leave Charlie alone or I'll tell Father you've been fighting again and you know what that means!" Not wanting to get into any more trouble with his dad, Thorne went off and chucked some children off the swings so he and his cronies could play on them. What Thorne had not expected was that Billy Lynch had come to the park to give Charlie a boxing lesson to prepare him for the upcoming tournament. He witnessed what happened and faced up to Lorcan Thorne. "Where were you the other night, Thorne?" Billy demanded to know. "I heard you said I'd chickened out of the fight, so how about us having a go right now?" he said as a way of insisting they should fight then and there. Billy was surprised when Thorne took off his coat and threw it to the ground. Concerned that Thorne's cronies might join in the fight, Billy was glad when his own cronies emerged from out of the smog like a horde of ghostly avengers.

It transpired that Lorcan Thorne was a far better boxer than Billy Lynch had given him credit for, and it was a closer match than most imagined. After knocking seven bells out of one another for over a minute, Margot Thorne stepped in to separate the boys. She told them to stop fighting and behave themselves. This they did immediately as Margot had a way about her that meant few argued with her. Billy went to shake hands with Thorne to show there were no hard feelings but he refused. Margot tutted. "He's always been like that. If he can't get his own way then he sulks. I'm Margot Thorne, by the way," she said, holding out her hand to Billy, "and before you ask, the answer is 'yes', I am Lorcan Thorne's sister," Margot added, wearing a mock grimace. Maggart Thorne piped up, "And I'm her twin," he said proudly. Billy took an instant shine to Margot, which Charlie noticed, and for some reason, which was mystifying to him, he did not like the idea of his cousin getting cosy with Margot Thorne. It gave him a knot in his stomach.

Margot introduced some of her friends to Billy, Charlie and the rest of the Carters. Talking to the Storm Hillers, Charlie discovered that the fever that had raged around Lemon Street was in fact not a fever but a case of food poisoning. How they knew they would not say. The significance of this was not apparent but when Nana Lyons looked deeper into the matter she discovered that the Storm Hill League of Welldoers had recently began providing the families around Lemon Street with free food. Poor people cannot turn down free food, especially if it comes with chocolate for their children. It was clear to the old woman that the Vampires had created the fake fever to separate children from adults but for what end she was unsure.

One of the Storm Hillers came and spoke to Charlie. "Hello," she said, "my name is Cho Lee. I understand you go to Penny Street School?" Charlie noticed Cho's enchanting accent. "Yes, yes I do. What school do you go to?" As Charlie spoke he was struck by the depth and beauty of Cho's almond-shaped eyes; he found them hypnotic. His obvious attraction for Cho irritated Margot Thorne, who butted in on their conversation. "She's starting at Penny Street

School tomorrow. Would you like to visit Storm Hill, Charlie? I could show you around. I think you'd like it there. You'd fit right in." Charlie did not really want to go to Storm Hill but out of politeness he replied, "That would be nice." A wagon suddenly appeared from out of the smog. Charlie was about to comment on its noiselessness but there was nobody around to mention it to. The Storm Hill children had already boarded the wagon and were waving goodbye.

"What the bloody hell are you playing at, Cho?" mumbled Margot through clenched teeth. "Every time I like a boy you do this. Well, you can't have Charlie, he's mine!"

"Oh, shut up, Margot. I can't help it if he finds me attractive," teased Cho, smiling.

"That was fun, wasn't it? You know? Sunday School and all that," interrupted Maggart Thorne, nodding at the Repeste drivers to remind the girls not to say too much in their presence. They got the message. They would not want their argument reported so they just sat smiling at one another for the rest of the journey. When they arrived at Storm Hill the girls went their separate ways, muttering how fed up each was with the other.

★

When Charlie returned to Evelyn Terrace he rushed inside to give his news to his mum and nana about the fever actually being food poisoning but they already knew. How Nana Lyons got to know was anybody's guess but Mary had been told by the Priest during Mass. After lunch, Nana Lyons took Charlie to the cellar kitchen and sat next to him on the couch, the one from which he had first seen Michael. He thought it now nice to think of the creature as Michael.

"Charlie Carter, I need to have a talk with you," said Nana Lyons, sounding serious.

"What about, Nana?" asked Charlie nervously.

"It's something I'd hoped never to have to mention but I must," she hiss-whispered. Charlie was a little frightened and concerned by his nana's words and tone of voice. "A long time ago, when I was a little girl growing up in the East End of London, my nana – well, she wasn't really my nana, more of an 'honorary' nana – my nana, Nana Alice, told me a story that after I heard it I never looked at things the same way again."

"Was that the same Nana Alice who brought you up?" asked Charlie, though he knew she must be.

"It was, son, it was. She took me in after my mother was taken by the Sweating Sickness. At least at the time I thought it was the sweats that got her. Nana Alice sat me down one day and told me what I'm about to tell you." Charlie went to speak but the old woman shushed him. "I need to pass this story on so it won't be forgotten." A noise from the coal cellar caused Nana Lyons to pause. "Michael knows what I'm going to tell you and he wants to join in but as he can't come up the stairs he'll just listen through the floorboards." After pausing to take a deep breath Nana Lyons continued. "A long time ago, nobody really knows when, some people lost their souls and in doing so they became Satan's Disciples."

"I thought you didn't believe in God and Satan and the Bible and all that."

"I don't know where you got that idea from. Just because I don't go to church doesn't mean I'm not a believer, Charlie. Anyway, these Satan Worshippers made a pact with Him for everlasting life and that's what He gave them but in return He took their souls. Since that time, they've been doomed to wander the Earth to create more like themselves in tribute to their Master."

"Oh, and how do they do that?" asked Charlie sceptically and at the same time expecting he was about to hear one of Nana's stories designed to frighten small children. The old woman gave Charlie an icy stare as payment for interrupting her.

"These Followers of the Dark Lord survive by feeding on the blood of the living. Sometimes, when the soul of their Victims can't take any more, they join the legions of the immortal dead." Michael made low howling noises in the basement. "But I must tell him. He must be prepared. We must prepare others too!" hissed Nana Lyons in reply to Michael's protests. The strange noises brought a number of grandchildren to see what was going on. "Get back up them stairs! Don't you dare come down, or Daddy Greenwood will come and get you!" yelled Nana Lyons. The children did not need telling twice. They scampered back upstairs as fast as their little legs could carry them and tried to listen in from the landing above the cellar kitchen.

"I need to prepare you for what lies ahead, Charlie. When I was a little girl, Nana Alice taught us a game to keep us safe from the forces of darkness. In playing it we became swift and agile and nimble, even in the smog, enough to avoid the clutching claws of the creatures that would carry us away. Vampires, they're called, and they'll take anything that has blood in them but mostly they want children, fresh young children that has young blood running in their veins. They prey on the poor because nobody takes notice if we go missing. If we disappear, everybody takes it for granted we've run away from our homes, our families, our responsibilities. That's what so-called civilised society thinks of people like us. So, we made a Treaty with the Vampires that they wouldn't take our children but they've gone back on their word." Charlie was lost for words so asked about the game Nana Alice taught her. "It goes by the name of Vampires And Victims but it's not really a game."

"If they're the Vampires are we the Victims, then, Nana?" spoke Charlie, asking the obvious. Nana Lyons nodded.

"I've already had a word with the Council of Crones and it's been decided that it's time every child learned to play Vampires And Victims to keep themselves safe when Vampires are out hunting." Charlie thought his Nana was telling him one of her famous stories but thought it best to play along with her.

"Are you going to tell everybody about the, erm, Vampires, then, Nana?"

"No! Of course not! We don't want to start a panic! Besides, nobody'll believe us. People don't believe what they see with their own eyes let alone what a bunch of old women tell them!" Charlie looked bemused as his nana continued her story. "At first, the children will think it's all just a game and that's the way it should be. To help with their training we're going to hold a competition. The teams will compete for a prize." Charlie went to ask about the prize but his nana got in first. "No, don't ask me what the prize is. There'll be a couple of teams from each of the schools in the Cauldron; we might even get some of the posh schools involved too. The winning team might even get a cup!" Charlie's eyes lit up at the idea of winning a cup.

"How do you play Vampires And Victims, Nana?" he asked enthusiastically.

"Here," she said, passing Charlie a piece of paper. "I've written the rules down for you to study. It's a simple game, so nobody should have any problems understanding how to play it. Now, let's get back upstairs before them kids listening on the landing get ear ache."

"Nana, why are you training kids? Why not our mums and dads?"

"Because, son, they've lost whatever it takes to believe in things like this. They'll get it back when they get older but until then it's up to us, us oldies and you youngsters, to save the world!"

"Save the world, Nana?" Charlie exclaimed incredulously.

"Only kidding, Charlie, only kidding," replied Nana Lyons, though she was not kidding in the slightest.

As Charlie and his nana left the cellar kitchen Michael gave a plaintive cry. They both instinctively understood what it meant: there was going to be trouble ahead.

★

Nana Lyons was perfectly correct about the rules of Vampires And Victims being simple. There are two teams, each consisting of thirteen players. The playing area is known as the Field of Battle and must be at least forty feet by sixty feet and contain within it structures such as swings, slides, monkey bars, advertising hoardings, back jiggers or derelict buildings.

One team plays the part of the Victims and the other the Vampires. It is the job of the Vampire team to turn all the Victims into Vampires by tagging them. At the start of the game, a child is chosen as the first 'Vampire' and Victims are given twenty seconds to disperse. Both Victims and Vampires must stay within the bounds of the Field of Battle. If a Victim gets tagged by a Vampire or goes out of bounds or touches the ground they must depart the Field of Battle to be replaced by a member of the Vampire team. If a Vampire goes beyond the boundary or touches the ground they are out of the game. A good tactic for the Victim team is to cause the first Vampire to fall to the ground and so win the game. Victims learning to move with agility and speed over, around, under and across obstacles is the key to not getting tagged.

The winning team is the one that either tags all Victims in the shortest time or in the event of Victims remaining untagged at the end of the game it is the team that has the most surviving Victims that is declared the winner.

By practising playing Vampires And Victims, children can avoid being captured by real Vampires, even in the densest of smogs.

★

What Nana Lyons did not tell Charlie was what drove Vampires to make a Treaty with Humans. In truth, they had little choice in the matter. While it is not easy to do, Vampires can be killed, or rather dusted, either by beheading them or driving a wooden stake through the organ that was once their heart. There are a whole list of things Vampires do not like, such as garlic and holy water; however, these are more of an irritant than anything fatal to them. Sunlight has a variable effect on Vampires depending on their Vage. Young Vampires of anything up to 200 or 300 years can stand a good degree of exposure to sunlight, suffering, perhaps, slight blistering, but older Vampires, especially Prima Generatie Vampiri, cannot be exposed to direct sunlight for more than a few seconds or they will burst into flames, leaving behind only a sprinkling of dust, often in the recognisable form of the fallen.

The answer to what it was that led Vampires to make a Treaty with Humans was that Nana Alice devised a way of killing them at distance, and with great accuracy, with a crossbow bolt. She discovered that dipping the tip of crossbow bolts into tree resin and then sawdust, white oak being best, was as effective as a wooden stake at dusting Vampires. It was as simple as that. One crossbow bolt, tipped with sawdust, through the heart exploded a Vampire into a cloud of fiery dust. Some Vampires took to wearing metal plates over their hearts but they can only stand metal being close to them for a very short time as it weakens, and even marks, them. A crossbow bolt through the heart of a Familiar will kill them, as it will for the various monstrosities that form the entourage of Vampire Houses or Nests. This hunting of Vampires greatly impacted their numbers, it taking so long to make a new one, and with Vampicide on the rise they had to reach an agreement with Humans or face extinction.

The Treaty reached between Nana Alice and the Supreme Council of Vampires stated that so long as Vampires, or nether-creatures under their control, stopped hunting and feeding on Humans, especially the poor, and more especially children, said Humans would stop dusting Vampires and assassinating their Disciples. During the early days of negotiations it was proposed that Vampires would feed exclusively on the rich, the influential, the Aristocracy and so forth. This was rejected on the grounds that if the life of a single member of the upper classes was taken it would be the end for Vampires and the poor would likely be held to account and punished as collaborators. Kill a hundred, a thousand, a million poor and nobody raises an eyebrow, but kill a single member of the upper classes and questions would be asked. Things would happen. Bad things.

Nana Alice initially demanded that Vampires feed only on the blood of animals but, as this would likely cause rebellion in Vampire ranks, she reluctantly agreed that they could feed on down-and-outs, reflecting that this would also solve a social problem. The blood of down-and-outs was not very nourishing but as it was better than a crossbow bolt through the heart the Supreme Council reluctantly agreed to Nana Alice's terms. The same terms were set throughout the length and breadth of every country around the globe; subsequently they were ratified by each successive generation of Humans with their local Vampire House. In this generation, for the Cauldron, the Treaty Scribe was Nana Lyons. She and Lord Harbinger signed the document at Mormant Hall when she was just thirty-three. She signed in red ink and he in her blood. There were parts of the Treaty Nana Lyons felt deeply ashamed of but she knew they were necessary in order to maintain peace and keep her nearest and dearest, and the nearest and dearest of people like her, safe, alive and free from predation from the legions of the undead.

Something which Vampires insisted be in the Treaty was that the game known as Vampires And Victims was banned for all eternity on the grounds that it kept their kind in the minds of mortals.

With the promise that no more children would be taken, Nana Alice agreed to ban Vampires And Victims. Nana Lyons knew resurrecting the game was a declaration of war. As far as she was concerned, however, it was a war which was far too long in the coming, a war she had been preparing for ever since her grandson, Charlie, had been fed on by a Moroi and bled dry.

CHAPTER 6

By seven o'clock on Monday morning Patrick Carter was at his work in Storm Hill. Meanwhile, in Evelyn Terrace, it was time for the children to get up, get washed, get dressed, have breakfast and get off to school. There were the usual Monday-morning malingerers claiming that they had this or that wrong with them or this hurt or that was swollen but neither their mothers nor Nana Lyons believed a word of it. All the children had to go to school, no matter what their state of health, that was that, as their mothers now had part-time cleaning jobs, arranged for them by Talon, so there would be nobody, apart from Nana Lyons, at home to look after them and she had made it clear she would not do so unless they had 'an arm or a leg hanging off'.

The Carter children slept much better at Evelyn Terrace than they ever had at Sanderson Street, meaning it was doubly difficult getting them out of bed, and when they did they fought and played with their cousins as they waited in line to wash, and again at the breakfast table. It was a good thing that Nana Lyons oversaw proceedings otherwise it would have been chaos. Jed wanted to know what Charlie and his nana had talked about the previous day, as he and the others listening on the landing hardly caught two connected words.

"So, are you going to tell us what you two talked about last night and what that strange noise was we heard?" asked Jed.

"No, and I don't know what strange noise you mean," answered Charlie off-handedly.

"C'mon, our kid." Jed always called Charlie 'our kid' whenever he wanted something. "Tell us what you and Nana talked about."

"Yes, Charlie, tell us or we'll tickle you till you pee your pants," said one of the other kids. Nana Lyons gave the children a 'look' to stop their prying.

"You'll find out soon enough," she added, casting another 'look'.

"Nana," began Jed cautiously, "tell us, what was that strange noise we heard when you and Charlie were talking yesterday?"

"Oh, that," she said, "that must've been Michael you heard." Charlie nearly choked at his nana mentioning Michael to the children. "He guards the coal cellar in case anybody dares to try and steal my coal. He'll rip their throat out if they do." The children stared in horror at their nana's words.

"C'mon, Nana, don't mess about," pleaded little Lilley Hawley. "Tell us the truth or we'll be too frightened to get the coal if you say things like that." The children nodded in agreement with Lilley.

"Don't worry, Lilley, Michael won't hurt you. Don't you think he'd've done so by now if he wanted to?" said Nana Lyons as if to comfort and reassure her grandchildren. Jed was not prepared to let it go.

"Okay then, Nana, how can this Michael rip somebody's throat out? Is he a wolf or a bear or something? Have you got a wild animal tied up in the coal cellar, have you?" Jed asked jokingly. The children waited in silence for Nana Lyons' answer. When it came it froze them to the spot.

"Michael's not tied up. He can come and go as he pleases. Why don't you ask Charlie, he's met Michael, haven't you, son?" Charlie was aghast that the old woman had asked him to tell the children about Michael. "Go on, Charlie, tell them what he looks like! His yellow eyes! His long sharp teeth and slavering maw! His claws that could tear you to pieces," she said, winking at Charlie. He did not know how to answer. Did she really want him to tell the children about Michael? She eventually broke the silence. "The looks on your faces," she laughed. "I'm only kidding. Now, you lot, get ready for school before I take my walking stick to the lot of ye."

Before Charlie left the cellar kitchen Nana Lyons whispered in his ear, "See what happens when you tell the truth, Charlie? How will anybody believe us if we tell them about Vampires?" That was a good lesson for Charlie and one he swore never to forget.

★

Only a few finger wisps of smog reached up to Evelyn Terrace that morning but the blanket of haze below was thicker than ever, it seemed. The scene created an eerie picture with the spires of churches poking through the smog like stakes through Vampire hearts.

The children left Nana Lyons' house and descended St George's Hill into the smog below. A wagon drawn by four massive black horses flashed silently past them to shouts of, "Get a move on, Carter," "You're going to be late for school, you dullard!" The voices belonged to Lorcan Thorne and his band of cronies. As the wagon was being swallowed by the smog, Charlie heard Margot Thorne yelling, "Shut up, Lorcan, you're so rude!" Her voice trailing off with, "See you in school, Charlieeeeee…"

The Evelyn Terrace tribe arrived at Dock Road in time for the Proddy Dogs of Penny Street and Cat Licks of Holy Cross to deliver a few friendly dead-arm punches to their mates before morning assembly. Charlie got a terrific dead arm from Sammy Irons, who was supposedly his best friend. He had not seen Sammy for nearly a fortnight, as his father needed him to help deliver coal. The Irons family was just Sammy, his two brothers and sisters, and his parents.

They did not have anybody else that anybody knew of – no cousins, no uncles or aunts, nobody. In fact nobody even knew where they came from. "Bloody hell, Sammy, that bloody well hurt!" yelled Charlie, rubbing his arm to take the sting away. Taking no notice whatsoever, Sammy jumped on Charlie, forcing him to the ground. "You need to toughen up, Charlie boy, we've got the boxing tournament next week," he said, laying into his friend with lefts and rights to the stomach and chest. Charlie was not all that interested in boxing, mainly because he was rubbish at it, but with his new-found confidence and sense of purpose he was determined to do well at the tournament. *If I can face something like Michael I can face anything*, he thought. "Our Billy's giving me lessons," said Charlie confidently. Sammy was sceptical. "But your Billy's a Cat Lick, so I doubt he'll teach you to box." After giving Sammy a revenge dead arm Charlie replied, "Oh, he'll teach me to box alright, once he knows there's a chance I might have to fight Lorcan Thorne." Just then Margot Thorne appeared. "Hello, Charlie; hello, Sammy," she said as she passed by. "How do you know her?" they chorused, each dismayed that the other knew Margot Thorne and she had said hello to them. Before they got a chance to get into an argument the school bell rang to call the children into morning assembly.

Glancing around the assembly hall Charlie noticed it was full to bursting with even more newcomers. Margot and Maggart Thorne went and sat either side of Sammy Irons and two new people sat either side of Charlie. "Hello," said the boy to Charlie's left. "I'm Maximillian Rune. My friends call me Max, and my friend next to you is Bogdan Radu," said Max, pointing to the boy on Charlie's right. "I'm Charlie Carter. Where are you from?" he asked. "A long way away from here; you won't have heard of it," replied Bogdan. Max laughed, "No, Bogdan, he doesn't mean what country are you from, he wants to know where you live. We both live in Storm Hill." Charlie was about to say something about there being so many children from Storm Hill at the school when Mr Bawles called for order.

"Good morning, children."

"Good morning, Mr Bawles," responded the assembly, accompanied by the usual sniggers.

"I have some good news. There never was any fever in Lemon Street, despite the people there showing all the signs and symptoms. They were, in fact, suffering from food poisoning, nothing more. Now, you'll want to know what's happening with your friends. Well, as you can see, many of them have already returned to school, while those who remain poorly are convalescing at the Storm Hill Sanatorium while they recover. We must write and thank Lord Harbinger for his kindness and generosity. Now, children, before we sing the first of our morning hymns I'd like to invite Father Grogan to the stage as he has an announcement to make." Father Grogan leapt onto the stage and he and Mr Bawles exchanged unfriendly looks.

"Good morning, children," cried the Priest.

"Good morning, Father Grogan," chorused the assembly.

"I bring you exciting news. This Easter a Jamboree is to be held at Mormant Hall." The children looked underwhelmed. "There's going to be competitions and prizes." The mention of prizes brought rapturous applause from children and teachers alike. "The prizes are going to be for a game that hasn't been played in these parts for a very long time." The children returned to looking underwhelmed. "It's a very dangerous game," announced Father Grogan with a glint in his eye. "It's a game your parents won't want you playing," he added. A game involving danger and one that their parents would not want them playing brought cheers from the children and concerned looks from the teachers. "You're going to have to practise playing the game three times a week after school and at weekends too." The children booed as they were not keen on giving up their evenings and weekends. "Those who come to practice get a hot chocolate." With hot chocolate as an incentive the children were ready to sign up; the kids from Storm Hill, however, were not interested in the slightest.

"Father Grogan, what's this game called?" asked Charlie knowingly above the hubbub of the assembly hall.

"You won't've heard of it, my son; it's called Vampires And Victims." For some reason the name of the game brought a deathly hush to the assembly, despite none of them, apart from Charlie, having heard of it before. "I'll pin the rules up on the noticeboard and those who are interested can come and see me in the playground at lunch. Now, I'll hand you back to Mr Bawles for him to lead the singing of hymns."

At the end of the assembly, Mr Bawles reminded the children, through gritted teeth, to read the rules of Vampires And Victims and to see Father Grogan during the lunch break if they were interested in signing up. He later approached the Priest. "So, what's all this about the children playing games instead of working on the school farm! You had this planned all along, didn't you?" hissed Mr Bawles. Father Grogan simply returned him a toothy smile. "You don't have the authority for something like this, Grogan. Who's behind it? Tell me! Who's behind it?" Father Grogan pushed the Headmaster into a corner and, pressing his mouth up against the Head's ear, whispered, "Don't be naïve, you know very well who's behind it. You'd better play along, or it'll turn out bad for you!" Mr Bawles went apoplectic with rage at being threatened after all he had done for the Cauldron in the past. "It's Elizabeth Lyons that's behind it, isn't it? Isn't it?" screamed the Head. Father Grogan nodded. "Does she know what she's doing? What she's starting?" cried Mr Bawles in disbelief. "You're either with us or against us, Bawles. Now tootle off and do keep your mouth shut."

★

Charlie and Sammy jostled one another on the way to the first lesson of the day. Their boisterous behaviour irritated everybody but as they had not seen one another in a while they did not complain.

"Are you going to sign up for Vampires And Victims?" asked Charlie. Sammy said he probably was but doubted he could make it to training as his dad needed him to help out with coal deliveries after school. The next thing Charlie knew he was flat on his back on the floor looking up at Lorcan Thorne, a couple of his cronies held Sammy Irons against the wall by his throat. "Just getting some boxing practice in. You don't mind, do you, Carter? I'm looking forward to giving you and your peasant cousin a good hiding next week." Charlie was about to say something when Maximillian Rune spoke. "You're tough when people have their back to you, aren't you, Thorne?" Max held out his hand and pulled Charlie to his feet. "Mind your own business, Rune, or I'll —" Before Thorne could complete his threat Max Rune butted in, saying, "Or you'll what, Thorne? I'm not scared of you. You Thornes think you're something special but you're not. You're pathetic, the lot of you. Now, why don't you try your luck with me?" asked Max, offering Thorne a fight. "I wouldn't normally waste my time with the likes of you, Rune, but if you think you're up to it then why don't you sign up for the boxing tournament and I'll see you in the ring." Thorne called his cronies to heel and they all left. After dusting himself down, Charlie thanked Max for stepping in to help him.

"We're not all like him, you know," said Max. Neither Sammy nor Charlie was convinced.

"You Storm Hill kids seem, I don't know, you seem stronger than us and I don't understand why," said Sammy. "Every time I come up against one of you lot I come off second best, and I'm very strong, I carry bags of coal, so how can that be?" Max shrugged his shoulders.

"I don't know," he lied.

"Are you going to try out for the boxing team?" asked Charlie. Max replied that he was. "What about Vampires And Victims?" added Charlie. Max said he would not be able to make it to training as he had to return on the wagon to Storm Hill with the rest of the children. Charlie suggested he could stay over with him at Evelyn Terrace.

"I'll think about it," replied Max.

Sammy felt a little jealous at being left out as Charlie was his friend and here he was inviting a newcomer to stay at his nana's house. At the sound of the late bell the boys gave one another a friendly dead arm and ran off to their classes.

★

A long queue formed in the playground during the lunch break to sign up for Vampires And Victims. Charlie was twelfth in line, and going by the faces of some of the children they were unhappy after speaking with Father Grogan. One of these sad faces belonged to his brother Jed, who walked sullenly back down the line of children toward Charlie.

"What's up, our kid?" asked Charlie. "You don't look very happy."

"It's that Father Grogan, he said I was too young and too little for Vampires And Victims. I'm small but I'm strong. And I'm nippy! You've seen me playing footy and on the monkey bars. I'm dead nippy, aren't I?"

"You are, our kid, but maybe you're a bit too young to play Vampires And Victims. I mean, it's a dangerous game."

"Just because Father Grogan says it's a dangerous game doesn't mean it is a dangerous game," whined Jed.

"I read the rules and it looks like it's a dangerous game to me."

"Ye can't tell by reading the rules. I should at least get a try-out."

"I'll put in a good word for you with Father Grogan." That seemed to satisfy Jed and he ran off to play football with the other V and V rejects.

"Ah, Charles Carter. So, you're interested in playing Vampires

And Victims, are you?" said Father Grogan, who already had a tick against Charlie's name.

"I am, Father."

"Well, that's grand, my son, you're in."

"Is that it? Don't you want to ask me anything?"

"It's not necessary, my son, your nana's been in touch and you're in," whispered Father Grogan.

"What's my nana got to do with this?" asked Charlie.

"Hasn't she told you anything about it, then?" enquired Father Grogan, giving Charlie a knowing look.

"Where my nana's concerned, I don't know what I can and can't say. Sorry," said Charlie unconvincingly.

"That's grand, my son, just grand. Don't worry, I understand. Best to keep your mouth shut until you know what's what. I'll see you on the Oller by the church for training after school?" Charlie nodded to confirm he would be there.

★

The very second Lorcan Thorne arrived back in Thorne Hill he went to see his father, Lucian. He could not wait to tell him about Father Grogan organising a revival of the banned game, Vampires And Victims, children of Familiars being under strict instructions to report anything they saw or heard in the outside world to do with Vampires. Lucian Thorne immediately left to report personally to Tyran Skel before anybody else got to him. "But, Father, I haven't told you what that bloody Max Rune said about us," bellowed Lorcan Thorne, but it was too late: his father was already out the door.

The Mutanti on guard at the entrance to Mormant Hall wanted to know what Lucian Thorne wanted. He told them that he had something of great importance to report to Tyran Skel and needed to see him immediately. Just then, Seren appeared from behind the guards. She asked Lucian what was so important that he had to see her Master personally. Even though Lucian believed Seren would not dare harm him, he was always extremely wary around her. She was, after all, easily capable of tearing him to pieces. From the first moment he beheld her gruesome form, Lucian Thorne hated Seren with a passion. Fear, hate and loathing aside, the Beast had far too many teeth and claws for his liking.

Seren, as with all Mutanti, is an example of Mother Nature at her cruellest; even taking account of creations such as Lupule, Lycanthropes, Repeste, and all the other unnatural nether-creatures that inhabit the Vampire realm, not forgetting Vampires themselves of course, Mutanti are the cruellest of all Her tricks. When a Vampire is made it can take on the characteristics of the animal or animals their Progenitor fed on before the moment of their creation, and in Seren's case the Vampire that created her had recently feasted on a particularly ferocious bear. In a one-in-a-million chance, the first time Seren's body took on its immortal form she transmogrified into a horrific, hideous, bearlike creature. Her form is not precisely that of a bear, though. She is not covered in fur; however, she has the claws, teeth and strength of a bear as well as the temperament of one that is angry all the time. Seren's head and jaw is extremely bearlike and when she drills into the fabric of her Victims with her piggy little eyes they find it hard to resist telling her the truth, oftentimes the truth Seren wants them to tell.

"You can tell me whatever it is you have to report and I will consider taking it to my Master," snarled Seren. Lucian Thorne knew better than to bargain with her but felt this was his one opportunity to get recognition in the eyes of Tyran Skel, perhaps even becoming his Conducere in the process. For some reason he had not appointed Conducere, which was of great concern to all Familiars in case it set a precedent.

"Certainly, Mistress Seren; however, if you will allow me to report to Vampire Skel personally I will be forever in your eternal debt."

"Why would I want somebody like you in my debt? What can you do for me that others cannot?"

"My children constantly bring me all manner of information, Mistress Seren, such as that which I have today, which I would bring first to you in future." It was not much of an offering but Seren knew that once this transaction took place she would own Lucian Thorne and could make greater and greater demands on him. During his servitude, she would record every act that could, in a certain light, be considered seditious; any wrong move on his part and she would be within her rights to feed on the juice of his innards.

"I will consider whether I will allow you to serve me after you've told me what it is you have for my Master."

"Thank you, Mistress Seren," answered Lucian Thorne respectfully. Before continuing, he cleared his throat as he was feeling, quite rightly, terrified. "A Priest visited Penny Street School today to announce the resurrection of the game known as Vampires And Victims—" Seren held up her hand to prevent Lucian from continuing.

"Oh? And who was it told you this?" Seren asked with uncharacteristic calmness.

"One of my sons, Mistress."

"Bring him to me!" This was precisely what Lucian Thorne had wanted to avoid but he had no choice in the matter.

When Lucian Thorne returned with his son, the Mutanti guards were nowhere to be seen; only Seren was there to greet them. Lorcan Thorne had never seen a Mutanto as horrific as Seren before, and at the sight of her, he made to turn and run away, but his father held him firm.

"Mistress Seren, this is my son, Lorcan. Today, while he was at school—"

"Silence! The boy can speak for himself! Can't you, boy?" Lorcan

Thorne, his eyes as large as saucers, nodded. He was so terrified he peed himself. "Well then, Master Lorcan Thorne, tell me all about the Priest that came to your school today. What did he say?" Lorcan's throat was too dry to speak.

"Speak up, son, nothing to be afraid of," whispered his father encouragingly.

"What could the boy possibly have to be frightened of?" asked Seren, baring her fangs in an attempt at smiling. "What have you to be afraid of, Master Thorne?" she asked, moving her head so close to the boy that he could feel the heat of her foul breath on his cheeks. "Here, boy, have a drink!" Seren handed Lorcan a gold chalice containing a light draught of Somnifir. "You'll talk after you've had a drink," she said to herself. Seconds later, Lorcan Thorne was in a trance-like state where nothing seemed real and rendering the Beast in front of him to appear harmless. "Now, Lorcan my boy, tell me what the Priest said today."

"He said there's going to be a competition with a prize for the winner," said Lorcan Thorne distractedly.

"What sort of competition?"

"It's to do with playing Vampires And Victims… there's going to be a prize for the winner." It was all Lorcan Thorne could do to stay awake.

"Is it just your school that's playing this game?"

"No. Coming back on the wagon all the children were talking about it. All the schools are entering the competition. They're starting their training tonight."

"Thank you, Lorcan. Now return home and don't mention our conversation to anybody," whispered Seren into Lorcan's ear. Whispers under the influence of Somnifir create obedience. The boy about-faced, robot-like, and returned home in a trance. "Come with me!" said Seren to Lucian Thorne.

★

The first thing Charlie noticed at V and V training was there was nobody from Storm Hill. There were lots of children from other schools, including half a dozen of his Catholic cousins, but not a sign of any Storm Hillers, not one! He asked some children if they knew if any Storm Hill kids had signed up for V and V training. They each gave the same reply, "No." Billy Lynch said there was something weird about them and he was glad they were not there. Charlie asked his cousin what he meant. "They're just different. And they're so strong, all of them! When Lorcan Thorne and me had that scrap I felt a terrible strength inside of him. If he gets any stronger I doubt I'll be able to beat him in a fight. And talking of fighting, Cousin Charlie, have you signed up for the boxing tournament yet?" Charlie said he had and wanted Billy to give him some boxing lessons. "There's no time like the present," replied Billy, taking up his favourite southpaw stance. Father Grogan interrupted proceedings, saying there would be no boxing that night, as they were there to concentrate on learning to play Vampires And Victims. "Anyway, our Billy, what are you doing here? Why aren't you and the other Cat Licks training with Holy Cross?" Billy gave Charlie a friendly dead arm. "That's for being cheeky. We're training with you Proddy Dogs because it's closer to our homes. With all that's going on, we don't want to be walking home in the smog by ourselves, if you know what I mean?" Billy's house was opposite Christ Church and just yards from the Oller but his answer was unconvincing as Billy Lynch was scared of nothing. *There's more to this*, thought Charlie. But there was not: Billy was just being his usual lazy self.

"Now then," began Father Grogan, "we have enough for three teams, so let's go over the rules to make sure you all understand them."

"The rules are nimps, Father," shouted Izzy Sanchez, "so let's get on with the game."

"You're right, Isabella, the rules are not complicated, and I can always put you right if you make a mistake. So, here's the teams."

Father Grogan handed out three sheets of paper for the children to see which team they were on. Billy and Charlie were on the same team. "Let's make a start with team one. Choose one of you to be a Vampire and the rest can watch how they do."

"We can't see much in this smog, Father," shouted Denny Lambert.

"That's the whole idea. In Vampires And Victims you have to react quickly to danger. When the game gets near the end there'll only be one Victim left and they'll have to avoid a dozen Vampires, so it'll be interesting to see how they do."

"I've a question for ye, Father," shouted Suzy McIver.

"What is it, Susan McIver?"

"If the idea is that the winning team is the one that lasts the longest, then why doesn't the Vampire just not catch anybody? You know, don't turn Victims into Vampires at all." Believing Suzy McIver had cracked the formula to winning the game the children repeated her words at Father Grogan.

"Now, that would be nice, wouldn't it, children? But this is only practising. It's not the real thing. In the real thing Victims who get tagged are replaced by Vampires from the other team, so they'll be trying to catch you and win the match." The children assimilated the information and after it sank in they emitted a collective 'ohhhhh'.

"So there's no way of us cheating to win?" Suzy asked disappointedly.

"I'm afraid not, young lady," replied Father Grogan unsympathetically. "Now, you lot, keep your eyes peeled and watch how the first team gets on. You'll all have a go then we'll get to the monkey bars to practise agility. Right, Victims, climb up the tins and don't fall off, otherwise you'll have to answer to Father Horan." This threat was enough for the children to be ultra-careful not to fall off the tins.

When practice was over, Billy gave Charlie some boxing tips. He showed him how to hold his fists to defend himself and how to attack from behind a straight lead. Afterwards, Billy told his cousin that he should practise all he could, "because you're not very good. I mean, you're me cousin and all that but I can tell you're just never going to be any good at boxing." Billy's words stung Charlie. "Don't worry, though, you're the best at Vampires And Victims so it all evens out. Nobody'll ever turn you into a Vampire." Knowing what he knew, Charlie hoped Billy's words were prophetic. "I bet you they make you the captain of the team and you win the competition!" Billy added to lift his cousin's spirits.

Charlie was glad of Billy's praise for his V and V skills but remained hurt by his comments about his lack of boxing ability. However, instead of giving up, as the old Charlie would have, the new Charlie was determined to prove his cousin wrong. *I'll show you, our Billy*, thought Charlie. "I'm going to practise day and night for the boxing tournament, I'll show you!" Charlie said aloud to laughter all around him.

Walking alone in the smog back to Evelyn Terrace, Charlie felt he was being followed. When he heard strange snuffling sounds getting closer he picked up the pace to get home as quickly as he could.

★

As soon as Charlie got through the front door Jed asked whether he had asked Father Grogan if he could join in with V and V training. "Sorry, our kid," said Charlie, "there was so much going on that I completely forgot to ask about it. I promise the next time I see Father Grogan I'll ask for you." Jed told Charlie not to bother. He was already fed up and this made him feel worse. Charlie put his arm around his little brother's shoulders and said, "Don't worry, our kid, I'll ask Father Grogan on Wednesday but don't get disappointed if he says 'no', okay?" Jed nodded and went off to bed.

Nana Lyons wanted to know how Charlie had done at V and V training but, as the fire was about out and there was no coal in the scuttle, Mary said he should have his supper and get off to bed. "Don't worry, Mum," Charlie replied, "I'll go down to the cellar and get some coal." Mary was shocked. "I thought you said you didn't like going down there after… you know, what you told me about that thing you said you saw when you were little," reminded Mary. "Just like you said, Mum," replied Charlie, "it was all just my imagination." Nana Lyons butted in, "I'm going to be up sewing for a while so go on, son, bring your old nana a bucket of coal so she doesn't freeze to death."

As he lifted the latch on the coal cellar door, Charlie heard a noise like a welcome coming from Michael. He felt in his pocket for his whistle but remembered he had left it in his bedroom. He turned to go and retrieve it when Michael made another noise, this one sounding like a sad sigh. For some reason, Charlie felt it would be okay for him to visit Michael without his whistle, so he switched on the light and descended the stairs into the coal cellar. The light bulb seemed dimmer than ever. "Michael?" Charlie hissed. "Michael? It's me, Charlie, I forgot my whistle." Walking to the middle of the coal cellar Charlie noticed two yellow eyes watching him from the space beneath the stairs. His courage failed him for a moment but before he had a chance to run away Michael blocked his escape route. "Michael, it's me, Charlie." The Lupulo snarled a greeting. "I'm here getting coal for Nana." These words drew no reaction from Michael. "I've just got back from Vampires And Victims training." Michael appeared alarmed by this news. "What's wrong?" asked Charlie. Michael held out a paw and took Charlie to his den beneath the coal cellar stairs. On a wall of the den was painted a strange-looking figure with a child draped in the crook of each of its arms. In the next panel the figure was holding the children to its mouth and in the final scene the children were standing either side of the figure holding it by the hands. "What's this about?" asked Charlie. Michael scratched the word 'Vampires' in the dirt with his claws, then pointed and said, "No! No!" in a crackly, croaky voice. Charlie turned to run but Michael was too fast for him. To reassure him that he was not in any danger, Michael gave Charlie a toothy smile and then helped him fill the coal bucket. Though frightened out of his wits, Charlie felt that he and Michael were now friends but he would check with his nana if that could possibly be the case.

"You took your bloody time, didn't you? What did you do? Mine the coal yourself?" Mary remarked sarcastically.

"Sorry, Mum, I couldn't find the shovel to fill the bucket."

"Now you've got the coal, get off to bed, you've had a long day and you'll be tired for school if you don't get some sleep."

"Mary love, why don't you go to bed and leave Charlie and me to talk for a while." Before she could object, Nana Lyons added, "Don't worry, I won't keep him long." Mary tutted and went off to bed mumbling and grumbling to herself about how her mother continually undermined her authority with the children.

"Nana, I saw Michael. And I didn't even have to use my whistle!" hiss-whispered Charlie excitedly.

"No whistle! I warned you, he's not a pet and sometimes he… oh, what's the use? You're okay, everything's okay, so tell me what happened, you were down there for quite a while. It was all I could do to stop your mother going to look for you."

"When I opened the coal cellar door, Michael made some funny noises that sort of invited me into the coal cellar. I wasn't feeling scared, so I went. He didn't like it when I told him I'd been training for Vampires And Victims. He grabbed my hand and took me to his den."

"You've been inside Michael's den?" queried Nana Lyons incredulously. "He hasn't taken me in there for ages. What's it like nowadays?"

"He showed me some paintings on the wall of a man and two

children," answered Charlie, sounding puzzled. His nana knew exactly who and what they were of.

"Stop right there. He showed you paintings of Lord Harbinger?"

"I've no idea who the paintings were of but after he showed me them he wrote the word 'Vampires' in the dirt on the floor and… and…"

"Go on, Charlie, did Michael speak to you?" The boy nodded. "What did he say?"

"He pointed to the word on the floor and then he repeated the word 'no' a couple of times. I panicked and went to escape, but Michael was too fast, I couldn't get away. I think he realised he'd frightened me, so he smiled to calm me down, at least I think it was a smile. So many teeth! There was no growling so I think it must've been a smile."

"So, Michael actually spoke to you."

"Yes, just like the creature that spoke to Jed. They must be the same. Was it Michael that spoke to Jed?"

"No, Charlie, it wasn't Michael that spoke to Jed, it was one of his kind, unless they've created more abominations up there at Storm Hill. So, Michael said 'no' when he pointed at the letters he'd written on the floor? I need to have a talk with him. But not tonight."

"What did he mean, Nana?"

"Michael realises we've started something, and I doubt he gives much for our chances of success."

"What is it we've started, Nana?"

"War, Charlie, we've started a war. It's been a long time coming but it's long overdue. I understand that now but better late than never."

"Who have we started a war with, Nana?"

"Storm Hill, son, we've started a war with the Vampires of Storm Hill. There must've been some changes up there. I'll need to find out what they are."

"How are you going to do that, Nana?"

"To be honest, son, I don't know. I'm not as young as I used to be. I can't go climbing over walls or shinnying up trees anymore otherwise I'd… never mind, never mind. Now get yourself off to bed and if you hear Michael grizzling and mizzling in the night just ignore him. Don't worry, he won't come out of his den, he'll want us to go to him."

"Instead of you going to Storm Hill to find out what's going on up there, what about getting Dad to help find out what's happening? He'll be able to find something out for you when he has his tea breaks and things?"

"That's a nice thought, Charlie, but do you remember when I told everybody about Michael and they didn't believe me? Well, imagine what your dad, or anybody, would say if I asked them to find out what's happening at Storm Hill? They'd ask a load of questions, and when I told them what I'm trying to find out they'd send for the men in white coats to take me away. People like your mum and dad are too set in their ways, too fixed in their thoughts and ideas to believe in the things that go on at Storm Hill. They've forgotten how to dream, Charlie. Now, for the second time, go to bed!"

"Before I do, can I ask you if Michael was out and about tonight?"

"No, I don't think so, why?"

"When I was heading home along Heatherfield Road after training I thought I was being followed. I heard a snuffling noise like Michael makes." Nana Lyons was alarmed at this development. It could mean Lupule were on the loose.

"It's not anything you should worry about, son. Now, get off to bed!"

"Okay, Nana, night night, sleep tight…"

"And don't let the bed bugs bite," added Nana Lyons, finishing the old saying. Charlie laughed whenever his nana said that but not that night.

As Charlie headed off to bed a thought occurred to him. *Why don't I ask Margot or Maggart or Max or Bogdan what goes on at Storm Hill? I'm sure they'll tell me. I'll ask them in the morning. I'll start with Max. Nana will be so pleased and proud of me!*

★

After Lucian Thorne gave his report to Tyran Skel about children doing Vampires And Victims training, Skel said, "Keep up the good work," and dismissed him, leaving Xenka Drach, Seren and he to discuss who and what was behind this declaration of war and what they should do about it.

Immediate retaliation was the first thing out of Tyran Skel's mouth. His idea was the Storm Hill League of Welldoers should stop supplying the poor with free coal. "But what about the smog?" queried Xenka Drach. "We need smog so we can move around the Cauldron during daylight hours." Skel had not considered that. "In any case, Master, the winter nights will soon be gone, so they won't burn sufficient coal to make smog," added Seren, attempting to rescue her Master's embarrassment. "Well then, let's stop the free meat. That'll teach them!" yelled Skel, leaping like a madman from his chair. "Stopping the meat will make them too weak to play Vampires And Victims!" Seren and Xenka initially thought this a good idea but concluded that if they did this then they would not be able to dose the local population with Somnifir. "I know what we should do," exclaimed Xenka, "we'll force up food prices in the shops. The poor hardly have enough money to buy food now, so they'll go even hungrier!" Tyran Skel clapped his approval of Xenka's idea like an excited child. "Yes! No food, no energy so no fight in them." Seren wanted to know why they were so set against Cauldronians playing Vampires And Victims.

"It'll occupy them and keep them from watching what we're doing. It's only a game!"

"A game? Oh, it's not a game, Seren, it's training!" hissed Skel. "Vampires And Victims firstly teaches Humans how to evade us, then they learn how to hunt us and finally they learn how to dust us. So it's not a game, Seren, it's far from a game!"

"It was a condition set down in the Treaty that Humans ceased playing Vampires And Victims and now we have this!" cried Madame Drach.

"Master, why then don't you just descend into Vampire sleep until this generation has passed away? Those that come after them will soon forget all about us. You know what mortals are like: out of sight out of mind."

"We cannot just stand by and do nothing! They've broken the Treaty!" yelled Tyran Skel indignantly. "Who's behind all this anyway?"

"I bet it's that Priest, Father Grogan, that's behind it."

"No, not him, he's just a lackey."

"What about Father Francis?"

"He's just a pretty boy with no brains in his head."

"Horan?"

"He's just an old drunk!"

"What about one of the old Crones?" Xenka suggested.

"Yes! Yes! I bet it's that interfering old hag Elizabeth Lyons what's behind it. She's had it in for us ever since Nisfara took her grandson!"

"But he was a Moroi, she knew that!" lamented Xenka Drach.

"We must find out if she's the one who's reviving Vampires And Victims."

"My Repeste could grab her. Her neighbours will think she's being taken off to the Sanatorium. They've thought her mad for years, so it'll come as no surprise to see the men in white coats taking her away."

"But what about her pet? He won't sit idly by and watch his Mistress being taken away from him," interjected Seren.

"He's just one Lupulo," scoffed Skel. "In any case, I don't think he's a houseguest, I think he's a prisoner."

"Do you seriously think a Human could keep a Lupulo prisoner all these years?"

"Who knows? Anyway, he's so old now he might be dead," laughed Skel nervously.

"I could always order my Mutanti to kidnap her?" suggested Seren.

"Your Mutanti, Seren? Since when did they become *your* Mutanti?" demanded Xenka Drach.

"Actually, I put Seren in charge of the Mutanti," admitted Skel. "You and I have enough to do, and I thought it a suitable reward for her loyalty during the rebellion," he added. Xenka was furious and showed it.

"Leave us, Seren," demanded Drach. The hideous Beast looked to Tyran Skel as her cue for what to do. He flicked his head toward the door, and she left the chamber. "Tyran, we, you and me, are equals in everything. We led the rebellion together, you with your Lupule and I with my Repeste. The Mutanti have always answered to the Prima Vampir, and with our Lord locked away we are Prima Vampiri, so why did you think it appropriate to give Seren control over the Mutanti?" Tyran Skel remained silent; he realised he might have made a colossal mistake. "There are more than enough of them to wipe us out and now that you have given them a leader they have a rallying point for rebellion. Have you noticed how many Mutanti are returning from exile since we incarcerated Lord Harbinger? Coincidence? I don't think so, Tyran, I don't think so!"

"If it makes you any happier, I'll keep an eye on her and if it looks like she's—"

"Tyran," interrupted Xenka, "I swear that if, even for just one second, Seren looks like she's about to betray us I will release Lord Harbinger from his captivity. He's the only one who can stand up to her and her kind!"

"And what will happen to us after He is freed?"

"We will throw ourselves at His feet to beg His mercy and forgiveness and hope that He is in forgiving mood. If He is not then I will end my own existence rather than have Him, who I still love and worship, do it."

"But He hasn't fed these past eighteen months. He's in no fit state to fight Seren?"

"Then we must start feeding Him. Not too much. Just a little every day, and be prepared to sacrifice however many it takes to restore Him to His full powers should the need arise," said Xenka matter-of-factly. Tyran Skel thought carefully before answering.

"Okay. But if He looks like He's getting too strong we must reduce the feeding," he replied nervously. Xenka agreed. There was something she had wanted to ask Skel for a while and this seemed the ideal opportunity.

"Tyran, we were all astounded, were we not, when the Lupule began breeding. Lord Harbinger said it was Mother Nature intervening after the Lycanthropes refused to create more of them. But what of Mutanti? Do you think they might be capable of breeding some day?" Tyran Skel considered the possibility and shook his head.

"No, Xenka. Mutanti are created in the same way as we and so they cannot breed," Skel replied solemnly.

"But what of the work going on inside the Sanatorium? What if, instead of creating Wraiths, they create Mutanti instead? What then?"

"Is it even possible to create a Mutanto?" queried Skel. He answered his own question. "Surely that is something nobody can know for certain," he sighed. "But if Mutanti are created instead of Wraiths then we can end them," he added, quelling his rising anxiety. "But there's nothing to say that is even possible!" he mumbled, concluding his self-argument. Skel's monologue hardly satisfied Xenka Drach but she was getting tired of their conversation.

"Tyran, Seren calls you Master. Tell me truthfully, are you her Master alone or are we both Masters to her?"

"Why, both of us, of course," Skel replied unconvincingly.

"Then why did she look to you when I ordered her from the chamber?"

"That's only natural. She wanted to check if we both agreed. I assure you that Seren is as dutiful to you as she is to me. There's nothing for you to be concerned about," answered Skel, trying to sound convincing.

Skel and Drach parted company on reasonably good terms despite the latter's unresolved concerns. As Xenka retired to her chambers in the galleries below Mormant Hall, Seren slipped silently out of her secret compartment from where she eavesdropped on those conversing in the Grand Chamber. She was extremely displeased with what she had overheard and wanted Xenka Drach out of the way more than ever. The Mutanto had long held ambitions to rule alongside Tyran Skel and ultimately alone. She now had to consider what to do about him and Drach reviving Lord Harbinger. However, she would not to interfere in case it gave them reason for suspicion. What intrigued Seren most was the part of the conversation concerning whether Mutanti could breed. She believed they could not but the thought excited to her.

For some considerable time, Vampire scientists had been attempting to create a Wraith. *So why not Mutanti too?* mused Seren. *Just throw in a bit of this and a bit of that and who knows?* spoke her inner voice in confidence to her. Following Seren's reverie, she returned to her quarters, chuckling as she went. Those that heard her believed she was suffering the aftereffects of imbibing the juice of some derelict whose entrails had gone putrid and delighted in thinking of her in agony.

CHAPTER 7

For millennia, Vampire Science has been far in advance of that of Human Beings. The fundamental reason for this is that Vampire scientists were not slaughtered by the Church for their art in the way Human scientists were. Science, and the enlightenment it eventually brought to Humankind, was believed by the Church to be unnatural, heretical, blasphemous, unholy and contrary to God's divine plan for His creation. If something practised by Humans was not mentioned in the Bible it was a lie and they had to either recant or die. An example of such religious barbarism is Giordano Bruno, the greatest Vampire Philosopher, Mathematician and Astronomer of his day. He was burned alive at the stake by order of the Catholic Church in 1600. His heart was later staked to put his spirit at rest with the Great Universe. Even when compared with his Vampire contemporaries, Giordano was a prodigy centuries ahead of his time. Many likened his genius to that of another netherworldly creature, Leonardo da Vinci. Giordano's theories around the infinite Universe and the multiplicity of worlds, in which he challenged the Church's geocentric astronomy, were groundbreaking. He theorised that the sun was merely a star, like all those which adorned the firmament. He claimed that the stars in the night sky were not placed in the Heavens simply for our delight, though it was perfectly acceptable to delight in them; they were suns just like our own. To illustrate this, Bruno explained that an object at close quarters seems large when compared to viewing that same object at distance. He speculated that the sun must appear as a star when viewed from a great distance, in other words when viewed from another star. The Church was incandescent with rage at Bruno's heretical, blasphemous, unholy and ungodly theories and ordered him to recant them. Being a creature of integrity, Bruno refused to retract a single syllable. The Church condemned Signor Bruno to be burned at the stake; he was the only Vampire scientist ever to suffer this way at its hands.

Not being shackled by religious persecution, the Vampire nation made great advances in science and medicine while their 'God-fearing' mortal counterparts were held back for fear of the consequences that came with angering the Church. Those few mortals who did openly practise science were careful to call it Natural Philosophy in dread of being bound hand and foot to a stake atop a pile of wood and having it set on fire beneath them. But for religion, by the epoch known as the Renaissance, Humankind would have vanquished every disease in creation and the Earth's inhabitants would have been travelling among the stars instead of living and dying in putrid squalor wallowing in their own filth. The grip the Church had on Humanity, especially the society of the poor, was total. For fear of being held up as a blasphemer or a heretic, or perhaps being excommunicated for some minor indiscretion, all society was forced to cower before an almighty Church. At various times throughout history the Church actually held more power than Kings, Tyrants or even Emperors, but thankfully their power and influence waned and hopefully one day it will vanish entirely.

Something that had long eluded Vampire scientists was the answer to why it took so long to make a new Vampire. Had Vampires been capable of 'reproducing' at the same rate as Human Beings reproduced there would not have been a problem but, with the overall Vampire population in decline, they were barely in a position to defend themselves against pitchfork-wielding peasants, let alone a well-trained and well-armed Human Army. Something had to be done to increase numbers. Then, by timely accident, a solution presented itself, one that would not only give Vampires a fighting chance in the population race but could possibly give them advantages never previously envisioned.

Ever since the time of the first Vampire, only Prima Generatie Vampiri were permitted to create new Vampires. To keep their Houses pure, they fed only on Victims with certain attributes. However, lower-order Vampires, Inferiara, began feeding on random Victims they just happened to encounter in their wanderings. This resulted in the creation of Pale Vampires of very inferior quality and sickly to look at. When discovered, they and their feeder would invariably be staked. What was remarkable was that Inferiara often needed only half a dozen or so feeds to create their Offspring. If Prima Generatie Vampiri could create new Vampires as quickly, then Vampire numbers would increase rapidly, but instead it often took decades to make a new Vampire. Very occasionally, a new Vampire was created after just a few feeds, but these 'quickies' took a long time to mature. This at least proved new Vampires could be made quickly; however, how and why this anomaly occurred eluded the best of Vampire scientists. Then, out of the blue, an Inferiara called Seraphina Sable made a new Vampire after just one feed. And, what was more, she had done so on purpose. She had fallen madly in love with the son of a Familiar and they cooked up a scheme that they could be together for all eternity. But they were uncovered, and she was denounced to Lord Harbinger by her Progenitor. The pair were taken before the Grand Council of the House of Mormant. Seraphina had broken two of the 'big' rules of the Vampire Code. Firstly, being an Inferiara, she was not legally allowed to create a Vampire and, second, Familiars can only become Vampires by special decree of a Prima Vampir.

Despite it being Seraphina's only transgression of the Vampire Code, she was ordered to be staked. The same fate was given to her lover, Daniel Lester. As Seraphina exploded in a flash of rapidly decaying light, a Vampire Priest screamed out from the darkened cloisters, "He casts a shadow! The abomination casts a shadow!" The Vampire Priest rushed forward holding a candle against the vast blackness of the Grand Chamber. It was true: Daniel Lester did indeed cast a faint but distinct shadow. The Grand Council declared there must have been a mistake, doubting that a Vampire had been created in the first place. "But we felt the passing of his mortal soul," cried the witnesses. If Daniel Lester was mortal, then what type of creature was he? Was the question from the thin, spiteful Recorder. Lord Harbinger called for the Grand Chamber to be cleared – all except Xenka Drach, Tyran Skel and Professor Grail. The Prima Vampir ordered the professor to study Daniel Lester and discover exactly what he was: Vampire or mortal? Xenka Drach and Tyran Skel were put in charge over proceedings and report progress. That was the biggest mistake Lord Harbinger had made in two thousand years.

★

Professor Grail established that no matter how much time Daniel Lester spent basking in sunlight he neither blistered nor burst into flames. Given his Vage this was not surprising, but what was surprising was he had a faint reflection and he bled real blood not Vblood; also, neither garlic nor holy water created any ill effects in him whatsoever. Was Lester's condition temporary? Would he change or revert over time? The professor could not say. Nor could he say whether Daniel was mortal and as there was only one of him he was not prepared to find out. Professor Grail did, however, eventually come up with a name for Daniel Lester's condition: he branded him a Wraith. Arguments broke out among Vampire Academics and Lore Keepers, as they already had a definition of a Wraith and as far as they were concerned Daniel Lester was not a

Wraith. Nevertheless, the term stuck. Henceforth, the official name given to creations of Daniel Lester's persuasion was Wraith.

The first thought of the Vampire scientists was to use Daniel for research into creating a vaccine to fight Spontaneous Combustion by Sunlight (SCS), something Prima Generatie Vampiri in particular would benefit from and so were keen to see this research undertaken as quickly as possible. Seren 'joked' to Tyran Skel that Wraiths would be ideal to replace Familiars. "No more worries about them having conflicts of conscience and betraying us," she suggested. Seren hated Familiars – 'filthy mortals' as she referred to them. She hated Lupule for the same reason but not quite as much. Xenka and Tyran Skel both saw possibilities in Daniel Lester, possibilities that would ultimately compel them to unite in a rebellion against the rule of Lord Harbinger.

Following Professor Grail's preliminary report, Tyran Skel and Xenka Drach asked Lord Harbinger's permission to look into creating Wraiths 'at will' using the 'Seraphina Sable Formula' by experimenting on derelict Human subjects. "Assuming you are successful, what would be in it for them?" asked Lord Harbinger. "In their anger and rage at being turned into Vampires they might rise up against us and then where will we be?" On the face of it this was a good argument but for one key factor. Wraiths were a type of Vampire with no opportunity of returning to their old selves or lives. They possessed a natural blood lust, as per Daniel Lester, and without the protection of a Vampire House they would be discovered, hunted down and dusted. "But why should true Vampires tolerate these so-called Mortal Vampires, these Wraiths?" was Lord Harbinger's next objection. "My Lord, Wraiths would be able to mix with Humans for the entirety of their lifespans. They will gain their trust and can identify suitable candidates for eternal life or a quick meal. And, as mortals, their natural ageing will lend Vampire Houses an air of respectability." It was assumed by all that as Daniel Lester cast a shadow and had a reflection he must be mortal and that others created in the same way would likewise be mortal.

Professor Grail was brought into the discussion. He added that most, if not all, of those 'chosen' would rejoice at being turned into Vampires. "What a change it would make in their lives. What an improvement it would be for them. They'd feel healthy, full of life, full of energy, all the time," he evangelised. "We would take the chosen from the ranks of the poor. They would no longer dwell in rat-ridden, lice-infested hovels. No more rolling around in filth and squalor and eating muck. Good work. Good homes. No hunger. No disease. No landlords bleeding them dry. No Church bleeding them dry. No shop owners bleeding them dry. No Trade Unions bleeding them dry. No Council bleeding them dry. Nobody whatsoever bleeding them dry after they become Wraiths. In fact, the opposite could be true. Under certain, pre-approved circumstances they could bleed some of those dry that had previously bled them dry. How they would enjoy that! They can revel in their new existence all thanks to Vampire Science," pronounced Professor Grail.

Vampire Science or not, good thing or not, Tyran Skel still had some misgivings about creating Wraiths. Seren wondered, if Professor Grail was successful, where Wraiths would leave her and her Mutanti and, when they heard the news, the Lupule were alarmed by Professor Grail's work. But they had been alarmed before and it had always turned out for the best, so why not so with the creation of Wraiths, whatever they were?

★

It was in Vampire laboratories that the eerily silent horse-drawn wagons were created. After experimenting with various combinations of materials, the rigs were mounted on pneumatic dampeners and the wheels fitted with double-skinned rubber tyres – the inner being solid and the outer pneumatic. The rigs are, in fact, not silent: they make a low rumbling sound, especially when being driven over cobblestones, but smog smothers what slight noise is created. The horses are shod with rubber booties. The inner layer of the booties is soft, the middle layer hard and the outer layer hardest, for obvious reasons. Just as with cart wheels, the horses make some sound as they make their way over cobblestones, but, again, the smog smothers what little noise they do make. The overall effect is supernatural as rigs race silently along smoggy roads. This brings up the question of how the rigs are able to drive so furiously fast through the densest smog. The answer is that Repeste wear special goggles fitted with a device which enables them to 'hear' obstacles, while the massive black horses are descended from a bloodline that was fed on by a Vampire with a penchant for feeding on bats. The result, in this case, was a horse capable of 'seeing' where none other could. This was just one of the many freakish 'accidents' that have occurred over the centuries.

Something Vampire Science has never been able to achieve is to brew a batch of Somnifir. No matter what, Vampire scientists never cracked the formula. The secret to brewing Somnifir lies with the Supreme Council who pass it down to Vampires that achieve the status of Prima Vampir, usually when they become Head of a House. Over the centuries, Vampire scientists learned that Somnifir required blood from a Prima Vampir to kick-start the process. The Vblood, as they called it, needed mixing with herbs and compounds and then exposed to sunlight to activate the Elixir. Without a Prima Vampir or a renegade PGV, little wonder Vampire scientists could not recreate Somnifir. Which was just as well, as in the wrong hands, and in sufficient quantities, Somnifir could wipe out the entire Vampire Creed.

For a year prior to Skel and Drach leading the rebellion against Lord Harbinger, they stockpiled Somnifir as they knew that after the rebellion he would cease production. Tyran Skel, however, came up with a plan to supplement the Somnifir supply, one which, if he were ever discovered, would bring the Supreme Council's Slayers down on him.

★

With Xenka Drach's words of warning about scientists creating 'test-tube' Mutanti rebounding inside his head, Skel wanted to know what they were up to in their secret laboratories deep inside the Sanatorium. He had not checked on them for a while. What if they had already created a Mutanto instead of a Wraith? Would they tell him? "No, they wouldn't, for fear of you putting a stop to their precious work!" screamed the voices inside Skel's head. "I bet they're keeping all sorts of things from you; not that you'd know, you wouldn't understand a single word they said!" continued the voices.

Skel resolved to pay a surprise visit to the Sanatorium. Leaving Mormant Hall via a secret door he made his way to the outer wall. When he got there he pressed several stones in sequence to reveal a handle. Pressing the handle downward a narrow section of the wall opened like a door. Once on the other side of the wall, Skel pushed the door back into place. He looked around and, seeing nobody, he made his way to the Sanatorium. Had he looked more carefully, Tyran Skel would have noticed a group of children of Familiars lurking in bushes close to where he emerged through the wall.

"Who was that?" enquired Noire Drabech, daughter of a level-ten Familiar. Like most of her friends, Miss Drabech had scant regard for her father's position and was always looking for ways to embarrass him.

"I'm sure I've seen him before," said Max Rune, son of Simeon Rune, Conducere to Lord Harbinger.

"He might be a spy!" speculated Bogdan Radu, orphaned son of a fourth-level Familiar. As with Human children, the children of Storm Hill's elite hang out together but there is always one who manages to get included and nobody quite understands how. In this group it was Bogdan Radu.

"Let's see where he goes," suggested Cho Lee, adopted daughter of Viserce, Xenka Drach's Conducere.

Many thought it suspicious that a Conducere had only one name. Those that knew the traditions of Mutanti believed her to be one of that kind. The truth was Viserce was not a Mutanto but a new kind of immortal created by Xenka Drach herself and then kept her 'condition' a secret.

The children followed the mysterious stranger at a safe distance. Arriving at the outer wall of the Sanatorium, Tyran Skel repeated the same trick he did at the wall of Mormant Hall to pass through it. The children agreed in future they would use this way to sneak into the grounds of the Sanatorium, and they planned to look for doors in all the walls around Storm Hill. After giving the stranger a thirty-second head start, the children opened the door in the wall of the Sanatorium. Thankfully, he was nowhere to be seen. They made their way round the side of the building to the only window showing a light, and once there they slowly and carefully positioned themselves to peep through it without giving their presence away. What they saw surprised and puzzled them. The room was full of Vampires standing to attention in front of the person they had followed. The Vampires then went down on one knee and, with their heads bowed, repeated, "Hail, Tyran Skel, Prima Vampir…" until he told them to stand. "Tyran Skel? Ever heard of him?" asked Cho Lee. "No, but what's concerning is they're hailing him as Prima Vampir. What's happened to Lord Harbinger?" whispered Max Rune. "Do you think Lord Harbinger's dead?" asked Bogdan Radu. "Shhhh. Shut up and listen," hissed Noire Drabech, though they could hardly hear anything of what was being said.

"My Lord Vampir Skel, to what do we owe the honour?" toadied Professor Grail, Chief Scientist at the Sanatorium.

"It occurred to me that I haven't been paying much attention to the important work you are doing here," replied Tyran Skel. Professor Grail was not fooled by Skel's words and knew that if this meeting went badly his research would be axed, and probably him along with it.

"It'll be my pleasure to show you what we've been doing. I'm confident you'll be suitably impressed, my Lord. I thought I'd start by showing you —"

"I want to see how far you've got with your work on creating a Wraith and if there've been any unexpected results." And there Mazus Grail had it in a nutshell. If his work did not please Prima Vampir Skel he would be axed. How he now regretted having gone along with the rebellion but Lord Harbinger had refused to allow him to fully explore the opportunities presented by Daniel Lester.

"Certainly, my Lord." Mazus Grail turned to one of his assistants. "Bring in the subjects." The assistant departed and returned five minutes later leading a line of bleary-eyed children. They appeared groggy as they walked Zombie-like to the centre of the room.

"Eight? I thought there were nine?" queried Skel.

"One child remains outstanding. His name is Jerad Carter. He and his family have recently moved into a house in Evelyn Terrace. Thus far we haven't been able to —"

"You've had long enough! Get this Carter child before he realises what he witnessed when he looked through the window that night."

"My Lord, I'm still not convinced that he or his friends saw anything that would jeopardise our work," said one of the scientists, speaking out of turn.

"Are you calling Seren a liar, Professor?"

"No, of course not, my Lord," grovelled Professor Zul. As required by the Vampire Code, after such impertinence Professor Zul bowed low, offering the back of her neck to Tyran Skel for him to rip out if he saw fit. He declined the gesture with a mere wave of his gloved hand.

"Now, Professor Grail, show me what you've achieved so far."

"As you can no doubt see, my Lord, the subjects remain Human but are beginning to show signs of transitioning."

"Transitioning, not transmogrifying?"

"Transmogrifying, my Lord? Transmogrifying into what?"

"Mutanti, Professor Grail. Transmogrifying into Mutanti. What else transmogrifies other than when Mutanti are created?" exclaimed Tyran Skel, exasperated.

"No, my Lord. Whatever gave you the idea that they could transmogrify into Mutanti? It's totally absurd to presume they could do so." Professor Grail realised his words were impertinent. "I apologise, my Lord, I did not mean to be disrespectful," he stuttered, bowing low and exposing the back of his neck to receive a Vampire Death Bite for his impertinence.

"Professor, please stand up. We can do with more honesty around here," said Tyran Skel, fooling nobody with his words of false comfort. "But what would you do, say, if you created a Mutanto by accident? I mean, accidents do happen. Look at how many Mutanti there are!" joked Skel, waving his hand in the air as if to imply Mutanti were everywhere.

"My Lord, our work here is to create a Wraith not a Mutanto, and if, by some accident of nature, one was created I would destroy it immediately." Tyran Skel was moderately satisfied with Professor Grail's reply.

"Very well, Professor. Then, tell me, why haven't you succeeded yet in creating a Wraith? We already have one, so why haven't you made more of them?"

"My Lord, when Seraphina Sable created Daniel Lester it was by accident. We are presently trying to replicate the circumstances of that accident. We've restored Seraphina's remains, such as they are, and we are using all our scientific knowledge to obtain her essence so that we might then use it to —"

"You've had long enough! It's not working! Try something else! Something different! Something new, drastic even!"

"My Lord, I'm not sure what you mean by something drastic?"

"Professor Grail, you have eight subjects, soon to be nine, and you may acquire more if needs be. You can have as many as you need, so why don't you get Inferiara, such as was Seraphina Sable, to feed on children exactly as she fed on Daniel Lester and then… well, you're the scientist, I don't need to tell you your business." Which was precisely what Tyran Skel was doing.

"That is something I've considered, my Lord," replied Professor Grail. The professor had, in fact, already carried out many experiments on the children using the blood of a cousin of Seraphina Sable he had discovered in the Vampire records. "We're being cautious because we were worried about losing subjects but if the rules have changed, and we can take children from the streets, then there's nothing to prevent us using Inferiara to experiment on them directly. I'll order testing to commence from tomorrow."

"No, show me now, I want to see. Round up some Inferiara and show me now." cried Tyran Skel. Professor Grail ordered his assistants to round up a couple of dozen Inferiara and bring them to the laboratory.

When the Inferiara arrived at the laboratory they feared the worst when they saw Tyran Skel standing there. As the Inferiara were bowing to Skel, Seren entered the laboratory. "Seren, what a nice surprise," he said, greeting her with a kiss on her cheek. Those in the room and outside looking through the window wondered how he could do so without retching. Few in Storm Hill had seen Seren but they knew of her by reputation. All found her form as terrifying and hideous as the stories of her cruelty. Now the Inferiara were really nervous. Tyran Skel whispered to ask Seren why she was there. She whispered back that she was curious to know why so many Inferiara had been rounded up and wanted to know the reason behind it. She asked Skel if she should leave. He replied she could stay if she wanted. Professor Grail instructed the Inferiara on what they were there to do. "You are here to feed on these subjects but not wantonly. This is a controlled experiment you are involved in. You will be instructed precisely what to do and you will follow your instructions precisely." Several Inferiara were visibly uncomfortable at the prospect of feeding on children, and others for feeding while being watched. "Now, the first eight of you come forward and stand directly behind the line of subjects." An assistant counted off eight Inferiara. When they were in position they were ordered to take one Cyathus from the subject in front of them: "No more, no less." As expected by the laboratory staff there was no effect. Then, subject four, Moey Groom, fell writhing on the floor. None of the children reacted to their friend hitting the ground as they were doped to the eyeballs with Somnifir. Professor Grail bent to examine the fallen subject, and as he did so the boy woke. He remained mortal but several Vampires had felt his soul tremor, meaning it had approached the threshold of the Great Universe.

"Excellent, Professor Grail, truly excellent. I believe we shall see quick progress now," Skel cried jubilantly. Professor Grail was relieved that at least one of the subjects had reacted positively.

"I too am pleased, my Lord. I will record all events meticulously so we might compare results between different combinations of subjects, Inferiara and volumes extracted and so forth – science stuff," stuttered the professor. Seren had a question for Professor Grail.

"Professor, what would you do if you created a Mutanto instead of a Wraith?"

"Mistress Seren, as I promised my Lord Skel, it would be destroyed. To be frank, though, I doubt Inferiara can create Mutanti."

"Why so? If there was any certainty in creation Mutanti wouldn't exist at all," hissed Seren craftily. Professor Grail could think of one Mutanto he wished did not exist.

"Come, Seren, let us leave our scientists to their work," interjected Tyran Skel, eager to be away.

"Before you go, my Lord, what shall we do about the adult Humans we have been preparing?"

"Carry on as normal, Professor Grail, the more the better!"

"Thank you, my Lord. We will, of course, use different Inferiara with them so we don't cross-contaminate the child subjects or…"

Tyran Skel was not interested in the slightest in Professor Grail's science wittering and rapidly departed the laboratory followed closely by Seren. The children watching through the window were deeply shocked by what they had witnessed.

"Did you see that thing?" gasped Noire Drabech, mimicking a dry retch.

"And that Skel bloke kissed it!" groaned Bogdan Radu, holding his stomach and also mimicking a dry retch.

"I've heard of creatures like that one before."

"I think I've actually seen a couple of them but nothing like that. It looked like it could've torn them all apart."

"Never mind that. Did you see what they're doing? They're experimenting on children," hissed Max Rune. "I wish we could've heard what they were saying."

"What are they doing to them, do you think?"

"Well, the feeding was minimal, so maybe they're just getting them used to… I don't know, being fed on, perhaps?"

"That's a good suggestion but what if something goes wrong and they kill one of them or turn them into a Vampire? If those children are not returned to the Cauldron all hell will break loose, and the last place they were known to be was here."

"I thought that if an Inferiara turns a Human into a Vampire they are both destroyed!"

"You seem to know a lot about it, Max?"

"My dad gives me all sorts of things to read and I'm studying Lore in Vampire school. I'm hoping to take over from my dad one day as Lord Harbinger's Conducere." The other children sniggered and pointed at Max but he took no notice.

"That Vampire, Skel, have any of you seen him before?"

"I recognised him but didn't know his name."

"I think he must be the boss; Professor Grail was terrified of him."

"If he's the boss then why did he leave Mormant Hall through a secret door in the wall? What do you think it all means?" asked Bogdan.

"I'm going to ask my dad if he knows anything about what we saw tonight."

"Do you think that's wise, Max? I mean, if there's something going on it could be dangerous just to know about it."

"I'm going to ask anyway."

"Don't do it, Max!" pleaded Cho Lee.

"Let's leave before the guards do another patrol."

When Max arrived home he went to his father to tell him about the night's events. Mr Rune shushed his son and ushered him into his study, locking the door behind them. He told Max to start at the beginning and be sure not to miss out any of the details. Max carefully and concisely told his father of the night's events. After which his father placed his head in his hands and emitted a suppressed cry of anguish so as not to alarm anybody in the house. Max asked his father if he knew anything about what he and his friends had seen. Mr Rune replied that he hoped the other children were going to remain silent about what they had seen. "Why?" asked Max. "Because what you witnessed could cost us your lives. It's too late to go knocking on doors, that would raise suspicions, but as soon as you see your friends tomorrow morning find out if any of them said anything to their parents. If they did then return here immediately, though if they have we'll probably get a visit tonight." Max had never seen his father like this before. "Sorry, Dad. I thought it would be fun to follow the man we saw go through the wall. Do you know who this Tyran Skel is?" asked the boy. "I do. He and Xenka Drach led a rebellion against Lord Harbinger eighteen months ago," replied Simeon Rune. Max wondered why his father had not mentioned this to him but then thought, *Why would he?* Mr Rune continued, "Son, you and your friends have to be wary of Skel and Drach, they are very dangerous Vampires. Since overthrowing Lord Harbinger they've broken the Treaty by experimenting on Humans. For what purpose, I shudder to think," admitted Mr Rune. Max was surprised by how much his father knew. "Dad, one of my friends is the daughter of Xenka Drach's Conducere. I hope she doesn't mention anything to her about tonight." Mr Rune said he hoped so too and told Max to get off to bed, as he had things he needed to do. Max had one more question for his father: "Is Lord Harbinger dead?" Mr Rune told Max that Lord Harbinger was, of course, dead in the same sense that all Vampires are dead, but he had not been destroyed, if that is what he meant. "He's being held under guard in a cell at the end of the fourth-level gallery below Mormant Hall."

★

Max rose early following a sleepless night. He rushed from his house to the pickup point to wait for the others to arrive. The first to arrive was Cho Lee. She looked unconcerned so Max was about to ask her if she had spoken to anybody about the previous evening's events when Lorcan Thorne showed up with Margot and Maggart. Noire Drabech and Bogdan Radu also arrived at the pickup point. Max flicked his head to one side to indicate that he wanted to speak with them all in private. They took themselves away from the pickup point, attracting the attention of Lorcan Thorne. He asked Margot and Maggart what they were up to. Margot replied it was none of his business. As he was still suffering the after-effects of meeting Seren and of the Somnifir potion, Thorne did not pursue the matter. Max told the others about his conversation with his father and how important it was that they did not discuss what they had witnessed the previous evening with anybody. They looked at him as if to say, "Of course not, we're not as stupid as you!" Before returning to the pickup point, Max told the others that Tyran Skel and Xenka Drach had led a rebellion eighteen months earlier against Lord Harbinger and that they had him incarcerated in a cell in the galleries deep below Mormant Hall. Bogdan Radu and Noire Drabech stared at Cho Lee. "Why are you looking at me?" she asked indignantly. "Mum doesn't tell me a thing about her work, so how would I know anything about a rebellion?" she whined. As the children seated themselves on the wagon, Max commented on how quiet Lorcan Thorne seemed. Hearing this, Thorne asked Max if he wanted to make something of it, which he could not be bothered to, so the pair left one another alone for the rest of the journey to school.

As the wagon drove down St George's Hill it passed close to Charlie Carter and his clan but Lorcan Thorne did not shout his usual abuse. Instead, he just sat in silence staring straight ahead. Margot, however, yelled, "Good morning, Charlie!" and ordered the Repeste to stop so they could walk the rest of the way to school together. "I think there's something going on there," remarked Max. "I've decided to let her have him," joked Cho. Max and Bogdan grimaced at Cho but she pretended not see them. Lorcan Thorne did not react at all to anything; he just continued sitting and shivering inside at the thought of the sight of Seren.

As the children filed into morning assembly they noticed Mr Bawles standing alone on the school stage. Where the teachers were the pupils could not guess. This was the first time any such thing had happened and it set all the children on edge.

"Good morning, children," said Mr Bawles in a tone that did nothing to set the assembly at their ease.

"Good morning, Mr Bawles," returned the children in the same tone. For the first time ever there was no sniggering after saying Mr Bawles' name.

"Please put down your hymn books." It was then the children noticed there were no hymns posted on the hymn board. "I have some sad news to share with you." A deadly hush descended over the assembly hall. The children feared the worst. "In the early hours of this morning, I received news that the children convalescing in Storm Hill – Maurice Groom, Steven Lewis, William Patterson, Stanley Kavanagh, Amy Collins, Sarah Keane, Angela O'Shea, Alan Moogan and Thomas Newcombe – all contracted Sweating Sickness and, tragically, passed away last night." The entire assembly erupted into wailing and howling. "I am sure you all share the heartfelt grief and sadness felt by their families and friends, and our thoughts are with them at this difficult time."

The teachers entered the hall to comfort the smallest of the children, cradling some of them in their arms like babies. Charlie Carter sat stunned. "No more Patto; no more Stevie; no more Moey," he muttered through trembling lips and began to cry. Margot held Charlie's head in her arms, gently brushing back his hair with her fingers. "Do you believe in God, Charlie?" she asked. "I don't know, I don't know. I hope there is a God and I hope they're all with Him." Mr Bawles spoke again. "I understand your parents rely on you being at school during the day but lessons are cancelled until tomorrow. Your teachers will stay to look after any children who wish to remain in school. Assembly is over but please stay in the hall as long as you wish." Mr Bawles left the stage via a side door. Before the door shut, Charlie saw the Head and Father Francis talking animatedly to somebody but he could not see who it was. A nudge in his back told Charlie the rest of the Carter children had come to their big brother for comfort.

"That's it, Charlie, that's it!" spoke Jed angrily. "I'm going to tell everybody what I know, they've done this on purpose!" he added, blubbering. Charlie put his arm around his little brother's heaving shoulders.

"What's he talking about, Charlie?" asked Effy, Agnes and Tatty together.

"Nothing, he's not talking about anything," replied Charlie reassuringly in an effort to calm his sisters.

"It could've been me, Charlie. I'm the only one they didn't get," said Jed.

"Will you shut up!" snapped Charlie. "You're upsetting the others!"

"I'm not staying here, I'm going to Nana's. Who's coming with me?" Patrick Jnr and the girls raised their hands.

"Aren't you coming with us, Charlie?" asked Tatty.

"I have a few things to do first but I'll be along later. Don't worry, Jed'll take good care of you. Holy Cross'll probably be having the day off too, so the Hawleys and the Morans'll walk home with you." Charlie kissed his siblings goodbye and went in search of Max Rune.

When Charlie found Max, the young Storm Hiller looked pallid like death. Charlie asked him why he was looking the way he was. He replied that he had hardly slept and was not feeling all that well. Unconcerned about how Max was feeling, Charlie grilled him about what went on in Storm Hill. Max was unhappy with the line of questioning and said so. Charlie said he did not care. "Look, Max, I want to know what's happening up there at Storm Hill and I think you want to tell me, I can see it in your eyes!" Max was not going to be drawn in by that old trick. "All you can see in my eyes, Charlie Carter, is tiredness. Now, I'm going to return to Storm Hill with my friends." Max left Charlie just as Billy Lynch appeared. This time there was no friendly dead-arm punch from his cousin. "Alright, our kid?" asked Billy with sadness ringing in his voice.

"Not really, our Billy, not really. There's something fishy going on at Storm Hill and I want to know what it is. How could Moey and the others have suddenly died? It's not possible." Billy was at a loss to explain. "I don't know, our kid, but I heard they've been cremated already. Apparently, the doctors said they couldn't risk the disease spreading, so they cremated them before handing them over to their parents. That's shocking, that is, isn't it, Charlie?"

This news made Charlie even more suspicious. He ran to look for Max Rune but neither he nor any of the other Storm Hillers could be found anywhere. Returning to Billy, Charlie said he should come with him to his nana's house to see what she had to say about all this!

★

When Billy and Charlie arrived at Evelyn Terrace they were greeted by the sight of a huge crowd gathered outside Nana Lyons' house. At first they thought the crowd had gathered in shared grief but as the boys drew closer it was obvious that they were angry with Nana Lyons and were calling for her to come out and face them. Charlie's mum emerged from the front door to boos from the crowd. "What do you lot want?" shouted Mary at the mob. "This has got nothin' to do with you, Mary, get yer mum out here. She's got some questions to answer about why our kids are dead and why so many of them are being taken away never to be seen again! She said they'd be home in a few days. She said they'd be okay, and now look what's happened!" Nana Lyons opened an upstairs window. "You all know me," she shouted to the raging crowd, "I've never let you down. When you needed something I was the first to give it. When you were ill it was me that brought the doctors!" These entreaties failed to placate the crowd. "You come out here right now, Elizabeth Rose Lyons, or we're coming in!" yelled one of the lynch mob. "I'm not coming outside with you lot in this mood but I'll allow a delegation inside if you want to talk. But at the slightest sign of trouble they'll get a fright they won't forget." Rumours about a vicious, bloodthirsty creature living in Nana Lyons' coal cellar had abounded for years, so the crowd took her threat very seriously. "Okay, Betty, have it your way. Just a few of us will come in," shouted Elsie Tatlock, who then selected two elderly women to join her. "Now listen," shouted Nana Lyons from the window, "go back to your homes and if you dare come back here I'll stiffen every one of yez!" There was something in Nana Lyons' tone that left the crowd in no doubt that she meant it and would do it too. Charlie and Billy passed through the crowd listening to what people were saying about Nana Lyons. They picked up words such as, 'witch' and 'traitor' and 'Devil Worshipper' and, puzzlingly to them both, 'Familiar'.

CHAPTER 8

Charlie and Billy entered the house close on the heels of Elsie Tatlock and her delegation. They went to follow the old women into the front parlour but were prevented from doing so by one of them.

"Hello, Charlie! And look, it's Billy Lynch, isn't it?" said the old woman. "You've hardly changed, either of you."

"Neither have you," replied Charlie out of politeness.

"Now, we all know that's a great big lie," replied the old woman, smiling. "You don't recognise me, do you? The last time I saw you two was… I can't remember but I know it's you," she said, speaking just like the boys imagined a Witch would speak.

"Are you going to be talking about Moey and Patto and Stevie and the others?" asked Charlie. "Because if you are we want to come in!"

"Well, you can't. Little boys should be seen and not heard," said another of the old women.

"Charlie," said Nana Lyons, coming down the stairs, "go and play with the other kids in the backyard. I'll talk to you later but for now go and play. First, though, go and get me some coal," she added with a wink.

"What was that wink for?" asked Billy.

"It wasn't a wink, I think Nana's got something in her eye." Billy was not convinced. He knew a wink when he saw one.

"Do ye want me to help you get the coal, then, our kid?" Billy asked Charlie.

"No thanks, our kid."

"Thank Christ for that, that place gives me the willies," said Billy with a shiver. "Have ye seen the size of the spiders down there? Sorry, Charlie, I didn't mean to… you know?" Charlie said he knew what Billy meant.

Nosily lifting the latch of the coal cellar door to alert Michael that somebody was visiting his domain, Charlie flicked on the light and descended into the shadowy gloom below. The light bulb seemed dimmer than ever and the cellar darker, danker and smellier than ever. Once standing underneath the dull cone of yellow light emitted by the puny light bulb, Charlie called for Michael to come out. To his surprise and then shock and then horror and then terror, two pair of yellow eyes glowed back at him from the space beneath the stairs. As with his previous encounter with Michael, Charlie thought of running but his legs refused to obey despite his rising fear. Out of the darkness emerged a pair of Lupule, neither of which was Michael. Charlie was really afraid. *What's happened to Michael?* he thought. But then a cat-like purr came from behind him; it was Michael. He 'introduced' Charlie to the Lupule, who performed a bow and scraped the dirt floor with their hind limbs. Charlie felt it only proper to return the gracious act, causing the Lupule to laugh and point at him. "Are you okay down there, Charlie?" shouted Billy into the coal cellar. "Do ye need any help?" At the sound of Billy's voice the Lupule slunk back into the shadows. "Nah," replied Charlie casually, "you're alright, our kid, I've just found the shovel so I'll be up after I've filled the coal bucket." As Charlie climbed the stairs he looked back and whispered to Michael, "Thank you for introducing me to your friends, I'll come back to meet them properly later."

After Charlie filled the coal scuttle with the bucket, he went out into the backyard to play with the other kids. The yard was very small so Billy suggested they have a game of V and V around the back jiggers. Charlie said there was not enough room for V and V but Billy answered, "All the better, now we'll get to see how good you are. I'll be the Vampire and you lot can be the Victims." At being told they were Victims, the younger kids screamed in feigned terror. "You've got twenty seconds to get away," said Billy and began counting up to twenty. "Twenty seconds? We'll only need two seconds in this place," replied Charlie. In their excitement to get away from Billy, the children yelled loud enough to wake the dead looking for places to hide. "Hey, you lot, it's not a game of hide and seek, it's a game of… oh, never mind," complained Charlie. "Annie, Lilley, Effy and me know the rules, so we'll be Victims with Charlie and the rest can see how the game's played," suggested Jed. Observing proceedings from a bedroom looking down over the backyard were Nana Lyons and the delegation of old women, all members of the Council of Crones. "I've heard Charlie's very good at V and V," remarked Minnie Chadwick. "We'll see," replied Nana Lyons sternly. "Why are you always so hard on the boy, Elizabeth?" asked Elsie Tatlock. "After all, he's your own flesh and blood," she added with a sly glance to see if Nana Lyons reacted, which she did not. There had long been rumours circulating around the Cauldron that Charlie was a swapling and the genuine Charlie Carter had perished when still a baby. Other rumours had it that he was the illegitimate product of a Lyons family member. Similar rumours abounded about forty or so other children of the Cauldron. "Charlie and Jed should be good at playing Vampires And Victims with all the time they've spent swinging on monkey bars and running along the top of the advertising tins!" interjected Minnie Chadwick to change the subject.

Almost immediately after Billy Lynch began hunting Victims he tagged Jed. Now there were two Vampires. Jed made a lunge for Charlie, who easily evaded his grasp. Lilley was the next to be caught and then Tatty. Anne, Effy and Charlie went and stood together on the roof of the outside toilet to tease the Vampires. Billy Lynch went one way, Jed, Lilley and Tatty the other to surround the remaining Victims. They tagged Anne and Effy but Charlie went on a daring dash along a back entry wall, the top of which had hundreds of rusty old nails and shards of broken glass cemented into it. One wrong move and it would be a trip to the hospital at the very least. Charlie sprinted along the wall like an alley cat on the prowl, picking his way between the glass and nails. Jed climbed up on one end of the wall and Billy the other and made their way toward Charlie, who was hopping from foot to foot teasing them. "Don't fall now," goaded Charlie to unnerve the boys, "it's a long way down, so whatever you do don't fall and end up with your head broken open." Jed could not stand it anymore. "Shut up, will you, Charlie, you're putting me off," he complained. Charlie replied, "You can't tell me to shut up, what if this was a competition? The other kids would be shouting all sorts of things to balk you." Charlie leapt across the five-foot gap in the entry to land on the backyard wall of the house behind Nana Lyons' house. He then jumped back again. "That's just showing off, Charlie, stop it!" shouted Jed, who then lost his balance, falling into the entry ten feet below. "I'm alright, I'm alright," he shouted to the others. "That's enough, Jed's hurt, no more playing!" shouted Lilley.

"Apart from the fall at the end, that wasn't too bad," remarked Maud Wainwright. "The boys have got the skills, I would say."

"They're just street kid skills. All Cauldron kids have got them. They get them from playing on the monkey bars and that. Charlie's nothing special," answered Nana Lyons. The other nanas were aghast at the old woman's lack of pride in her grandson but she spoke the truth; all street kids played on the monkey bars and had honed their skills on them over many years, but Charlie's nana was incorrect saying he was nothing special as the boy was exceptionally agile.

"Why do you keep playing the lad down, Betty?" whined Elsie Tatlock. "He did very well, and given the right training he could do even better."

"I don't want anybody to go praising him just because he's my grandson, that's all."

"We wouldn't do that, Betty. It could put the lad in danger if we did that. Call him in so we can meet him properly." Nana Lyons slid open the sash window.

"Charlie," she called. The boy looked up in surprise, as he had not realised he was being spied on from above.

"Sorry, Nana," he replied, automatically thinking he was in trouble. Charlie was born with a guilty conscience, always thinking he was in trouble even when he was not. "Jed's not hurt, honest. He only fell ten feet. He'll be alright, I'm sure of it."

"That's okay, son," shouted Nana Lyons from the window. "Kids like Jed bounce, so he'll be fine. Come on in, we'd like to have a chat with you in the front parlour."

"You've had it, Charlie," whispered Billy Lynch. "They're always nice to you when you're really in trouble; it's so you'll go quietly and won't run away." But Charlie knew there was no point running away; he had to go and accept whatever punishment his nana had in store for him.

When Charlie arrived outside the door of the front parlour he knocked very quietly in the hope that nobody would hear him and then he could tiptoe away, claiming to have knocked but received no answer. "Come in, Charlie," called his nana, opening the parlour door. He had only ever been inside the front parlour twice in his entire life. On both occasions it was to file past the casket of a dead uncle before attending their funeral; he wondered if this was his funeral for almost killing Jed. Nana Lyons introduced Charlie to her Council of Crones. "This is Minnie Chadwick; we've known one another ever since I moved to Ravenport." Minnie aimed a sweet old lady smile at Charlie. "This is my friend Elsie Tatlock, and the one on the end is Maud Wainwright; we were in London together." Nanas Elsie and Maud likewise smiled benignly toward Charlie. It was then he realised the so-called delegation was a ruse to disperse the angry crowd and the old women were, in fact, Nana Lyons' friends.

"Nana, what was that all about in the street? What did they mean when they said you've got some questions to answer about their children being dead? They don't blame you, do they, Nana?"

"They don't really mean it, son, they're just angry. I tried to reassure everybody that the children would be okay, but… do you remember I told you we'd have a talk one day?" Charlie nodded. "Well, today's the day. You're going to hear some things that are going to shock you. I told you about Nana Alice signing a Treaty with the Vampires, remember?" Charlie nodded. "And I told you that Vampires feed on blood?" Charlie nodded again, concerned where this was going.

"You're making a right mess of telling the lad," interrupted Nana Elsie. "Let me tell him. What your nana's trying to say is that when Nana Alice signed the Treaty with the Vampires she agreed that they could feed on as many down-and-outs from off the streets as they wanted so long as they didn't feed on the poor."

"But aren't the down-and-outs poor too?" asked Charlie.

"They are, son, but Nana Alice knew that Vampires crave Human blood above all other blood, and so that was the price she agreed to pay. Nobody is bothered if people like us go missing and even less so if a street drunk goes missing," said Nana Elsie coldly. Charlie was shocked, though he knew what she said to be correct.

"That's awful," said Charlie in the saddest voice he had ever used.

"There's more to it, son," said his nana. "Every generation must renew the Vampire Treaty and when I was a young woman it was me that signed it."

"No! No, Nana! No!" cried Charlie, not willing to believe his nana would commit such a heinous act to allow Vampires to feed on Humans, albeit derelict Humans. He burst into tears.

"I'm afraid it's true, son. I didn't have a choice. Had I not signed the Treaty then the peace would be broken and I didn't want

Vampires feeding on me or my family or my friends. I couldn't just stand by and let that happen." Nana Lyons wiped the tears from Charlie's face and continued. "I met the Prima Vampir at Mormant Hall that day," she said, holding back the name of Lord Harbinger. "He signed the Treaty and I signed after him and that was that. I got the feeling he was… I nearly said 'a man of his word' but it amounts to the same thing. I felt he wouldn't break the Treaty but, with all that's gone on and is still going on, I'm not so sure. I have a feeling deep within me that all is not right at Mormant Hall."

"Aye, Charlie, and there's lots going on, lots you don't know about," added Nana Minnie. "And what with all those children from Storm Hill filling up our schools! What's that all about? What's going on up there? What are they up to?"

"Shouldn't you go to the Police or the Church and tell them what you know about the Vampires?"

"I've told you before, Charlie, nobody cares about what happens to us poor. Besides, we've got no proof of anything."

"But that shouldn't matter to the Church. If you go to a Priest and confess to him what you know they're bound to do something!"

"Go to a Priest? Never do that, Charlie, never go to a Priest about anything to do with this! So many of them are what we call Familiars. For long enough Familiars within the Church have been in league with the Vampires doing their bidding no matter what." Charlie recalled that some of the crowd had called his nana a Familiar. "And as for the Police? They're infested with Familiars. The Town Council too!" Charlie wondered where it all ended. What about his teachers? Were they Familiars too?

"No, Charlie, if you go to the Police or the Church and tell them about Vampires you'll get a visit from the men in white coats and you'll get carted off to Storm Hill and you don't want that. No. Charlie, it's best we sort things out ourselves."

"There are dark days ahead," said Nana Minnie sagely.

"We knew these days would come. It's time we began getting the kids ready for the fight ahead. They're the only ones that can do it, Charlie. The older generation can't do it because they're too busy to lift their heads and look around to see what's going on; only children know the way." Charlie could hardly believe what he was hearing. *The fight ahead! Children are the only ones that can do it. Only children know the way? The way to what?* he thought.

"That's right, Charlie, the children are the only ones that can do it," said Nana Minnie, as if reading Charlie's mind. "But we're not alone, Charlie. There are some at Storm Hill who will help us and tell us what goes on up there."

"There's something I've got to tell you…" Charlie blurted out but then stopped in case he was about to say the wrong thing.

"Go on, son, go on," urged Nana Lyons. "I think you were going to tell everybody about Michael. Go ahead, don't worry, they already know about him." That was not what Charlie was going to mention but thought he would tell the old women what happened earlier in the coal cellar instead.

"Okay. When I went down into the coal cellar before I went to play in the backyard… I don't know what to say," said Charlie nervously. The nanas brushed Charlie's hair from his eyes.

"Just tell us what you saw, love."

"There's three of those things down there now!" he exclaimed. "Honest a God, three of them!" he said, holding up three fingers. The old women laughed.

"Actually," said Nana Minnie, "there are four but one of them's a bit mischievous, she likes hiding and jumping out and frightening people; we call her Trixie. She'll probably get you next time you go down the cellar to get some coal." Charlie tried to laugh it off but he was terrified at the prospect of a Lupulo jumping out on him in the dark of the coal cellar.

"Get on with the story, Betty," hinted Nana Maud, sounding irritated. "The poor lad doesn't want to hear all this nonsense."

"I've got something else to tell you," mumbled Charlie, half hoping the old women did not hear him.

"Then get on with it!" chorused the nanas.

"You said there are some people at Storm Hill trying to help us, tell us what's going on up there? Well, after my talk with Nana the other day, I spoke to one of my school friends, Max, about what goes on there."

"Oh, you shouldn't've done that, love," interrupted Nana Maud; the other nanas nodded in agreement.

"He might tell the Vampires that you're nosing around."

"He helped me fight off a bully called Lorcan Thorne, so I feel I can trust him. He didn't answer my questions but I know he wanted to. I'm sure he'll tell me one day."

"This Max, what's his surname?"

"Rune," replied Charlie. The nanas stared at one another, aghast.

"Oh, Charlie, you couldn't've picked a worse one, his father's Conducere to Lord Harbinger." After saying His name, the old women crossed themselves and then Charlie.

"What exactly did you say to him?" asked Nana Elsie. Before Charlie could answer his nana butted in.

"No matter, it's too late now, but keep away from him in future, Charlie, I mean it!"

"I think you're all wrong about Max," yelled Charlie, defending his friend.

"Wait a bit, though, ladies, Charlie could be right. Maybe we're being too hasty," said Nana Minnie, wearing a sly grin. "We've been suspicious for some time now that something has happened to Lord Harbinger, and who better to know than Max Rune's father, and he'll have told his son!"

"Are you saying we abduct young Master Rune, sling him in the coal cellar and let Michael interrogate him?" enquired Nana Elsie, rubbing her hands together.

"No!" yelled Charlie. "You can't do that to Max, he's my friend."

"We wouldn't do that, Charlie," answered Nana Lyons. "Nana Elsie was only joking but from now on remain cautious of the boy. If he comes to you with information be wary of it, he might be acting under orders."

"Now then, young man, you'll need to keep yourself fit for playing Vampires And Victims," said Nana Maud, changing the subject, "so we'll cook you up something special to build you up."

"You don't mean pigs' trotters and tripe, do you? I can't stand that stuff!"

"But it's good for you, Charlie, it'll make you strong!" said Nana Maud, rolling up her cardigan sleeve and showing her bicep.

"No thanks, I'm okay with stew, that'll do me fine," griped Charlie. The nanas laughed and then ordered the boy from the parlour as they had other matters to discuss.

"You know, Elizabeth, the lad's got himself in there with Max Rune. But let's keep a close eye on things and if it looks like he's in trouble we'll step in to protect him."

The nanas were not specific about what form of action they would take to protect Charlie but they tacitly accepted it would not end well for Max Rune.

★

The following morning was bitterly cold, as if to remind everybody that winter had not gone away. During the night Jack Frost had spread his sparkles everywhere, taking many dozens into his chill embrace while they slept their final sleep. They were safe. No Vampire could touch them now. As the Evelyn Terrace clan descended St George's Hill into the smog, its wisps clung to their clothes like coffin shrouds. Right on time the Storm Hill wagons passed on their way to school. Lorcan Thorne shouted his usual abuse at Charlie Carter. "He's back to his normal self," everybody remarked as they walked holding hands two and three abreast to school.

Understandably, given the events of the previous day, the school assembly was a muted affair. Mr Bawles read out the school notices, as usual, then they sang two hymns as usual and said two prayers as usual, the second being for the children who had died from the Sweating Sickness at Storm Hill. By the end of the assembly a good portion of the younger children were crying, so Mr Bawles handed them into the care of their teachers. Just as the hall was emptying, Mr Bawles returned to the stage. "Children, children," he called, "just to remind you that there's Vampires And Victims training with Father Grogan outside Christ Church after school. All those that have been selected should make their way there when your lessons are finished for the day. Anybody who wasn't selected is asked not to attend. Thank you." Jed Carter reminded Charlie to ask Father Grogan if he could join a team. Charlie promised his little brother that he definitely would not forget this time.

★

The very first thing Charlie Carter did when he arrived at V and V training was to ask Father Grogan if Jed could join one of the teams. "Tell you what, Charlie, we'll make him first reserve," replied the Priest. "Hang on, Father Grogan, I thought you said our Kenny was first reserve," complained Masie Smith. "That's right, Masie, he is but only for your team, Jed'll be first reserve for Charlie's team." This should have been the end of the matter. "Wait a minute, Father Grogan, a few kids have said that their mates are the reserves, what's going on?" The penny dropped with the Priest. "I think what's happened here is that Fathers Francis and Horan have been getting involved where they shouldn't have, so tell all your mates that unless I said they're a reserve then they're not a reserve." The children were far from happy. Father Grogan came up with what he hoped would be an amicable solution to the situation. "Tell you what, all those who have been told that they're a first reserve, not second or third reserve but a first reserve, can form a team and train. But they won't be playing in competitions unless somebody from one of the other teams gets injured or something. I'll have a word with the good

Fathers so they understand that I, and only I, can say who's in and who's out. Is that clear to you all?" The children grunted a noise that Father Grogan took to mean they understood. As he went to check his paperwork, Father Grogan heard Fathers Francis and Horan laughing drunkenly behind the oak doors to the church. This was typical of the practical jokes the Priests played on one another and Father Grogan swore he would have his revenge on them.

This time around, the V and V Field of Battle was ringed with fire baskets to drive the smog away so everybody was able to see what was going on. Charlie Carter was chosen as the first Vampire. After Father Grogan blew his whistle it only took Charlie four minutes to tag all the Victims. None of those he had turned into Vampires tagged a single Victim; Charlie got them all. Father Grogan was very impressed but the Victims were far from happy. "Ar'hey, Father Grogan, we hardly got a go, don't pick Charlie to be the Vampire again," complained Suzy McIver. But Father Grogan was under strict orders from the nanas to test Charlie to the limit and so he had chosen him to be the Vampire and would continue to do so. "It's not a matter of who gets tagged and who doesn't or how fast they get tagged, I just need to know who's who and what's what," spoke the Priest, getting irritated. "This time the Victims will be Billy Lynch's team." This was incendiary. A Proddy Dog Vampire chasing Cat Lick Victims. Everybody expected there to be blood. Billy Lynch came up to Charlie and greeted him with a friendly dead-arm punch, which Charlie returned with interest. "That's a good punch you got on you there, Cousin Charlie, you'll need it for the boxing tournament next week." Billy hoped he would get drawn against Lorcan Thorne. "Now, children, remember, this is only training, so no going mad and killing one another," yelled Father Grogan. He blew his whistle for the second round of V and V to commence.

Charlie tagged four Victims in less than a minute but they refused to act as Vampires and hunt down their Holy Cross School mates.

Instead, they baulked Charlie to prevent him tagging more Victims. Father Grogan did not intervene. Fathers Francis and Horan came to watch the proceedings. "I've a shilling that the lad will end up at the bottom of the tins," said Father Horan, burping a pungent-smelling whiskey belch. "You're on, Father, I bet he'll catch them all in under five minutes," countered Father Grogan. As difficult as the bogus Vampires were making things for Charlie he still tagged Victims, with six of them falling from height while trying to escape and ending up in crumpled heaps on the slag cinders of the Oller below, causing deep abrasions to elbows, arms, knees and legs. Charlie left his cousin Billy Lynch until last on purpose. "Just you and me now, Billy boy," yelled Charlie to taunt his cousin. "I think this has gone far enough, boys, the game is over," shouted Father Grogan. Neither of the cousins took any notice of the Priest. "Leave the lads alone," yelled Father Horan, rubbing his hands in anticipation and taking another swig of whiskey.

The advertising hoardings being used for V and V training were known locally as 'the tins' and were made up from three sections of billboards thirty feet high, supported from behind by structural metalwork. The tops of the tins were wooden beams barely four inches wide. Street kids would make dares with friends and enemies alike that they could not run along them at full speed. Nobody had died so far but there had been many close calls. What the cousins did next took things to a level of recklessness nobody imagined they could. Billy Lynch stood atop the tins at one end and Charlie Carter the other. They looked like two musk oxen getting ready to charge one another. "Come down, boys," yelled Father Grogan in a panic. Billy Lynch ran full pelt toward Charlie but jumped down onto a metal cross-strut before getting tagged. All the Cat Licks cheered, while the Proddy Dogs booed. Charlie was on Billy in a flash. The pair were like Quicksilver darting this way and that, but, as is so often the case, the advantage lay with the hunter. One wrong move and the hunted would be tagged. Billy found himself once again standing atop the tins but this time Charlie was only feet from him. Anticipating Billy's next move Charlie arrived at the cross-strut ahead of his cousin. The pair collided as they both made to jump for the same strut. Their fall was broken, if bouncing off metal beams can be described as breaking a fall, to find themselves lying next to one another on the slag cinders covering the Oller in front of Christ Church. "Your mum's going to kill you when she sees the mess you're in," laughed Billy. "That's nothing. Here's your mum and she's got your dad's belt in her hand," cried Charlie in mock-horror. Billy's mum was not there but out of fear of a leathering Billy got up and ran away. "See? They're both fine," slurred Father Horan, swaying left and right in a drunken stupor. "Now then, Father Grogan, what about I give them a drop of the hard stuff from the old country to revive the lads? It'll fix them up a real treat!" gabbled the elderly Priest incoherently as he swirled the contents of a half-empty bottle of whiskey in the air. "You can't go giving kids whiskey, Father Horan," gasped Father Francis, shocked at the thought. "I'm prepared to have a try," answered Billy Lynch, having returned after realising Charlie was only joking with him. Father Horan touched the lips of both the boys with the neck of the bottle. "Sláinte," said the old Irish Priest in a toast of good health, "and may ye both be in Heaven half an hour before the Divil knows yer dead."

Four Repeste watched the V and V training that night from the house of a Familiar situated opposite Christ Church, and as soon as it was over they returned to Storm Hill to make their report to Xenka Drach. She immediately went to see Tyran Skel. "It's true, they are preparing for war, Tyran, and we must prepare also." He seemed unconcerned. "What have we to fear from a bunch of children and old women?" he scoffed. "Better prepared than not," responded Xenka Drach, furious with Skel's attitude. "Then I say we form V and V teams from the children of Familiars so they can study the mortals' progress," stammered Skel. Xenka Drach was amazed that he had come up with such a good idea and added, "But we'll need to keep an eye on them in case they get too attached to the children and lose their nerve when their time comes." After agreeing things with Tyran Skel, Xenka Drach went off with her Conducere, Viserce, to create V and V teams made up from the children of Familiars.

★

The freezing cold weather continued over the next few days and the smog was unrelenting. Jack's tally ran into the dozens as down-and-outs, the infirm and the elderly succumbed to his touch each night. The people of the Cauldron had never known a winter like it for cold or smog, or the number of deaths. The Vampires of Storm Hill were none too happy either, as so many deaths created a shortage in the food supply, such that the more desperate of them visited Vampire-owned farms to feed on the livestock. They were always careful to rinse and gargle afterwards so as not to carry anything away with them which they might inadvertently pass on to a Devotee. What disgusted the higher-order Vampires most was having to feed alongside Inferiara.

Meanwhile, the experiments on the child subjects continued. Though none, thus far, had passed beyond the threshold of the mortal veil into the nether-world, there were definite signs of their souls twisting and wrenching to escape their hosts.

"Grail…" growled Seren menacingly.
"Mistress Seren, what a pleasant surprise seeing you here, you don't visit us often enough," replied the professor, bowing low.
"Don't be such a weasel, Grail, I know you can't stand the sight of me," spat Seren as Professor Grail thought how anybody could stand the sight of such a hideous Beast without retching was beyond him.

"To what do I… I beg your pardon, Mistress Seren, to what do we owe the honour?" toadied the Professor.

"Get them out of here," snarled Seren through slathering fangs.

Professor Grail ordered everybody from the laboratory. "What progress are you making?"

"We are making great progress with the subjects. One in particular, Maurice Groom, the one who fainted the other night. He almost passed over the threshold in the early hours but his soul fought back; I don't think it'll be long now."

"You know what I'm talking about, Grail, are you able to create Mutanti?"

"Mistress Seren, the answer to that is in the lap of the gods," answered Professor Grail, which surprised Seren, as it was extremely unusual for a Vampire to say anything that referred to dependency for anything on the will of a deity.

"Do you believe in God, Professor? Are you a Relignik, perhaps? A secret worshipper of the Enemy of the Great Progenitor?"

"Mistress Seren, I am a scientist not a Priest. Now, as I have said previously, there is no way of telling whether an Inferiara can create a Mutanto, as it's never been done before. We'll just have to wait and see."

"I don't have time to wait and see, I must know," screamed Seren. She wandered around the laboratory as Professor Grail remained silent and still. He did not turn around, even as Seren circled him, but he did brace himself for an attack that never came. "What we need are more subjects!"

"Lord Skel did say we could get more subjects but —"

"No buts, Professor, no buts! I don't care for taking tiny little steps, endlessly recording this and that. Too much writing and not enough action!"

"But if we create a Mutanto and don't record the steps we took of how we did it, then how can we then repeat them to make more?"

"You need to create at least one pair of Mutanti: a male and a female. And breed them. Just like Lupule, they might not breed straightaway but Mother Nature will find a way. They'll breed, Professor, they will breed one day. I'm certain of it!"

"If I create Mutanti, Mistress, Tyran Skel has ordered they be destroyed. I cannot go against his will and nor can my fellow scientists."

"Then, Professor Grail, we must take a different path. We must do something else. I have found a building in the Cauldron that will suit our purposes perfectly. My Mutanti will snatch children from the streets as you need and they will help carry out the work in the laboratory – under your guidance and instruction, of course."

"If we are found out, Mistress Seren, we'll be destroyed."

"If we're found out, Professor Grail, I will order my Mutanti to rise up against our Vampire overlords and wipe them out. They'll destroy those filthy Familiars too. They'll like that."

"But what of the other Vampire Houses? In London and Budapest and Paris and around the world? They will join forces and crush us if we rise up against the House of Mormant."

"Have you noticed how more and more our brother and sister Mutanti are returning from exile? Their numbers grow daily. There are too many of us for the Vampires to deal with, and with Harbinger locked away the House of Mormant won't stand a chance. And now, Mutanto Grail, obey the word of your Mistress and make me some Mutanti!"

"I promise you, Mistress Seren, I will do my best not let you down," said Professor Grail in such a way that she believed he was being sincere, or perhaps he was in fear of her ripping him apart.

"By the by, Professor, Skel and Drach have secretly ordered Simeon Rune to commence feeding Harbinger small animals, and his Somnifir doses are to be reduced. What do you make of that, Professor Grail?" asked Seren serenely.

"I don't understand. Lord Harbinger will destroy them if he regains his strength. Why are they doing this?"

"I suspect the leaders of the rebellion believe a Mutanti revolt could be on its way and are hedging their bets."

"That could mean bad news for our ambitions."

"Then do your work quickly and do it well," roared Seren.

As Seren turned to leave the laboratory, Professor Grail bowed low, exposing the back of his neck so that she might tear it out if she so wished, but that was merely standard protocol for Mutanti parting company and was seldom acted upon. Mutanti took this affectation from Vampire protocol, believing it put them on a par with their betters. Professor Grail's mutation was so slight it was easily kept hidden from Vampires, Familiars, Mutanti and Lupule. Being a Mutanto, he was under the control of Seren, and following their meeting he set about making preparations for the child subjects he would acquire for use in his experiments into creating Mutanti.

*

Before boarding their wagons for school, the Storm Hill children were gathered together and ordered to form V and V teams and join in the training with the Cauldron children. "But, Sir," said Lorcan Thorne and Max Rune together, "it is against Vampire Law to participate with Humans in any matters concerning Vampires." The pair could hardly believe they were agreeing with one another. To show there were still hard feelings between them Lorcan Thorne dead-armed Max Rune with a sly punch. Max simply brushed his upper arm, saying, "I think a fly just landed on me." The entire wagonload of children, including Thorne's cronies, burst into laughter.

Halfway down St George's Hill, Margot Thorne ordered the Repeste to stop for her to get off the wagon. Cho Lee alighted with her. This was not part of Margot's plan. She asked Cho Lee what it was she wanted. "I thought I'd walk the rest of the way to school with you. It'll give us the chance to have a nice chat along the way. Oh, look, isn't that Charlie Carter ahead of us?" said Cho, pointing. She and

Margot ran to catch him up. As they reached him Cho took hold of Charlie's hand. "Hello, Charlie, have you heard the latest?" she asked. "What latest?" he asked nervously. "We're all going to be playing Vampires And Victims together. Isn't that nice?" And with that Cho Lee let Charlie's hand go to take up the hand of Edward Lambert, a handsome lad of five foot five inches. "I wanted to tell him that!" shrieked Margot. "Yes, Charlie, it's true, we are going to join the Vampires And Victims club, or whatever it's called. We can be on the same team!" Charlie did not want to say anything but Jed did. "Listen, you, you can't be on Charlie's team because it's full and I'm the first reserve! I think you're better off sticking to your own team, Thorne!" Given how nice Margot had been to everybody Charlie thought Jed was being too unkind to her, despite her being Lorcan Thorne's sister. "Look, Margot, why don't you come along to training and see how it goes? You never know, there might be a place." Jed was very unhappy at Charlie sucking up to a Thorne and walked on alone to school.

★

Over the following days school was just normal, ordinary and uneventful, but when Friday came all hell broke loose. There was just a week to go before the boxing tournament, plus there were V and V matches on the Saturday morning. All Penny Street School were keen to see just how good Charlie Carter was at V and V and how good a boxer Lorcan Thorne was, while all the time hoping somebody would chin him and sit him on the seat of his pants.

At assembly, Mr Bawles announced that all lessons were cancelled in favour of boxing practice.

"You lot had better not let the school down!" said the Headmaster, frowning from the stage. "We did very well last year and we're going to do even better this year!" This was a false hope, as all the kids who were good at boxing had left school the previous summer. It was widely touted that Penny Street were in line for a wooden spoon. It appeared their only hope was Lorcan Thorne, that is, if he was as good as he said he was, and having seen him up against Billy Lynch the kids gave him every chance of saving the school's honour.

Boxing practice was held in the school hall and was little more than a free-for-all. Not only had all the good boxers left school but the teacher who had trained them had moved to Kirkdale Middle School. They were being tipped to win the whole thing. Miss Williams, Miss Cartwright, Mr Griffin and Mr Casson were 'volunteered' by Mr Bawles to run the training. When it became clear that the teachers were hopeless, Max Rune stepped in to organise sparring so they could at least see who could box. It was pitiful to watch. When Charlie Carter entered the sparring ring Lorcan Thorne pushed his way through knots of children to get into the ring with him. Max Rune told Thorne that it was not his turn but he took no notice. "I've been looking forward to pulverising you, Carter!" snarled Thorne. Charlie did not fancy his chances but nevertheless he took up the boxing stance Billy Lynch had taught him and invited Lorcan Thorne to attack him. Which the lad did with considerable ferocity. Despite Charlie's undeniable agility, along with his street and V and V skills, he found himself on the floor of the ring three times in the first round. The bell sounded to save him from further punishment. As Charlie made his way to his corner, Lorcan Thorne snuck up behind him and hit him on the back of his head, sending him flying through the ropes. The kids in the hall booed Thorne. In response he raised his hands above his head in victory and then squirted the first four rows of children with water.

After checking that Charlie was okay, Max Rune jumped into the ring and shouted for Lorcan Thorne to return or be called a coward. Thorne was so confident that he could beat Max he accepted the challenge. The fight was stopped by Miss Williams at the end of the second round, much to the annoyance of the crowd. The two boys had beaten the living daylights out of one another but it was clear that Max had won on points. Lorcan Thorne could not accept this and tried the same underhand trick he had done with Charlie but Max was waiting for him. With Thorne closing in on him from behind, Max turned and, ducking beneath Thorne's swinging blow, he delivered the bully a thundering uppercut to his chin that lifted Thorne off his feet. As Thorne hit the canvas, he just lay there motionless. His cronies ran forward to see if he was dead. As they surrounded him he shouted, "Get away from me! I don't need your help. Did you see what that Rune did? He cheated. He hit me after the fight was over." Strictly speaking, Thorne was correct. He had not hit Rune but Rune, however, had hit him. Lorcan Thorne called for Max Rune to be barred from taking part in the boxing tournament. The kids in the hall went apoplectic with rage. "Ye can't bar Max, Miss Williams, he's our only hope of winning a match!" Miss Williams saw what had gone on and said to Lorcan Thorne, "If I bar Master Rune for hitting after the bell then I shall have to bar you too, Master Thorne, for hitting Charlie Carter on the back of the head when the round was over." Thorne was about to accept Miss Williams' ban but then he thought about Billy Lynch and how much he wanted to pan his face with his fists. "Quite right, Miss Williams, what was I thinking, of course you cannot bar dear Max, what would we do without him on the team?" Lorcan Thorne walked over to Max Rune, offering him a handshake. As Max took the offered hand Thorne pulled him in close. "Listen to me, Rune, if you get in my way during the tournament my father'll make sure you fail the Vampire Lore exams, then there'll be no cushy Conducere job for you." Max did not take Thorne's threat seriously but thought he had better mention it to his dad in case Lucian Thorne could scupper his career plans.

★

It was strange having the Storm Hill children at V and V training. They formed two teams, adding to the existing three, making the Field of Battle very congested. Father Grogan insisted the Storm Hillers showed him what they had. Lorcan Thorne nominated himself as Vampire, and Father Grogan told the Victims to, "disperse yourselves amongst the advertising tins and for Christ's sake don't fall off. Master Thorne, count to twenty before going after your Victims." It was obvious to all that the Victims let Lorcan Thorne catch them, and the game was over in a minute. His self-satisfied grin showed he was rather pleased with himself.

"That was terrible, the Storm Hill teams are banned from training and competing," announced Father Grogan to cheering from the Cauldron kids. Lorcan Thorne could not believe it.

"Why are we banned? I caught all the Victims. Isn't that the idea of the game?" he whined.

"The idea of the game, Master Thorne, is not to cheat, and your Victims let you catch them, and that is cheating, Master Thorne, cheating," responded Father Grogan.

"Give us another chance," shouted Max Rune, "but this time let's see how Thorne gets on against Charlie Carter's team."

"I'll take anybody on, nobody from the Cauldron stands a chance against me and my team," bragged Thorne.

"Tell you what, Thorne," interjected Charlie Carter, "I'll be the Vampire and you and your cronies the Victims, and when I tag them they won't join the hunt, it'll just be me that hunts you." Lorcan Thorne thought all his Christmases had come at once, a chance to show Charlie up or perhaps even get the chance to injure him.

"What do you say, Master Thorne?" enquired Father Grogan.

"I say he won't be feeling quite so cocky by the end of the game."

The Storm Hill Victims positioned themselves on the tins in such a way as to protect Lorcan Thorne. He was standing atop the central hoarding of the tins, arms in the air, beckoning Charlie to catch him. "No showing off now, Master Thorne, it's a long way down," shouted Father Grogan but Lorcan Thorne took no notice as he pranced along the top of the tins to taunt Charlie, who leapt onto the superstructure like a Jaguar. Charlie was immediately hit with a dropkick from one of Thorne's cronies. He barely prevented himself from hitting the ground and handing victory to Thorne. The crowd booed and called for the crony's blood but Billy Lynch shouted, "Shut up, you lot, and stop being babies. Charlie can take care of himself. Go on, our kid, show them!" yelled Billy to encourage his cousin. Then, gripping the underside of the ironwork with both hands, Charlie walked on all fours like a chimpanzee to the top of the tins, bypassing Thorne's cronies, who all fell to the ground trying to stop him reaching Lorcan Thorne. Billy Lynch made sure they stayed there. "No more going on the tins for you, boys and girls," he whispered to each of them and then following up with his trademark dead-arm punch.

"C'mon then, Carter, see if you can catch me!"
"Be careful, Thorne, you're not a street kid; you're not used to this. You'll fall just like your mates did and you might not be so lucky."
"What's up, Carter, scared?"
"Look, Thorne, I've played on these tins just about every day of my life. I know every inch of them and what you can do and what you can't do on them. I don't like you but I don't want to see you get hurt."
"Shut up, Carter, you're not my mum. Tell you what, why don't we have a little boxing match up here? Eh? Give you a chance for some revenge for the other day."
"I'm not interested in revenge, I'm only interested in finding out what goes on up there at Storm Hill. Tell you what, Thorne, if I catch you before the time limit will you answer my questions about Thorne Hill?"

"If that's what it takes to shut you up, then fine. If you catch me before the time is up I'll answer any questions you have about Storm Hill." This was the break Charlie had been waiting for. If Max Rune would not tell him about Storm Hill, then Lorcan Thorne would have to.

With the grace, speed and agility of a leopard climbing a tree, Charlie bounded across the tins from support strut to support strut, hunting Thorne down by cutting off his every escape route. The Storm Hill boy became mesmerised by Charlie's movements, and in an attempt to outmanoeuvre him he ran full speed along the top of the tins, something only experienced street kids should attempt. In a mighty leap, Charlie landed just feet in front of Thorne. "Give in, Thorne, you've lost." Instead of surrendering, Lorcan Thorne saw his opportunity to knock Charlie to the ground some thirty feet below but, as he swung, Charlie ducked beneath Thorne's flailing fist, causing him to lose his footing. Seeing that Thorne was going to fall, Charlie grabbed hold of him by his arm. Thanks to Charlie's quick thinking, the pair fell just six feet onto a cross-beam. Charlie felt like he might have cracked a rib but Thorne was in a bad way, having landed awkwardly. Father Grogan mounted the tins and carried both boys to the ground. Onlookers were impressed by the Priest's athleticism and strength. "You know what, I reckon Father Grogan'd batter Bawlesey in a fight," said Izzy Sanchez, repeating an earlier statement she had made on the likely outcome of a fight between the Head and the Priest.

As Lorcan Thorne was being attended to, a wagon drawn by two massive black horses silently emerged from the smog, pulling up right alongside the Priests. Two men in white coats loaded Thorne onto the back of their wagon and shot off into the smog. The street kids were stunned by the sight but not so the Storm Hill children. With Thorne being taken care of, Father Grogan blew his whistle and ordered the next team up onto the tins. After half a dozen rounds of V and V it was clear that the Cauldron kids were superior in every way to the Storm Hill kids. When training was over, Max asked Charlie why he had saved Lorcan Thorne. "Don't know. Instinct, I suppose." Before Charlie had time to ask Max some questions about Storm Hill, he and the other Storm Hillers were loaded onto wagons for them to return journey home. "They could've offered you and Jed a lift," said Billy Lynch, staring in the direction the wagons had taken. "I mean to say, you live on their way back to Storm Hill after all." Charlie shook his head. "I didn't want one," he answered, trying to sound defiant. Charlie put his arm around Jed's shoulders and, tired and sore, the pair made their way back to Evelyn Terrace.

CHAPTER 9

The Storm Hill children disembarked the wagons in a sullen mood having performed so badly against the kids from the Cauldron. They would need to improve, and quickly, if they were to make the Vampires proud of them. Some children observed Lorcan Thorne being discharged from hospital, which surprised them considering how badly injured he had been. "What are you lot looking at?" was all he said. The children ignored Thorne and, with their heads hanging in shame, trudged home.

When Max Rune entered his house his mother and father, Amriel and Simeon, were in the hallway waiting for him. They asked how the V and V training had gone. "Badly, very badly. They humiliated us," said Max almost inaudibly. Amriel and Simeon tried to console their son by saying they were certain he had tried his best and that there was always next time.

"But, Dad, we're so much stronger and healthier than them, so how could they have beaten us so easily?" asked Max, angry and confused.

"They had home ground advantage but it won't always be that way," answered Simeon kindly. "Amriel darling, would you mind if Max and I had a father and son conversation?"

"Of course not, darling, I'll leave you to it. Max darling, there's something in the oven for you. It's your favourite, steak and kidney pie, peas and potatoes."

"I don't deserve my favourite," answered Max in a pout. "I just want to go to bed."

"Now, now, Maximillian, don't be so hard on yourself. Maybe it was the fault of the others that you did so badly at your game. Maybe they let you down?"

"No, we were all awful and they were better than us." This was a hard thing for Max to admit.

"There, there, son, you'll feel better after something to eat and a good night's sleep. Don't keep him up too late, darling," whispered Mrs Rune to her husband, then kissed him and her son on the cheek before going off to bed.

"Come with me, son, I've got something to tell you."

"But what about the V and V report I have to prepare for the Vampires?"

"Never mind about your report. Fetch your supper and meet me in my study… and close the door behind you."

Max could tell by his father's tone of voice that he had something serious to discuss with him. When he entered his dad's study Max was shocked to find a Vampire sitting behind his father's desk.

"Son, this is Xenka Drach," said Simeon Rune respectfully. "Convention dictates you bow low to show fealty."

"Simeon, leave the boy be, it's not necessary that he bows to me before he's of age. Do you know who I am, Max?"

"No. I mean, I've heard of you but I'm not sure what to believe."

"That's very wise of you, Max, very wise. It's extremely important to be careful who and what you believe. I understand you have a close friend at Penny Street School?" Xenka waited to see if Max offered up a name but as he did not she continued. "Charles Carter?" she suggested. Max nodded his head. "He has a brother? Jerad?"

"Jed, they call him Jed."

"It has come to my attention that you and the daughter of my Conducere, along with two others, were spying on Professor Grail a few nights ago when you saw something you should not have?"

"Indeed, Madame Drach, but —"

"Do you know what it was you saw, Max?"

"No, Madame Drach. I'm not really sure what I saw," mumbled Max. From what Xenka had said he understood that Cho Lee must have mentioned to her stepmother, Viserce, about them witnessing Inferiara feeding on the Cauldronian children and was unsure what he should admit to.

"Did you recognise the subjects? The children?"

"Some of them, Madame Drach, but not all."

"Who are they?"

"They're from the Cauldron. I think some of them go to Penny Street School."

"Indeed. Do you know why they were there?"

"No, Madame Drach," whimpered Max but could contain himself no longer. "The Headmaster said those children were dead but they are not! I saw them being fed on! What's going on?" raged the boy. At such impertinence toward a Vampire of Xenka Drach's status Simeon Rune begged forgiveness for his son's lack of respect.

"Simeon, I appreciate your son's frankness. You are quite right, Max, the children are alive. They were guilty of the same crime as you and your friends: spying on things they should not have been spying on. They looked through the windows of the Sanatorium and saw, so Seren claims, people long thought to be missing being experimented on. You must have seen Seren, she was the one —"

"Don't worry, I can guess which one Seren was," interjected Max, mimicking Seren's hideous face.

"Seren claims the children recognised people long thought to have gone missing but I believe she was lying." Madame Drach paused to consider how much she should tell Max. "There were nine children that spied through the window that night but only eight have been acquired. The ninth child is Jerad Carter."

"Why are you telling me this?"

"So you can tell Charles Carter that his brother is in great danger. He's going to be taken."

"What? You want me to warn Charlie Carter, a Human, that his brother is going to be kidnapped by Vampires?"

"Yes, but leave the Vampire part out," teased Xenka. "Instead, tell him the men in white coats are coming for Jerad."

"Then what?"

"That's enough for the time being. I sense things will soon come to a head. Now, Simeon, give your son your news."

Simeon told Max that Madame Drach had ordered him to commence feeding Lord Harbinger small animals to build up his strength and that the Vampires guarding him had been replaced by Repeste and that they were reducing Harbinger's Somnifir doses. Max had no idea what Somnifir was but guessed it must be potent as his father had told him how powerful Lord Harbinger was. What Max did not know was Somnifir can be deadly to Vampires and if Lord Harbinger was given as little as a teaspoon of it in a single dose he would most likely combust. Max's head was in a spin. He could not understand why he was being taken into Xenka Drach's confidence. Then she dropped the bombshell.

"Do you know why your little friends in the Cauldron are training for the game called Vampires And Victims?"

"Yes, there's a prize for the team that —" Madame Drach laughed out loud, causing Max to stop speaking.

"You must at least be suspicious that something is going on?"

"I… we… we all know not to get involved in anything concerning the word Vampire, and when we heard about this game and the competition we avoided it like the plague. To be honest, we were shocked when we were told to form teams and join in with the Cauldronians."

"Vampires And Victims is not a game, Maximillian. It's training," uttered Madame Drach coldly.

"Training? For what?"

"To hunt us down and destroy us; all of us. Vampires, Familiars, Repeste, Mutanti, Lupule; and all those crawling things below and between."

"How can puny Humans possibly kill Vampires?" asked Max, forcing a phoney snort of derision.

"Oh, they know how to do it alright. They know very well how to do it. We haven't had a war in a long time but there's one coming and, most likely, we will lose it!"

"If Humans can kill Vampires, shouldn't we all run away?"

"It's too late. The only way to avoid the inevitable is to stop what we're doing and sign a pledge swearing that henceforth we will conform with the Treaty."

"What Treaty?" asked Max, puzzled.

"I knew you'd ask. The original Treaty was signed four hundred years ago but that fizzled out. Then, a couple of Human generations ago, somebody known as Nana Alice came up with the idea of reviving it. I met her a couple of times. I could smell straightaway she was a Lycanthrope but what a Vampire she would have made."

"I don't understand about the Treaty. Why was one necessary?"

"Because Nana Alice had trained an Army of children in the art of Vampire dusting. She pretended it was all a game. After they became expert at playing Vampires And Victims she told them about us and showed them how to hunt us down; afterwards she showed them the secret of how to dust a Vampire."

"Surely you can protect yourselves or attack them?"

"If we attack them we are doomed. Do you know how long it takes to make a Vampire?" Max shook his head. "Often decades and then, at the last moment, when they stand on the threshold you can lose them to the Great Universe and all your work has been for nothing. But Humans! Humans breed like rabbits! They make new Humans by accident all the time! If they rise up against us we will be annihilated, slaughtered in our thousands, all over the world. We won't stand a chance." Max had to ask the question uppermost in his mind.

"Madame Drach, how do you kill a Vampire?" he asked slowly and deliberately. Mr Rune squirmed uncomfortably on his seat at his son daring to ask such an impertinent question.

"If we are beheaded we die, or as good as, but the way to kill us, destroy us completely, is to drive a wooden stake through the organ that was once our heart. We are then free to join the other souls in the Great Universe."

"Then keep away from people holding stakes!" was Max's simple solution to the problem.

"Well, Max, while that is excellent advice, it doesn't help against Nana Alice's invention. It was too simple for words, and why nobody until then had thought of it is a mystery. Nana Alice discovered that if you dip the head of a crossbow bolt in tree sap and then sawdust it works just as well as a wooden stake. Better! They don't need to get close to us. They simply take aim and…" Xenka made a 'puffff' sound and with her hands mimicked something going up in smoke. Max was astonished. Should he tell his friends about this? "Max, do not tell any of your friends about this," said Xenka, as if reading his thoughts. "The hour is late, and mortals need their sleep. You have a big day ahead of you tomorrow, Maximillian Rune. Do your best at V and V but, more importantly, keep your eyes open and keep a watch out, especially for rancorous old women."

All throughout Storm Hill children had to confess to their parents how badly they had done at V and V. They dreaded the thought of the first competitive games which were due to be held the following day.

★

Arriving back at Evelyn Terrace after training, Charlie and Jed discovered a pot of piping hot stew waiting for them on the stove.

On the table next to their bowls were two slices of crusty bread either side of a thick slice of meat. Charlie asked his mum what the treat was for; she replied it was a gift from the old women. "The Council of Crones," Nana Lyons corrected her. As the boys ate their supper, they regaled the matriarchs with tales of derring-do from the evening's V and V training. The women made encouraging noises and tutted at the antics of Lorcan Thorne.

After supper Jed was ordered to bed as Nana Lyons said she wanted to have a private talk with Charlie about the V and V competition the following day. Before leaving them to it, his mum told him to 'play fair and don't cheat, not even if you're tempted to by the Devil'. His nana was not so inclined and told Charlie he must win at any and all costs.

"What is it you want to talk to me about, Nana?" asked Charlie, expecting some underhand tactics to guarantee victory, but that was not what was on his nana's mind.

"Have you told me everything about tonight?" she asked her grandson accusingly.

"Not quite," answered Charlie apprehensively.

"What did you miss out?"

"I made a deal with Lorcan Thorne that if I tagged him before the time ran out then he'd answer my questions about Storm Hill."

"I see. I thought you were going to convince Max Rune to tell you what's going on at Storm Hill, so why have you now chosen to alert this boy Lorcan Thorne when you've said he's untrustworthy? He'll go to his father with this information and he'll go straight to his Masters and they'll concoct some plan to commit some skulduggery against you. You've made a big mistake, Charlie, a big mistake."

"But, Nana, we need as many irons in the fire as possible so if Max won't tell me about Storm Hill then Thorne will have to. Besides, he's changed lately," Charlie lied.

"Well, it's too late to do anything about it now, but promise me you won't be putting any more 'irons in the fire'."

"Okay, Nana, I shan't in future. If he's at the competition tomorrow we'll see what he has to say for himself." Charlie decided not to mention to his nana the fall Lorcan Thorne and he had taken. In his mind he convinced himself that did not want to upset his nana but in reality he was just being devious.

★

As Nana Lyons had predicted, Lorcan Thorne did indeed go running straight to his father to tell him of the 'deal' he had made with Charlie, and Lucian Thorne went running to his Masters to tell his tale. When Seren arrived in the Grand Chamber to find out what Lucian Thorne had to report she was angry to find Xenka Drach in company with Tyran Skel. She had to form a plan to build mistrust in Skel's mind such that he would not want Xenka Drach anywhere near him.

★

"Before you pop off to bed, Charlie, you should visit the coal cellar. There's a surprise waiting for you down there," said Nana Lyons.

"Isn't it a bit late, Nana? I need to get my rest for the competition tomorrow."

"You don't fool me, Charlie Carter, you're frightened that Trixie will get up to some mischief, aren't you?"

"Well, yes. To be honest, I was frightened when there were three of them but when I found out about Trixie it put me off altogether. What sort of stuff does she do?"

"Don't worry, son, I'll go down with you. Now, where's my walking stick?" Nana Lyons regularly used a walking stick, though going by the way she moved she hardly needed it. She was always careful never to let anybody touch her stick or even get near it, which raised suspicions about it.

As they entered the coal cellar, Nana Lyons emitted a curious call. She was answered by a similar call from Michael's lair beneath the stairs. He had been busy; the den was far larger than when Charlie had first visited it. Inside, the three Lupule greeted Charlie. All he could think about was where Trixie was hiding. The Lupule parted, and lying there in a newly dug alcove were four cubs. They were all snuggled together on what looked to Charlie like his best Sunday coat. "Don't worry, son, I'll clean your coat tomorrow after I find them something for the cubs to lie on," whispered Nana Lyons. As Charlie approached the cubs, the two Lupule he did not know snarled at him. Michael nipped them on their ears for doing so. Next, Charlie felt a tap on his shoulder. He turned around to see who had done it but there was nobody there. When he faced forward again he almost jumped out of his skin as he came face to face with a Lupulo he assumed was Trixie. She had been hanging from the joists and had dropped to the floor to surprise him. It was more than a surprise as Charlie nearly messed his trousers with the fright of it all. To break the ice with Charlie, Trixie made a farting noise and pointed at Charlie's backside while holding her snout and wafting away an imaginary fart. The Lupule 'laughed' and so did Nana Lyons. Next, Trixie pointed at Charlie's chest and when he looked down to see what it was she ran a paw up to his nose and tweaked it. The Lupule laughed again and so did Charlie. He liked Trixie and was no longer afraid of her.

What was most noticeable about Trixie were her eyes. Unlike the yellowy eyes of the other Lupule, Trixie's left eye was bright blue and her right glowed a bright green. Charlie asked his nana if Trixie could see as well in the dark as the other Lupule. She answered that she must, as she never had any problems chasing down prey. It then occurred to Charlie that he did not know what Lupule ate. "What do they eat, Nana?" he asked. She replied that they were carnivores and usually fed on anything small. This news sent a shiver down Charlie's back. He took another look at the cubs. They had their mother's eyes, one green and the other blue. This made them special for Charlie and he asked if he could name them. Michael spoke to the other Lupule about his request. After a fair bit of snarling, Michael held up one claw. "That means you can name one of the cubs," said Nana Lyons. Now all Charlie had to do was think of a suitable name for a nether-creature.

Before Charlie went to bed that night his nana still needed to have a word with him about the V and V tournament the following day.

"Now, Charlie, listen to me. You'll need to be more careful than ever tomorrow. There'll be people there watching that are Familiars and will report on you to their Masters."

"How can I tell if somebody is a Familiar, Nana?"

"It's not easy, son. It takes years of practice, and even then you can get it wrong. First, I need to warn you about a particular group of Familiars: Priests." Charlie was shocked.

"Priests? What, like Father Grogan and Father Francis and Father Horan? But I suppose you're right. When Jed had his fall the other night, Father Francis came to the house with a couple of men in white coats to take him to Storm Hill and —"

"Whoa, whoa, whoa, Charlie, slow down. Father Grogan and the others aren't Familiars – a drunk, an idiot and a fancy Dan, but not Familiars. That Father Francis hasn't got half a brain, so he won't've realised what he was doing bringing the men in white coats to cart Jed off to Storm Hill."

"Well, who then, Nana?"

"As I said, son, it's not easy telling if somebody is a Familiar but watch crowds of spectators carefully. If any of them slip quietly away or they watch somebody too closely then they might be a Familiar. The Vampires will want to know who's who and what's what when it comes to Vampires And Victims, so try not to do too well, otherwise it could end badly for you."

"Oh, thanks for the warning, Nana," replied Charlie sarcastically.

"By the way, where's the tournament being held? Is it the Christ Church Oller?"

"No, it's round the back jiggers off Kirkdale Road," replied Charlie.

"Who the hell decided it was going to be held there?" gasped Nana Lyons in disbelief.

"I don't know, we were just told that's where it's going to be."

"In that case you'll need to be doubly extra careful, there'll be all sorts of things for you to watch out for with that Kirkdale Road lot. They used to have a nasty habit of laying booby traps the night before a competition, and I doubt they'll have changed through the generations."

"What sort of booby traps?"

"Loose bricks or smearing them with oil so you can't get a grip to shinny up the walls between jiggers. But worst of all they put metal spikes in places where kids are likely to put their hands. Keep your eyes open tomorrow, Charlie."

"I will, Nana, I will," answered Charlie in fright.

"Now, lad, get off to bed and get a good night's sleep." As if Charlie could sleep with all the excitement of Lupule cubs, news of Familiar Priests and warnings of foul play by the Kirkdale Road gang in the V and V tournament.

★

After Lucian Thorne delivered his message about Charlie Carter trying to find out what was going on at Storm Hill, Xenka Drach and Tyran Skel, with the unasked-for assistance of Seren, considered their options. Should they feed this Charlie Carter with disinformation to deceive him and his interfering grandmother, or simply eliminate him with a swift Vampire Death Bite? This way of despatching was devastating, and resulted in decapitation. Xenka, unhappy at Seren's presence, dismissed her from the chamber. "This is not something for you to be concerned about, Seren, leave us." This time Seren did not look to Tyran Skel to sanction her dismissal; she simply bowed, turned and walked away. Once outside the Grand Chamber, Seren looked about to make certain that she was not being observed before slipping into her secret compartment to eavesdrop on the conversation.

"Why do you treat Seren so?" asked Skel.

"You know why, or have you forgotten that we agreed to be careful around her?" returned Madame Drach. Skel turned his back on her without replying. She asked him, "Did Seren report about the Lupule as you asked her to?"

"Yes, of course she did," he lied. "Why are you asking about it, Madame Drach?" Xenka doubted Seren had told Skel about the Lupule, otherwise he would be more concerned.

"I was wondering what you intend to do about them?" she asked nonchalantly, not wanting to insinuate that he was unaware of the situation with the Lupule.

"I am undecided on the matter but as I value your opinion, Xenka, what do you propose I do about them?"

"I suggest you establish the extent to which Lupule can speak." Surprised by this news, Tyran Skel returned Madame Drach a blank stare. "They have their own language, of course, but they can also speak, or rather croak, Human words. Did Seren not inform you of this?"

"I already told you she did but I have more important things on my mind than whether Lupule can or cannot croak words."

"Important things like experimenting on the children locked away in Professor Grail's laboratory?" Madame Drach asked contemptuously. "Tyran, we are supposed to be partners in everything. This is the second time you have betrayed my trust lately." Skel deemed Madame Drach impertinent and changed into his Vampire form before delivering his threat.

"I warn you, never speak to me in that way again, Madame Drach, or you will regret it. Now leave before I set my Lupule on you!" At their Master's words a dozen massive Lupule emerged from the shadows, their eyes shining yellow, their maws dripping drool from their deadly fangs.

"Your Lupule? Your Lupule?" mocked Madame Drach. "What of those Lupule deserting in their droves? Whose Lupule are they, Tyran Skel? Who is their Master, oh Lord of the Lupule?" she laughed and left the Grand Chamber to find Seren standing on the other side of the door.

Madame Drach pushed Seren aside. As the Mutanto Beast went to turn on Xenka, Viserce dropped from the ceiling and came to stand between them. "Beware, Mistress Seren, beware," hissed Viserce. "I am not afraid of you and you would do well not to spy on my Mistress." Seren looked shocked that Viserce knew of her secret compartment. Xenka asked Viserce what she meant. "The creature has a secret place from where she listens to all that goes on in Grand Chamber," answered Viserce. Before Xenka could challenge Seren to tell her the truth she disappeared into the Grand Chamber and bolted the door behind her. "Come, Viserce, we have work to do," whispered Xenka, beckoning her Conducere away. "What news of Lord Harbinger? Is his strength returning?" asked Madame Drach. Viserce told her Mistress that Simeon Rune had begun feeding their Master but he was far from being strong enough to defend himself against an assassin. "You think our Lord to be in danger?" Xenka asked. "If the creature was in her secret compartment when you and Skel agreed to feed our Lord then he is in danger," replied Viserce coldly. To counter any threat to Harbinger's existence, Xenka ordered a doubling of the Repeste guard. "They are to be armed with Somnifir bombs sufficient to repel a Vampire attack, and Mutanti are forthwith barred from the fourth-level gallery. Hopefully that will be enough to keep our Lord safe while he regains his strength." Meanwhile, inside the Grand Chamber, Seren dripped her poison into Skel's ears.

"Master, what are you going to do about Drach?" asked Seren, exposing the back of her neck, inviting Tyran Skel to deliver a Vampire Death Bite for her insolence. "My Lord, she undermines you with her every word and action. My agents report that she's holding secret meetings with Harbinger's Familiar, Simeon Rune, and others, and —"

"She's changed, Seren, my darling Xenka's changed," interrupted Skel dejectedly. "When we began the rebellion she wanted what I wanted, what all Vampires wanted: pride in what we are, a sense of purpose and our rightful place in the order of things."

"And better food," added Seren slyly. Skel smiled ruefully.

"Yes, and better food."

"She's plotting against us, my Lord; against you, I mean. I believe she's —"

"Seren…" spoke Skel hesitatingly, "why didn't you tell me that the Lupule can speak just as we are now?"

"Lupule can speak, my Lord? Speak?" asked Seren, sounding incredulous. "They growl and gnash in their own strange language but it's not speaking as we know it, as we would recognise, it's just Lupule speaking Lupul, that's all, just Lupule being exactly what they are, animals."

"Then they don't speak Human words?"

"Ha! See for yourself, my Lord, summon the Lupule Captain and have a conversation with him about literature," mocked Seren. "Or you can talk together about the weather or philosophy or Vampire Lore or science or history," she ranted. "No, Master, Lupule cannot speak, though some do croak a few words as a parrot does." Seren's insolence was calculated to deflect the conversation, she having made a pact with Lupule Leaders not to share their dirty little secret with their boss lest he slaughter them as abominations.

Tyran Skel recalled Xenka Drach having recently used the word 'croak' in this context and wondered if it was just coincidence that Seren had used it too. It was at times like this that his inner voices spoke to him.

"You're a fool, Tyran Skel, a weak fool, a weak, pathetic fool. Who do you think you are leading a rebellion against the Vampire that loved you like a son? Traitor! Traitor! You're a traitor to your Lord and your kind, Tyran Skel. Mark our words, you will be the doom of the Vampire Nation, not its salvation, its doom!"

"Don't ever mock me, Seren," hissed Skel, "It is not for nothing I am known as the Sorrow of Praha!" To demonstrate fealty, Seren knelt and exposed the back of her neck for her so-called Master to deliver a Vampire Death Bite if he so wished but she did not apologise.

"Master, I was merely illustrating how Madame Drach is rumourmongering to spread confusion and sow the seeds of doubt to distract minds while she goes about her wicked work!" said Seren, seeking reassurance, but none came. "My Lord, with your permission, I will have Drach watched and report her every transgression to you so you may act as you see fit." Tyran Skel nodded his assent reluctantly.

"Now go. Go about your work and do not get discovered in it," muttered Skel dejectedly.

After Seren left the Grand Chamber, Tyran Skel asked the Captain of his Lupule guard, "Can you speak, my Guardian Angel? Can you?" As the Lupulo Captain made no reply, Skel thought more favourably toward Seren and less so toward Xenka Drach. Deep down, though, he was feeling out of his depth and regretted ever having rebelled against his Progenitor.

★

By six thirty on Saturday morning Patrick Carter Snr was preparing to leave Evelyn Terrace for his job in Storm Hill. As was now usual, he had woken feeling bright and breezy after an excellent night's sleep. His wife, however, had woken several times during the night to pee, as the baby growing inside her had taken to dancing on her bladder. Patrick was about to flick the front-door latch when he noticed light coming from the floor below. "Hello, who's there?" he called. Charlie answered that it was only him and wished his dad a good day. Patrick leaned over the bannisters and hiss-whispered to ask Charlie what he was doing up at that hour and if he was okay. Charlie replied that he had been unable to sleep due to all the excitement of the V and V tournament. Patrick made to go downstairs, panicking Charlie as Michael and Trixie were eating the rodents they had caught during the night. "Don't come downstairs, Dad," hissed Charlie. "Why not, son, what are you up to down there? I'm coming down!" Charlie had to think quickly. He shoved Michael and Trixie out the backdoor with his boot. "What the hell was that?" cried Mr Carter, having caught a glimpse of something hairy disappearing behind his son's back. "It was just a stray dog I've been training but it's gone over the wall now. Talking of going, you're going to be late for the wagon if you don't hurry." Mr Carter took his son's advice and left the house. It did not occur to him until later that day that a dog could not climb the wall of the backyard.

Charlie went outside to apologise to Michael and Trixie for treating them so roughly but they were nowhere to be found. Thinking they had probably entered the coal cellar via the hatch he went looking for them there, calling as he went, but there was no reply. As he turned to leave, something landed on Charlie's head. It was a 'present' from Michael and Trixie, who were hanging upside down from the joists and had flicked something at him for the way he had treated them. Charlie put his fingers into whatever it was and then smelt the substance. It was sticky and it stank. He dreaded to think what it was. Just then, the cubs appeared from under the stairs. Charlie saw his opportunity to inspect them at close quarters. Trixie was fine with this but not so the cubs' aunts and uncles. The coal cellar suddenly seemed rather full. Charlie counted the eyes. There were eight or nine pair of yellowy eyes and, counting the cubs, five green and blue pairs. Alarmed at being so outnumbered, Charlie spoke to show he was not afraid. "So, erm, which one of them do I get to name?" he asked, pointing at the cubs. Trixie made a sign that it was up to him. Charlie liked the smallest cub best and named him Midget, which is Pitic in Lupul. The Lupule clan approved of the name and celebrated with a collective, though muted, howl.

Nana Lyons arrived just as Charlie was closing the cellar door. She asked him what he was doing up so early on a Saturday morning. "I was too excited to sleep so I visited the Lupulos and named one of the cubs Midget," he replied. He also mentioned the increase in the Lupule population of the coal cellar. "I don't like it," said Nana Lyons, more to herself than Charlie. "There's something going on up there at Storm Hill." Charlie suggested Michael go and take a look around. Nana Lyons answered, saying that it was too dangerous for Michael to show his face in Storm Hill as he was not very much liked there. "I suppose not then. Anyway, Lorcan Thorne still owes me an explanation of what goes on up there." Nana Lyons counselled caution in the boy. "Even if he tells you anything it'll probably be lies. Do not trust the Thornes!" she said as though she knew them. "Anyway, the tournament doesn't start until this afternoon, so you should grab yourself a few hours' kip." Charlie felt tired enough to sleep so took his nana's advice and went to bed.

★

Only seven teams turned up for what was the first V and V tournament in over fifty years. There were two teams from Penny Street School, two from Holy Cross School, two from Kirkdale Middle School and one from Storm Hill, though why they had their own team nobody could say. An announcement that the posh schools were a no-show brought jeering and catcalling from the Cauldron kids, together with choruses of 'bock, bock, bock' chicken noises.

Before the tournament got underway, Charlie spied Lorcan Thorne and went to ask him if he was okay from his fall and if they could meet up afterwards to talk about the goings-on at Storm Hill. Thorne looked around and, seeing nobody was looking at them, whispered, "Get lost, Carter, who the hell do you think you are sticking your peasant nose where it's not wanted?" and punched Charlie in the stomach, sending him sprawling to the ground. Margot Thorne saw what had happened and raced over to check if Charlie was okay. "I'm no expert but I think your nose might be broken," she said, kissing Charlie's nose better. When Billy Lynch showed up he wanted to take on Lorcan Thorne there and then but Charlie convinced him that he should save it for the boxing tournament.

Father Kenny was chosen as referee. He began by reading out the names of the children and the team they were representing. Sections of the audience either booed or cheered depending on who was being called out and what school they were from. The first match was the big one: Penny Street School versus Holy Cross School. Father Kenny pointed out the Field of Battle boundaries and repeated the rules for the benefit of those who might claim ignorance of them and dispute being tagged. A time limit of ten minutes was set for each match. If after ten minutes there were Victims remaining, the team with the most survivors would be declared the winner. If the numbers were tied, then whoever caught their first Victim fastest would be the winner.

The fog rolled right in on cue. It soon turned to smog after mixing with the smoke from hundreds of chimneys throughout the Cauldron. A coin was tossed and Holy Cross School chose to be the Victims; Charlie Carter was chosen as the first Vampire. The back jiggers of Kirkdale Road were extremely dangerous places under normal circumstances so great care was required to play V and V in the smog. As no player was allowed to touch the ground, Victims and Vampires alike would have to run along jigger walls topped with glass or shinny up between houses to run along rooftops. In all, there were over 400 yards of jiggers that could be run; this was a large Field of Battle.

Before the match began, Charlie eyed the opposition to work out the order in which he would tag his Victims. They were given the usual twenty seconds to disperse. Three of them jumped for the same jigger wall, bumped into one another and hit the ground. They were out of the game, replaced by three Penny Street Vampires. The Holy Cross School V and V coach screamed, "I told youz lot not to go for the same wall. Didn't I just tell you that just thirty seconds ago? And what do you do? Idiots!"

Charlie told his Vampires to cut left as he cut right to form a pincer movement. Though desperate to tag Billy Lynch, Charlie wanted him left until last. Three Victims were tagged in quick succession, with two more soon following. Having shinnied up a jigger wall between the rows of houses, Billy Lynch took to the roofs. Standing atop a chimney stack, he surveyed, as best he could through the smog, what was left of his team and those Vampires pursuing them. One of the Vampires tried to sneak up on Billy but lost his grip due to bricks having been coated with lard by the Kirkdale Road gang the previous night. He took one of his Vampire teammates with him as he fell to the ground. Both were eliminated from the game.

Even before half the time was up, Billy Lynch was the only Holy Cross Victim remaining. But he being so fast, strong and agile, four Vampires fell to the ground trying to tag him. With other mishaps there were soon only three Vampires remaining. Charlie told his teammates to take up station at either end of the jigger where they had Billy Lynch cornered.

"Come on, cousin, come and get me!" taunted Billy Lynch defiantly.

"Which one of us are ye talkin' to, our Billy," Savanah Lyle shouted back.

"Our Charlie of course! Who else did ye think I was talking to? Anyway, I want it out with him to see who's best so youz two can get lost."

"Take no notice, Savvy," said Charlie, "the name of the game is winning. You and Izzy close in from either side and I'll go up the middle."

"What's up, Charlie, are ye chicken or what?" shouted Billy, trying to goad his cousin.

"I'm no chicken, our Billy, I just want to win, that's all."

Billy leapt from wall to wall back and forth across the jiggers and then shinnied up a drainpipe onto a nearby roof. Following on his tail, Charlie hauled himself to within ten feet of Billy. "Give it up, our Billy, you've lost." But Billy Lynch was not the type for giving up. He slid down the roof of the house and then leaped onto its backyard wall. How he accomplished this was incredible, even to Charlie. At a boundary wall between four houses, Billy sidestepped Izzy Sanchez. She was furious with herself. To celebrate his escape, Billy was doing a victory dance when he slipped and, reaching out to grab anything that would stop him hitting the jigger floor, his hand found a booby trap. It was a rusty metal spike and it had gone right through Billy's hand. He screamed in agony. A halt was called to the match. Charlie looked around to see if any of the Kirkdale gang were looking pleased with themselves for laying the booby trap but instead he saw Father Kenny slipping away. "That's exactly what nana told me to watch out for," Charlie muttered to himself. Before he could make ground on Father Kenny to see where he was going, Father Grogan held up Charlie's hand, declaring Penny Street School the winners. In the reverse match, Holy Cross School failed to tag Charlie, Sammy Irons or Izzy Sanchez, leaving bragging rights with the Proddy Dogs.

Having won all their matches Penny Street School won the tournament. The losing schools shouted they would have their revenge at the boxing tournament. As Charlie went to pick up the winner's trophy he noticed Father Kenny had returned. He was standing at the back of the crowd talking to an old woman. Charlie could not make out who she was, and before he could get through the crowds of spectators to get a better look at her she had disappeared.

With no word of farewell, the Storm Hill children silently boarded their wagons for their journey home. None of them was looking forward to telling their parents they had come last. Though, to his credit, Lorcan Thorne had given a good account of himself; he had seemed superhuman at times. His performance, however, was entirely due to the treatment he had received following his fall from the tins. As Thorne's therapy had proven so successful, future Storm Hill V and V teams would be given treatments prior to tournaments but not training sessions so as not to raise suspicions.

★

Simeon Rune descended to the fourth-level gallery where he was stopped by a phalanx of Repeste guards armed with axes, spears and a host of Vampire repellents. After showing his pass he proceeded along the gallery to the very last cell on the right, where eight Repeste armed with Somnifir Bombs were standing guard. Conducere Rune was carrying with him a covered cage from within which came scurrying sounds. The Repeste inspected the contents of the cage before admitting Rune into Lord Harbinger's cell.

"My Lord," whispered Simeon, his eyes blinking in the twilight of the cell.

"Simeon, I sense a change, what's going on?" gasped Lord Harbinger, weak from being given daily doses of Somnifir since the rebellion.

"Xenka Drach has banned Mutanti from the fourth-level gallery and replaced the Vampire guards with Repeste."

"Is that for me?" asked Lord Harbinger, looking hopefully at the covered cage.

"It is, my Lord." Simeon Rune removed the cloth cover from the cage. The piglets inside it smelled Lord Harbinger's Vampire scent and went berserk.

"They sense their end is nigh," murmured Lord Harbinger, relishing the fear felt by the piglets enlivening their blood and making it all the more delicious. Simeon Rune opened the top of the cage for his Master to reach inside and grab His lunch. Lord Harbinger bled the piglets to the very last drop. Simeon understood there would be a Porcine after-effect from his Master feeding on the piglets but he also knew it would not last very long.

"My Lord, while you are temporarily indisposed, I shall bring you up to date with the news. It is not all good, I'm afraid. You'll need to brace yourself for a shock. I couldn't tell you before because…" Lord Harbinger gestured with His hand for His Conducere to stop wittering and get on with it. "My Lord, Professor Grail, under Skel's orders, is performing experiments on Cauldronian children to turn them into Wraiths." Lord Harbinger writhed in apoplectic rage on His stone bed at the news. "The children have previously been reported as having died from the Sweating Sickness. Thus far, since Daniel Lester, no further Wraiths have been created. And, my Lord, I believe Daniel Lester is being held in the custody of Seren." Lord Harbinger's Porcine side-effects were beginning to diminish. "Xenka Drach is appalled by the experiments and confronted Skel about them and so the pair are no longer in cahoots." Conducere Rune paused to think. "What else? What else? Oh, yes, the townsfolk of the Cauldron have recently revived the game of Vampires And Victims." This news was enough to restore Lord Harbinger to full consciousness.

"What!" screamed the Vampire Lord so loudly it shook the cell walls. "Tell me, Simeon, who is behind this treachery?"

"We believe it is Old Mother Lyons who is behind it, my Lord."

"Of course, it had to be her! Elizabeth Lyons, protégée of Nana Alice. I met Nana Alice while negotiating the Treaty. I could smell straightaway she was a Lycanthrope but what a Vampire she would've made. Magnificent. I had been tempted to feed on her during her youth. I wish I had now," reminisced the former Prima Vampir. "We must put a halt to all this or it'll mean war, and no matter what anybody says we cannot defeat the Humans, there are far too many of them and far too few of us!"

"Madame Drach shares your concerns, my Lord. What is your command?"

"I command you bring me some proper food so I can be restored and get out of here to put things right!"

"I'm afraid I'm not allowed to do that, my Lord, and if I tried, the Repeste guarding your cell would kill me."

"Then why am I being fed piglets?"

"Because Tyran and Xenka need you to build your strength in case Seren and her Mutanti rise up and —"

"Seren's Mutanti? Seren's Mutanti? Since when are they Seren's Mutanti?"

"My Lord, Tyran Skel, foolishly he now admits, placed all Mutanti under Seren's control. They become bolder each day and many exiles are returning to their Vampire Houses. Xenka believes a Mutanti uprising is on its way." At this news Lord Harbinger let out a Vampire Wail which was felt by every Vampire in Storm Hill. It made them afraid.

"Leave me, Simeon, I must think."

"Before I do so, my Lord, I must inform you that it is Tyran Skel's and Xenka's intention that in the event of a Mutanti uprising they will feed you as many Familiars as are necessary to restore your powers to you."

"Including you, Simeon? Will they feed you to me?"

"My Lord, if it comes to it I will gladly give myself to you."

"Are they expecting mercy?"

"No, my Lord, they are not."

With those words singing in His ears, Lord Harbinger stretched out on His stone bed, crossed His arms over His chest, closed His eyes and descended into a deep Vampire Sleep, the deepest and most satisfying Vampire Sleep he had taken in more than a millennium. Simeon Rune later swore that the Grand Old Vampire went to sleep with a smile on His face.

CHAPTER 10

Following Penny Street School's victory in the V and V tournament, children chanted, "Charlie, Charlie, Charlie," as they carried him shoulder-high along Evelyn Terrace like a hero of old. Their cheering brought all the households onto the street. Nana Lyons stood and watched impassively on her doorstep. Catching Charlie's eye, she beckoned him into the house with a flick of her head. She wanted to know how things went and whether there were any potential Familiars observing the proceedings.

"I think I spotted a Familiar, a Priest called Father Kenny. He disappeared, and when he returned I saw him talking to an old woman at the back of the crowd. I tried to see who she was but before I could get close enough she'd disappeared," whispered Charlie to his nana in confidence. "And guess what else? You were right. The Kirkdale Road lot put booby traps out and our Billy got a spike right through his hand. There's no chance he'll be able to take part in the boxing tournament next week, and —"

"Take a breath, son, or you'll pass out," joked Nana Lyons.

"Who do you think the old woman was, Nana? She was definitely in cahoots with Father Kenny by the way they were talking together."

"Well, let's not go jumping to conclusions, Charlie. Now tell me all about the tournament, every little detail, so we can fine-tune your training." It was news to Charlie that he was going to be fine-tuned.

After Charlie giving his nana a blow-by-blow account of what had happened at the V and V tournament she told him to get something to eat and then get to bed as he had church in the morning followed by chores. Charlie was hoping he might be excused church and chores so he could train instead. As things turned out, he did an hour's training after church when the Council of Crones took him to a derelict factory and put him through his paces. When Charlie returned to Evelyn Terrace he still had his chores to do but, as it was breaking coal, he did not mind because it gave him the opportunity to see how Midget was getting on. There were now thirteen Lupule living in his nana's coal cellar and the smell was starting to get noticed.

★

At morning assembly, Mr Bawles announced that the funeral of the children who had died from the Sweating Sickness was to take place the following morning at ten o'clock. He said that anybody wishing to attend the funeral could do so as the school would only open in the afternoon. Father Grogan then mounted the stage and, in sombre mood, told everybody that Penny Street School had won the weekend's V and V tournament, thanks to Charlie Carter. At the mention of Charlie's name, half the school cheered while the other half booed. The teachers clapped vigorously, with Miss Williams jumping down from the stage and gave Charlie a big hug and a kiss on the top of his head. Father Grogan finished by announcing that as other schools, in light of their poor performances, had instigated a more rigorous training regime, their own V and V training would, henceforth, be held nightly, commencing that evening. This announcement was greeted with groans from all except the Storm Hillers.

That night, V and V training was carried out around the jiggers behind Sanderson Street to simulate the Field of Battle they had encountered the previous Saturday. This time, though, there were no booby traps, though Izzy Sanchez said they should have some to keep everybody on their toes. Father Grogan considered the idea for a brief moment but it would, "not sit well with his boss," he said, pointing to the Heavens. Unable to train because of his injured hand, Billy Lynch watched the Storm Hill children training. He noticed a massive improvement, despite them being hopeless only a few days earlier. They were just like alley cats the way they were able to run flat out along glass-topped jigger walls and leap clean across them like people-sized frogs.

On Tuesday morning the streets of the Cauldron were lined six deep by the thousands upon thousands of people who had come to pay their last respects to the children who had died from the Sweating Sickness while being cared for in Storm Hill. Their parents walked at the head of the funeral cortège. Many of them had to be supported by family members to prevent them from falling down in their grief. Everybody wore special bereavement clothes or their Sunday best on such occasions, and as mortality rates were so high people got good use out of them.

After the funeral procession passed along Kirkdale Road the crowd thinned as adults dispersed to their favourite pubs and mourn the loss of the young lives by getting blind drunk. This ritual is universal and not confined solely to the poorest in society, as claimed by those in high society. Most of the child mourners went to school after lunch but no action was taken against those that did not.

V and V training on Tuesday evening was held on the site of a derelict building opposite Christ Church. Priests lit fire baskets inside it to disperse the smog and allow them to observe the training. Father Kenny turned up uninvited and made notes throughout the training session. The children from Storm Hill showed a massive improvement on their Saturday performance, arousing further suspicion about them.

On Wednesday and Thursday, instead of lessons, every school in the Cauldron concentrated on getting their pupils ready for the Inter-Schools Boxing Tournament. The kids from the posh schools had their lessons as normal, as they expected to win the tournament despite Kirkdale Middle School being favourites. V and V training on those evenings took place on the tins in front of Christ Church as Nana Lyons was of the opinion that along with home advantage they would ensure certain victory for Penny Street School when they faced the Storm Hill team.

There was to be no V and V training on Friday evening due to the Inter-Schools Boxing Tournament being held during the day but a second V and V tournament was arranged at short notice for Saturday afternoon on the site of a derelict warehouse down by the docks. Nana Lyons was concerned about the venue as she had long suspected that abandoned warehouses were being used by Vampires and 'others'; for what she did not know though rumours had it that a hideous 'bearlike' creature had been seen stalking the area.

★

Friday morning, the day of the Inter-Schools Boxing Tournament, had finally arrived. There was a buzz of excitement everywhere, including the pubs lining Dock Road. Adults were betting on which school would win overall, as well as the results of individual bouts. Billy Lynch was deemed unfit to box due to his hand injury. "Ar'hey, let me fight, will yez?" he whined. "I can beat any of this lot with one hand tied behind me back. To give them a chance I'll even tie me good hand behind me back and box them with the one with a hole in it," was what he said, which made everybody laugh. Dejected, Billy sidled up to Charlie. "Alright, our Charlie? I'm gonna give ye me best move but don't use it all the time, okay?" Charlie nodded. "Now watch me feet. See? See me stance? Now watch. That's what we boxers call a switch. You start orthodox, with a left-hand lead, and then you go southpaw, with a right-hand lead, and while your opponent is figuring it out you plant them with a big left hook or a right uppercut. Got it?" Charlie nodded again. "Now show me," said Billy. Charlie followed his cousin's instructions but, despite getting a thumbs-up for his efforts, Billy was sceptical he could pull the moves off in the ring. "Just do ye best, our kid, that's all anybody can ask," were Billy's final words of encouragement to his cousin.

The fourth bout promised to be a sizzler. It was between Tyler King of Kirkdale Middle School, an odds-on favourite to win his weight and age division, and Bogdan Radu representing Penny Street School. On paper, everybody thought Tyler would win the fight easily but word went round that Bogdan was going to be no pushover. When the pair entered the ring, Bogdan removed a cloak from across his shoulders to expose a square and very muscular body framed by a boxing vest. All in the hall fell silent. Tyler King muttered something to Mr Jones, Kirkdale School's boxing coach, who then called out to the referee, "Hey, Ref, isn't he supposed to be working down on the docks?" he said, pointing at Bogdan. "That lad's never a school kid! Look at him! He's got muscles everywhere!" All the children laughed though some booed Mr Jones. Some even yelled out, calling him a traitor!

Half the hall erupted into shouts for Bogdan while stamping their feet in time with their chanting. It ran: "Bogdan," dum, dum, dum, "Bogdan," dum, dum, dum, "Bogdan," dum, dum, dum, "Bogdan," dum, dum, dum. In response, the children of Kirkdale Middle School began a chant of their own: "Tyler," dum, dum, dum, "Tyler," dum, dum, dum, "Tyler," dum, dum, dum, "Tyler," dum, dum, dum. Mr Bawles leapt into the ring waving his arms around like a demented daddy longlegs to demand silence, which he eventually got, but as soon as he left the ring the chanting erupted again.

What Bogdan Radu lacked in boxing skills he more than made up for in sheer power. At the break in between the first and second rounds, Mr Jones threw in the towel, much to the disgust of Tyler King, who, some say, wanted to go on, plus the kids yelled in anger because they wanted to see more blood. "What d'yez expect?" shouted Mr Jones at the crowd. "That lad's a ringer!" he ranted, pointing at Bogdan Radu. "Look at him! He's built like a brick outhouse!" Bogdan ignored Mr Jones' remarks and simply left the ring to make way for the next bout. Next into the ring was Lorcan Thorne and one of Charlie's cousins, also one of Billy Lynch's younger brothers, representing Holy Cross School, Kenneth 'Kenny Boy' Lynch. It was a massacre. Thorne sat Kenny on his backside four times during the first round and broke the lad's nose. Thorne celebrated his victory by jumping around the ring like he had won the world championship. After proclaiming that he was from Storm Hill and not Penny Street School, Thorne glared at Charlie Carter, pointing at him and saying he was next. Charlie did not react; he just sat impassively waiting for his first fight.

Despite some fine footwork, and excellent switching from orthodox to southpaw and back again, Charlie lost his bout on points. He was badly banged up by his Sefton Park opponent and had the makings of two lovely black eyes. Billy came up to Charlie after the fight to offer his commiserations and a running commentary on where he had gone wrong. Much to the disappointment of many but much to the relief of Charlie Carter, there was no matchup between him and Lorcan Thorne. Charlie knew he was no match for Thorne in the boxing ring but fancied his chances against him on a V and V Field of Battle and planned to prove it the following afternoon.

It was a shock to everybody that the posh kids of Sefton Park Private School won the tournament, but Bogdan Radu was crowned overall champion, having won all his bouts. Penny Street came last overall.

★

Walking back to Evelyn Terrace following the boxing tournament, where Charlie lost his one and only bout, Billy Lynch shadow-boxed to demonstrate what he should do next time. The boys were dead-arm punching one another as they went up St George's Hill when Charlie commented that the smog was not as dense as it had been lately and there was a feeling of spring in the air. "No more Jack Frost," commented Charlie, taking in a deep breath of cool clean air through his nose. "No more going to bed early and having to put up with me brothers' smelly feet waving in me nose," laughed Billy, who then said, "I wonder if it'll always be like this?" and sighed. "What do you mean?" asked Charlie. "You know, struggling and that. Smog, not enough food and no prospects for the likes of us is what me ma and da say; no, there's nothin' for the likes of us, they say. Will it be like this forever? Is this what we've got to look forward to for the rest of our lives? I think the dead are better off than us." Billy's words depressed Charlie into silence as they continued on their walk to Evelyn Terrace.

Once inside Nana Lyons' house Billy and Charlie regaled everybody with a blow-by-blow account of the boxing tournament. Aunts Lilley and Alice said boxing was barbaric and should not be allowed but added that they were proud of them and their cousins all the same for coming second against the odds. The boys had lied to them about the results.

"Hey, Charlie, where's our Jed?" asked Mary. "Is he coming along later?" Charlie and Billy were surprised that Jed was not home.

"Jed was in front of us, wasn't he, Billy?" remarked Charlie. Billy nodded.

"Yeah, Aunty Mary, we saw him walking up St George's Hill. He was well in front of us. He should be here, unless he's gone to one of his mates' houses."

"None of his mates live up this way, they're all down in Sanderson Street. Where could he have got to?" Mary asked in a panic.

"He's probably up to no good, you know what he's like, always up to no good, that one, but he always turns up," said Nana Lyons reassuringly.

"Oh, I know what he's like, alright, but this is different. He hasn't done anything like this since he had his fright."

"What do you mean, 'his fright', what happened, Mary?" asked Lilley.

"Nothing," interjected Nana Lyons, "it was just a bit of nonsense, that's all, just a bit of nonsense."

"I'm worried, Mum," admitted Mary, looking scared for what might have happened to Jed. Seeing the fear in her daughter's eyes, Nana Lyons believed there must be something amiss.

"A mother knows best," she said, "so all of you get out looking for Jed. Charlie and Billy, you go down to Sanderson Street in case he ducked down Heatherfield Road. You can get the families down that way to look too. Someone will know where he is. The rest of you, get gone! What are you waiting for? Get out and find Jed!" yelled Nana Lyons. With that everybody put on their coats and headed out in all directions looking for Jed.

★

The Repesto driver pulled into the Sanatorium. Removing the cover from the cage she flung open its door. Lying dead still on the floor was a bundle wrapped in rough sacking. She flung it over her shoulder. "I got him," she cried. "Excellent," replied Professor Grail, clapping and rubbing his hands together in childlike joy. "That's the last of them," he smirked. "Take him to his friends, I'm sure they'll have a wonderful reunion." The Repesto carried the bundle into a twilit room, flinging its contents onto an empty bed and handcuffing a bare wrist to the bedframe. Before leaving the room, the Repesto went to inspect the children. She was curious to see if any of them had passed over into the nether-world. When she got to bed number five, the subject was wide awake, eyes aglow and staring at the ceiling. "Hello," said the Repesto. The child turned her head toward her and smiled. "Hello," she replied in a hollow, echoey, otherworldly voice. "Who are you?" she asked. "I'm Dragana," replied the Repesto. "Dragana who?" asked the child. "Just Dragana," replied the Repesto. "Come closer," whispered the child. "It's so dark in here and I want to see what you look like. I bet you're beautiful." Dragana leaned forward, and as she did so the child changed form and cut deep into the Repesto's throat with her Death Bite Fangs. Dragana ran screaming from the room, leaving behind her a thick trail of blood. The transforming was felt by the Vampires working in the laboratory. They ran into the room but by then the child had returned to her normal form and was pretending to be asleep. Had they gone to her bedside they would have seen she was smiling and had the Repesto's blood on her lips.

★

Hundreds of Cauldronians combed the streets looking for Jed. They searched everywhere they thought he might be but without success and so at eight o'clock Mary Carter went to the Police Station to report her son missing. Patrick Carter, having arrived back to an empty house, was told about Jed being missing and as the search for him had turned up nothing Mary had gone to the Police Station. Being infested as it was with Familiars and Vampires, the Ravenport Police were neither sympathetic nor helpful to Cauldronians. They looked upon them as peasant scum barely fit to feed on. At ten o'clock Mary and Patrick gave up begging the Police Sergeant behind the desk to do something to help them find Jed and returned to Evelyn Terrace torn with trepidation over what might have happened to their son.

Hungry and exhausted after running round Jed's haunts searching for him, Charlie arrived back at Evelyn Terrace just after his mum and dad. He went to go into the front parlour but was prevented from doing so by his nana. "Follow me, we need to talk," she said, leading Charlie away by his elbow. She took him to the coal cellar where a dozen pair of yellowy eyes glowing in the dark greeted them. "I think Jed's been abducted and taken to Storm Hill," declared the old woman solemnly. Her words caused consternation among the Lupule. Michael and Trixie came forward and put a paw on Charlie's shoulder to comfort him; they looked sad and made sad sounds. One of the Lupule let out a howl of lament but was quickly hushed by the others. "Why are the Lupulos acting this way?" asked Charlie. "They suspect I'm right," replied Nana Lyons, barely able to keep herself from bursting into tears. "But why would they take Jed? The other kids are dead, so why take him?" asked Charlie, puzzled. "What do you mean, 'the other kids are dead, so why take Jed?'? What's his connection with the dead children?" Charlie told his nana about the night Jed and his mates went snooping around the Sanatorium. "They looked through a window and saw Stevie Lewis' dad. Jed said he was strapped down on a bed. Stevie kept shouting to his dad but the other kids panicked and ran because they were scared of getting caught but Stevie stayed behind. He got grabbed. Then Patto got run down by a rig and Stevie got burned when his house caught on fire. Then there was the bogus fever down by Lemon Street. One by one, they were taken to Storm Hill and ended up dying from the Sweating Sickness. There was only Jed left." The door to the coal cellar opened. "Are you down there, Charlie? Nana? We heard a strange noise like a dog howling," called Lilley Hawley down the coal cellar stairs. "It must've been outside. We're breaking coal. We'll be up in a minute," shouted Nana Lyons sternly to deter further conversation on the subject. Lilley closed the coal cellar door and returned to the back parlour to report what she had been told. "If Jed's been taken to Storm Hill, then what can we do, Nana?" asked Charlie. "This shows the Vampires mean business. It's clear they don't want peace, they want war, and if that's what they want then that's exactly what they'll get!" Charlie had hoped for a different answer. "But, Nana, we got to do something now!" he said with great urgency in his voice. "Charlie, we can't just go marching into Storm Hill, we'll be slaughtered. No, we need to prepare for war, which for you means you need to get some sleep before the Vampires And Victims tournament tomorrow." Charlie was shocked by his nana's lack of action. "I can't go to bed while Jed is missing. I can't go playing games when Jed is missing. I can't —" Nana Lyons cut Charlie off. "Listen, Charlie, I've told you before, Vampires And Victims isn't a game, it's training, and after the tournament tomorrow I'm going to teach you how to hunt down and dust Vampires so we can rescue Jed together. Now, get off to bed and no back-chat."

Michael and Trixie ushered Charlie from the coal cellar and returned to discuss the situation with Nana Lyons and the other Lupule.

★

Despite all that was going on, at six o'clock the next morning Patrick Carter Snr was up and ready for his day's work. He was under strict instructions not to eat anything other than his sandwiches, nor drink anything other than tea from his can. Nana Lyons had told him to pretend to eat the food but not eat it under any circumstances. "But why not?" Patrick asked. "Because I think it's being tampered with," answered Nana Lyons in frustration. "Rubbish! The food they give us is delicious and it's free, so I'm going to carry on eating it!" Nana Lyons forcibly explained to Patrick that no matter how delicious the free food was he was not to eat it, plus he was to make notes of everything that went on around him, plus, if he got the chance, he was to take a look behind closed doors to see what went on there. Patrick eventually agreed to do as the old woman 'requested'.

Despite all that was going on, Charlie Carter slept soundly until ten o'clock, at which time his nana came into the bedroom wielding her walking stick. "Who's been sleeping in my story house?" she chanted. "Only Daddy Greenwood," she continued. "But don't take none of my fine chickens… only… only… only… only… this fine one!" At the end of her chant Nana Lyons grabbed Charlie by the ankle, giving him a fright. "You scared the life out of me!" he yelled. "Don't be such a baby, I was only doing the Daddy Greenwood. You know it always ends with me giving you kids a good fright, you know that. Or would you prefer I give you a good hiding with my walking stick?" she said, smiling at Charlie, but he was not in the mood. "What time is it?" he asked. "It's time for you to learn how to dust Vampires," she replied coldly. "I like to use this to deal with the other things that lurk around Storm Hill," she added, drawing a sword out of her walking stick. "You know, Familiars, men in white coats, Repeste and, on the odd occasion, Lupulos too," she said, swishing the air several times before sliding the weapon back inside her walking stick. Charlie was astonished. He had never imagined for one moment that his nana's walking stick had a sword hidden inside it; but, then again, very little now surprised him about his nana.

After scoffing down a late breakfast, Charlie met up with his V and V teammates outside Christ Church, and from there they strolled together to an old bonded warehouse down by the docks. Penny Street School were the first team to arrive so they checked the Field of Battle to see where they might gain some advantage. The other teams arrived fifteen minutes later. This time, there were eleven teams, including from Sefton Park Private School. After their victory in the boxing tournament they were feeling cocky. Charlie spoke to a few of the Sefton Park kids and had to say he quite liked them. They were not as snobby or standoffish as he thought they would be.

As neither of the Fazakerly School teams turned up, Father Quinn was designated to referee the matches. He deputised the children from Fazakerly that had come along to support their teams as Marshals. They were to ensure compliance with the rules as there had been some disputes the previous week. Some teams claimed the Fazakerly kids were biased against them but Father Quinn said it was more likely that they were disappointed at, "not being able to cheat this time!" Billy Lynch and some of the reserves volunteered to be Marshals and posted themselves along the far wall of the warehouse as that was likely to be where all the action would take place.

Team names were put into a hat to be drawn out one at a time. The first team drawn would play the second team and have the choice of whether to be Vampires or Victims and so on. At the end of each match the teams would reverse roles and play each other again. There was only time for sixteen matches, so not every team would play against every other team. To the great disappointment of the children and the Priests, Charlie Carter's and Lorcan Thorne's teams were not drawn to play one another. Right on cue, the fog rolled in off the river but it was nowhere near as dense as it had been recently – a sure sign that spring was on its way.

First up was Storm Hill versus Sefton Park Private School. As usual, Lorcan Thorne nominated himself as first Vampire. He was lightning-quick hunting down the Sefton Park Victims. He neither wanted nor needed help from his teammates. It was all over in under six minutes. When it came time for Sefton Park to play the part of the Vampires, Lorcan Thorne sent their first Vampire crashing to the ground, thereby claimed a stunning victory for Storm Hill. Their band of supporters yelled and whooped and screamed in excitement. They were ecstatic after the shambles of the previous week, all, that was, except Max Rune; he just sat and watched impassively before walking off by himself to stand away from everybody.

The final match of the day was Penny Street School versus Kirkdale Middle School. All the matches thus far had been extremely tough, and with so many injuries Tyler King, captain of the Kirkdale team, could not field a full side and so had to forfeit. "Hang on a minute," yelled Lorcan Thorne, "this is a fixup! If the match is forfeit, then Penny Street School win the tournament." Which they would not have if Lorcan Thorne had allowed his teammates to tag Victims instead of him insisting on being the lone Vampire. "What do you propose we do about it, Master Thorne?" asked Father Quinn derisively. "Storm Hill should join with Kirkdale to make a full team," he insisted. "What do you think of that, Master Carter?" asked Father Quinn. "Okay by me," replied Charlie, "but we'll have Billy Lynch and Savanah Lyle on our side, as we're carrying a few injuries ourselves." Father Quinn looked across at Tyler King and Lorcan Thorne. "Well, what do you say?" he asked. "That seems fair to me," said Tyler King, shaking Charlie's hand sportsmanlike. "Fine by me too, so let's get on with it," snarled Lorcan Thorne. "And don't expect any favours this time, Carter, or you, Lynch," he said to stir the pot. "What the hell is he talking about?" asked Billy Lynch. "I have no idea," replied Charlie.

For the first round Storm Hill were the Victims and Charlie Carter played the Vampire. "Watch out, Charlie, remember what Thorne did to the Sefton Park Vampire," whispered Izzy Sanchez. Don't worry, Izzy, I've a plan up my sleeve," replied Charlie, giving Billy Lynch the thumbs-up. As soon as the match began Charlie tagged the injured Tyler King. Despite him being upset at being caught so quickly, and being very sporting, Tyler immediately swapped out for Billy Lynch to become the second Vampire. This infuriated Lorcan Thorne; his worst two enemies would be out to get him and he was not wrong. Charlie and Billy ignored all other Victims to hunt down Lorcan Thorne. They cornered him, and though he sent Billy Lynch crashing to the ground Charlie Carter tagged him. "You missed," yelled Thorne, scampering away from the scene.

"No he didn't," called out several of the Marshals. Lorcan Thorne went apoplectic. "You cheaters! You cheaters! You know he missed!" yelled Thorne, incandescent with rage at the Marshals. "No I didn't, Thorne," returned Charlie Carter, "and you know I didn't, but if that's the way you play then let's just you and I go at it! Winner takes all." Lorcan Thorne ordered everybody else from the Field of Battle.

"So, Carter, which of us is to be the Vampire?"

"I'll go first," said Charlie, who, after counting to twenty, went springing from wall to wall to come to land just feet from Lorcan Thorne, who tried to cause him to fall, but Charlie tagged him by the arm. "I think that was about ten seconds, Thorne," bragged Charlie after the tag was confirmed by a Marshal.

"You can't do that! That's cheating! I wasn't ready!" whined Thorne.

"Master Thorne, you were caught fair and square so take yer medicine," yelled Father Quinn, who smiled to himself after turning his back on the children.

"Alright then, Carter," said Thorne, leaping toward Charlie to tag him before he had taken his twenty seconds, dispersal time, "Got you!" he cried, lunging at Charlie. But the lad missed his target as Charlie effortlessly sidestepped Thorne's clumsy grab. Being completely off balance, Thorne fell twenty feet to the warehouse floor below. A hush came over the crowd as everybody thought the boy must be dead. Astonishingly, Thorne scrambled to his feet and dusted himself off. He was badly banged up but refused any help to walk.

"Another victim of Vampires And Victims," joked Father Quinn with a wry smile. As with previous injuries sustained by a Storm Hill child a wagon arrived on the scene from out of nowhere to whisk the injured away.

"Well, children, that's that," shouted Father Quinn at the dispersing crowd. "I declare Penny Street School the winners and accordingly award them..." The Priest stopped speaking as there was no one there to listen to him.

★

Following the V and V tournament at the warehouse it was declared that, in future, there would be just one team allowed from each school so a full Round Robin could take place to 'ensure fairness to teams, players and schools'. The Council of Crones guessed it was Storm Hill that complained as they had expected to beat all the other teams and thereby prove their superiority.

★

Charlie arrived home at exactly the same time as his father. He appeared to the boy to be pale-looking and shaken. Charlie asked his dad if he was feeling alright but got no answer; his dad just walked into the house ahead of him where Nana Lyons greeted them both. She took one look at Patrick and hauled him into the front parlour where the Council of Crones were in session. Charlie went to follow but his nana told him to go down to the coal cellar and tell Michael all about the V and V tournament. "But what about you training me to hunt Vampires, Nana?" complained Charlie. "I know it's late but you promised." Nana Lyons closed the parlour door so no others could hear what she had to say to Charlie. "Keep your voice down, son, you never know who is listening," she whispered, as if hinting that somebody untrustworthy was close at hand. Charlie went to reply but his nana shushed him. "I'll show you later on how to hunt Vampires but for now you need to go to the coal cellar to tell them all about today's tournament." Charlie hesitated. "Go!" ordered Nana Lyons, handing Charlie his whistle and kicking him up the backside.

As Charlie made his way to the coal cellar Effy poked her head between the banisters to tell him that the Police had been at the house earlier with Jed's clothes. "They said they found them down by the river and were searching along the shore for his body. They said that they think Jed might have drowned. He can hardly swim, so what was he doing by the river? Especially this time of year!" Charlie desperately wanted to tell his sister that he and Nana believed Jed was probably alive and being held in Storm Hill but how could he? "We've got to hope and pray that Jed's okay; now go and play, I've got to break some coal for Nana." Effy asked Charlie if she could help him break coal. "You don't want to go down there, little sister, it's full of spiders and all sorts of things," he said to put her off. "I know, I've seen them." The way Effy spoke it was as if she had seen the Lupule. "What do you mean?" asked Charlie, hoping Effy's answer was not going to be anything to do with the Lupule. "I don't know what you call them. They look frightening but they're nice. I haven't told anybody about them in case they think I've gone mad and send for the men in white coats to cart me off to the loony bin." Charlie hardly knew what to say for a second. "You're right, don't go telling anybody in case they think you're mad. Now, I've got to break some coal or Nana will freeze to death and we don't want that, do we?" Effy shook her head. "Say hello from me, Charlie," said Effy as she made her way upstairs. Charlie was not sure who she was referring to: Nana or the Lupule? "Alright, I'll say you said hello, now get up them stairs before Nana does the Daddy Greenwood on you." At the mention of Nana's terrifying chant Effy shrieked with mock dread and ran upstairs to join her siblings playing tents in the bedrooms.

As Charlie descended into the coal cellar he wondered why his nana had handed him his whistle as he had no need to use it after the first time he visited Michael; then the answer became obvious. Straight ahead of him stood the largest and most fierce-looking Lupulo he had ever seen. This one was different in colour to the rest and looked as though it could even be a different breed. One thing was for certain, though: it was the leader of the pack, as all the Lupule fell in behind it. Charlie dropped his whistle in terror and then blew it as hard as he could, causing the Lupule to cover their ears and snarl at him. Michael came forward and bowed to Charlie but instead of returning it he raised the Lupulo's head to look at him eye to eye. "I wish we could speak one another's language, Michael, then you could tell me what's going on." Michael pointed to the large Lupulo and coughed, "Nezok," in his strange croak. Following this introduction the monstrous Lupulo bowed to Charlie and scraped his claws on the coal cellar floor. Charlie recalled that when he had returned this action previously the Lupule had laughed at him but he was not going to be put off. He returned Nezok's bow and as he went to scrape the toe of his shoe along the floor Trixie rushed forward and removed his shoe from his foot. This time no Lupule laughed at him. Charlie told the Lupule that his nana had ordered him to tell them about the V and V tournament at the warehouse. He was uncertain as to how this would work, but felt the Lupule would understand him more than they could speak. The Lupule formed an arc in front of Charlie with Nezok at its centre as if they were at the local music hall waiting for the star turn to sing.

Meanwhile, in the front parlour, Patrick Snr, after being dosed with one of Nana Lyons' powders, began telling the Council of Crones what had happened at work that day. He started nervously with his arrival at Storm Hill. The powder suddenly took effect. Patrick slumped in his seat and then spoke as if in a trance. He told how he and his workmates were given a broth to start the day with but he had poured his down the sink. After ten minutes a man in a white coat entered the canteen and asked Dracaena Zayne if the men were ready. At the mention of Dracaena Zayne the Council of Crones looked at one another. Patrick began to shake uncontrollably. Nana Lyons blew some powder into Patrick's face and a minute later he was calm again. He told how he and his workmates were taken to a room full of beds where a woman wearing a white coat told them what work they would be doing that day. "She then called a Professor Grail into the room. He had a dozen people with him. He uncovered a cage and the people inside it were told to feed. They were handed animals and a woman wrote down which animal they got." Patrick hesitated but the effect of the powder overcame his reluctance to continue. Patrick suddenly blurted out that the people in the cage transformed into hideous creatures with long fangs which they used to suck all the blood out of the animals. He said after the creatures fed they changed back into people and those in white coats took blood from them, which they squirted into glass tubes. What Patrick told the Council of Crones next caused them most concern. He told how the people in white coats mixed the blood with potions and then injected him and his workmates and made notes about who had been given what. He said the pain was excruciating and the after-effects almost unbearable but he refused to show any sign that he was conscious. After Patrick and the others were returned to the factory they were sprinkled with sawdust and wood shavings so the story they were given about the work they were supposed to have done would seem real to them. Patrick ended his tale with, "I'm never going back there again. Never!" Nana Lyons told Patrick that he had to go to work as usual to find out as much as he could about the goings-on at Storm Hill. "How can I do that? Tell me, Elizabeth, how can I do that? There are hundreds of them up there and they watch us like hawks. What can I do against hundreds? What happens if whatever they're doing to me kills me or something? Eh, what then? Sorry, but I'm not going back there ever again." Nana Lyons said she would give him time to think by telling his workmates he was unwell and needed a few days off work. After Patrick left the front parlour, Mary told him about the Police finding Jed's clothes down by the river. He thought about going back and confronting the Council of Crones but instead he marched to the nearest pub where he drank himself senseless.

★

After Charlie finished telling the Lupule about the V and V tournament, they entered into a heated argument and as he did not understand Lupul he left them to it. Arriving at the front parlour door, Charlie knocked and was told to enter. He thought the Council of Crones looked crestfallen so he asked them what the matter was.

"Things have taken an unexpected turn," said Nana Lyons.
"Is there anything I can do to help?" asked Charlie, not knowing what help he could possibly be. "Anyway, I met Nezok. He appears to be the leader now. He's huge, isn't he? Where did he come from?"
"Where else? Storm Hill, of course. Until yesterday evening he was Captain of the Southern Guard. He had over a hundred Lupulos under him. But now he's on the run. He said he wasn't going to —"
"That's enough, Elsie! Charlie doesn't need to be involved in our business."
"I do! I do! You must tell me everything!" Charlie cried.
"Not tonight, Charlie," said Nana Lyons. "There's enough to be getting on with without you getting involved in Lupulo politics." Charlie needed to mention something that was weighing heavy on his mind.
"Nana, you once told me that Lupulos spoke a language that not many people understand but I think you understand them perfectly well and they seem to understand us."
"It's not that straightforward, son. You see, some Lupulos are what you might call 'traditionalists'. They refuse to speak English or any other Human language, but they pick up the odd word here and there. Other Lupulos are all for learning what they can and many want to learn English because they see it as a way of gaining independence from Vampires. There's more to it than that but I'll teach you what I know of their language on condition that you promise me that you will follow my instructions to the letter, no matter what." Charlie quickly agreed to his nana's terms. "I'll teach

you one or two words every day or so and you can practise them on Michael. Don't worry if he or any of the others laugh at you, they'll be impressed that you're at least trying to learn their language."

"I want to be able to ask them their names."

"For all the good that'll do you! Anyway, it's late and we've a lot to do tonight. It's time for you to learn how to hunt Vampires." Charlie was excited to be moving to the next phase of his training.

Before Charlie and the nanas left the house, Nana Lyons went to her secret cupboard and retrieved several items which she wrapped in a blanket. The children were very curious to know what she was carrying. "It's the axe Daddy Greenwood uses to chop up his victims," she replied in a menacing voice. The children laughed until Nana Lyons poked the head of an axe out of the blanket and told them he was on the prowl. They shrieked in mock terror and went running around like they were possessed, crashing and banging into doors, walls and one another.

When Charlie and the Crones reached the old Army Barracks at the end of Evelyn Terrace, Nana Lyons dropped the blanket to the floor. "For beheading Vampires," she said, holding an axe, "and a crossbow and bolts for dusting them." Nana Lyons told Charlie that the best sawdust to use on the tips of the bolts was white oak but any sawdust would do. She also told him that if a bolt missed a Vampire's heart but hit some other part of their body it caused them to lose their strength to the extent that he should be able to pin them to the ground and dust them with a hand-held stake. "Don't do it if you can avoid it because they can still bite you. While we're on the subject, a Vampire has two types of bite. The first is the feeding bite. This bite, as the name implies, is for feeding. Feeding Fangs extend to about an inch long. They are used to pierce a Victim's neck so they can feed on their blood." Charlie wobbled and went pale at the thought of flowing blood. "The second type of bite has various names but I know it as the Vampire Death Bite. This bite, as the name implies, is for killing things. Fangs are extended to about three inches long. They use these fangs to tear into their Victim's neck. It's not unknown for the Victim to be decapitated depending on the ferocity of the attack. The Vampire can still feed on the blood so long as they're quick, because feeding on anything not living can destroy them." By now Charlie was ready to vomit. "You also need to know that Vampires use their bite to make new Vampires out of Victims but this is a complicated process that can take years. Imagine that, Charlie, being kept hanging in limbo between life and death for years. My advice to you, if you're taken to be made into a Vampire, is kill yourself if you can. Now then, son, how about some training?" Charlie was willing to do anything to take his mind off any further talk of blood.

"You're to only use your axe as a last resort," began Nana Lyons. "If you're close enough to a Vampire to use an axe then you're too close, remember that! Use your crossbow to dust them and always aim for the middle of the chest. That way if you miss the heart you're bound to hit something and that'll weaken them. You can finish them off with the axe or put a bolt through their heart. It's up to you, your choice," said Nana Lyons, smiling. Charlie thought she was attempting humour with her last piece of advice. "Now, Charlie, pick up the crossbow, draw back the string until it hooks behind the clip; then place a bolt in the groove and you're ready to dust a Vampire."

"Nana, this bolt has a metal tip."

"I know, I'm not going to waste a perfectly good Vampire Duster on practice."

"Okay, what do I do next?" asked Charlie after loading the bolt into the groove.

"Line up the 'V' with what you want to hit, then pull the trigger and you'll hit it. It's as simple as that." Charlie took aim on a wooden beam and pulled the trigger. There was very little kick from the crossbow but the power was tremendous. The bolt went clean through the wooden beam.

"Wow! That felt great, Nana! Another! Another!"

"Hang on a minute, Charlie, I think we've got company. Show yourselves!" yelled Nana Lyons into the dark recesses. Two Inferiara emerged from the shadows. "Perfect," she whispered to Charlie, "we don't want anything too difficult for your first time."

"What do you mean, Nana, 'my first time'?" asked Charlie, nervous at the answer he was half expecting.

"These are what we call Pale Vampires, Charlie. These two have been coming here for a while feeding on rats but recently they've been taking cats and nobody, but nobody, hurts cats! Now you're going to set them at peace, Charlie."

"What do you mean, Nana?" he asked, still nervous at the answer he was half expecting.

"You're going to dust them but don't worry, they're not really alive, so you can't be done for murder. Anyway, when you set them at peace they'll burst into flames, only leaving behind a small pile of ash, so there'll be nothing for the Police to go on." Charlie could hardly believe he was in this situation. "Now, Charlie, as they're only Pale Vampires you're okay to use the axe but they can still bite you, so be careful." With this last piece of advice, Nana Lyons handed Charlie the axe and shoved him toward the Vampires. They snarled, transfigured into their Vampire form and bared their fangs in response.

"Wow, Nana, it's as light as a feather!" gasped Charlie, stunned by the lack of weight in the axe. He was worried that such a light axe was not going to be of any use but after testing it on a wooden beam his concerns evaporated.

"It's made from a star that fell from the sky," shouted Nana Lyons.

"It's called a meteorite," Charlie answered helpfully.

"I know what a meteorite is, thank you, Charlie Carter, now stop messing around and deal with these Vampires before they deal with you!" Charlie took up a stance. "Oh, before I forget. You have to be quick dusting them because they won't get tired but you will and if that happens it's all over for you, boy!" At that moment two of what appeared to be Angels landed on top of the walls of the derelict building. They folded their wings and peered down on the scene as into an amphitheatre. Charlie froze.

"What are they, Nana?" he hissed.

"They're what's known as Mutantos. There are lots of different types of them and, as you see, these ones can fly. They're just interested in watching to see how you do, so get on with it!" The winged Mutanti were then joined by two more.

The Pale Vampires separated to attack Charlie from opposite directions. He looked from one to the other and back again. Nana Lyons shouted to him to remember his V and V training so he ran along a wooden beam and leapt onto a wall to come to stand within a few feet of the nearest Vampire. Up close they were far more frightening to look at. The Vampire jumped straight at Charlie, her fangs extended and snarling at him. To get away, Charlie folded his arms and pencil-dropped onto the beam below. As the Vampire passed over him Charlie chopped off her foot, causing her to scream and howl as if in pain but she felt no pain; they were screams and howls of anger. The severed foot burst into flames before it hit the floor. The other Vampire came at Charlie from behind, and as he spun round he slipped and fell to the floor. Both Vampires were on him in an instant, pinning him to the ground with their bony hands covered in semi-translucent skin. The female Vampire was about to bite into Charlie's neck when Nana Lyons drew a sword from her stick and beheaded her. The other Pale Vampire burst into flames after Nana Maud shot it through the heart with a crossbow bolt tipped with sawdust. Charlie thought he was done for and felt mightily relieved that the Vampires were 'dead'. He then had pangs of deep disgust that he felt happiness that something, albeit a Vampire, was dead. Killing did not sit well with him.

"That wasn't too bad for your first time, not too bad at all," said Nana Lyons, patting Charlie on the head. "What do you think of that?" she shouted to the 'Angels'. They made no reply, they simply flew away.

"They could've killed me!" shrieked Charlie, shoving his nana's hand from his head.

"Rubbish, we had you covered all the time. We weren't going to let you perish on your first go," claimed Nana Elsie.

"No, that would be a waste," laughed Nana Minnie.

"You did well for your first time," said Nana Maud sincerely.

"But they're so fast and so strong. I'll never be able to beat them!"

"Oh yes you will, it's all just a matter of training, but now it's time for you to dust your first Vampire," said Nana Elsie, sporting a homely smile.

"What do you mean?" asked Charlie.

"The one your nana beheaded needs finishing off."

"What Nana Elsie means is you need to set it at peace so its soul can join all the other souls in the Great Universe," said Nana Lyons, handing Charlie a wooden stake and a mallet. "Now, son, place the point of the stake in the middle of its chest and hit it hard with the mallet. Don't be afraid, you're doing it a kindness."

"Can't I just shoot it with a crossbow bolt?"

"No! I'm not going to waste a perfectly good bolt on a thing like that. Put the stake on the middle of its chest and hit it hard with the mallet. Now go on!"

Charlie did as he was instructed. He placed the point of the wooden stake in the middle of the Vampire's chest over the heart and hit it hard with the mallet. As the stake drove through the organ that was once the Vampire's heart its remains burst into flames. The flash of light from the combusting Vampire was so bright in the darkness of the old Barracks that it dazzled Charlie, leaving him with spots before his eyes. Seconds later there was nothing left of the Vampire but a body-shaped pile of dust-like ash. Charlie thought he heard a voice on the wind saying, "Thank you, Charlie Carter, thank you." To which his Nana replied, "Now go, be at peace with the Great Universe." At these words the nanas crossed themselves. Charlie asked how the Vampire knew his name. "Who knows? It's a mystery," Nana Maud replied unhelpfully, though Charlie felt she did know and so did the other nanas.

The walk back to Nana Lyons' house began in silence. On the way Charlie thought, *How can God just sit there and let this happen? How can He allow these things to feed on His flock? Why did His Angels stand by and do nothing?* He arrived at the conclusion that there was no God. "Nana? Those Angels, why did they just stand there and do nothing?" he asked. "I told you what they are, Charlie, they're Mutantos and definitely not Angels," she answered. "How many of them are there?" he asked, keen to understand as much as he could about these wonderful creatures. "I honestly don't know, son, but not all Mutantos are like those we saw tonight. Some of them are monsters and terrifying to behold." When they reached home, and having had more than enough for one day, Charlie said he was going straight to bed. "Night, night, Nana, see you in the morning," he said, yawning a pretend yawn. "Night, night, Charlie. I love you, boy," replied the old woman. She felt hurt when Charlie did not return his usual, "I love you too, Nana." Instead he took the stairs two at a time to his room, closing the door behind him, shutting his nana and everything else out.

CHAPTER 11

When Charlie woke on Sunday morning, he told his mum he was never going to church ever again and that he did not care what people thought of him for not doing so. She said that she did care what people thought of her and her family, and he was going to church whether he liked it or not. "It's bad enough that your dad has left the faith and converted us all to Methodists, God forgive him, but that doesn't mean it's not a proper church and you're all going to church and Sunday school as well. All, Charles Carter! Do you hear me? All. You're going to church every Sunday until you die." Charlie answered, saying that he did not care what his mum did, he was never going to church ever again and that was that. Later, when the family were at breakfast, Mary told her mum what Charlie had said. "I don't know what to do with him, Mum, he seems so determined." Nana Lyons stomped upstairs banging her walking stick on the treads as she went, chanting, "Who's been sleeping in my story house? Only Daddy Greenwood. But don't take none of my fine chickens… only… only… only… only… this fine one!" The old woman grabbed Charlie by the ankle, making him jump in fright, even though he knew it was coming.

"Now you listen here, Charles Carter," scolded Nana Lyons, "you're going to church whether you like it or not; even if you do skip Sunday School to play on the swings. You mustn't change anything you do otherwise you'll come to people's attention, and you don't want to do that with the tournament at Mormant Hall coming up. Look, son, I understand last night was a big shock for you," said the old woman as sympathetically as she could.

"Those Vampires very nearly killed me!" whined Charlie.

"Don't be so dramatic, you big baby! There wasn't one chance in Hell of you getting so much as a scratch with us there. Even if they'd have been proper Vampires we'd've handled them easily, don't you worry," said Nana Lyons confidently. "I wouldn't let anything happen to my Charlie," she added, ruffling his hair. "You need a haircut. Now get up, get dressed and get down them stairs for your breakfast, and then get off to church."

"What are you going to be doing while we're at church, Nana?"

"Never you mind!" the old woman replied in such a way as to deter further discussion on the subject. "When you get back this afternoon, we're going to the old Barracks so you can learn where you went wrong."

"I'll look forward to it," Charlie replied sarcastically.

"Don't be like that, son. You need to do this so you can help me save Jed."

"If he's still alive. What if he's already…" Charlie couldn't say the word.

"He's alive, son. You have to keep believing he's still alive."

★

When Jed eventually came round from the effects of the Somnifir the Repeste had doped him with, he went to get up but was dragged back by his wrist handcuffed to the metal bedframe. He pulled and pulled against the handcuffs until his wrist was raw. Patto called out to him, "Don't bother, Jed, you're wasting your time. You won't be able to break free. You'll only make your wrist sore." Jed was shocked and yet happy to hear his friend's voice. "Patto! You're supposed to be dead! Everybody thinks you're dead!" The next voice Jed heard belonged to

Moey Groom. "How did they get you?" he asked. Jed was unsure how they got him; his head was still befuddled from the Somnifir. "Moey? Are any of the others here?" asked Jed, raising his head to look around the twilit room. They were all there. All nine of them that had looked through the window of the Sanatorium that night and saw Mr Lewis strapped to a bed. Suddenly, there was a noise outside the room. Jed copied the other children in pretending he was asleep.

"It's no good pretending to be asleep," said Professor Grail to the children. "We can hear a whisper from a mile away," he exaggerated, "so we can certainly hear your loud mouths from the next room. Now, sit up, all of you, I want to check how you are progressing."

"Why are we here?" asked Jed.

"Ah, the new one," snarled Seren from behind a line of people wearing white coats. Some of the children screamed when they caught sight of her. "What are you lot screaming for?" she asked. "Have you never seen anything so beautiful as me before?" she laughed.

"What are you?" asked little Amy Collins, pointing.

"What are you?" mimicked Seren, pointing a claw at Amy. "Is she one of them?" Seren asked Professor Grail.

"Yes she is, and so is he," replied Professor Grail, pointing at Moey Groom.

"Is that all?" Seren asked. Grail nodded. "Why them and not the others too?"

"We think we have the answer but we need to make sure."

Professor Grail beckoned a group of Pale Vampires forward. They each took position next to one of the seven unaffected children, blew Somnifir into their faces and commenced feeding – if it could be called that as all they took was the merest Cyathus measure of blood from each child.

Even in their Somnifir-induced state the children knew what was going on but were powerless to do anything about it. Amy

Collins and Moey Groom observed the feeding impassively at first but they soon became agitated and then angry, causing them to change form, with Death Bite Fangs cutting the air and ready for action. Moey and Amy gave an ear-splitting screech that was answered with howls from nearby Lupule and even some Mutanti. Seren and Professor Grail looked at one another but dismissed the behaviour of the nether-creatures without further thought. Seeking a private conversation, Seren beckoned Professor Grail away from the children's room.

"The other two looked like they wanted to rip us to pieces," remarked Seren. "What could they have done to us?"

"Recently, one of them tore out the throat of a Repesto, so we might expect the same treatment if ever they get loose. But don't worry, once they accept what they are they'll be fine."

"You're positive they'll accept their new form?"

"Of course, Mistress, and those that don't will be destroyed. But what choice do they have? They're nether-creatures now." Seren was not convinced. She knew the character of Cauldronians as contrary creatures prepared to cut off their noses to spite their faces on matters of principle or honour, or just out of sheer bloody-mindedness.

"Why has no progress been made with our project? You created two Wraiths but no Mutanto yet. Why not?"

"The Mutanti project is following the work here, so I'm sure we'll soon have success."

"If there are no results by Easter you must expand the experiments. You must do all and everything to create Mutanti from the child subjects. You've done it with Vampires, so you must be able to do it with Mutanti!"

"Mistress," said Professor Grail in his meekest toadying voice, "what do you want them for? I only ask because —"

"Soldiers, Professor Grail, I want them for soldiers. Ever since the Prima Generatie Vampiri forbad the creation of any more of our kind we have been in decline, but thanks to Vampire Science our numbers grow once again. We shall never perish!" spoke Seren as if making a speech to an invisible horde. "That is why it is vital you create new Mutanti and once they can breed —"

"But, Mistress," interrupted Professor Grail, "there's no guarantee that, even if we are successful, the Mutanti we create will ever be capable of breeding."

"I find your lack of faith disturbing, Professor Grail. Do you doubt that Mother Nature will not take care of us as She has the Lupule?"

"Mistress, several hundreds of years elapsed before Lupule were able to breed, and they are mortal." Seren went to speak but the professor continued on, "It is yet to be established whether Wraiths are indeed mortal. All we have so far is the word of a Priest because Daniel Lester cast a shadow. We don't yet know what Wraiths are and the same will surely apply to any Mutanti we create, if and when we create any, that is. We must bear in mind, Mistress, that if Wraiths and similar kind are indeed immortal, no undead has ever bred," ended Professor Grail solemnly.

"Then find a way, Professor Grail, find a way! You're a scientist, aren't you, so find a way!" screamed Seren at her terrified underling.

"Be assured, Mistress, I will do everything in my power to ensure the success of our project," toadied Professor Grail to quell Seren's rising anger and frustration with him.

Seren left Professor Grail a jabbering, quaking wreck not knowing what to do for the best. He did not want to create so-called mortal Mutanti, but being a closet Mutanto he was afraid of exposure that would, no doubt, end in him losing his hard-earned position in Vampire Society. He had wanted to challenge Seren's claim that no more Mutanti were being created, as he knew differently and believed she did too. Despite the Supreme Council banning further creation of Mutanti, some were occasionally created by Vampires who, instead of waiting for the animal blood they had feasted on to become inert, too soon fed on a Human. Mutanti had always been created this way and continued to be so. To keep their dirty little indiscretions secret, Vampires would destroy the evidence but some were not up to the job and Mutanti that were barely distinguishable from Vampires, such as was Professor Grail, remained within Vampire Society, while the others roamed the Earth as the stuff of Human nightmares.

*

Following the events of the previous evening Charlie wanted to tell the whole world what he had seen and what he had done but brought to mind the day Nana Lyons had told everybody about Michael and how they thought it was all just one of her nana tales and did not believe her. To convince people of the existence of Vampires, Charlie knew he would have to bring one before them and despatch it into flame and dust in front of the eyes. Then he considered that they would think it was a trick, an illusion, that he had conjured up for his own aggrandisement. *People are so stupid! They don't believe what their eyes can see and yet they believe in God and that He exists. When it comes to the truth they need to believe in it before they accept it. They always make excuses, anything to pacify their minds! Why am I thinking like this? What is wrong with me?* Charlie asked himself. He went and sat apart from the other children in case he was contagious. He would not wish whatever it was he had on anybody, *except Lorcan Thorne*, Charlie mused with a broad smile. *I wonder what he knows about Vampires? Does he know about Vampires?* he continued. *He must, he has to, and I have to get everything out of him so I can rescue Jed!* Rescuing Jed would be a highly dangerous undertaking and something likely to lead to disaster should Charlie go it alone.

Instead of attending Sunday school, Charlie took his siblings to the park to play on the swings. There were fewer children there than usual. When Charlie asked around, a girl said, "Since those poor children died from the Sweating Sickness most kids are going to church instead of bunking off to the park." Another said they were going to church to preserve their immortal souls. "But not me, I don't believe in immortal souls or God or any of that stuff, I like playing on the swings instead."

From out of the thinning fog came Margot Thorne and Cho Lee. They wandered across the grass to sit either side of Charlie. He asked them what they were doing there as he thought they were not churchgoers. They said they were not but knew when church let out and had come to play on the swings and meet up with their friends. Charlie asked them if they really thought of the kids from the Cauldron as friends, as it was his belief that anybody from Storm Hill was not allowed to make friends with 'people like us'. Margot said there was some truth in what Charlie had said, while Cho said it was nonsense and they could make friends with whomsoever they wished. Cho went to play on the swings, leaving Charlie and Margot free to talk. "I made a bet with your brother and if I won it he'd tell me what goes on up at Storm Hill," said Charlie. "I bet he didn't keep his word?" replied Margot, sliding closer to Charlie. After what he had witnessed the previous evening, he moved to keep distance between them as he believed anybody from Storm Hill could be dangerous. "Margot, as your brother broke his word to me there is a family debt of honour and so you should tell me what goes on up there at Storm Hill." Margot thought for a moment before answering, "What do you mean exactly by 'what goes on up there at Storm Hill'? It's just a place like any other, so there's not much to tell, to be honest." Charlie contemplated whether he should take a risk. "Margot, what if I told you that Storm Hill isn't a normal place and I fought with two of its inhabitants last night? What would you say to that?" Margot looked Charlie up and down before replying, "You should stop fighting and concentrate on your studies. Education is everything. It has the power to set you free."

Charlie could tell he was not going to get anything from Margot and as he went off to play with his siblings he noticed Lorcan Thorne watching him. He was astonished to see him there after the fall he had taken the previous day. He was about to go over and speak with Thorne but he turned his back, making it clear he wanted nothing to do with Charlie.

Before Margot left the park, Charlie asked her how come her brother had recovered so quickly from his fall. She simply replied that the doctors in Storm Hill were better than those in Ravenport at fixing people up. "Charlie, if you're so interested in what it's like in Storm Hill, then why don't you ask your father about it? He works there, I believe." Charlie asked Margot how she knew that. She replied that her father had mentioned it. "My father knows everything that's going on; he's very important. He's due a promotion, so I heard him say to mother at least." Just then a whole bunch of Lynch kids arrived in the park. Charlie asked his cousin Billy to watch over Patrick Jnr and sisters and make sure they got home safely. "Why, where are you going?" asked Billy. "I've got some training to do for the next Vampires And Victims tournament," Charlie lied. "You're going to need it, the way those Storm Hill kids are coming along," laughed Billy. "Makes you wonder, though, doesn't it? You know, how they managed to go from being rubbish to being so good. Especially that Lorcan Thorne. He's had a couple of bad falls lately, yet there he is looking like brand new again. There's something going on up there at Storm Hill." Margot Thorne heard what Billy had said. "Oh, not you too! Look, if you like I'll invite you both to stay at my house and we can all have a good look around together. You can even have a sleepover if you like." After fighting Vampires the previous evening Charlie was not keen on visiting Storm Hill, so said he would think about it. Billy Lynch, however, accepted the invitation without hesitation, despite Charlie signalling him not to. That was not in Margot's plan so she conveniently forgot about the whole thing.

When Charlie arrived back at Evelyn Terrace, he dashed downstairs to the coal cellar to find his Nana and Nezok in conversation. "I knew she could understand them!" muttered Charlie to himself. He went and stood behind the rows of Lupule that were listening intently to the proceedings. They made chuntering noises every now and then to express their views on what was being discussed.

As soon as the pow-wow was over, Nana Lyons grabbed Charlie by the arm and rushed him to the old Army Barracks, where they were met by the other nanas of the Council of Crones. The plan was for Charlie to understand where he had gone wrong the previous evening. Nanas Maud and Minnie played the part of the two Pale Vampires and Nana Lyons coached Charlie on how he should have proceeded against them. They went over the scenario time and time again, adjusting this and that, covering all eventualities, until they were satisfied he could handle two Pale Vampires. As Charlie went to pack up the axe and crossbow to leave, Nana Lyons said, "And where do you think you're going, Charles Carter?" in such a way that Charlie was worried at what was coming next. From out of the shadows Nana Elsie emerged with two Pale Vampires on the end of chains. "Give them a few minutes to recover from the effects of the metal and then Charlie can show us what he can do," said Nana Elsie.

As the Vampires came round, several children appeared outside the Barracks. They were egging each other on, daring one another to go inside the 'haunted Barracks'. Nana Lyons left to shoo them away. As she did so Nana Elsie let slip the two Pale Vampires. They moved as though they had not been effected by the metal at all and rapidly closed in on Charlie, their Death Bite Fangs fully extended, ready to decapitate him. Nana Maud aimed her crossbow at the nearest Vampire but missed. This distraction, however, gave Charlie time to gain the high ground. "Come on! Come and get me," he shouted, taunting the Vampire nearest him. This challenge from a callow youth greatly enraged the Vampire. She flew at Charlie in a temper, which was the worst thing she could have done. Using his V and V training, Charlie leapt atop and then over a pile of rubble and came to land behind the Vampire. As she turned to face him, Charlie decapitated her with a single swing of his axe. By now, Nana Lyons had returned to the Barracks. Taking in the situation, she gave Nana Elsie a look the old woman would never forget before lining up her crossbow on the second Vampire. "Nana! Stop! This is my game!" screamed Charlie. However, instead of dusting the second Vampire, Charlie spoke to him. "I know it is your nature to do these things, but you were Human once. Can you not stop? Must you continue this existence?" The Vampire retracted his fangs and took Human form again. He asked Charlie if he had a cure for him, a cure that would allow him to re-join society. "Of course you don't, how could you, nobody does. I know I will meet my doom here, but I go willingly to the Great Universe." Born in Devonshire 227 years earlier, these were the final words of Jonas Clarke before he hurled himself onto a pile of splintered wooden beams, one of which penetrated his sad heart. Jonas' body burst into flames in an instant, leaving behind only a pile of dust. He was at peace and finally able to take his place in the Great Universe.

Taking a wooden stake, Charlie approached the headless Vampire and plunged it into the organ that had once been her heart. She burst into flames before settling into dust. Rising from the dust the Vampire's soul sighed and kissed Charlie on the cheek, "Thank you! Thank you, Charlie Carter! Ahhhhhhh," she gasped contentedly. Charlie looked wildly around at the nanas, asking, "Did you see that? Did you? Did you hear?" he screamed. "She was alive! Alive!" he howled. "We've all heard such things, Charlie, and they caused doubt in us too. They do it so that you might hesitate next time, and if you do it'll be you that will be killed. Be assured, young warrior, she was a Vampire and would've killed you given half a chance," spoke Nana Elsie earnestly. "Right, let's all go home so we can hold close those whom we love." The nanas walked Charlie home and then went their separate ways. Nana Lyons, walking stick at the ready, scuttled after Nana Elsie to ask her what she thought she was doing releasing the Vampires when she did. "But that's what you wanted. That's what your note said. I followed your instructions to the letter," she swore. "Show me the note," demanded Nana Lyons. "I burnt it, just like you instructed," answered Nana Elsie. Nana Lyons was not convinced by Nana Elsie's story. She had been on her guard ever since Charlie had told her about the old woman he had seen talking with Father Kenny and wondered if it was Elsie.

★

Throughout Monday, all of Penny Street School were talking about was the Vampires And Victims tournament the previous Saturday. As the day wore on, exaggerations grew larger and larger until the showdown between Charlie Carter and Lorcan Thorne took on epic dimensions. Rumours even circulated that Lorcan Thorne's fall had in fact killed him and he had been replaced by his twin brother. If Lorcan Thorne had a twin then he behaved exactly like the real Lorcan Thorne at school that day, as he and his cronies took their temper out on anybody they heard mention the V and V tournament or his fall. He openly accused Charlie Carter of, "Cheating as usual," and challenged him to a fight at the end of the school day. After battling Vampires that weekend on top of the V and V tournament, Charlie felt physically and emotionally drained and despite the 'bock, bock, bock' chicken noises hurled at him, he declined Lorcan Thorne's invitation to have it out after school. More than anything, though, Jed was on Charlie's mind, and now he knew how to dust Vampires he was resolved to pay Storm Hill a visit and look for his brother.

All that week, Charlie was suspiciously quiet. He went to V and V training as usual and practised with the Star Axe, as he had named it, and crossbow afterwards. He visited the Lupule regularly and even got to hold Midget on one occasion. Charlie believed Trixie to be a good mother, even though she pranked her own cubs. *Must be in her blood*, he thought. Michael could tell something was going on with Charlie and spoke to Nana Lyons about it. On the Thursday of that week, she asked him if he was having difficulties coming to terms with destroying Vampires. "No, I'm fine with it, I think, but Jed's on my mind. We can't just sit here doing nothing," Charlie cried. "Who said anything about not doing anything? For your information, we are doing something! When I spoke with Nezok last night he told me that a Vampire called Tyran Skel and another called Xenka Drach led a rebellion against Lord Harbinger about eighteen months ago and that's why things have changed. He thinks old Harbinger's still alive, if you can call it that. I paid the gatehouse at Mormaont Hall a visit this morning but there was nobody there, or at least they didn't answer the door. Never mind, we'll get a better look around the place during the finals of the V and V tournament." Charlie had clean forgotten about the Easter camp at Mormant Hall. Despite this giving him the perfect opportunity to snoop around Storm Hill he wanted to pay the place a visit beforehand to have a look around for himself. Something else was on Charlie's mind, "Nana, exactly how much of the Lupulos' language can you speak?" he asked. "Not much. I understand more than I can speak, and as they understand more English than they can speak we get along fine." Charlie was unconvinced his nana was telling him the truth and wondered why she would lie to him.

★

Much to Seren's chagrin, no new Wraiths had been created and those that had already crossed the threshold refused point blank to feed on their friends. Professor Grail had even waved juicy little piglets in front of Moey and Amy to get them in the mood but to no avail. According to him, they had no trouble transforming but they simply refused to feed on their friends even after he had them smothered in blood like gravy on a Sunday roast. Seren ordered Professor Grail to stake Moey to encourage Amy to feed, but he just begged her to do it and Amy said that no matter what happened they would not feed on their friends. "We'd rather die," they said. "You're Vampires, you're already dead!" replied Seren. "Then kill us again! We don't care!" screamed Amy at the top of her voice. "These people from the Cauldron, they really will cut off their noses to spite their faces," said Professor Grail, reminding Seren of the nature of Cauldronians. "There must be something we can do," cried Seren.

"Hey, ugly mush," shouted Moey Groom to Seren, "what wagon ran over your face to make you look like that?" Amy Collins added, "You look like a cow's backside that's been battered with an ugly stick!" Seren flew at the pair in a rage, and as she did so Moey and Amy transformed in a split second, complete with Death Bite Fangs. They lunged at Seren's throat, catching it by a tiny fraction of an inch. "How can they do that?" shrieked Seren, covering her throat with a paw. "Vampires need time to extend their fangs but not them. Why?" she demanded of Professor Grail. "This is new. I've never seen them do that before. Perhaps that was how they managed to attack the Repesto. She must've been taken by surprise." Moey and Amy grinned ghoulishly. "Come closer, come closer, we can hardly see you in this gloom," they said, their voices echoey, disembodied and ethereal. "They are too dangerous!" exclaimed Seren. "You must destroy them!" she demanded. Professor Grail whispered, "Let us not be too hasty, Mistress. Who knows how we might yet use them?" Then, for effect, he shouted, "No, Mistress Seren, no! I say to you that I will not destroy them for to do so would betray the trust placed in me by Tyran Skel." And with that, Professor Grail and Seren flounced out of the room like actors leaving the stage after a bad play. Walking away, Seren and Grail were left to ponder what they had witnessed. "Perhaps they are not Wraiths after all, but Mutanti!" whispered Professor Grail. "If so, then our work is done," answered Seren in a whisper of glee. "But how can we get them to cooperate to make more?" hiss-whispered Professor Grail. "We'll dose them with Somnifir until they won't know whether they're coming or going!" answered Seren.

Inside the children's chamber, Amy asked Moey, "Did they mean for us to hear them whispering?" Moey replied, "I've no idea but I'm not doing anything they want me to do." Amy said the same. "Moey… Amy," croaked Jed, recovering from the effects of the Somnifir. "What's going on? What have they done to you?" They told their friends how they came to be as they were and how Professor Grail wanted them to make Jed and the others the same as them. Jed had a flash of inspiration. "Did you see how terrified they were of Moey and Amy?" The others nodded. "So why don't you bite us so we do become like you and the next time they come to see us we'll attack them!" said Jed. The others nodded again but Moey and Amy were against the idea. "It'll be fine," argued Stevie Lewis, "it'll wear off after we go home." They all desperately wanted to get back home to see their mums and dads again. "C'mon, Moey; c'mon, Amy," urged Jed, "we all want to go home. Bite us and make us like you. They'll shit themselves when they find out." Jed dragged his bed toward Moey's. When he got close, he lifted his chin, exposing his throat to Moey, and whispered, "C'mon, our kid, do it!"

★

As soon as Charlie thought everybody was asleep, he slid out of bed and went downstairs to the coal cellar to pick up his Star Axe, crossbow, white-oak-tipped bolts for dusting Vampires and several steel-tipped bolts for killing non-Vampires, and a large hunting knife. Michael barred Charlie's exit from the cellar but was pulled out of the way by Nezok, who said to Charlie, "Go! Go!" in his croaky voice. Before leaving the coal cellar, Charlie ruffled Midget's hair as a kind of goodbye in case anything should happen to him.

In return, Trixie ruffled Charlie's while hanging upside down from the joists. Michael made to leave with Charlie but Nezok prevented him from doing so, causing Michael to howl a lament. The friends touched hand to paw as Charlie left the coal cellar bound for Storm Hill to look for Jed. Michael said to Nezok, "If anything happens to the boy, Eshirona will never forgive you and neither will I." Nezok placed a paw on Michael's shoulder. "Faithful old Ryrnyr, if he is the one, this is his chance to prove it," answered Nezok.

Charlie arrived outside the walls of the Storm Hill Sanatorium around midnight. He knew from his nana that Vampires had no need of sleep, so he would have to be careful and quiet. Scaling the perimeter wall was easy for a street kid like Charlie. Once beyond the wall, he made his way toward the light that was coming from one of the windows. As he got near, Charlie heard talking coming from his right. He dropped flat to the ground. Parting the branches of the bush concealing him from view, Charlie spied a shadowy group making its way toward the front doors of the Sanatorium. His attention was drawn to a hooded figure at the head of the group, which turned and looked in his direction. He stopped breathing, hardly able to believe what he was seeing. "What the hell is that?" he muttered under his breath. The sound of Charlie's whisper drew the attention of others in the group. "What was that?" asked as Vampire. "It sounded like it came from inside," answered another. Charlie remained dead still lest he give himself away. As the group entered the Sanatorium, Charlie noticed a Priest and an old woman toward the rear. He squinted to see who they were. "It's Father Kenny," he said to himself, "and he's with the old woman, from the other day." He focused hard, trying to identify the old woman but could not make out her features. "I'll teach them to betray their kind," he mumbled as he grabbed his crossbow, but before he could load it he was grabbed from behind. Try as he might, he could not break free. "Stop struggling," hissed Charlie's captor, "you'll bring them down on ussssss." The next thing Charlie knew he was tucked under his captor's arm and carried over the wall of the Sanatorium. He knew that whatever had captured him was not Human as no Human could perform such a feat. *What kind of creature is this that can carry me like I am an infant?* he thought.

Inside the Sanatorium, the shadowy group were brought before Tyran Skel. The old woman told him about Nana Lyons planning to attack Storm Hill the coming Sunday night, "while you are at your worship, my Lord," she whispered as if in confidence.

"And what reward would you feel appropriate for giving me this information?" asked Tyran Skel.

"Immortality, my Lord," replied the old woman. Skel returned her a snarl.

"If I've told you once I've told you a hundred times: you are too old. It could take decades to make a Vampire out of you, and at your age you will most likely expire along the way and we will have wasted our valuable time for nothing!" he yelled.

"That is a risk I am willing to take," began the old woman, ceasing only when Tyran Skel changed into his Vampire form.

"Do not try my patience, old woman; and you, Priest, what is to be your reward?" snarled the Vampire.

"I am content to have your gratitude, my Lord," replied Father Kenny, bowing low and exposing the back of his neck, "and a few pieces of gold would be welcome too," he added with a sly grin. Tyran Skel threw several gold pieces onto the floor, which the Priest gathered up speedily.

"Leave. And only return if you have fresh information." The Priest and the old woman bowed low and retreated from the chamber, keeping the backs of their necks exposed should Tyran Skel wish to deliver them a Death Bite for their insolence. "Pass the word, Seren, there will be no worship this Sunday. Instead, all Vampires are to remain in their chambers below Mormant Hall and must not emerge until commanded to do so." Seren smiled as this suited her scheme.

"Yes, Master. I will personally see to it that every Vampire hears your decree."

*

The creature dosed Charlie with Somnifir and then loaded him into a coach. In his dreamlike, semi-conscious state, the boy could do nothing to escape even though he was not tied up. In fact, he was not restrained in any way and could have jumped from the coach and run away if he had have wished but he did not. After what seemed like a second to Charlie, but it could have been ten or twenty minutes, the creature dragged him from the coach into a house. "Take him in there and tie him up," said a male voice. "There's no need, he's had enough Somnifir to down a pack of Lupule," replied Charlie's captor. The creature shoved Charlie into a room, forcibly plonking him down onto a chair.

"Don't give him the antidote yet," said a female voice. Charlie's mouth was as dry as sandpaper. Somebody handed him a glass of water, which he downed in one go, making him burp. "Charles 'Vampire Killer' Carter, I presume, going by the white-oak-tipped crossbow bolts in your knapsack."

"I wasn't going to kill a Vampire," spoke Charlie drowsily, "I was going to kill Father Kenny and the old woman," he answered, unconcerned how this female knew his name. "And how do you know my name?" he asked after a pause. "Anyway, who are you?" he added, sounding drunk.

"My name is Xenka Drach. Why were you going to kill the Priest and the old woman?" she asked.

"Because they are traitors."

"How can you be so sure?"

"They were in company with Vampires, so I'm sure."

"But, Master Carter, you are in company with a Vampire right now, so are you a traitor?" Charlie raised his head and stared at the female sitting opposite him. She was beautiful. Her skin alabaster, her hair corvid black and her eyes emerald green.

"You look so perfect… beautiful," muttered Charlie involuntarily. "How can you be a Vampire?" he asked naïvely. Madame Drach slowly, deliberately slowly, changed into her Vampire form and extended her fangs to their full length. For some reason Charlie was unafraid.

"Aren't you scared, Master Carter?" spoke a female voice behind him. Charlie turned to see what he took to be the creature that had kidnapped him. She removed her top to expose scale-like skin. "What about me, Charles Carter, are you afraid of me?" asked Viserce, flicking a forked tongue out from between her lips.

"I don't think either of you will harm me," Charlie replied, trying his best to sound confident.

"Is it you? Is it really you sitting here before me? You who survived Nisfara? Or are you an enchantment of the Strigoi?" whispered Vampire Drach into Charlie's ear, her voice metallic, ethereal, disembodied, dreamlike.

"Mistress, to be certain, taste him," urged Viserce. Madame Drach's fangs reduced in size for feeding.

Bringing her horrific visage close to Charlie's face she delicately pricked his neck with the very tips of her fangs, barely taking but a Cyathus of blood from the boy. The effect on her was immediate and terrible. Vampire Drach dropped to the floor, writhing and screaming in agony. Several minutes passed before she was herself again. It was fortunate she had taken so little blood and then only on the tip of her tongue.

"It cannot be!" sputtered Madame Drach. "Return the boy to his home, unharmed and with no memory of these events," she ordered.

"Yes, Mistress," replied Viserce. After dosing Charlie with more Somnifir, Viserce whisper-wiped his memory of Xenka Drach's reaction to tasting him and along with it went most of the evening's events.

"If he is the Prophecy then we are doomed," spoke Madame Drach out loud but to herself.

"Way do you mean?" asked Viserce. She received no answer.

"When you return, I want you to check on the Repeste guarding Lord Harbinger, I have a feeling something is amiss." Viserce departed with Charlie tucked under her arm to carry out her Mistress' commands.

"Madame Drach," said Simeon Rune after Viserce had left the room, "may I ask about —"

"No you may not!" she screamed in a rage. "Now go and find out what's happening to the subjects in the laboratory and be sure nobody sees you!" Simeon Rune bowed low, exposing the back of his neck should Madame Drach wish to tear it out for his insolence. She dismissed him with a mere flick of the back of her hand to send him on his way.

Madame Drach was sitting alone in her chamber, reflecting on the evening's events, when Seren burst in and blew a massive quantity of Somnifir into her face, rendering her immediately catatonic. Simeon Rune had been captured during his spying mission and, under torture, had told Seren everything. She went to Tyran Skel and informed him of Drach's treachery in allowing a Human to see her in Vampire form and not kill him. "She is planning a coup against you, my Lord. She must be stopped before she destroys us all. Did you know that she has banished my Mutanti from the fourth-level gallery and replaced the Vampires guarding Harbinger with her Repeste? They're armed with Somnifir bombs." The voices inside Skel's head woke and spoke to him: "This is your chance to demonstrate your quality! Your opportunity to show you're not the weak-minded pathetic fool they believe you to be! If you do not destroy Drach you will not realise your destiny. With her gone the Repeste will answer to you. With her gone every Vampire in the

House of Mormant will answer to you and you alone," echoed the voices over and over. "Have Drach arrested!" he cried. The voices fell silent. "Have her placed in the first-level gallery, far away from Harbinger." Seren was not happy with this. "But, Master, we must destroy her before it is too late!" But that was a step too far for Skel to take. "No, Seren, do as I say," he answered calmly. "We may yet have need for her in the coming war." Seren would never blatantly disobey Tyran Skel but she planned to dust Drach and blame it on some poor creature before tearing it apart in feigned anger, leaving none to contradict her version of events.

★

It was nearly three in the morning when Charlie was dropped off at Evelyn Terrace. The Repeste leaned him up against the frame of the door before administering the Somnifir antidote and driving away at speed. When he came around he found himself staring into Trixie's heterochromatic eyes. She had been out hunting and seeing the Repeste wagon racing away she went to investigate. Soon there were four Lupule around the boy. They picked Charlie up, took him to the cellar kitchen and placed him on the once grand settee from where, as a child, he had first seen Michael. "Hello," said Effy, "I couldn't sleep." Charlie jumped up with a start. Looking around he wondered where the Lupule were. They were gone. He began to think he had imagined it all. "I couldn't sleep either," he replied. "I'm really thirsty!" he said, smacking dry lips together. Effy brought him some water in a chipped enamel cup which he swallowed in two gulps. "I heard you sneak out, and I've been waiting up for you to come home," said Effy, taking the empty cup from Charlie. "Don't worry," she continued, "I won't tell mum or dad or nana." A voice spoke from behind Effy. "You won't tell Nana what?" asked Nana Lyons. "Oh, nothing," replied Effy. "Anyway, I'm tired," she said, stretching and pretend-yawning. "I'm off back to bed." And off she trotted upstairs to bed. Nana Lyons sat staring at Charlie, silently coercing him into speaking. He could not resist and soon told her everything; everything he could remember at least. "So, you met the great and powerful Xenka Drach, did you? And lived to tell the tale! You're a lucky boy, Charlie Carter, a very lucky boy! Don't you go doing anything like that ever again! I can't afford to lose you," admitted Nana Lyons. "Do you know this Xenka Drach?" he asked. "We were never formally introduced; I more know of her than know her. Whenever there was a gathering between Nana Alice and the Vampires she used to look into the eyes of the children as though she was searching for something. I think the other one you mentioned is probably her Conducere, Viserce. Nana Alice knew them all, you know. Yes, Charlie, she knew them all," spoke Nana Lyons with a faraway look in her eye. Charlie thought he might slip away while his nana was reminiscing but no such luck. "So, Charlie Carter, no sign of Jed in Storm Hill and, yet again, you failed to identify the old woman with Father Kenny. That really isn't good enough, we must have a traitor in our midst and it's important we ferret her out. You have to do a better job next time!" chastised the old woman. Charlie asked what should be done about Father Kenny and was surprised when his nana replied, "Nothing," and refused to elaborate.

Though she was no expert, it seemed to Nana Lyons that Charlie, from his 'patchy' story, had most likely been dosed with Somnifir, and from what she knew of it, he would not easily find sleep, and so the pair talked until her other children were up and out of bed. After feeding the kids their breakfast, Nana Lyons told Charlie to come straight home after his V and V training as he would need to gather his strength before the next tournament, the last before the tournament at Mormant Hall.

★

Simeon Rune staggered through the door to his house just as Max was getting ready to leave for school. He was wheezing, his clothes were bedraggled and he had marks and cuts to his hands and face. Max was shocked; he had never seen his father in such a bad state. Mr Rune beckoned the boy into his study. "Max, something terrible has happened. Xenka Drach has been arrested and her Conducere, Viserce, is missing." Simeon told Max about the previous evening. "I fear for the safety of Lord Harbinger. You must tell Charlie Carter everything. Everything! I mean it, including the experiments they are conducting on children." Max was not sure that was such a good idea. "Please, son, you have to trust me, tell Charlie Carter everything you know. Help him. You must help him in whatever way you can." When Max arrived at the pickup point there were no children or wagons to take them to school. A Repesto told him there was not going to be any further schooling in Ravenport. Max was convinced he had to find Charlie Carter and tell him all about the Vampires of Storm Hill.

★

That morning, the assembly hall was half empty. "The Storm Hill kids are late for school," chorused several children, laughing with glee. "They're never late!" answered other children. Heads turned this way and that with children whispering behind their hands, asking one another what they thought was going on. Mr Bawles mounted the stage. "You will notice there are no children from Storm Hill in school today. I've been informed that they are staying away as a precautionary measure. For what, I am uncertain, but as soon as I find out I'll let you all know. Now, if you'll turn your hymn books to 'Guide Me, O Thou Great Redeemer'." After his adventures of the previous evening, Charlie thought the absence of the Storm Hill children had to be something to do with him. As soon as assembly was over, Charlie gathered his V and V teammates around him and, as a subterfuge, told them he suspected the Storm Hill team were up to something. "Don't you think it's suspicious with the competition coming up at Mormant Hall they're not at school today?" he asked. "And I bet they don't show up for the tournament tomorrow. They're probably practising like mad up there and we've got to do the same down here!" Charlie wanted each and every one of them all to be as prepared as they could possibly be because he had a bad feeling about what was now likely to happen between Cauldronians and the Vampires of Storm Hill.

Throughout the day, Charlie's head was in a swirl thinking about Jed and what was going on at Storm Hill. His imagination was running wild. The aftereffects of the Somnifir made Charlie paranoid. As soon as the school day was over, Charlie and his teammates ran along Dock Road to the Oller for V and V training. When they arrived at Christ Church there was no sign of Father Grogan. Father Horan shouted, "You lot, get on with your practising. Father Grogan will be back any minute now." But Father Grogan did not show. Charlie thought that yet another sign things were about to get bad.

After V and V training, Nana Lyons, just like Father Grogan, was nowhere to be found and no one knew where she was. Feeling totally drained through lack of sleep, and with a thumping post-Somnifir headache, Charlie wolfed down his supper and went straight to bed. Following a dose of Somnifir, sleep usually goes one of two ways: you can have a black dreamless sleep from which you wake totally refreshed, or you have unending nightmares which seem to last years. For Charlie it was the latter. After a hellish night during which he died several times in the most gruesome ways imaginable, the boy woke at eight o'clock in a lather of sweat. He was alone in the bedroom. All was still and quiet throughout the house; suspiciously quiet, he thought. Reaching under his bed, Charlie took his crossbow from its cover and loaded it before stealthily making his way to the top of the stairs. He listened hard but not a sound was heard throughout the entire house. The hair on the back of Charlie's neck stood stiffer than he could recall. Soundlessly, Charlie tip-toed his way downstairs to the cellar kitchen. "Well done, son, well done," said Nana Lyons, emerging from the cellar parlour and congratulating Charlie. "What's going on?" he asked in a fright. "I was testing to see if there were any lasting effects from the Somnifir but there don't seem to be any. Now, put the crossbow down, we need to talk. Oh, by the way, in case I haven't mentioned it before, Vampires have really excellent hearing, so it pays to be extremely quiet when hunting them." Charlie was angry at his nana testing him. What if I'd've shot somebody? What if I'd've shot you? What would we have done then? How could we fight the Vampires then? Anyway, where is everybody?" Nana Lyons took the crossbow from Charlie, sat him down and poured him a cup of weak tea. "I sent the children off to the park to play before they do their chores. Your mum and your aunties are out shopping. They took your dad with them, though I got the feeling he'd've rather gone to the park with the kids. He's just a big kid himself really," chuckled Nana Lyons. An odd feeling came over Charlie; something felt missing. "Where are the Lupulos, Nana? I can't hear them scrabbling around in the cellar." She told him that they had up and left during the night. "What, all of them?" he asked disbelievingly. "Yes, all of them, even Midget," replied Nana Lyons unconcernedly. Charlie asked why they had left. "I think you know why, Charlie. War is coming and they have their part to play in it." Charlie was distraught at the thought of never seeing Michael or Trixie or Midget ever again. Nana Lyons assured the boy that he would see them again.

★

Only six teams turned up for the V and V tournament. Penny Street School easily won but to Charlie it felt like everybody was just going through the motions; they all seemed preoccupied. "Hey, youz lot," shouted Billy Lynch, "what's up with yez? Ye weren't really tryin'." Tyler King stepped forward. "Don't you feel it, Billy?" he asked. "Feel what?" he asked. "Something's not right," said Suzy McIver. "First Patto gets carted off, then there was the fire, then the fever that turned out not to be fever but they took the kids to the Sanatorium and now they're all dead. And what about the Storm Hill kids, eh? Where have they disappeared off to then? There's something going on, Billy. There's definitely something going on and things don't feel right. To be honest, everybody's a bit scared." Billy tried to reassure them. "Don't be daft, there's nothing to be scared of," he said, trying to sound confident in his words. "And what's happened to all those other kids, then, Billy? All them that got taken away by the men in white coats? Eh? The quiet kids. The ones that just sit there that nobody notices but we noticed they weren't there yesterday when the assembly hall was only half full. Where are those kids, eh, Billy? Where?" Billy Lynch had no answer; nobody did. All they knew was lots of children had gone missing over the past year and nobody knew where they were or what had happened to them. Billy asked Charlie if he wanted to go and play on the monkey bars but after the flop of the V and V tournament he was not interested. "No thanks, our kid," he said, "I'll see you in the park tomorrow after church."

It was especially dark that moonless night for Charlie's walk home, like somebody had thrown a blanket over the sky. Halfway along Heatherfield Road Charlie felt a presence behind him. He turned around to confront whoever was stalking him.

"Who's there?" he shouted into the dark.
"It me, Max. We need to talk."
"There's only one thing I want to talk to you about, Rune, and that's what's going on up there at Storm Hill."
"That's what I've come to talk to you about but we can't talk here."
"I'm not going anywhere with you, or anybody from Storm Hill," replied Charlie after noticing several figures lurking in the shadows behind Max Rune.
"You must trust us, Charlie," called Bogdan Radu.

"Who else is with you? Come out," yelled Charlie. The figures emerged from the darkness to encircle Charlie.

"You know Bogdan and Cho, and this is Noire Drabech," said Max. "We've come to warn you."

"Warn me about what? And keep your distance!" Charlie cried, pulling a crossbow bolt from his knapsack.

"Oh, don't worry about that. We've no desire for an argument with your Lupule." As Max spoke, Charlie heard snuffling sounds he recognised. He called for Michael and the others to come to him but they refused to draw near.

"Okay then, Rune, what is it you have come to warn me about?"

"War is coming between the Cauldron and Storm Hill."

"You lot know all about the Vampires up there at Storm Hill," said Charlie, pointing at Max and the others, "but you say nothing, you do nothing. What kind of people are you? Are you Human? Is Bogdan a Vampire? Or Cho or any of the others?" cried Charlie.

"No, of course not, we are just the children of those who serve Vampires."

"Why do they do it? Why do they go against their own kind?"

"It's not easy to explain," answered Max. "But we want to make a clean breast of things. Will you at least hear us out?"

"Okay, I'll listen but keep your distance," said Charlie, waving his crossbow in the air.

"First, I want to tell you that your friends, the ones who were supposed to have died from the Sweating Sickness, are alive. Or at least they were a few days ago."

"And Jed? What about Jed?" he asked.

"We believe Jed's with them but we can't be certain." Charlie went to speak. "Wait, there's more. The children that have been taken away recently by the men in white coats are being forced to work as slaves in mills and factories owned by Vampires. They only took a few at first but then they took more and more and filled the gaps they left in schools with us," said Max, pointing at Cho,

Bogdan and the rest. Charlie was astonished; he could not believe what had gone on right under the noses of the authorities.

"What are you going to do now? Will you come with me to the Police or a Priest and tell them what's going on at Storm Hill?"

"It's not that simple, Charlie. The authorities are run by Vampires: the Police, the Church, politicians, the military, councils, trades unions, employers, charities, everything!" It was as though a bright light had been shone in Charlie's eyes; for the first time he saw everything as it really was. All the corruption, all of the stacking of the odds against the poor, all the ways people like him were kept down, oppressed and controlled and abused by those in authority.

"So, what can be done? What can we do?" asked Charlie despondently.

"We need to strike a blow against them. A blow that will be felt throughout the whole Vampire nation," answered Max.

"You should meet my nana and tell her what you've told me. Come with me to Evelyn Terrace."

"We dare not. We're being hunted. They're probably watching Evelyn Terrace because they know Lupule have taken shelter there."

"Where will you go?"

"There are a couple of places we can hide in but it's best I don't tell you about them. Dozens of kids have left Storm Hill. The Vampires are afraid we'll tell everyone in the Cauldron about them though even if we did we doubt they'd believe us, so we won't!"

"Come on, Max, you can trust me. Tell me where you're going in case I need to get in touch with you."

"It's better that I don't in case you're captured and taken to Seren. Nobody can keep secrets from her." Max went silent for a moment. "There's something else you should know. The Vampire you met, Xenka Drach, she's been imprisoned, and her Conducere, Viserce, is on the run. My dad's worried that Lord Harbinger and Madame Drach are going to be assassinated. I don't know where it will all end." Charlie could see Max was upset, so he placed a comforting arm around his shoulder. "We'll stay close by in case we can be of any help. Goodbye, Charlie, I hope you don't think too badly of us."

"Listen, Max, I found out some things from my nana the other day, so I know we're not blameless in all this, so I won't think badly of you. At least you came good in the end. Good luck to you all."

As Charlie made his way up St George's Hill he was aware of the tell-tale pitter-patter-paws sound of Lupule all around him as they kept watch to make sure he came to no harm. Arriving safely home, Charlie hiss-whispered into the darkness, "Goodnight, Michael. Goodnight, Trixie." His words were answered by low, mournful howls. Once inside the house, Charlie told his nana what Max Rune had said. She acted as though she already knew most of it. What Charlie was unaware of, and his nana chose not to tell him, was that she had convinced Patrick Snr to return to work to spy on Storm Hill.

CHAPTER 12

After a fitful night's sleep, Charlie woke early that fateful Sunday morning. Making his way downstairs he saw the front door close out of the corner of his eye. He was about to go and see who it was had just left the house when his nana called him.

"Charlie! Come down here, I've got something to show you." Nana Lyons beckoned Charlie toward the coal cellar door. "Have a look down there," she said. Charlie opened the cellar door, turned on the light and descended into the gloom. Before he reached the bottom of the stairs he saw two heterochromatic eyes peering at him from beneath the treads.

"Trixie?" he called out.

"Better than that," answered his nana from above, "it's Midget. Trixie thought you might like to raise him." Charlie picked up the cub and, pulling him close to his chest, spun around and around until he was dizzy.

"How will I feed him?" was Charlie's question.

"Don't worry about that, he'll catch his own food," replied Nana Lyons. Charlie did not like to think about what that meant.

"Nana," said Charlie, "who was that leaving the house just now?" he asked.

"That was your dad," the old woman replied nonchalantly.

"He's up early, where's he off to?" enquired the boy.

"Storm Hill… to work," replied Nana Lyons innocently.

"I thought he said he wasn't going back to work at Storm Hill ever again?" the boy recalled.

"He had to go back, we need information," replied Nana Lyons casually.

"How can you have let him go back to work there after what we spoke about last night?" cried Charlie, concern for his father reverberating in his voice.

"Because, son, we need to find out about what's going on in Storm Hill," responded the old woman coldly. Charlie was furious with her.

"How could you, Nana, how could you? You've put Dad in danger!"

Charlie ran to the front door to call his father back but he was too late: the wagon had already picked him up to take him to Storm Hill.

★

When they arrived, Patrick and his workmates were taken to the canteen where they were served a delicious breakfast. Those supervising the proceedings were so used to this routine that they did not bother to ensure everybody consumed their Somnifir-laced food. Determined not to be experimented on again, Patrick only pretended to eat his breakfast. After the men finished eating Dracaena Zayne ordered the guards to remove them to room 414. Patrick overheard them saying that room 414 was a feeding chamber; he realised that he and his workmates were about to be feasted on by Vampires. Not just any old Vampires: Prima Generatie Vampiri, as they always had first dibs on Humans. As the men were marched from the canteen, Patrick ducked beneath a table. He was not missed until roll call was taken and then all hell broke loose. After all that had gone on during the past few days, a Human running around Storm Hill on the loose was the last straw. The Captain of the Northern Guard ordered his Lupule to hunt down the escapee and bring him back. "He can be the dessert," joked Madame Zayne.

It was obvious to Patrick Snr that all the hullaballoo that was going on was to do with him not being where he should be. Rather than risk capture, he decided to abandon his mission and return to Evelyn Terrace without delay. On reaching the outskirts of Storm Hill, Patrick took to the woods and continued on south. Picked his way through the undergrowth, he heard branches and twigs snapping behind him, followed by sounds he did not recognise. "Sounds a bit like a dog snuffling," he muttered to himself. Emerging into a small clearing, Patrick turned around to check he was not being followed. He saw the bushes at the far end of the clearing part. Poking through them came a head, followed by another and another and another. They were not heads Patrick recognised because he had never seen Lupule before. He went to run but found himself face down in the dirt with a huge Lupulo on his back. The creature pressed its fangs into Patrick's neck in such a way that he knew it wanted him to surrender, which he immediately did for obvious reasons.

Suddenly, the Lupulo that was holding Patrick down went flying through the air.

"Let him alone," hissed Viserce in Lupul. In her Serpent form with venom dripping from her six-inch-long fangs she was truly terrifying to behold.

"We'll be rewarded well for bringing in a traitor such as you, Viserce," said Wahron, Captain of the Northern Guard. He and his cohort cautiously edged their way toward Viserce.

"Wahron, surrender and join us," growled Nezok, former Captain of the Southern Guard. At these words, Nezok's band of renegade Lupule emerged from either side of the clearing. Wahron and his cohort were outflanked and outnumbered.

"I always hated you, Nezok Rat Eater, now we shall see which of us is best," slathered Wahron through gritted teeth.

"Nezok only eats rats because that's all your mum serves for breakfast!" howled Trixie in reply.

Patrick wondered what the hell was going on as all the creatures around him, bar one, were laughing like drains, if indeed they were laughing and not choking. Archivists later recorded Trixie's words at the Battle of Forest Glade, as it became known, as the first 'Your Mum' jibe but they were incorrect in this. Your Mum jibes have been around for millennia. Many were recorded in ancient Egyptian hieroglyphs, as several Egyptian animal-headed gods were, in fact, Your Mum jibes. The easiest to spot, and probably the funniest, is the hippopotamus-headed goddess, Taweret. The battle that followed was short and terrible and when it was over dead Lupule littered the small glade. While Lupule can be gentle, loveable creatures, their fangs and the ferocity with which they can use them are legendary. Patrick made to surreptitiously crawl away from the scene on all fours but he was blocked from doing so by bumping headfirst into Viserce's scaly legs. He pretended to pass out in order to give himself time to figure out whose side this terrifying creature was on and if he was in any danger.

★

Despite all his objections, Charlie was packed off to Sunday school by Nana Lyons as she had 'things to do that she'd tell him about later,' but for now he and his siblings had to go to Sunday school, even though she knew they would be straight out the back door and into the park.

An hour later the park was packed with kids running about and playing on the monkey bars, swings and slide. There was a lot more playroom without the Storm Hill kids there. Billy Lynch showed up after Mass and Charlie went over to speak with him. He told his cousin all that Max Rune had told him. "Do you believe him?" asked Billy. "Yeah, I do," replied Charlie. "So what are you going to do about it?" asked Billy. "You mean what are *we* going to do about it. You're not getting out of it, even with your gammy hand," laughed Charlie. He then told Billy about him being taken captive, and even about Xenka Drach and Viserce. "I think you must've hit your head and made your brain wonky," remarked Billy but Charlie convinced him he was telling the truth. "In that case I'm definitely not going anywhere near Storm Hill if they've got things like that running around loose up there."

Sammy Irons, Izzy Sanchez and several other members of the V and V team came over to see what was going on. Billy told them what Charlie had told him. "Look, youz, we've known for ages that something's going on up there at Storm Hill," said Izzy Sanchez, "so I reckon it's about time we did something about it, because nobody else is going to help us." When Izzy put it that way it made sense. "When shall we go then?" asked Billy, knowing full well what his cousin would say. "There's no time like the present. We'll drop by Evelyn Terrace first, though, to pick up some weapons." At the mention of weapons everybody was keen to get involved.

★

News of the Battle of Forest Glade spread like wildfire, causing panic throughout Storm Hill. Professor Grail ordered the child subjects be dosed with Somnifir and removed to a chamber in the first-level gallery below Mormant Hall. Once there, for everybody's safety, they were to be handcuffed through metal loops embedded in the stone walls. One of the Familiars tasked with this job had her throat ripped out by Amy Collins after she administered the antidote too soon. The Mutanti guards only just managed to lock the chamber door before Moey and Amy could get at them. As Somnifir was now in short supply, mainly because the Repeste had used it to make Somnifir bombs, Professor

Grail decided they could not afford to dose the children again and they were allowed to roam free around the chamber until supplies could be replenished. "There's definitely something going on," said Jed to the others. "We might not be so lucky next time, so you've got to turn us into Vampires," he urged Moey and Amy. "But it doesn't work, we tried," replied Moey. "Yeah, when we tried before it didn't work," added Amy. "But we can't just give up. You've got to try again," begged Stevie Lewis. "C'mon, Amy, c'mon, Moey, give it another go. Please! I want to see me mum and me dad and me brothers and me sisters again, so please give it another go!"

★

At midday, Simeon Rune dragged a large cage into Lord Harbinger's cell. This time it contained two fat pigs for him to feast upon. "This was the best I could do," Simeon said, opening the top of the cage for Lord Harbinger to gorge on its contents. While his Master was feeding, Simeon Rune updated him on events, the main one being that Seren's Mutanti now controlled all the upper galleries, and only the fourth-level gallery remained out of their hands.

"Find a key to unlock these," said Lord Harbinger, shaking his chains at Simeon Rune. "I must be freed before they dust me," he said with urgency ringing in his voice.

"I will do my best," replied his faithful Conducere.

"And I'm going to need more than just these swine if I am to have energy for the fight ahead." Once again, Simeon Rune offered Lord Harbinger his own life blood and once again Lord Harbinger refused, saying to him that he was more valuable alive than dead. "If things get bad throw a couple of Repeste in here," whispered Lord Harbinger.

"But, Master, if you feed on them there'll be none to protect you. And besides, they're not very nutritious."

Before he left, Simeon Rune told Lord Harbinger that Xenka Drach was being held in a chamber in the first-level gallery, 'next to that occupied by the child subjects'. The former Prima Vampir replied, "I know," indicating to Simeon Rune that his Master's powers were returning. After Rune departed the cell in search of a key to unlock Harbinger's chains, the ancient Vampire, strengthened by his feedings, closed his eyes. *Xenka*, he called with his mind. "Yes, my Lord," she answered in her Somnifir-induced stupor. Lord Harbinger chastised her for her treachery and then, in a fatherly voice, forgave her sins. The pair formulated a plan for the Repeste guards to sacrifice themselves to him should the need arise, *"for the good of the House of Mormant,"* cried the Prima Vampir through his mind. Madame Drach promised she would order Viserce to ensure the Repeste did their duty.

Tyran Skel was sitting alone with his thoughts when Seren came bursting through the doors of the Grand Chamber. She told him the Repeste were still preventing her Mutanti from entering the fourth-level gallery despite the imprisonment of their Mistress, adding that she was fearful they would release Lord Harbinger. "Let them. What can that weak old fool do against us? If He tries to climb out of His hole I'll tip ten thousand tons of rocks on top of Him." Seren had already thought of this but wanted more immediate action. Skel, however, was not going to be drawn, despite the voices inside his head arguing on Seren's side. "We will consolidate our forces in the top three galleries. That's where the Humans will attack tonight. They'll hope to surprise us at worship but we'll be waiting for them, and when they enter the tunnels we'll wipe them all out, every last stinking one of them," said Skel with glee resounding in his voice. "Can I then destroy Harbinger and Drach?" begged Seren. Tyran Skel agreed that after they had dealt with the Humans she could do with them as she pleased. But instead of waiting, Seren ordered a Mutanti attack on the fourth-level gallery. "I'll say the Repeste released Harbinger and my Mutanti had no choice than to bomb

Him with Somnifir," spoke Seren's inner voice, bolstering her self-confidence for what she was about to do. She had never imagined in her wildest dreams that she would destroy two such Vampires in one day. "Just one more and it'll be me what wears the crown," she snarled and made her way to the Mutanti's secret lair.

★

By three that afternoon Charlie, Billy, Sammy, Izzy and the others were making for the mills and factories to the north of Storm Hill. "So, run this plan of yours by me again, will ye, Charlie," said Billy. "C'mon, Lynchy, it's not that hard to understand," groaned Sammy. "It's a good job yer a handsome lad, Billy Lynch, because you're not very bright," teased Izzy Sanchez, prodding Billy in the back with an axe. "Okay, Billy, listen up. Vampires can't stand sunlight," began Charlie once again. "And who was it that told ye that?" asked Billy. "His nana!" chorused Izzy and the others. "Weren't you listening?" Charlie outlined the plan again for Billy's benefit. "And as Vampires are unlikely to be in the mills or factories during the day, because they can't stand sunlight, we'll free the slave children, and when the Vampires come to see what's going on we'll rescue Jed, Moey, Amy, Patto and the rest," concluded Charlie. "Nimps," echoed the rest of the gang to Billy.

★

By three thirty, Nana Lyons received word that Charlie and some of his mates had stopped by Evelyn Terrace and had left carrying 'loads of axes and crossbows and all sorts of things'. Guessing what her grandson was up to, the old woman rushed home to bring her plan to attack Storm Hill forward, when she was clubbed from behind and thrown into the coal cellar. Nana Lyons' attackers were about to finish her off when they heard a gentle purring coming from the shadows. "What's that?" asked one of the men. Two blinking lights appeared from beneath the stairs, one green, the other blue. The purring turned into a snarl, and into the dim electric light of the coal cellar emerged Midget. The attackers laughed and went to stroke him. The first to get close to Midget's maw lost three fingers. Small though he was, Midget was like a raging beast, snapping and biting and clawing at Nana Lyons' assailants until they took to their heels. After they fled, Midget stood guard over the old mother Lyons until help arrived.

★

At twenty-five minutes to four a tremendous howling and wailing went up throughout Storm Hill. "That sounds like Lupulos calling to one another," guessed Charlie. "I think it's begun," he said to the others. "What's begun?" they chorused. "The war! The war's begun! We are at war!" Half a mile away, two lines of Lupule faced one another across the open green in the centre of Storm Hill. "Mhyrly," shouted Nezok to the huge Lupulo at the head of the larger of the two Lupule forces. "Too many of our brethren have died for them over the centuries. More of us have died today and more will die now unless we leave Vampires to fight their own battles." Nezok's words caused a murmur on Mhyrly's side of the green. "Silence!" screamed Mhyrly, Supreme Commander of the Lupule. "We are not all traitors, Nezok Rat Eater." Mhyrly could not understand why his words drew raucous laughter from Nezok's forces. "You laugh at a time like this!" he yelled. Thinking quickly, Nezok replied, "We laugh in the face of death if it brings us freedom from enslavement to Vampires. All our kind should be free!" Nezok instigated a paw-clapping chant of, "All Lupule should be free! All Lupule should be free! All Lupule should be free!", which was joined by the Lupule on Nezok's side, and it began raising a chorus on Mhyrly's side too. Mhyrly could see he was losing the loyalty of his Lupule Army and so yelled, "Death to the traitors! Death to the traitors! Forward, my Lupule! Forward!"

After ten paces, Mhyrly looked back and saw only a quarter of his Lupule were with him, now he was outnumbered. He stopped and shouted to his Lupule Army, "It's me or Nezok! Which of us do you follow?" It is invariably a mistake to deliver an ultimatum because they speak to the emotional side of the brain, meaning the decision comes from the heart and not the head. An example of this is when somebody cannot decide on this thing or that thing, so they toss a coin. If they are unhappy with the result, then they know deep down what they really and truly wanted all along. "Mhyrly, it's over! Let us all live together in peace as brothers and sisters." Commander Mhyrly had worked long and hard to get where he was and was not going to give it up easily. "Never! I will never surrender!" At his words one third of the forces that had followed Mhyrly deserted him. Mhyrly had to act quickly and decisively or lose the day. "I challenge you to mortal combat, Nezok Rat Eater!" screamed the giant Lupulo. These words again brought raucous laughter from Nezok's forces. This infuriated the Supreme Commander of the Lupule. In anger, he rushed at Nezok, his maw gaping, his fangs dripping with drool. Nobody gave Nezok a chance in a fight with Mhyrly, including Nezok himself. The result of the fight was taken out of both their hands when Mhyrly was felled by a crossbow bolt. From nigh on eighty feet away, Max Rune had drawn a bead on the Supreme Commander of the Lupule, hitting him right between the eyes. After initially being stunned into silence that the great and mighty Mhyrly had fallen, Lupule jumped into the air and rejoiced at his passing.

★

Charlie and his gang heard a loud cheer some way away in the distance. It sounded like a victory cheer but for which side none could guess. "Now, are we all ready?" asked Charlie. Everybody looked at Billy to see if he had any questions. "What are you lot looking at?" he asked indignantly. "Just wondering if you had a question," said Izzy. "Of course not," Billy replied. "Let's get on with it, unless youz lot have forgotten the plan," he added sarcastically.

Charlie and Billy loaded white-oak-tipped bolts into their crossbows, just in case there were any Vampires hanging about, while Sammy and Izzy loaded steel-tipped bolts into theirs to deal with Familiars and the like. All was silent. Up at the windows on the first floor of the building the gang saw figures passing to and fro behind the frosted windows. "Be careful," warned Charlie, which brought an exasperated sigh from the others as if they would be so stupid as not to be careful. Entering the mill, the rescuers made their way to the first floor. Inside the main room they saw guards watching over children as they worked. They were unarmed, so Charlie and his Army burst into the room.

"We're here for the children. Don't try and stop us or you'll get hurt," cried Charlie, waving his crossbow in the air.

"And what are you going to do with those?" asked one of the guards as he changed form into a Vampire. Charlie took aim, dusting him with a bolt through the organ that was once the Vampire's heart. The sight of a Vampire bursting into flames brought screams of panic from the child slaves. Other crossbows were pointed at the remaining guards, who dropped to the floor.

"We're not Vampires! We're not Vampires!" they screamed. Charlie was not convinced.

"To be on the safe side we're going to check to see if you bleed. Do the honours, will you, Billy? We'll cover you."

Billy was not thrilled at being handed this 'honour' but not wanting to show any fear he marched toward the nearest guard. As he drew close, she transformed into a Vampire, snarled at Billy and bared her fangs. He dusted her with a single crossbow bolt to her heart and shouted for Sammy and Izzy to load up. The remaining guards were checked; they were all Human. Charlie and the others released the children from their manacles, placing the guards in them before evacuating the building in triumph. No sooner had they got outside than a shot rang out, wounding one of the children.

"Duck for cover!" yelled Charlie. It quickly became apparent they were facing a force of at least eight armed guards.

"That's great, that is, we've brought medieval weapons to a gunfight," observed Izzy Sanchez dryly.

"Shut up, will ye, Izzy, you're frightening the kids," shouted Billy Lynch. "Don't worry, kids," he said soothingly, "you'll be alright. We'll have yez out of here in no time."

The guards closed in on Charlie and the others. Three more children were wounded but thankfully none seriously. Unwilling to see any more children hurt, Charlie shouted to the guards that they were going to surrender.

"No!" screamed Billy. "We can't surrender! We can't let these kids down! What'll happen to them if we surrender?"

"It's no good, Billy, we're surrounded and we don't have enough bolts to fight our way out. If we surrender then at least we'll be alive and while we're alive we have hope."

"Hope? Hope! Hope of what? Hope they don't eat us? Hope they'll let us work as slaves in their factories? Hope that our mums and dads won't miss us? If that's the hope you're talking about, Charlie, then we have no hope!" Billy's words stung Charlie but this was a time for cool heads not hot blood.

"I don't like it any more than you do but we've got no choice. Do you want the deaths of these kids on your conscience, because if we carry on we'll have their blood on our hands."

"Promise you won't let them eat me, Charlie," cried Sammy Irons in terror. "Promise me, Charlie!"

"I promise, Sammy, I promise," Charlie replied calmly. "If it comes to it I'll do us both before they take us," he said, throwing down his crossbow and slipping his hunting knife in his waistband.

As Charlie, Billy and the others raised their arms in surrender, Vampires sheltering nearby screamed for the guards to bring the ringleaders to them. Then a child's voice called out, "Dad! Dad! It's me, Dad. You've got to let them go. You've got to let them all go!" cried the little girl. Another voice called out, "Listen, all of you. This is Max Rune. You all know my father. You closed your eyes and ears to what Tyran Skel was doing but today your eyes and ears must open. My father is freeing Lord Harbinger as I speak. He will soon be back in charge and anybody against him will surely perish." The guards surrendered immediately. Max ran to Charlie and the others. "Thank you, Max," cried Charlie in frenzied excitement. "Thank you. Now, let's get to the factories and free the slaves there." Max grabbed Charlie by the arm. "No, Charlie, they will have to wait. Jed and the others have been taken to the underground galleries. Their lives are in danger, we must rescue them first." Charlie knew Max was right. "Okay, show us the way to the galleries."

As Charlie was rallying the slave children to join him in their fight for freedom, Seren was on her way to finish off Xenka Drach when she encountered Tyran Skel. "Where are you going?" he asked. "I'm on my way to finish off Drach. She was accidentally overdosed with Somnifir when she was taken, so I'm going to put her out of her misery," she replied. Skel noticed Seren no longer referred to him as her Master. He told her that Madame Drach would have to wait, as he had sensed a strengthening in Lord Harbinger's powers. "If He gets much stronger He'll break free," said Skel, peering into the dark depths of the shaft leading to the galleries below Mormant Hall. As Seren believed this to be more important than finishing off Xenka Drach she said she would accompany Tyran Skel. Then came a crossbow bolt whistling over their heads, hitting the rock wall and clattering to the ground. This was followed immediately after by a deafening pre-pubescent roar as over 200 children armed with wooden this and that ran toward Tyran Skel and Seren. Even with their powers they doubted they could fend off so many, particularly as some were armed with crossbows.

"Run!" shrieked Seren. "Run!" The pair made it to the comparative safety of the first-level gallery where Seren ordered the Mutanti guard to prevent the invaders from rescuing Xenka Drach, dusting her if necessary. She and Skel continued their descent to the fourth-level gallery to destroy Lord Harbinger. "The old woman lied to us. She said the attack would come during worship!" screamed Seren. "This has nothing to do with the attack planned by Old Mother Lyons and her geriatric army. Did you not hear? They are all children! They must've escaped from the factories," replied Tyran Skel. "How could they break free?" cried Seren. "They must've had help. Probably from Simeon Rune or his damned son. Curse them!" howled Tyran Skel, dodging crossbow bolts fired into the dark from above.

As the main body of children reached the head of the shaft that led to the galleries, a force of twenty Mutanti set on them. However, with their superior numbers, the children drove their larger opponents back, pushing many of them down the shaft. Those Mutanti that could, fled for their miserable lives. Charlie surveyed the scene; though injured children lay everywhere he knew the fight was not yet over. They needed to press on but first he ordered the smallest children back to the surface with the wounded. "This way to the first-level gallery," cried Max Rune, pointing into a pitch-black hole. "How many galleries are there?" asked Charlie nervously. "Four in all. Lord Harbinger is imprisoned in the furthest cell of the deepest gallery." Fortunately for all concerned, Max knew where they kept the tar torches which they lit and passed around.

On reaching the first-level gallery Charlie shouted, "You," pointing to half the children, "stay here and —" He was interrupted by the unmistakeable sound of a large pack of Lupule heading toward them. Charlie hoped they were not looking for a fight. At the head of the Lupule pack were Nezok and Trixie. Charlie asked them about Michael. "Dead," growled Nezok sadly in his croaky voice.

Before Charlie could react to the sad news, he heard his father calling. "Son! Son! Is that you, son?" Patrick Snr emerged into the flickering light of the tar torches, waving his hands like a man possessed; behind him came a hissing sound. It emanated from a creature Charlie recognised from his meeting with Xenka Drach. "Don't shoot!" he yelled to his comrades in arms. "She's a friend."

While the children were welcoming the newcomers, a large number of Mutanti came out of the darkness of the gallery tunnel, taking Charlie and the others by surprise. They fell back under the weight of the attack until they could fall back no further. They were literally up against the wall. Seeing her chance, Trixie bounded over the heads of the Mutanti, eluding their grasping claws, to place herself at their rear. As she landed, Trixie sensed Xenka Drach behind one of the doors but she also sensed something behind the door next to her cell, something that filled her with hope and fear.

Half a dozen Mutanti split off from the main body attacking Charlie and his Army to attack Trixie. Before they got to her she opened the door next to Xenka Drach's cell and out of it poured a horde of terrifying creatures with fangs like kitchen knives. Moving like a gathering Tsunami, the Wraiths ripped their way through the Mutanti in front of them and then turned on those attacking Charlie's Army. At the sight of the Wraiths, most of the Mutanti fled rather than standing and fighting. As the creatures came to stand to face Charlie he levelled his crossbow at the nearest of them. He had but one bolt left but the creatures halted their advance.

"Charlie!" called the creature at the head of the horde. "It's me! Jed!" Recognising his brother's voice Charlie fell weeping to his knees in joy.

"God! God!" he shouted into the vastness of the cavern, his words echoing loudly before disappearing from hearing. "What have they done to you? What have the Vampires done to you?" he cried. It was all Charlie or any of the others could do to contain their shock and outrage.

"It's okay, Charlie, it's okay, honest," replied Jed calmly. "We'll be okay. Nana'll know what to do." The Wraiths returned to their Human form as Patrick Snr pushed his way through to hug Jed.

"They said you were dead, son," he whimpered. "See! See, Charlie! Jed's alright. He's fine! Didn't I say he'd be fine?" wept Patrick.

"Let's hope so," answered Charlie as Max shook his head in response to Charlie's unasked question.

Three galleries below Charlie and his Army, Tyran Skel, Seren and 200 Mutanti fought their way past an equal number of Repeste to gain access to the fourth-level gallery. The poor Repeste were simply no match for a Vampire like Skel, a Beast like Seren and a horde of Mutanti. Skel marched to the furthest cell door and kicked it open. There, on the slab of rock where Lord Harbinger had lain, was Lucian Thorne, now just a wrinkled husk drained of every drop of his blood. At the side of the slab lay the bodies, or rather shells, of eight Repeste. Realising his former Lord and Master was on the loose, Tyran Skel fled the cell, closely followed by Seren. Before they made twenty strides, they were confronted by a silhouette spread spectre-like in the twilight of the gallery.

"Tyran!" spoke Lord Harbinger in an ominous tone. "I loved you like a son and you betrayed me!"

"No, 'Father', it was you who betrayed me! You betrayed your own kind; you betrayed the Vampire Nation and brought shame on the House of Mormant," replied Tyran Skel defiantly as Seren, with her back flat to the wall of the gallery, edged closer to Lord Harbinger.

"Neither of you shall leave this place," spoke the Vampire Lord calmly.

"You are still weak, Morfeo, I can sense it," said Skel confidently.

"Such meagre fare as you have had today will not restore your powers after such a prolonged fast," gloated Seren.

"I have enough in me for both of you!" Lord Harbinger answered coldly.

"But what of the 200 of my Mutanti at your back, my Lord?" uttered Seren with glee.

"Did you hear, Tyran? Her Mutanti, she calls them her Mutanti. I warned you, I warned you not to make her their leader. Mark my words, her aim is to destroy us all."

"Upon my command, Harbinger, my Mutanti will tear you apart. But as a consideration to your former greatness, I will allow you one minute to prepare for your journey to join the Great Universe!" screeched Seren, exciting the Mutanti to shriek in response.

As Skel and Seren were preparing to dust Lord Harbinger, inside the first-level gallery Simeon Rune freed Xenka Drach. She was still in a bad way from the Somnifir overdose Seren had given her. Charlie called for everybody's attention. "Listen, we've rescued everybody we can from here, so let's go and free the others from the factories and mills," he shouted. "We can't leave, Charlie, we still have work to do here," cried Max Rune. "What do you mean?" asked Izzy Sanchez. "My father has released Lord Harbinger. He's lying in wait to challenge Tyran Skel to a fight to the death. Whichever of them is victorious will have the loyalty of the entire House of Mormant; that's over 300 Vampires. All of whom are presently locked inside their chambers in the galleries below us and we have to make sure they stay there!" Charlie returned Max a blank look. "How the hell are we going to keep 300 Vampires locked up?" asked Billy, which was the question everybody was thinking. "The debris that was excavated by the miners that dug the galleries is piled up near the top of the shaft. We can entomb the Vampires by filling the shaft with boulders." This idea seemed ludicrous to everybody except

Max and his dad. "How the hell are we going to fill a massive shaft, that's God knows how deep, with rocks? It'll take ages!" remarked an exasperated Billy Lynch. Everybody nodded in agreement with him. This was Billy's second valid point of the day; he was on fire. Simeon Rune answered him: "Don't worry, there are pneumatic engines to tip the rocks down the shaft. They were left behind after the galleries were excavated in case they were needed to bury the Vampires to keep them safe from attack by Humans or other Vampire Houses." Charlie was impressed with the plan. "We won't need to fill the whole shaft, there are chicanes and narrowings above and below each gallery entrance designed to wedge falling rocks tight." Convinced the plan could work, Charlie ordered everybody to the top of the shaft. When they got there Mr Rune fired up the pneumatic engines. Their roar was loud enough to be heard throughout Storm Hill and the galleries below its surface.

"What's that?" shrieked Seren. "It's the engines! They're going to entomb us in the galleries!" cried Tyran Skel in a panic. "We have to get out of here!" Seren ordered a cohort of Mutanti to attack Lord Harbinger to give her and Skel enough time to escape. It did not take long for Lord Harbinger's Death Bite Fangs to despatch the Mutanti, but it was long enough for Seren and Tyran Skel to make their way to the end of the gallery. There were over a hundred Mutanti standing between Lord Harbinger and his quarry. He still had sufficient power to lay waste to fifty of them in as many seconds, causing the rest to flee in panic. As they reached the end of the gallery, the Mutanti had to take shelter from the huge rocks crashing onto the floor in front of them, several being squashed flat by falling boulders.

One gallery up, Tyran Skel and Seren were taking shelter from the falling boulders. Some of which became wedged in the shaft such that Skel and Seren were able to use them like steppingstones to race toward the surface. As they climbed, Seren shrieked for her Mutanti horde to attack those dropping rocks on them. She had no idea that they had been vanquished and were long gone. Seren's shrieks, however, served notice to warn those doing the rock-tipping that she was on her way. "And Skel is with her," gasped Xenka Drach, sensing his presence. "They'll be on us in less than a minute!" Xenka's words caused panic in the ranks. "Father, what can we do?" asked Max Rune. "We're almost out of ammunition and there aren't enough of us to fight Seren and Skel." Simeon Rune thought for a moment and in that moment Seren leapt from out of the mouth of the shaft, tearing at the air with her massive claws. Behind her came Tyran Skel, his Death Bite Fangs fully extended. With the last of his white-oak-tipped crossbow bolts, Charlie drew a bead on Tyran Skel and fired. He hit dead centre of Skel's heart but the bolt fell harmlessly to the ground. Everybody was shocked and stunned that Skel had not been turned into a pile of dust. He rapped his knuckles against his chest. "Iron," he said, laughing. "Your feeble weapons are no match for my armour!"

Viserce stepped forward in Serpent form; her fangs were twice the length of Skel's and were dripping blood-red venom. "Come, my Lord Vampire, come close and taste my venom. I will be your doom!" Seren was almost speechless. "You're a Mutanto!" she shrieked. "How could I not sense you? How did you keep your secret from me?" she howled. "If I told you then it would no longer be a secret," answered Viserce, hissing and flicking her forked tongue from between her lips. Seeing Lupule gathered milling around, Tyran Skel ordered them to attack Viserce and the Humans. Many of them were powerless to resist their Master's commands, and though they fought the urge they eventually succumbed to his will, though as many did not. There followed a short but bloody battle that later became known as the Battle of Pit Head. And just like at the Battle of Forest Glade, the Battel of Pit left many Lupule lying dead on the ground.

During the fighting, Simeon Rune slipped quietly away and located the valves to Storm Hill's water supply. The water in the pipes was under thousands of pounds of pressure, which he turned on Seren and Tyran Skel, lifting them off their feet and smashing them against the wall of the cavern before tumbling back down the shaft. Mr Rune continued to allow the water to flow until the entire shaft was filled. Charlie and the others believed that the galleries below would likewise be flooded but that was not the case as each was fitted with watertight doors. This was not to prevent the Vampires from drowning, for they cannot drown, it was to keep them dry while waiting for their Familiars to rescue them.

The top of the shaft now looked so much like a pool that the children were tempted to take a dip in it but Charlie called them away, saying they had work to do. He looked about the cavern. "So much death and destruction," he muttered. Charlie blamed himself for all the injuries and deaths. *I am too reckless, too headstrong, I am not fit to lead*, he thought solemnly. Putting his thoughts away, Charlie ordered everybody in the shaft to attack the mills and factories to liberate the remaining child slaves. Before departing the cavern, several Lupule went to the newly formed pool to wash the blood of their brothers and sisters from their skin and hair. Then, from out of the water-filled shaft, rose Seren like a leaping salmon, slashing and biting and ripping and tearing at all those around the pool before disappearing back below the surface. Mr Rune fired up the pneumatic engines and tipped the rest of the rocks down the shaft to seal in every living and undead thing. "Trixie!" called Charlie. "Trixie!" he yelled, but no answer came. At the far side of the pool, Charlie saw the faint flicker of a blue eye next to a green eye. He knew straightaway they were Trixie's eyes. He held her close to his chest as her life-force ebbed away and she passed into the Great Universe.

Charlie's Army met with virtually no resistance from those guarding the slaves in the remaining factories and mills. All the Vampires had long since fled, leaving only their Familiars behind for Charlie and his Army to deal with. Victory belonged to the street kids of the Cauldron. It was time to go home; it was time to take the children home. "But what about Jed and the others, what'll we do with them?" asked Billy Lynch. "They're coming home with us," replied Charlie without a second's hesitation. "But what about…" began Billy slowly. "You know?" he added with a nod toward Jed and the others. "What about nothing!" snapped Charlie. "Who will take them in if we do not? Nobody cares for the likes of us so we have to care for one another. I don't have all the answers, Billy, in fact I don't have many answers, but I know this, my brother is coming home with me." There was no point arguing with Charlie in this mood. He and Max Rune commandeered Storm Hill's magnificent black horses and ordered riders to go on ahead to Evelyn Terrace to tell his mum he was bringing Jed home.

Sitting astride a black stallion like an Emperor, Charlie led the columns of children away from Storm Hill. Max Rune was at his side and behind them rode Billy Lynch, Sammy Irons, Izzy Sanchez, Jed, Moey, Stevie, Amy and the others. Billy was not happy that Max was riding alongside Charlie. "That should be me that's riding alongside our Charlie, not that bloody Max Rune. Who the hell does he think he is riding up there anyway, he's the enemy! It should be me! I should be the one riding next to our Charlie!"

★

By the time the procession arrived at the top of St George's Hill, news about the victory at the Battle of Storm Hill had spread like wildfire and thousands upon thousands of Cauldronians had gathered to welcome the conquering hero. When Charlie saw the crowds he could not believe it. Parents came rushing forward when they saw the children they believed they would never see again. They kissed and hugged them tightly, causing them to complain, but the parents did not care; they had their kids back and promised them they would never let them go, no matter what. Having escorted Charlie's Army home, the Lupule raised a wailing chorus, about-faced and disappeared into the night.

Nana Lyons arranged a street party to welcome the children home. As poor people do everywhere they brought far more than they could afford so they could show their friends, relatives and neighbours that they were not as poor as they thought they were. The Council of Crones pulled Charlie to one side, demanding he give them every detail of what had gone on. He told them as much about the Battle of Storm Hill as he could remember and then went to join the party. Try as he might, Charlie could not find Billy Lynch anywhere. As the night wore on, loads of Storm Hill kids showed up. Margot Thorne danced with Charlie and kissed him full on the lips before she and the other Storm Hillers made their way home.

Nana Lyons and the Council of Crones kept themselves to themselves for most of the night as they were on the lookout for Familiars, assassins and the like.

"Does Charlie know Vampires can't be drowned?" enquired Nana Minnie.
"Clearly not," answered Nana Elsie.
"Shall we tell him?" asked Nana Maud. Nana Lyons shook her head.
"No. I'll tell him in the morning. Let him enjoy himself tonight."

EPILOGUE

Even heroes must go to school, is what Nana Lyons said to Charlie after he begged her to be allowed to stay home.

"But, Nana, it's Monday. I have the rest of the week to catch up," Charlie pleaded, but Nana Lyons knew there was more to it than that.

"What's up, son?" she asked.

"I don't feel like a hero, Nana. In fact I feel the opposite of a hero. I feel terrible. So many dead and injured. I can't believe I'll never see Michael or Trixie ever again," said Charlie, sighing deeply. "They're the heroes, not me," he added, shoving his head into his nana's ample old woman's bosom.

"Charlie, listen to me! Heroes exist in the hearts and minds of people, so whether they think they're heroes or not is not for them to say."

"Nana? Can I ask you something?" said Charlie, refusing to make eye contact with her.

"Of course you can, son, of course you can. You can ask me anything you like. I can't guarantee I'll answer but that shouldn't stop you asking," teased the old woman.

"While we were tending to the wounded, Max overheard something. He told me that Xenka Drach said that I am the Prophecy and that Viserce told her the Prophecy was an old wives' tale. What was she talking about, Nana, do you know?"

"Just like with heroes, prophecies exist in the hearts and minds of the people, and if they want to believe in them then they will believe in them. Think of it this way: if something happens that has been foretold, is it a prophecy that has come to pass or did circumstances make it inevitable? People see prophecies where they want to see them. Some people live their lives according to prophecies so that they can fulfil them and be the Prophecy. The Bible is full of such people. There are also self-fulfilling prophecies but that's another thing entirely."

"Do you believe in prophecies, Nana?"

"I believe in lots of things. Now, let's get you off to school, and don't forget you're at Vampires And Victims training tonight. Just because you're the big hero doesn't mean you can relax."

"But why do I have to go to Vampires And Victims training? The war is over."

"Oh, Charlie, I wish it was, I truly do. The battle was won alright, but the war is far from over. In fact, it's only just begun."

"But, Nana, we drowned all the Vampires. They're dead and gone!"

"Ask yourself this, son. If something doesn't need to breathe, how can you drown it? It's true that Vampires don't like being immersed in water, not even for a minute, it makes them all sluggish, but their Familiars have probably freed most if not all of them by now. No, Charlie, the Vampires of Storm Hill are far from dead and gone. They're probably sitting around a table plotting our destruction as we speak. But don't worry, we've got you," said the old woman, ruffling Charlie's hair. "Now, Charles Carter, get out of bed, get dressed, get down them stairs, get your breakfast and get yourself off to school."